I0772742

Free Me

CONSUMED SERIES
BOOK 3

Tris Wynters

Tris Wynters Publishing

Contents

"Even in times of trauma, we try to maintain a sense of normality until we no longer can. That, my friends, is called surviving. Not healing. We never become whole again—we are survivors. If you are here today, you are a survivor. But those of us who have made it through hell and are still standing? We bear a different name: warriors."

~Lori Goodwin

Free Me

Playlist

(The playlist can also be found on YouTube Music)

1. **Break Stuff-** Limp Bizkit
2. **Taki Taki (feat. Selena Gomez, Ozuna & Cardi B)-** DJ Snake
3. **Wrapped Up In You-** Garth Brooks
4. **Paint The Town Red-** Doja Cat
5. **Sickick -** Official SickMix Part 3- Sickick Music
6. **Alone-** Kim Petras and Nicki Minaj
7. **Tag, You're It-** Melanie Martinez
8. **P.I.M.P-** 50 Cent
9. **Can I Be Him-** James Arthur
10. **Dandelions -** Slowed (Remix)- Muppet DJ & SECA Records
11. **Milk of the Siren-** Melanie Martinez

Warning

The Consumed Series is a dark, contemporary romance with adult themes. The female main character has multiple love interests and will not have to choose between them. The present love interests are not the dark and broody types but her past and future have plenty of darkness that will force our female to shine.

While I would love for you to enjoy this book, please keep your mental health a priority. This book is very different from the others. Unlike some books, this book will not only focus on Annie's trauma. The guys will all be dealing with their own primary and secondary traumas, as well. While some instances are not "healthy", they find out what supporting each other really looks like.

All too often we, as a society, forget that secondary trauma is real. Because of that, I felt it was important to dive into the experiences and thoughts of The Gospel Boys as they navigate through their traumas and help Annie overcome hers.

Please be aware of your triggers and limitations.
A more defined list of content/trigger warnings can be found on the next page.

Content/Trigger Warnings

Adult Language
RH
Polyamory
Bi-awakening
MM
MF
MMFMM
BDSM references
Graphic Sex Scenes
Inability to wake
Hospitalization with restraints
Nightmares
Discussions of past stabbing/betrayal/rape/forced drug use
PTSD
Body Dysmorphia
Anxiety and Panic Attacks
Disassociation
Trauma Healing- Primary and Secondary
Dizzy Spells/Almost Fainting due to lack of eating (Accidental)
Mention of child injury at pool (not on page)

If you have any questions about content or trigger warning, please reach out to triswyntersbooklover23@gmail.com.

1

Annie

Where am I? What is happening? Why can't I open my eyes? Am I dead? I'm floating in a never-ending pit of nothingness. Nothing is here. No one is here.

But, I can hear something beeping away like a bomb ready to explode. *What the hell is that sound? Someone turn it off, please!*

Fire and ice slide through my veins. I try to move. I try to scream. Lightning crackles behind my eyelids. *I can't breathe. I can't breathe. I can't...*

Darkness blankets me. It's so peaceful. No pain. No fear. No panic. Just me and the darkness, holding me tight.

2

Cory

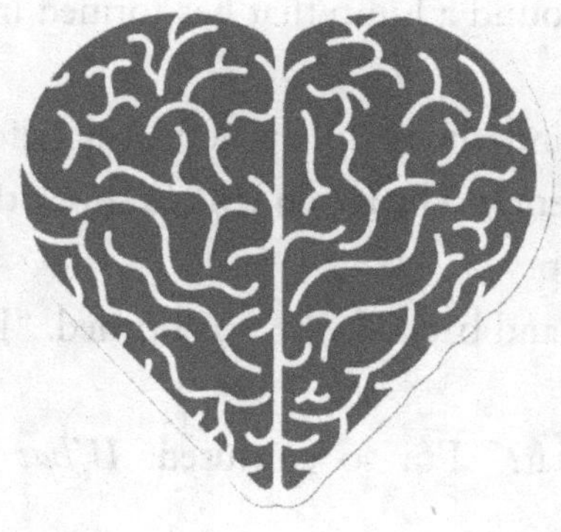

Gunfire erupts around me, echoing around the dungeon. The sickly scent of sweat, blood, and mildew fills my nose and I fight back a gag. I walk through a door and am immediately met with pain. Blood obstructs my vision; pain sears my body. I fight. Swinging, kicking, and screaming in fury and rage. "Annie! Annie! Where's Ann..."

"Cor! Cor. Wake up, bud." My eyes fling open as I suck in a painful gasp.

My heart feels like it's actively trying to beat out of my chest as panic continues to strangle me. Fear consumes me as my eyes dart around the dark, unfamiliar room before being sucked into stormy green eyes.

It takes me a moment to connect that I vaguely remember seeing an open door on the other side of the room with a light streaming from it. The light filters across the room, causing his green eyes to shimmer.

"Hey. You ok?" Jenson's whispered tone is laced with concern and a hint of fear flashes behind his eyes. I stutter on an inhale at being the sole focus of Jenson's attention. His brow furrows the longer I stare into his eyes without responding.

I see slight movement in my periphery, but I don't bother looking away. I swallow around a lump that has formed in my throat, blinking slowly.

"Cor?" His hand slides up my left arm before resting on my bicep, squeezing gently. The touch sends a shock through my system, causing me to jump.

He yanks his hand back like he was burned. "I'm sorry, Cor. Are you ok?"

"O-Okay? What?" I'm so confused. *What happened? Where are we?*

"Yeah. You were thrashing and screaming in your sleep. Bad dream?" He's still whispering which confuses me more.

Then the rest of what he said processes through my brain.

"Oh. Yeah. Sorry to wake you." I close my eyes, needing to break eye contact and remind myself he's just being a good friend. My emotions have been all over the place since Annie went missing and I'm not about to let a bad dream make me feel things that aren't there.

I sigh heavily and run a hand down my face, hissing in pain. "Careful, Bad Boy. Don't need you ripping your stitches." Jenson whips the blanket off of him and walks across the room to the bathroom.

My heart has finally settled and my eyes have adjusted thanks to the bathroom light. I remember that we left the medical unit late last night when I was finally cleared to "go home". Right now, home is the hotel room we're all sharing. It's simple but large enough we can all move around without bumping into each other. Nick and Vince share the bed next to ours; closest to the bathroom.

I turn my head towards the nightstand sitting between the beds and see the bright red numbers glowing. It's 5:30 am. This means it's been a little over 24 hours since we raided Lukas' warehouse.

Movement across from me has me shifting my eyes to the other bed and I notice Vince and Nick are both sitting up, looking at me with concern. "You ok, man?" Vince asks.

I exhale roughly and slowly start sitting up. Grinding my teeth through the pain in my ribs, and now my head, I finally position myself into a somewhat seated position. Nausea is rolling through my stomach and it takes me a moment to breathe through it; pursing my lips and concentrating on calming it.

After a moment, I think I have a handle on it so I can respond. "Yeah. Sorry to wake y'all."

Before I even finish, Vince is shaking his head as Jense makes his way from the bathroom. "No worries. None of us were sleeping all that great anyway. I'm sure it will take some time given what we've all been through."

As Vince stops talking, Jense hands me a bottle of water and two pills. I look at them in question before he smirks and says, "Nothing heavy. Nausea tablet that dissolves on your tongue and a strong acetaminophen. Promise."

I nod my head, knowing he wouldn't lie, and take the pills. By the time I down half the water in the bottle, Nick is sliding out of his bed and walking over to the bathroom. He closes it just enough to give him privacy but still allows some of the light to spill into the otherwise dark room.

It takes a moment for my brain to realize that Jense is still standing in front of me in his briefs; his dark, skin-tight briefs that leave nothing to the imagination. Goosebumps skitter across my arms and I have to force myself to look away, slowly leaning over and setting the water on the nightstand.

"Need anything else?" Jenson's voice sounds even more sultry in the dark. My dick takes note and hardens, seeming to reach out for him. I close my eyes tightly; visualizing muddy tires, greasy fingernails, and books that are falling apart at the seams. Anything, *anything,* to get my mind off of Jenson and the way I want to lick him from tip to... *Nope. No way. Think about little kids serving themselves at a buffet.*

Shaking my head, I glance at Jense before pulling the blanket a little higher on my chest; needing the extra layer of protection. "No. I'm good. Thanks, though."

His head tilts, a tender smile gracing his face, as he says, "Ok. Just let me know." He makes his way back to the other side of the bed we're sharing just as Nick walks out of the bathroom.

He stands there for a moment, looking between the three of us before asking if we're officially up or need some more sleep. We all shake our heads, knowing sleep wouldn't be coming for any of us, now. Vince leans over and hits the button on the lamp, illuminating the space around us. Nick slides in next to Vince, on top of the covers, and rests his head on his chest. Their contented sighs soothe something in me and I feel myself relax a little.

Feeling like I'm intruding on a private moment, I quickly look away, picking at the stitching that lines the coarse blanket. Silence fills the room as we all get lost in our heads.

Movement to my left steals my attention and I see Jense lying back, on top of the covers, with his right arm resting beneath his head. He looks trapped in a memory while staring at the ceiling. I watch as his brows furrow, and a frown crosses his handsome face. Whatever he's thinking about, it's hurting him.

"Hey", I whisper. "Penny for your thoughts?" He rolls his head towards me and his bicep flinches with the movement; causing the lines of his raven and skull tattoo to ripple. It's my favorite tattoo he has. Although, I don't think I've ever told him.

When he first got it, he had just finished a book of Edgar Allen Poe's works. We spent so many nights talking about the different literary works and the images they painted in our minds. It was so funny hearing the similarities and differences in our perspectives based on our views of the world. It's crazy how, like art, literary works can evoke different thoughts and emotions in people based on their backgrounds and circumstances. Those are some of my favorite memories with him. In fact, it was our conversation about "A Dream Within a Dream", paired with copious amounts of whiskey and laughter, that led to the night that we do *not* discuss.

Shaking my head like an etch-a-sketch to keep my brain from going down that road, again, I lift my eyes back to his. His brows are furrowed and drawn down like he's waiting for an answer but, I know he didn't ask anything. I tilt my head in assessment and watch as his brows soften and a small smirk lifts the corner of his mouth. "I'm just glad you're ok."

Closing his eyes, he takes a deep inhale, then blows it out roughly. When he opens them again, tears have settled against his lower eyelids, threatening to spill over. "I-I..." He coughs to clear his throat before trying again. "Cory, I saw you come out of the back door and you looked..." He swallows audibly, unable to finish his thought. "I was stuck between getting the women out and wanting to rush to you. Once I saw Enzo's guy had you, it helped a little but, you were basically out after that." He closes his eyes, shaking his head for a moment. When he meets my gaze again, his eyes hold so much fear and pain that I can't help but reach my hand out, lying it on top of his elbow.

"I know. I'm glad you were there. But, I'm glad you got the girls out. I'm ok, Jense. And I really appreciate you staying with me."

I don't realize I'm rubbing my thumb across his arm until I feel him flex. Snatching my hand back, I give him a reassuring smile before clearing my throat and turning away to grab my water.

As I take a swig, I notice Vince rubbing his hand through Nick's hair as he scrolls through his phone. They are so damn cute it hurts.

Chuckling to myself, I finish off the water. Twisting the cap back on, I start tapping it against my thigh. "So," I say loud enough to carry through the room. I sneak a peek at Jense, making sure he's paying attention, before looking back to Vince and Nick. "What now? I'm guessing you haven't heard anything?"

Vince sighs heavily, taking his left hand and rubbing it over Nick's, lying on his chest. "Haven't heard yet but, that's nothing to worry about. They were all dropped off with no names or anything. It's going to take some time for all of them, not just her, to be identified and families contacted. First, they have to go through injuries and make sure they're stable. I'm sure they're working on it."

We're all nodding our agreement because that does make sense and we were prepared for that. Honestly, it just feels good to know that she is, in fact, safe.

In true Jense fashion, he voices the question we're all skirtin' around, "So, what happened with everyone?" His left arm reaches across his chest as he turns his body towards me, sliding his hand to rest between his head and left arm. His bright green eyes search mine with an intensity that causes warmth to fill my body.

After a tense moment, I look away, not able to voice my experience as the nightmare is still too close to the surface. I turn my head towards Vince, raising my brows to hopefully signal that he needs to go first. He doesn't say anything about my past, but his eyes tell me that I will *absolutely* be sharing before we leave this room. With a deep sigh, I give a brief nod in understanding. We all know what can happen if we bury things too long and, fortunately, *and* unfortunately, we've all known each other long enough to know when to push and when to pull.

3

~

Annie

Hands grab at me. Pulling, tugging, squeezing. "No! Not again! I won't go back! Nick!!!"

My heart pounds in my ears, now overriding the beeping sounds, but I can't get in a full breath. *Fight, Annie. Fight. Don't let them take you back.*

Something heavy presses across my chest and arms. "Nooo! Help! Vince!"

I kick and scream and fight. *I can't go ba...*

Then I'm floating into darkness once again.

4

Jenson

Vince, Nick, and I spent about an hour telling our version of the events that took place almost 30 hours ago. It all happened so quickly that it almost doesn't feel real.

But, it was. It *absolutely* was.

We all sit in silence as we replay the stories through our minds. Vince was shot, and yeah, it's more than a damn graze. *Stubborn ass.* Nick got to hold Annie all the way to the hospital, and me, well, I got to help free almost a dozen women. Thankfully, Nick was the only one who didn't have to kill someone but, that's probably best given his past. Then again, having to let Annie go wrecked him in more than ten ways.

Vince raises his arm and hisses in pain. Nick immediately starts

3

〜

Annie

fussing over him and telling him that he needs to clean and redress the wound. Vince huffs in annoyance but Nick levels him with a glare. Within seconds, Vince concedes with a nod and Nick slips off the bed and rushes to the bathroom.

Cory and I chuckle, causing Vince to whip his head towards us with a glare before muttering, "Fuck off." And we lose it, laughing so hard that our faces are red and we're gasping for breath.

Nick comes out of the bathroom, stopping at the end of their bed, then pops his brow up and glances between us. Cory and I just continue laughing. Vince shakes his head and rolls to his side so Nick can get his wound clean. It's that movement that makes me suddenly realize that no one has checked Cory's wounds since we left the medic area last night.

"All right, you too, Bad Boy," I say, rolling off the bed and walking towards Nick. He snaps his head up and raises a brow in question. I smirk at him, tossing my head towards Cory. "Oh trust me, you'll understand once you get Cory's story. I only know some of it but it's enough to say that he's no longer a book dragon but a certified badass." Nick and Vince raise their brows in surprise and their eyes widen with shock and intrigue.

As I round the bed, I smirk back at Cory and tilt my head; making sure he knows damn well that he hasn't gotten out of storytime. But, the look I get in return makes me pause. His eyes look...haunted. My chest aches while wondering what the hell happened in that back room.

Humor gone, I quickly maneuver to the side of their bed and grab a few supplies. Once I have what I need, I walk back to the bathroom and grab two washcloths. I turn on the hot water, grab the bar of soap that we already unwrapped, and begin lathering it into one cloth. Then, I turn the cold water on and soak the other before ringing it out. I grab a larger hand towel, then wrap up all of the supplies in it before returning to Cory.

Nick and Vince are already cuddled back up and scrolling their phones. Grinning a little, I slide back onto my side of the bed before unwrapping the towel and laying out the supplies. I glance at Cory through my lashes, and watch as he stares down at the blanket; subconsciously running his fingers over the same spot repeatedly.

"Cor?" I try to say his name lightly but he still flinches in surprise. His eyes instantly widen as he whips his head towards me. I raise my hands a little and give a small smile before tilting my head. "Sorry, Cory. You were a little lost in your mind there and I need to clean up your cuts."

For a moment, he appears to be looking through me, and his eyes are pinched in confusion. Then he blinks a few times and his eyes clear in recognition. He half-heartedly grins before huffing out a laugh. "Sorry. Yeah. Sorry, I'm just still tired I guess."

I can tell that is only half true but decide to let it slide for now. "No worries. I get it." I reply mildly. "So, I'm going to check the back of your head first. Then clean your stitches and I need to check your ribs. Ok?"

His mouth pulls tight in a firm smile as he nods once. He slowly rolls his body forward as I lean in and begin to probe through his hair. He hisses when I make contact with the bump but, thankfully, it hasn't gotten too much worse. I take the cold cloth, press it to his head, and ask him to hold it for me. "It's the best I can do until I run to the ice maker".

He shrugs noncommittally, then leans back while keeping the cloth on his head. The blanket slips down his chest a little, giving me a peek at the light spattering of blonde hair on his chest.

Closing my eyes, I quickly clear my head of the thoughts that try to creep in. We promised each other we would never bring that night up but, fuck, it's so damn hard. And now, seeing him hurt physically squeezes my heart in a vice.

When we left the warehouse, I refused to leave his side from the moment I hopped in that van. It felt like a piece of my soul was being sliced away with every grunt, every groan, every stuttered breath.

But, I know where I stand and I refuse to make him uncomfortable. We've always been best friends. Sure, we've relied a little more on each other the last couple of weeks but that's probably because of our mutual feelings for Annie. Once she's back with us, the fleeting glances and light touches will go away. We just needed a little more support to cope with it all. Yup.

You're an idiot. Stop! Don't go down this rabbit hole again. It will only hurt worse.

Clearing my head, again, I get to work peeling off the bandage covering his stitches. I quickly use the soapy cloth to wipe away the little bit of blood, wincing when Cory flinches in pain. "Sorry," I mutter and quickly make sure the whole area is clean before re-dressing it.

"Ok, one more place. I need to check your ribs." His eyes snap towards mine in what looks like fear. "Cor, come on. It's me. I just need to make sure they're healing right. I've got some ointment for the bruising."

He considers me for a moment, eyes flicking between mine, before sighing loudly. He nods once and starts to bring the blanket down his chest. I swallow roughly as I watch the fabric slowly inch its way down, revealing more of his blonde curls. His muscles aren't as defined as Vince's but damn do I want to trace the outlines with my tongue. The fabric moves agonizingly slowly until it pools just below the band on his briefs. I suck in a breath through my teeth, hoping he doesn't hear it. My eyes trace over the lines of his Adonis belt without my permission.

Shifting to hide my growing erection, I open the tube of Arnicare, squirt some along my fingers, and gently massage it into his growing bruise across his ribs. He jolts in pain but lets me continue to work the ointment into his skin.

A few seconds later, I feel his body relax into the bed as the cooling effect takes over. I sit there for God knows how long, completely transfixed on the ministrations of my fingers and how his muscles bunch under my touch.

Eventually, I realize that all the ointment has been rubbed in and I am, well, being weird. I blink away the fog and swallow hard.

Suddenly remembering my surroundings, I hastily start cleaning up the supplies before flying off the bed like my ass is on fire. *Get it together. You can not lose it like this.*

Rushing back to the bathroom, I throw away the trash, rinse out the cloth I used to clean him, and set the rest of the things on the counter. I take a moment to stare at my reflection as I try to calm the pounding of my heart.

My feelings for Cory are becoming a problem. I've been attracted to him for the last few years. Watching my little book nerd spill all of the information needed about starting our own business lit me on fire. He had always been smart, but rarely showed pure joy. That day, though, he had bullet points, graphs, and more information than any of us knew what to do with. He left me in awe as he shared everything he had found with as much excitement as a three-year-old talking about bubbles. But, it was more than that. He wanted to open the business as much as we did and, honestly, we wouldn't have been half as successful without him. His mind blew me away and I wanted nothing more than to kiss him and share in his excitement.

Of course, I did nothing of the sort. I spent months watching as he went from a semi-quiet, slightly anal brainiac, to a confident man knowing exactly enough about *everything* in our lives to make sure we were all successful, safe, and set up for the future. That is definitely his love language, and he loves us all.

But then, I screwed up. One night he caught me reading "The Murders in the Rue Morgue" and looked at me like I had sprouted legs from my ears and his laugh echoed around the library. I've never really been the smartest of the group but I secretly loved to read. It wasn't that I was purposefully keeping it from the others, I guess. It's just, sometimes I longed to get lost in a different world. I found out a lot about myself through books and character interactions that I may not have ever considered.

Eventually, he calmed his laughter when he processed the look of shame and embarrassment on my face and quickly made amends. Apparently, Poe was one of his top 3 favorite authors so he was eager to talk with someone about his different works. After that, we agreed to make time to read and talk together. Two or three times a week we read the same thing and then talk about what we liked, hated, or didn't understand. Those nights led to some of the best conversations I've ever had.

Of course, it also led to a drunken night that we promised to forget about. I didn't want that. At all. But, when we woke up the next morning, after spending hours exploring each other's bodies, he freaked out.

I remember reaching out to rub the dimple I knew was hiding near his mouth but the moment my hand touched his face, he reared back like I had hit him. His head snapped towards me and I saw it all. His eyes swirled with fear and shame. My breathing stuttered as I asked him what was wrong, then solemnly guarded myself, expecting the worst.

The image of his brows pinching in irritation as he huffed out a humorless laugh is forever ingrained in my mind. "What do you mean what's wrong? We got plastered and could have ruined our entire friendship."

While *those* words stung, his next play in my head almost daily. "I'm sorry. We were wasted. I don't remember most of it. I'm sure it's fine. We don't have to bring it up ever again. Right?"

His eyes were wide with unshed tears and I knew right then; *I* had fucked up. I acted on my own stupid feelings and caused him to feel regret and shame.

"Right. Yeah." I chuckled, but I was filled with sorrow.

"Promise? We're good and we don't ever talk about it again?" No one knows, but that's the moment my heart fractured. It took all I had to muster up enough false positivity to respond; promising we would never speak of it again. Dropping my usual jokester mask in place, I jostled him around in a bro-friendly manner before tapping my hand on his shoulder, then slid off the bed.

Leaving the room was the most painful experience I ever had, next to my mother basically abandoning me. The difference was; that I expected it from her. I didn't see it coming from him.

"Jense, you ok in there, man?" Vince's voice carried through the bathroom, pulling me out of my head. I clear my throat, before telling him I'm good and am just cleaning up.

Looking into the mirror, I realize that I've had tears pouring down my face. *Nope. Not here. Move the fuck on, man.*

I quickly flush the toilet for some reason, brush my teeth, and rinse my face. Then I open the bathroom door and stride around to the other side of the bed while keeping my head down. I snatched up my sweatpants, tugging each leg through the holes, before throwing on a shirt from my bag.

"Where are you going?" Nick's voice is laced with concern and I can feel all of their eyes boring holes through my skull.

"Running to the ice machine, then to track down some coffee. I need coffee." I mutter the last bit to myself before swiping a key card off the dresser and walking straight the fuck out of the room. I didn't want any more questions. My emotions from the last few weeks have been too high, too raw, and I can't be the happy-go-lucky Jense they need right now.

I stroll down the hall and click on the elevator to take me down. But, I could feel the tears fighting to be let loose. I swear under my breath then turn towards the stairs, hoping it will help me clear my mind. *I don't need this. Not today. Not when we're still waiting for*

*news about Annie. And definitely not when I don't have my own room
to fall apart in.*

5

Vince

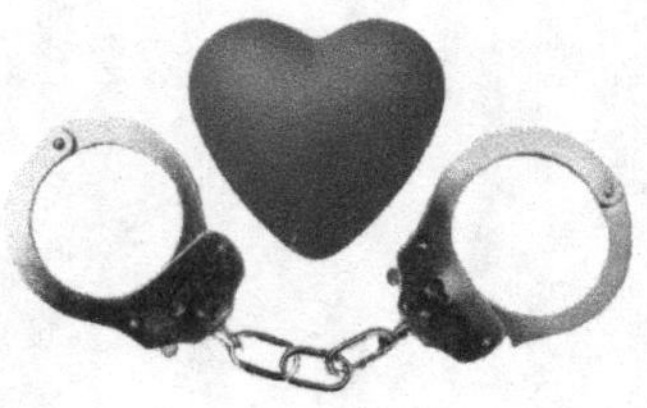

After Jenson returned with a bucket of ice, coffee, and bagels, Cory finally shared what he went through. The pain and fear in his voice almost crippled me. I don't know what we would do without Cory. He's the glue that holds us together. He's family and we would absolutely be lost without him.

We all hugged it out, then spent time wrapping our minds around the fact that we're all safe and relatively okay. Ten minutes later, I decided to get cleaned up. While Nick and I showered, Jense held the cloth filled with ice on Cory's head and ribs while Cory dozed.

Coming out of the bathroom, I feel so much better than I had before. Glancing across the room, I look at Jense, watching over Cory like a little mother hen; or like someone who's in love and won't admit it. I smirk, shaking my head. *One day those two will figure their shit out.*

I let out a quiet whistle to let Jenson know he was up next for a shower. He quickly checks over Cory's still sleeping form before sneaking off to the bathroom.

Nick raises his brow at me and smiles wide. "And they said we were bad," He mumbles out. We both chuckle and lean back against the headboard.

Turning on my tablet, I cue up the next episode of Lucifer. Nick always jokes that I'd prefer Tom over him but, honestly, I wouldn't be able to handle all that. Tom is probably a top and that is firmly my position. Although, the accent absolutely does things to me.

* * *

I startle awake when the sound of my phone ringing drifts through the room. I take a quick look around and notice that everyone else has also fallen asleep.

My phone rings out again and I swipe it from the nightstand. I inhale a gasp as I see my Captain's name flash across the screen. I quickly hit 'answer' as I slide off the bed and move towards the bathroom. "Daniels," I answer, hoping my voice doesn't convey my guilt.

A deep sigh filters down the line before he speaks. "Vince. I, uh, I know you're on leave this week but there's been a development in two of your cases. I knew you'd want to hear about it as soon as possible."

His voice, usually so strong and sure, trembles just enough to signal his concern. I take a deep breath, summoning up my most professional voice as I respond. "No problem, Cap. Glad you called. What's up?"

"It's about the Black Thorns." My spine straightens as he pauses much longer than I'm comfortable with. Fear tingles down my back as I prepare for him to tell me that I've been caught. That he knows we intervened and crossed legal lines. That my life is over.

Papers rustle in the background, bringing me out of my swirling thoughts of doubt. "I heard from CLSPD today. A warehouse and a home were attacked. Preliminary investigations assume someone knew about Lukas and his dealings and blew it all to kingdom come."

"Holy shit, Cap. Are there any survivors?" I try to hide the relief tinged with fear from my voice but, given the circumstances, maybe he won't find it odd.

"At this time, no. But, Vince," He exhales raggedly, after taking a deep breath. "The pictures of what's left of the warehouse; it's bad. They were definitely storing product there."

His throat clears, and his voice lowers. "Including women. I-I can't... I don't want to freak you out but, they were definitely held there." His loud sigh permeates through my brain.

"Are they safe?" My voice comes out raspy and thick with emotion. Yes, I know the answer, but it still feels surreal. Like it was all some fucked up nightmare. I didn't see the cells, the fucking dungeons like Jense and Cory did, but I know enough that it still rattles me. And the images my brain conjured up may not live up to reality, but it's enough for me to want to light it all ablaze; again.

Thankfully, Captain's voice pulls me out of my own head. "Fuck, Vince. They are. Well, the ones that were dropped off at the hospital."

"Dropped off? What do you mean?" I say, my voice regaining some of its strength.

"I don't even know. A bunch of mercenaries or something dropped the women off. All the cameras were wiped and none of the staff or other patients could identify anything other than black clothes, black beanies, and black marks covering their faces. Whoever they were, they didn't want credit for it." He snickers quietly before proceeding. "I'm sure they didn't want to get charged for the men they killed and the buildings they blew up. I mean, if they did all that, they're probably not on our side of the law. But, between you and me,

I'd shake their fucking hands. Those women were saved and that's a moral compass I can get behind."

I let out a strangled chuckle, agreeing with his assessment. Then, I release an unsteady breath. "An-Annie? Was Annie one of the women?"

He takes a moment before answering, causing me to panic. *What if something happened? What if she had injuries and died? Oh, God, I couldn't live with that.*

"Honestly, I don't know yet. They're still working their way through the victims. A couple of them needed surgery. They're all going to need psych evals. The officers are all so swamped and technically, it's not my jurisdiction, so I'm sure I'll be one of the last notified."

I nod my head and spend a couple of seconds in silence. Then, his soft laughter fills my ear, confusing me. "You ok over there, Cap?" I ask.

He chokes on his laugh before clearing his throat. "Yeah. One of the girls told the investigating officer to "go fuck himself" when he started asking about the men who brought her in. She was all too willing to give every detail about the men who had been keeping her and how they treated everyone. But the moment he asked about the people who got them out, she shut him down. Told him that even if there was something to say about them, she wouldn't. He tried to explain they needed to talk to the guys and ask them questions, too. That's when she told him to "go fuck himself". Said she knew if the police didn't know about them, that meant they were guardian angels and she refused to see an angel behind bars." I joined him in his laughter, praying that Annie kept her strength, as well.

"Can't say I blame her." I chuckle.

"Agreed. She mentioned she and the other girls had already agreed while they were being transported to the hospital. They will talk about anything else, but not the people who saved them."

"Damn. Talk about appreciation." I remark, thinking about what they all must have gone through. And, yet, they still have fire in them. They didn't let those assholes snuff them out completely.

"Yeah, I agree. And I don't blame them." He sighs out again. "Anyway, I just wanted to let you know. As soon as they have time to send me IDs, I'll let you know."

"Thanks, Cap. I appreciate it. And, let me know if I need to come back early."

He waited all of two seconds before responding. "Nah, you finish out your leave. I'll keep you updated. There will be plenty for you to do once you get back."

I grunt in agreement before we end the call.

6

Jenson

While Vince was in the bathroom, the rest of us stirred from our mid-morning naps. We can't make out much of his conversation, but we're all hoping it's going to be the news we've been waiting for.

Vince comes out of the bathroom with his hair ruffled and looking exhausted. Nick slides off the bed and slowly approaches him. When he places a hand on his shoulder, Vince jumps and looks around frantically before meeting Nick's eyes. "Sorry, what?"

Nick's grin can be seen from across the room. "I didn't say anything. You just looked..." he flicks his hand from his body to his face, "frazzled."

Vince nods a couple of times before swiping a hand through his hair roughly before sighing. "I'm good. Cap just called. He officially knows what happened. Well, what the Clear Lake Shores PD has told them. They don't have identification on all the women, yet, so we're still supposed to be blind about Annie." He gives us each a pointed look, causing me to roll my eyes in exasperation.

Once he forces us to voice our agreement, Cory begins shifting his body up. Hissing and grunting through the pain, he finally reaches a seated position; sweat dotting his brow. His head tilts toward me, likely feeling my glare burning through his head. "What?"

I shake my head and huff out an irritated breath, rolling my eyes as I scoot off the bed. "Stubborn asshole."

Once my feet hit the ground, I rush towards the window where our shoes are and slide my Asics on. I don't know why I'm so damn pissy but watching him be so fucking pigheaded and not asking for help just set me off. I have to get out of here. I know I'm not thinking clearly. I do. So, I'm removing myself to make sure I don't say anything I'm going to regret.

"What's wrong? Am I missing something?" The concern in Vince's voice stops me, right in the middle of tying my shoes. I only pause for a second before shaking my head and muttering, "Nothing".

Once I'm done, I stand up, and cross the room towards the door, swiping a set of car keys as I go. Right before I get to the door, I mumble, "Going for food. I'll be back." I flip the latch off the door, slam down the handle, and swing the door out wide before disappearing out into the hall.

I don't even bother with the elevator as I hook a left at the end of the hall. I slam into the Exit door and immediately race down the stairs. The sounds of my feet thumping against the cement echo through the narrow passage. I get a little thrill as my heart rate bumps up just a little. *Maybe I should find out if this place has a gym. Work off these stupid emotions.*

Hitting the final landing, I slam into the door, startling a few people in the main area. "Sorry," I call out as my cheeks heat. I quickly walk towards the front lobby and out the automatic doors. The chill in the air causes my skin to break out in goosebumps and I take a moment to let the fresh air fill my lungs and flow through my body.

Feeling a little more centered, I head towards the two cars we had parked in the lot. I glance down to see that I grabbed Cory's black Suburban keys. My eye twitches in irritation; the universe laughing at me as I try to run from the feelings pressing down on me. I angrily give the sky a middle-finger salute. I'm not even sure why, but it felt good for a moment.

Unlocking the SUV, I climb up and slide onto the smooth, leather seats. Slamming the door a little harder than necessary, I press the ignition button and take my phone out of my pocket. I need to get out of my head or get a release or something. I feel like I'm crawling out of my skin and I don't know if I want to scream, or cry, or find someone to go ten rounds in the ring with.

I scroll through my phone to find a song. I know the guys will pester me if I come back pissy so I need to use this time to my advantage. Limp Bizkit catches my eye so I scroll through before landing on Break Stuff. The first two chords vibrate through the SUV and I turn it up a little more, hoping to get out of my head, heart, whatever, and come back with a clear head.

I start screaming the song along with Fred Durst as I search up the little seafood restaurant we fell in love with a few years ago. It only takes me a few seconds before I find the address to Joe Lee's and hit the button to start the directions. I continue letting my rage match the song as I drive away from the hotel.

Halfway into the next song, I'm pulling into the small parking lot. The small building isn't much to look at, minus the red-lined roof and sides and the red and white striped tilted window coverings. But the food is to *die* for!

My shoes scrape across the cracked parking lot before I swing the front door open. Deep-fried bliss fills my nose as I turn and head for the counter. The little girl behind the register can't be older than 22, and she instantly makes me think of Jodie; the girl from the warehouse. My heart beats painfully in my chest and I absently rub it, hoping for relief.

"What can I getcha?" The girl asks, thankfully stopping the images from the other night from playing through my mind. Blowing out a breath, I summon my most charming smile and order our lunch to go.

Once I fill our drinks, I sit at one of the small wooden tables, leaning forward in a hard metal chair, as I wait for our food to be ready. My eyes roam the walls and ceiling as I spot some additions to the wacky decor. The entire left and back walls are lined in corrugated galvanized steel pieces; similar to what you would see on a small shed or warehouse roof. Attached to the steel pieces are random pictures of famous people who have eaten here, a bunch of random signs, and of course, fishing decor. Right in the center of the back wall is a bright neon Budweiser sign, hanging above a bunch of framed photographs. A large nautical rope bounds across the left and back walls and they also have large plastic fish hanging around.

I am sitting next to the front wall, which is basically a giant window complete with the American flag hanging from it. Across from me, the television is tuned into a local news station. A reporter fills the screen and my breath gets caught in my throat as I realize *where* she is. The cameraman zooms out and shows the woman standing in front of the destroyed warehouse. It's mainly a pile of broken cement with metal pieces sticking up all over the place, but those aren't the images *I* remember.

I shoot up out of my chair and rush over to the cashier. Her eyes widen as I approach, no doubt sensing the crazed energy coming off of me. "I'm sorry to startle you but, since there's not many people here, can you turn up the tv for just a minute? Please."

She warily looks at me for a moment before glancing at the TV; her eyes widening with intrigue. Looking back at me, she nods quickly and runs to the back. I turn and walk right back to the table as the reporter continues to review the damage.

Suddenly, blue numbers appear on the top right of the screen, signaling the volume going from 0 to 28. I turn with a smile and a wave as I shout, "Thank you" before turning back.

"... are still working through this section but what they've already found has been as shocking, as it is disturbing." The live feed switches to multiple images of the dungeon areas. The reporter drones on about the various tools and crates that were found but I zero in on the second, smaller dungeon area. While most of the main dungeon had been destroyed by the blast, chains, cuffs, and obvious cell bars were found in the rubble of the bottom dungeon. The images disappear before showing the reporter, again.

My mind doesn't process the next few words she says before she turns the report over to a man at a different location. He stands a few houses away from a giant structure that has also been blown to bits. People in safety gear are running all around the area, sifting through the rubble. With the house flattened, you can see the bay stretch out on the backside. "...have reason to believe the two bombings are related as both buildings were bought by known associates of the Black Thorns Gang. At this time, police have recovered 14 bodies between the two locations, but not a single survivor."

The ringing in my ears drowns out the rest of the report as a strange, euphoric feeling race through my body. *We really fucking did it. It wasn't a weird, fucked up dream. It happened. And we know we got Annie.*

A smile tugs at the corner of my mouth as peace, and a little bit of joy, thrum through my body.

"Your order's ready, sir." I jump at the girl's voice and she giggles out an apology. I smile wide, walking back to the counter and slipping $20 into the tip jar before thanking her. I take the bags of food, and the drink carrier, back to the SUV.

Feeling much lighter than I did when I left the hotel, I press the ignition button and click on my Jammin' mix. Taki Taki by DJ Snake with Selena Gomez, Ozuna, and Cardi B bump through the speakers. I smile wide, moving my body to the rhythm as I roll down the windows and exit the parking lot. I can't help it, the beat is so easy to get lost in, and it is just so fun to sing along. Besides, now my body is filled with excitement, and it needs to go somewhere.

Parking in the still-open spot next to Vince's truck, I roll up the windows, and jump out of the SUV. I feel a little pep in my step as I round the car, open the passenger door, and take out our lunch. I do a goofy white-boy jig, close the door with my hip, and chuckle at myself. *Yup, leaving was exactly what I needed to release the tension.*

I feel like I'm gliding through the foyer; high on life and ready for whatever comes next. Hitting the elevator button with my elbow, I wait and sway to the beat in my head. When the doors slide open, I strut in and hit the third-floor button. A smirk pulls at my mouth when I realize that not even the boring elevator music can bring me down.

The elevator bings, alerting me of my arrival, and whooshes open. I step out onto the blue and cream carpet and bee-line for our door. Kicking out twice, I holler through the door that I have food. Five seconds later, I'm strolling in; still rockin' a little swag as I move. I walk right over to the little table that sits by the window and start opening the bags. "Okay, I got everyone a Kemah Combo."

I open the first one and quickly walk over, pushing it into Nick's hand. "Catfish, oysters, and butterfly shrimp for you." Then I walk back over and open the last three boxes, setting the one aside that's mine. Taking the other two in my hand, I hurry over to Vince. "Stuffed crab, crawfish tails, and Flounder for you," passing it off quickly, I then turn towards Cory with the last box, "And, of course, chicken tenders, popcorn shrimp, and crawfish tails for you."

Hurrying back to the little round table, I grab the drinks and pass them out before sitting with a loud and carefree sigh. I take out the container of shrimp coleslaw and crack open the lid then free a fork from the utensil wrap. Just as I stick my fork in my coleslaw, I realize that no one has moved, or talked, or anything, since I walked in. I mean, I know *I'm* excited but, did I miss something completely?

I raise my head and take a quick look around the room. Nick is standing next to his bed, food and drink in hand, not moving a muscle. I dart my eyes to Vince who is sitting on the edge of the bed, having put his drink on the nightstand and food next to him as he looks at me like he's waiting for an answer. *Shit. Did I miss a question? I must have really been in my head.*

"Uh, sorry. Did you ask something? I was a little lost to the music in my head." I jokingly pull my smile back down my throat, hoping to convey that it was an accident. But, after another moment of silence, I start to get nervous.

I quickly glance at Cory, who looks at me like I'm a wounded animal. I can't handle any look from him right now. Not after I just got back to myself.

I avert my eyes and land back on Vince, lifting my brow in question. He takes a deep breath and I slowly lower my takeout container to my lap. "What happened?"

The room freezes with a tense silence before Vince stands up and slowly makes his way towards me. As soon as he gets close enough, he kneels down while his brows pinch with worry. "Melissa called."

I tilt my head, completely confused. Then it hits me like a hand upside the head. "She did! What did she say? Is it Annie? Is she ok?"

Vince turns back to look at Cory, then Nick, before returning to me. His eyes bore into mine as he takes a few controlled breaths. "Annie *is* in the hospital. She's *mostly* okay. But,"

I wait, or I try to, but the tension pulls so tight, I'm afraid it will snap. "But *what* Vince?" I didn't mean to snap at him but he needs to spit it the fuck out right now or I'm going to lose it.

"She's having a hard time waking up, *and* staying calm when she does." His eyes dart between mine like he's hoping he doesn't have to say more.

"Okay," I said slowly. "So she needs more rest. I mean, that shouldn't be surprising right?" I shrug my shoulders because *of course*, she needs to sleep. Lord knows how much she got in that hell hole.

Vince shakes his head slowly before glancing down. I hear him swallow hard before he looks up at me again. "No, she's stuck between *there* and *here; in her mind*. She's become combative. They've had to restrain her because she panics and immediately goes into fighting mode. Once she does, they sedate her again."

Anger builds inside me but, also, a little pride. I knew my little Hellcat wouldn't go down without a fight.

"Well," I start, then give in to the need to take a deep breath. "Good."

"Good?" Nick's voice strikes out across the room causing Vince and I to both turn towards him. His face is contorted in anger and I can hear the styrofoam takeout box compressing as he squeezes it.

"Yes, *good*. Even if she's stuck in a dark place now, she's fighting. *Literally* fighting. *That*, my dear friends, means she was probably fighting there, too. Our girl is strong as fuck and I, for one, am proud of her."

Nick goes to talk but I hold a hand out to stop him. "I am *not* happy she's stuck. I was a little angry, *at first*, that she's being restrained but she's *safe*. She's ok. She's alive. *And*, she's *fucking fighting*." I give each of the guys a pointed look before shrugging my shoulders. Grabbing the coleslaw container I pull out the perfect bite, with a tiny shrimp in the middle of my fork, and point it at them, "It's not the best case scenario, but it sure as hell isn't the worst. Our girl's fighting and we should abso-fucking-lutely be happy about *that*."

I pop the slaw in my mouth and close my eyes with a smile as the flavors erupt on my tongue. Not too much mayo, or sugar, or salt. Simply. Perfect.

Once I swallow, I open my eyes to find the guys all looking at each other and nodding in agreement as my words settle over them. A smirk of satisfaction tips my lips as they all tuck in and begin eating.

We spend the next fifteen minutes eating and talking about plans for the next day or so. No one is allowed to see Annie, yet, so Melissa plans on going up tomorrow after the kids are dropped off at school. With any luck, we'd get to see our girl by tomorrow afternoon.

7

Nick

Jense was obviously in a better mood after his lunch trip. He never could sit still for long. Being cooped up in the hotel is probably working his nerves.

After lunch, we all decided to watch a few episodes of *Lucifer*. We have to stay hidden for a bit longer so no one can connect our involvement with the Black Thorns crap. Plus Cory definitely needs to rest and heal as much as possible. He's being a little shit about taking pain meds even though he very clearly needs them. *Maybe that's also part of Jenson's little tantrums?*

We're almost finished with the second episode when our phones all ping with a message. Glancing at each other in surprise, we all rush to open our phones. A collective sigh of disappointment flies around the room. We all tense at the sound, and then immediately start laughing. Clearly, we're all a little disappointed that it isn't news about Annie.

Cory looks over at Vince, "I really want to go but, I may need a shoulder to lean on." Behind him, I see Jenson turn his brows down and tense his jaw. *Oooo he's big mad right now.*

Vince must catch it, too, as it takes him a moment to respond. "Of course, we aren't leaving you here. I'm sure Jense and I can manage to get you down to the conference room at dinner time."

Cory nods silently before leaning his head back against the wall behind him. His Adam's apple travels with the movement of his heavy swallow. I swear it looks like he's trying to focus anywhere except on Jenson. But I mean, judging by the glare Jense is using to burn a hole through Cory's face, I'd probably be avoiding him, too.

I steal a glance at Vince, who appears to be watching the same show I am. However, *he* must feel my eyes on him as he slowly turns his head towards me with a raised brow and conniving smirk. I know that look and, no, we absolutely will *not* be trying to push them together. There's too much going on right now and that has "Bad Idea" flashing in neon lights around the room. I try to convey as much as I narrow my eyes and a slow shake of my head. A wide smile spreads on my face and I have to swallow my chuckle as Vince's body slumps forward with a heavily disappointed sigh. Besides, Enzo just asked us to come down for dinner tonight to discuss the information he collected from all of his men post-mission. So, yeah, no one is in the right headspace for all of *that* right now. *Now* needs to be about resting, planning, and waiting to see My Siren.

At 6 o'clock, we head down the elevator to the lobby. Cory has his arm draped over Jenson's since he's still getting dizzy spells and the bruising around his ribs and abdomen from the fight is making it difficult for him to walk without pain.

Once we make it to the first floor, we head to the conference room Enzo has rented out for the evening. It is a large space filled with three long tables and enough chairs to seat at least 30 people. The same blue and cream carpet from the hall upstairs fills the space and the windows to the outside are blocked by the closed blinds. The scent of garlic and tomatoes wafts through the air, tickling my nose and causing my stomach to growl.

Enzo, naturally, sits at the head of the middle table, eyes sparkling with adoration at Gina; who sits on his left. Rocco and Mateo both sit on her right side, leaning forward on the table, and are equally looking at her like she is the sun, the moon, and all the stars.

Vince clears his throat, breaking their trance. Enzo stands, quickly buttoning his suit jacket, strolls over with a genuine smile on his face, and shakes all of our hands. "So good to see you all, again. Come on over. I've had a local Italian restaurant deliver. I hope you don't mind."

"Sounds amazing!" Jenson replies with a smile of his own. We walk over to the table, take turns shaking hands with Mateo and Rocco, and giving gentle hugs to Gina, before sitting on Enzo's right.

Matteo and Rocco start taking the aluminum covers off the pans set out across the table. Steam curls up to the ceiling, carrying the scents of oregano and garlic around the room. Gina hurriedly stands up and passes out plates, utensils, and napkins to each of us. Her pale cheeks redden as she murmurs, "I'm so sorry. I was going to have them out when you got here but, I, um, got distracted." Her little giggle makes me smile as Vince assures her it is more than fine.

We all start digging into the platters of chicken parmesan, spaghetti with meatballs and Italian sausage, chicken alfredo, antipasto salad, and garlic bread. I never shy away from good Italian food so I have a scoop of each. The mixture of flavors explodes on my tongue and a moan falls from my throat.

I startle as a big, warm hand lands on my thigh; squeezing tightly. I glance at Vince out of the corner of my eye and smirk at the tension set in his jaw; his eyes close as he inhales deeply.

Turning back to my food, Enzo begins sharing the information he received from each of the guys we raided Lukas' house and warehouse with.

Just as Enzo finishes talking about what went on in the house, Vince's hand tightens on my thigh. I shoot my head over to him, tilting forward to look at his face. His eyes are unfocused and the bumpy rise and fall of his chest tells me he's having a hard time catching his breath. "Vince," I whisper.

When he doesn't so much as blink, I realize everyone else has gone quiet, likely sensing that something is wrong. I fold my hand on top of his, squeezing hard, as I try to get his attention again. "Vince, what's wrong? What happened?"

His eyes are still glazed over and unfocused when he utters, "I, I was right there. She was right behind me the whole time."

Jense leans over the table to look at Vince. "Yeah," he says slowly. "I thought you knew Mikas had taken her and passed her to Nick?"

Vince is already shaking his head, pulling both lips over his teeth and biting down. "I guess, it just didn't really connect until right now. But," he swallows hard as tears fill the bottoms of his eyes. "I, I saw the room before we left. The guy had his shirt off and pants down..." Vince pales and his body begins to tremble. "What if he," he clears his throat and turns towards me.

Enzo holds his hand up and gives Vince a stern look, "I'm going to stop you right there. I talked with Lars, the guy who opened the door and found her. He said he was just pulling his pants down. We won't know for sure without a doctor's input but, there was no reason to believe he had..." Enzo's hand flits through the air as he struggles with the words.

"Started," Gina provides with reddened cheeks and sad eyes.

Enzo snaps his head towards her. Sympathy shines in his eyes as he reaches towards her with a loving smile. He cups her face, rubbing his thumb over her cheek. "Yes, Mia Regina."

Vince swiftly wipes his eyes and takes three large gulps of his water. When he clears his throat, he nods and gives a subtle smile to Enzo and his family before saying, "Thank you. All of you. We really couldn't have done this without you."

Rocco pointedly coughs out, causing us to turn towards him. His eyes hold Enzo's and a silent conversation passes through them. Unease ripples through me as Enzo closes his eyes and sighs heavily. Opening his eyes, he levels each of us with a look that implores us to let him explain before jumping in. "We heard from the Cosa Nostra. After running the facial recognitions that we could, one person was actively missing from the destruction that night."

I suck in a breath, already knowing where this is going.

"Lukas was not in the wreckage of the house. We reviewed the footage and there was a blind spot in coverage. Once the door was blown, he snuck out, like the cowardly bastard that he is. We caught a glimpse of him on a camera a few houses down. He had stolen their boat and high-tailed it out of there. Apparently, he caught up with the cargo ship moving the product they were able to offload."

Jenson groans, tugging his hair, Cory looks like he's about to cry and Vince's whole body is vibrating with barely contained rage. Me, well, I've gone numb. *After all that and the asshole still slipped through our fingers?*

Enzo clearly notices our plummeting moods as his tone changes. It lands somewhere between comforting and assuring. "But...the Cosa Nostra caught him when he tried fleeing from the ship. Once they boarded, he tried to jump off the side. *Idiot.*" He scoffs, rolling his eyes. "He broke his leg with the impact of the fall to the deck and they were all too happy about exacting revenge on the actual person who wronged them."

He lets that piece of information fill our veins as we slowly come to terms with the fact that, he may be alive, but he's been caught by the biggest and baddest there is.

Clearing his throat, he adds, "They were able to recover the women, set them up in a hospital, and worked with local law enforcement to track down their families. As far as Lukas, let's just say my contact has informed me that they're going to make sure Lukas feels every ounce of pain that he has caused; ten-fold."

The thought of him being mercilessly tortured by one of the largest mafias in the world should make me feel bad, I think. But, honestly, I'm glad. *Fuck him and all he's done.* I hope he spends whatever time he has left on this Earth in complete agony.

Looking up, I see the others wearing soft, unsure smiles before nodding in acceptance. Jenson's voice calls out as he raises his glass, "To new friends, good family, and gettin' a little justice." Everyone cheers and clinks their glasses together before refocusing on the delicious meal.

We spend the next hour sharing funny stories and keeping the conversation light. When we started talking about our venture with the youth center, Rocco's eyes lit up. By the time we finish dinner, we promise to send him what our plans are for the next six months so he can do something similar in their community. It filled my heart to hear that our little program to help the local youth may spread to other areas; even if it does contradict the typical "scary mafia guy" cliché.

After dinner we slowly savor dessert; tangy Italian lemon cream cake and fresh cannolis. I sit back and silently observe everyone, talking vibrantly and laughing together, and am immediately struck by the complete absurdity of it all. We're sitting here, casually talking about family recipes and where the best vacation spots are, with people who lead a whole damn syndicate. They have known associations with the Italian Mafia for cryin' out loud! *But*, after what we've all been through, they're family. They love deeply and truly care about those in their circle. How Enzo talks about his men makes it obvious that he not only respects everyone in their ranks but genuinely cares about their well-being. He's not some crazed tyrant trying to kill everyone with a Tommy Gun. *I know, I watch too many movies.* Instead, he takes into consideration everyone's strengths and uses those to make moves across the cities he leads to make improvements. Whether it be farming, giving torn-down areas much-needed facelifts, or making sure the worst of the worst don't take advantage of innocents, he and his people have a hand in it all.

As Matteo begins stacking up the dirty dishes to throw away, Gina starts talking about how awesome it would be to visit next summer. Excitement rolls off of her in waves as she bounces happily, clapping her hands, and talking about all of us going fishing, cruising around in one of Enzo's boats, spending the day at NASA and another at Kemah.

As she continues to plan all the things we can do together, I feel a smile pull at my lips. Our little family has grown. I have no doubt that we would do anything for them, and they have clearly done the same thing. I just hope Annie will want to be part of it.

8

❧

Annie

I startle as I fall out of the darkness. A strange light burns through my eyelids and I struggle to breathe. Panic wraps its hand around my throat as I choke and heave for breath. My heart bangs roughly against my ribs, causing pain to spread through my chest.

"...nie. You're ok. We've got you." I man's voice spears through my panic but it isn't familiar. *I never got out. It was all a dream. Nick wasn't there. The guys hadn't come for me. And I'm still a prisoner.*

I scream out as agony pierces my heart. *I need to fight. I need to get free.* I raise my hands but am held down. Again. Something is

43

wrapped around my wrists. I try to kick out instead, but my ankles are shackled, too.

"Noooooo! Let me go. I'm not yours. I'm not y..."

A cool, calming sensation races through my veins. I can feel it soothing a path through my body, causing me to unclench my fists, and relax back into the comfort of darkness once again.

A feather-light touch across my forehead forces light into my world. My head is so foggy, my limbs are heavy and worn. But there's a soft, female voice. It's kind and loving. I find myself leaning into it, wanting to soak in the warmth it fills me with.

She's speaking just above a whisper and I try desperately to hold onto the words. "...and Josh decided he wants to try baseball next season. I told him we could talk about it. Oh! And the kids enjoyed laughing at me. They had to teach me how to feed Reginald. I don't know how you can handle having bugs living in your house but watching them smile and giggle about his bug salads is definitely sweet."

The words make their way through the murkiness that fills my brain. They're familiar and comforting; pulling on the strings of my heart and slowly unraveling it. Intense sadness slices through my heart and a soft whimper escapes me.

The pressure on my forehead stops suddenly before gradually sliding down my cheek. Another joins it on my other cheek and some-thing larger, warmer, leans against my forehead. "Please, baby. Please come back to me." The gentle whisper squeezes my heart and I feel a splash of liquid fall against my cheek, sliding down.

The pressure in my chest increases as fatigue pulls me back. I try to fight it, I do, but I'm just so, damn, tired.

9

~

Cory

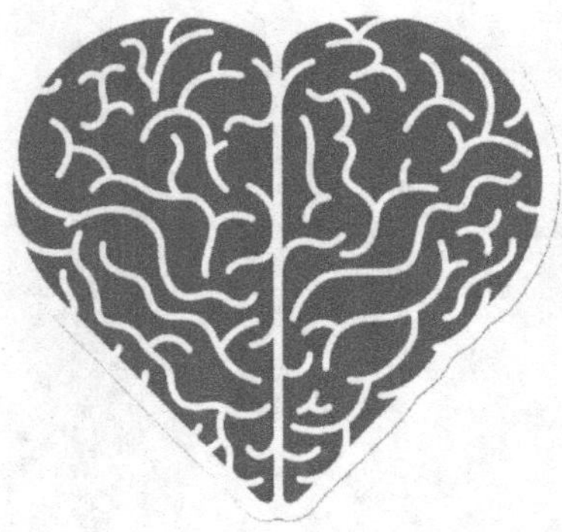

I jolt awake and immediately curl into myself from the pain. Sweat coats my body and my heart thunders in my chest. The nightmares are really starting to irritate me.

A hand on my shoulder, tenderly rubbing up and down, helps to settle me as my eyes adjust to the darkness of the room. The last frames of the nightmare fade away as I remember where I am and who I'm with.

Turning slowly, I face Jenson. His eyes are still closed with sleep even as his hand makes calming patterns down my arm. "Sorry for waking you," I whisper.

His hand stills for a second before continuing with his comforting strokes. "I was already awake. I've got you. Go back to sleep."

Pinpricks sting my eyes as they form tears and I've never been so thankful for the dark. I reach my right arm over my body, as gently as possible, before finding his hand and grasping it. His movement halts; causing my heart to break. But then, I feel just a ghost of a touch from his thumb skimming the skin on my shoulder. Still trying to comfort me; letting me know he's still got me.

I press his hand in a silent thanks before dragging my arm across my body and letting it drop back to the bed. Concentrating on the sounds of his breathing, and the featherlight touches on my arm, I coast back into a much more relaxing sleep.

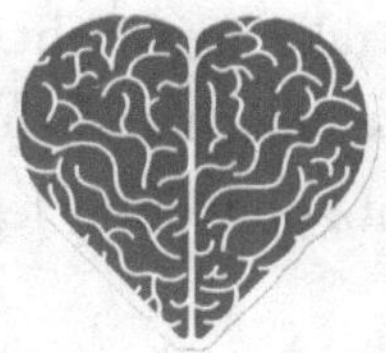

The click of the door closing pulls me from my peaceful slumber. My eyes flutter as I try to adjust to the light given off by the open bathroom door. It takes a minute for my brain to come back online as the last pieces of sleep disappear.

At some point, I must have rolled to my side, as I'm now facing Vince and Nick's bed. Only Nick is in bed, hair wet from what I can only assume is a recent shower. He's dressed in black ripped skinny jeans and a heather blue Nirvana tee. Leaning over his laptop, he clicks a million miles a minute while he does whatever his genius tech brain is trying to do.

A smirk pulls at my face; then the sound of water cuts off. I hadn't even realized it was on, but now the silence is deafening. However, it does nothing to coax me out of the bed. *Although, I do need to pee.*

I lie there for another minute or so before reaching my hands down and pressing them to the bed. Inhaling deeply, I begin to lift myself to a seated position. My arms struggle to hold my weight as I do everything in my power to not move my core too much. The bruising may be fading, a little, but the internal bruising is excruciating. *Not that I'd tell any of the guys that.*

It takes longer than I'll admit to get my feet to dangle off the bed and prepare myself to stand. Thankfully, Nick is too engrossed in what he's working on to notice my movements. I haven't looked behind me but I assume Jense must still be asleep. If he was awake, I already know he'd be all up in my space like a mother hen. Not that it's bad, it's just... I like him taking care of me a little *too* much.

Feeling brave, or stupid, I plant my hands on either side of my hips and slowly let my feet take my weight. I bite my cheek to prevent from groaning out as my stomach and chest protest the movement. I'm feeling a little like Bambi on wobbly legs but I do, in fact, manage to stand unassisted.

Exhaling roughly, I make my way between the two beds, then stop at the dresser. My bladder is officially about to explode so, the closer I am when Vince comes out, the better.

I grasp the handle on the dresser in a death grip as my body trembles with lack of movement. I don't care. I will do this. I *need* to do this.

Another minute passes and I'm starting to worry that my legs may give out if Vince spends any more damn time primping. *Jesus, he's getting almost as bad as Jense.* I chuckle to myself as I think about how long Jense takes to manage all that hair. Hair that I want to comb my fingers through and- *Nope! Down boy.*

The moment my thought subsides, the bathroom door swings open, and steam rolls in waves over the top of the door frame. And out steps Jenson. He's only done up his hair in a half man-bun today, letting the rest of his hair fall just below his shoulders. And sweet baby

Jesus, he's only in a towel. *I mean, of course, he's in a towel. That's not new but, um,* fuck. *I can't handle this right now.*

A water droplet runs down his neck and my eyes decide to follow it all the way down. It travels a path I've often dreamed of doing; hooking from ridge to ridge, then slipping down the line of his V... until it soaks into his towel. I feel myself swallow thickly around a rock that has formed in my throat. Quickly clearing my throat, I brashly ask, "You done? I gotta use the bathroom?"

I quickly glance at his eyes before looking into the bathroom. My vision starts to double as I stare at it like it might magically lift me over his head so I don't have to make my way around him. "Yeah, sure. Sorry. I'll check on your stitches aft..."

"No. I'm fine. I've got it now. Thank you." My voice comes out a little harsher than I meant for it to but he's been so hot and cold the last few days. And I think I'm getting a little cabin fever.

I straighten as much as I can, sucking a breath through my teeth from the stretching in my chest and abs, then force myself to walk as steadily as possible past him. The man-sized pain in my ass doesn't move an inch, forcing me to brush against his bare arm that's still warm from his shower.

As soon as I step into the bathroom, I close the door and release the breath I've been holding. His citrus and leather scent clings to the steam still wafting through the room, further irritating me. I stumble over to the shower, angrily ripping the clothes from my body as I go; pain be damned. I reach down, biting off a groan, and turn the shower to ice cold. Not only will it help me with the pain coursing through my head and upper body, but it will tame my hardening dick.

I stare down at the treacherous bastard, standing proud and leaking from the tip, before rolling my eyes and stepping under the icy cold spray. Hissing out a breath, I force myself to stand still as the cold pelts my body like needles and begins to inject a chill through my body. The ache in my muscles slowly begins to lessen; along with my protruding cock.

As I watch the water swirl down the drain, my mind flips through the last two months. The extreme highs from being with Annie and the partnership with the Youth Center were some of the most important experiences in my life. But the lows; so many damn lows. From Annie being taken, to weeks of no information, to the attack at the warehouse, and now my mind and heart are blurring the line between Jenson and me...

I absently rub at my chest, willing the ache to recede as tears mingle with the shower water. I slowly lean my back against the far side of the shower and slide down until the back of my head is resting on the bathtub ledge, extending my legs out so the icy water hits directly on my abdomen and chest.

And for just a moment, I allow myself to feel, to fall, to break.

10

Vince

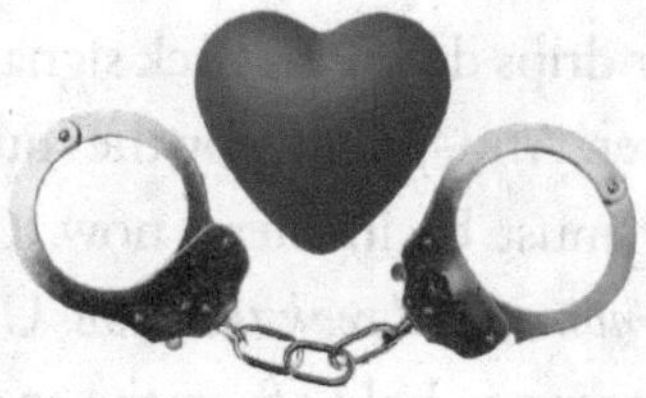

Right around thirty minutes ago, Nick and I took advantage and had some private shower time while Cory and Jense slept. We needed a minute to reconnect, to remember that we're both still alive, and to just bask in each other's presence.

Once we got out, we settled on the bed minutes before Jense woke up and decided to shower, too. The shower had barely turned on before my phone started ringing. When I silenced it and saw that Melissa was calling, I hopped out of bed and made my way into the hall so I didn't disturb Cory. He's been fighting nightmares and, honestly, he looks like shit.

After talking with her, I grabbed us all some coffee and muffins from the breakfast downstairs. I knew that once I told the guys what Melissa revealed, they'd all be ready to sprint the hell out of here.

Stepping off the elevator, I briskly move down the hall and tap the bottom of the door with my foot. I let Nick know I would need help opening up before I left the breakfast room. He clearly must have been waiting because my foot barely connected with the ground again before he was swinging the door open.

A huge smile stretches across his face and his eyes look brighter than they have in days. I am so damn thankful we decided to spend some time together this morning. It clearly did wonders for us both.

I step in and he takes the drinks from my hand, placing a gentle kiss on the side of my mouth before spinning and heading over to the table across the room. Closing the door with my now free hand, I turn and make my way toward Nick and catch Jense bending over the bed tying his shoes. Water drips down his back signaling that he probably just finished his shower. And, judging by the sounds of water rushing through pipes, Cory must be in there, now. *Good, they're going to want to head out the moment I break the news.* Unfortunately, Cory *is* in the shower so I'm going to hold off on the good news. Lord knows he needs to care for himself, too.

Jense, Nick, and I spend the next ten minutes chomping down on the muffins and soaking up the coffee. My leg bounces with excited energy. I can feel Nick's gaze flicking back and forth between me and his laptop. Another minute passes before he slams it closed and turns toward me. "Dude, what gives?"

"Uh, nothing. Just antsy. I hate waiting in this damn room." The other two nod their heads, accepting my statement as being restless from lack of movement; instead of restless from the information that is bursting to come out.

Not able to take it anymore, I shoot to my feet and stomp over to the bathroom door. I land two solid knocks before screaming through the door. "Hey, Cor! You 'bout done in there? I'm getting restless and need to get the hell out of here. Chop-chop."

Smiling at my ability to joke around like we used to, I wait for his response. But, the longer I wait, the more my smile fades. Another second passes before I call out again, "Cor, you ok?"

Nothing.

It's then that I realize I don't hear the lapping of scoops of water splashing in the tub. Instead, it's a steady stream of water pelting down. No movement; just on and spraying down with nothing blocking its path.

Unease creeps up my spine and I take half a step back to glance at Jense. His gaze is already trained on me. His brows are high on his forehead and wrinkled in the middle. His eyes are wide, sparking with fear. *Yeah, he has no clue why Cory isn't answering either. Fuck it.*

I don't knock again, I just turn the handle and walk right in. Cory's eyelids are swollen from tears and pair perfectly with red streaks that have overtaken his normally white sclera.

In three long strides, I'm at the edge of the tub, leaning down and shutting the water off. "Get up."

I turn and grab two towels off the wired shelving unit and begin unfolding them. By the time I turn back around, Cory's grunting as he slowly rolls over onto his knees and braces his hands on the side of the tub.

His entire body is shaking uncontrollably and is distorted in a painful blue color. "Dude, what the fuck were you doing?"

He turns to look at me over his shoulder before mumbling, "Figured the cold water would help with the pain."

Shakily, he brings himself to stand. I knew better than to try and help because he's so damn used to doing everything himself that he has a hard time accepting it. And hell would freeze over before he *asked* for help.

I quickly wrap a towel around his lower body then drape the other one over his shoulders, tying it off like a cape. "I get that but, one, that was too fuckin' long, and two, you should have at least told one of us. You still have a concussion, man. The last thing we need is for you to have slipped or something and busted out that beautiful brain of yours." I give him a grim smile, praying that he can not only see the truth of my words, but also the worry.

He stares at me for a moment, shivering from head to toe, before tilting his lips in a chastised smile. "Yeah. You're right." He exhales heavily. "Sorry, I guess I'm not doing all that great right now. But, you said you wanted to get out for a bit, right? That may be exactly what I need." His smile grows a little more and his eyes shine with a hint of excitement.

I nod then pat him on the shoulder. "All right, I'll bring you some clothes. If you need something, tell us Cor. Don't you dare struggle alone. You know better. Big or small, we're brothers, family. Let us be that for you."

He nods his head in acceptance and I turn out of the bathroom and walk towards his bag. Jenson is sitting at the end of the bed, boring holes into my noggin. As I grab the last of Cory's things, I face him and level him with a hardness in my eyes that I usually save for men I'm locking up.

"Jense, we're all hurting, we're all emotionally fucked up after the last few weeks, but you two need to get it together. You're both spiraling and pulling away from each other and you know damn well how pointless that is."

His eyes widen in shock and, while I want to say more, I don't. Not right now. Not when I have information that will change everything.

I head back to the bathroom and put Cory's clothes on the counter. As I turn to leave, Cory murmurs, "Th-thank you. I know I'm being a pain in the ass. I ju-" He inhales deeply and then releases it before continuing. "I just don't know how to get help for stupid shit like standing. Especially when every one of you needs help, too. I just don't want to add to it."

I face him fully and take the last step between us. I tentatively place both hands on his shoulders and make sure that he has no choice but to look at me. "I get that, I do. But if we all turn in on ourselves, we'll destroy this entire family. We've always been there for each other, and this shit isn't changing that. Testing it; maybe. But not changing it. Got it?"

My eyes bounce back and forth between Cory's until he smiles and nods. "Got it."

"Good. Now get dressed. We're getting the fuck outta here." With that said, I leave the bathroom, close the door behind me, and swipe my truck keys, wallet, and hotel card.

I turn back to the other two and lift my mouth into a mischievous smirk. "Once he's out, we're leaving. Grab whatever you need to hold you over for a few hours." Jenson and Nick both raise their brows at me like I'm insane but I can't be bothered to care. Today is everything and I can't wait to tell them where we're going.

11

Nick

The truck ride was maybe seven minutes but I swear to all things holy if Vince doesn't go faster, I'm going to throttle him. The second Cory came out of the bathroom, Vince smiled like a kid who had just been told he had an all-access pass to Main Event for the day. We were all dressed and ready to go, wherever it was he decided to go, but his energy seemed a little too high given we were just supposed to get out of the room for a bit.

Jenson asked why he was being weird, which made Vince laugh. It was warm and rich and boomed around the room, initially causing me to flinch in surprise. But, once the sound penetrated, I couldn't help but smile with him. I've missed *that* Vince. The happy, playful, confident Vince. But his next words have been playing on repeat in my head for the last eight minutes. "Melissa called. She's with Annie and wants us to join her. She woke up once, panicked, and they put her back to sleep. But, an hour later, she was talking to her and she swears Annie responded in her sleep. She wants us to visit and is hoping that, if Annie hears our voices, it will rouse her from the dark place."

We all stared at him in disbelief. But once the words sunk in, we basically crashed on top of each other to get out of the room. Even Cory didn't hesitate to get help walking a little faster. *Poor bastard.*

We all piled into the truck and shot out of the parking lot in under three minutes. Wrapped Up In You by Garth Brooks plays quietly, giving a glimpse of Vince's mood change since the attack. I even caught a glimpse of Cory and Jenson bouncing their heads to the playful, light rhythm.

The hospital comes into view and it suddenly feels like someone vacuums out all of the oxygen. We have clips, images, and possibilities of what we may encounter once we walk in, but none of us can truly be prepared for what we will find; even with Melissa's warnings.

As the truck pulls into a spot, a couple of rows away from the entrance, knots form in my stomach. *What if she hates us? What if whatever she went through, she turns away and no longer wants to be with us?* I mean, we can't blame her. We had *just* started the relationship before she was taken. But, we wouldn't be able to push like we had before. We'd have no choice but to let her go, and silently pray that she becomes interested again.

I jolt as Vince's hand finds mine and squeezes. "I know. I know. But if nothing else, we want her to know we're here. No matter her decision." Tears fill my eyes as one escapes his own.

Vince sniffs once, before looking back to Cory. "Remember our story about your injuries?"

Cory nods emphatically, "Yup, car crash. Owie," He fake pouts then chuckles; sounding lighter than he has in days.

With a final look around, all of us smiling and bursting with joy, we pile out of the car and head towards the entrance. Vince pulls out his phone. "Room 218. I'm going to let her know we're here," He remarks before sending Melissa a message.

The elevator is stuffy but, thankfully, it's a short ride. The energy bouncing between all of us is a chaotic mix of excitement and terrified. Truthfully, it's taking every ounce of willpower I have to not sprint down the hall the moment the elevator bings and whooshes open. Vince must know that because he hasn't released my hand since he pocketed his phone in the lobby.

Cory's hand rests on Jenson's shoulder and I'm relieved to see that he legitimately appears to be walking a little easier today. But, we'll have to make sure our little bookworm sits down once we get into the room.

The overwhelming stench of antiseptic and cleaner hangs in the air as we walk down the white-floored hallway. The walls are also white but they at least painted the handrail against the wall a deep, navy blue. Other than that, it is all so, blindingly, *white*.

As the numbers on the doors count closer to 218, my palms begin to sweat and my heart rate picks up. Once we pass 212, our strides become longer, and our pace faster. Then we come to an abrupt stop outside of 218. And, none of us move. Fear, excitement, anxiety, stress, worry; it all looms over us like a tsunami of epic proportions.

I glance over at Vince and study the rapid rise and fall of his chest as he stares down the door. We all wait as our non-official leader prepares to toe the line between officer and criminal, friend and boyfriend. And we let him. After all, he's been with Annie from the beginning and is the only one of us who has spoken to Melissa.

After almost a full minute, I notice him blinking his eyes rapidly, then suck in a deep breath, before reaching out and knocking gently on the door. Right away, a feminine voice penetrates the door, "Come in." Vince gently pushes down on the door handle and walks through; never releasing my hand. I can hear Jense and Cory's quiet footsteps squeak across the floor behind us.

Shock punches through me at the instantaneous surge of familiarity I feel when I lay eyes on Melissa. She is *absolutely* Annie's mom. Other than short, brunette hair and hazel eyes, she could be Annie's sister. When she glances towards Vince, recognition filters through her eyes before she reveals a bright smile; *so damn similar to Annie's*.

We stop right inside the door, next to the bathroom. While we can see an ugly orange armchair in the left corner, we can only make out the end of Annie's bed as a thin blue curtain is still pulled halfway across the room.

"Vince! You're here! It's so good to see you." She beams quietly as she makes her way over to us. She doesn't even hesitate to push up on her tiptoes and wrap her arms around his neck, squeezing tightly. Vince drops my hand to return the hug and the hushed tones of her cries wash over us.

Choking back a sob, she steps back, brushes the tears from her eyes, and looks up at him in every way you would hope a mother would look at a child. "I'm so glad you're here."

Her smile grows and her eyes begin to flit between the rest of us.

Vince clears his throat, batting away his own tears, and makes introductions. Melissa hurriedly bundles me up in the most soul-fixing hug I think I've ever received. At first, I stiffen but, not even a second later, I find myself totally relaxing into the hug. Even crazier, I actually return it. Once she moves towards Jense, I suck in a rejuvenating lungful of air, feeling surprisingly content considering I usually shy away from physical touch.

After giving Jenson the same hug, she wraps her arms around Cory. He hisses out in pain, causing her to startle back, pausing to quickly scan her eyes over his body and face. "Oh my God! I'm so sorry! The light isn't on over here and I didn't really pay attention. Are you ok? What in God's name happened?"

She looks between all of us before Cory responds, "Just a car accident. Still a little sore."

Her eyes fill with worry and she tentatively reaches her hand towards the stitches on his head. She doesn't touch, though, but something must snap in her head. She moves right into what I assume is 'Mom mode' and begins fussing over him. "Oh gracious child, you come right over here and sit down. I don't know how I missed the shiner but the gash on your head looks downright awful." She bustles around the room, moving things off of the armchair before patting the chair for him to sit in.

When he doesn't make an immediate attempt to move, she fixes him with a hard stare that screams, "Don't mess with Mama." We all snigger as he slowly shuffles his feet over to her and gently settles into the chair.

"Thank you, ma'am." She lightly pats his shoulder and rolls her eyes. "Don't you ma'am me. Call me Melissa." She says it with such a bright smile that I can't help but smile with her.

Vince, Jenson, and I step the rest of the way around the curtain and we all finally have eyes on Annie. Jenson sucks a breath in through his teeth and Vince's hand immediately finds mine and squeezes. *Or, maybe I found his.* Either way, she looks so pale; sick almost. Her face is bruised, her lip is split, and her hair is drenched in sweat, causing it to stick to her forehead; almost covering a set of stitches near her hairline. Even in sleep, she looks haunted. It's taking every fiber of my being to stand in this spot and not run over and scoop her back into my arms. *Wait, arms. What the actual fuck?*

Before I can investigate the jagged cuts down her arms, I hear footsteps scrambling backward before the bathroom door closes with a *snick*. The sounds of Jense losing his breakfast follow. *Same, bro, same.*

I chance a look at Melissa to see how she's doing. She must feel my eyes on her as she glances from the bathroom door to me. Sympathy, understanding, and heartbreak clash in her eyes. She gives me a grim smile before walking back next to Annie and holding her hand.

A few seconds later, the toilet flushes and the sounds of the sink coming to life fill the room. When Jense is finished, he slowly comes back out and walks over to Cory's chair, placing a tentative hand on his shoulder.

None of us move; none of us talk. Heck, I'm not even sure if we're breathing at this point. But I know we're all taking in the state of the woman who captured our attention and then stole our hearts; praying that she makes her way back to us soon.

12

Jenson

The woman lying in the bed, brows furrowed and face covered in bruises, is not my Annie. Cuts mark her perfect face and there are a few longer, gnarly ones on her arms. I squeeze my eyes shut and ground my molars together, which results in an audible *pop* echoing through the room. Not that anyone noticed as they continued to visually catalog every mark on Annie.

The rise and fall of her chest through the blankets, and the incessant beeping of the heart rate monitor, at least tell me that she is alive. But, she is definitely not well.

A groan rips from her lips and my head shoots up towards hers. Her body squirms a little as her face pinches in pain; *or is that fear?* Sweat has already glued her hair to her face and I have the overwhelming urge to brush it from her forehead so I can take full inventory of every line, every bump, every cut. *Damn, now I wish I had someone to kill all over again.*

A clanking sound brings my attention to her hands once more. "Why is she still strapped down?" I'm aware I said it through gritted teeth and I'm pretty sure I snarled but, thankfully, Melissa doesn't get mad at me for being a douche. I remember Vince told me but, I didn't realize they left them on.

Her sweet voice comes out just above a whisper. "When she tries to wake up, she, well, she fights. She clocked one of the nurses earlier and gave her a bruise on her cheek. It's to protect herself and the staff. The things she screams..." Melissa hiccups a sob as tears stream down her face. I remember Vince telling me that but, hearing it and seeing it are two very different things.

I don't know Melissa, but I have the overwhelming need to protect this woman, my girl's mom, at all costs. In a few strides, I'm right beside her, pulling her into a hug, and rubbing her back gently. I let her cry into my shirt and hope that she can feel all the strength I'm attempting to lend her.

After a couple of minutes, she sniffs and lifts her swollen eyes towards me. "Thank you," she whispers. "I can see why Annie fell for you all. You'll be good for her. I just know it."

I feel myself tense and turn my head towards Vince, lifting a brow and trying desperately to communicate "What the fuck did you say to her?" Our relationship is nowhere near conventional and I know Annie would be pissed if we had blabbed to her mom without her there. She's so shy and vulnerable; maybe even more so now.

Vince lifts his own brow in challenge and smirks, shaking his head at me. Melissa steps out of my hold and looks between Vince and me. "Oh please. I knew before Annie did." She giggles softly to herself, drying her eyes with a tissue. "As long as you all treat her the way she deserves, I don't have an issue with it. Love is love."

She glances down at Vince and Nick's joined hands, her smile widening before glancing between the four of us. "As long as everyone is cared for and happy and growing together, who cares what that love looks like? And my girl here, she has a lot of holes from people who took what wasn't theirs to take."

She sighs heavily before slipping her hand into Annie's and rubbing her thumb across the top. Her voice comes out even quieter as she says, "Some of us may need more than one person to help fill those holes. And if it makes my daughter, and grandkids happy, then I couldn't be more excited." She looks back between the four of us, beaming with a smile so bright there's no way to not return it. *Now I see where Annie gets her light from.*

Suddenly, Annie gasps a deep breath, and whimpers out a low, "No." My heart drops straight out of my ass as I watch her face twist in agony from whatever is in her head. Stepping back, I collapse on the edge of the three-seater couch near the window and put my hands on my head, pulling the hair by the root to help ground me.

A voice pulls me from my inner turmoil and I look up to see Nick approach the bed. He stares at her for a moment, indecision warring all over his face before he slowly slides his hand along the bed sheet, up to meet her fingers. He gently inner-laces his fingers with hers. It's only about halfway, not even touching her actual hand, but seeing him be the one to initiate is absolute insanity.

He leans down, just a little, and carefully brushes the damp hair from her forehead. From my spot on the couch, I'm sitting at the perfect angle to see the adoration glowing in his eyes. The way he looks at her makes my own damn heart squeeze. Then, he slowly leans down, a tear falling from his eyes and landing on her arm, and whispers, "Siren, come back to us. P-please. We've missed you." Tears fill my own eyes as I watch him continue to lean over her and run his fingers through her hair.

"N-Nick..." It's barely audible, hardly a whisper, but there's no doubt that we all hear it. All heads snap toward her. My eyes widen and my breath stutters to a stop.

"Hey, Siren. I'm here. You're mama, Jense, Cory, Vince; we're all here. We're just waiting for you to come back to us." Other than the beeping of the heart rate monitor, no sound exists in the room. My head feels like it's swimming and I have to blink back the spots that float through my vision.

Suddenly, her left arm moves, like she's trying to reach for something, but it's stopped by the soft cuffs. And then the sweet moment turns to absolute shit.

13

Vince

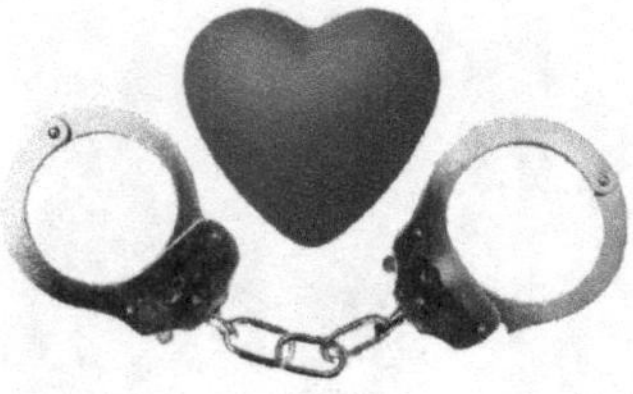

One second, my heart is in my throat as I swear we're about to watch Nick coax Annie back to life. The next, I'm frozen in a deep-seated fear that I don't think I've ever experienced before.

Annie goes to move her left arm but the second the cuffs stop her, we lose her again. Or, to be more accurate, *she* loses it.

"Noooo! Let me go!" She thrashes and screams, her whole body twisting in the sheets as her face twists in rage and agony. "Let me go back! Let me go! I need to get back to Cory."

I blanch and look over at him, still sitting in the orange chair. His face has paled and tears freely run down his cheeks. He leans forward and puts his head down on his arms, resting his elbows on his knees.

"P-p-please! Jenson! Please! Let me say goodbye! Please!" Melissa and Jenson wrap around each other, quietly sobbing as Nick continues to hold on to Annie's right hand. He moves from her fingers to grasp her whole hand, trying to shush her and soothe her but it's not working. She's too in her head to hear it.

"Siren, baby, please come back. We're here. Cory and Jense are here. Come on Siren." Nick's voice cracks in heartache and tears fall on her shoulder. The monitors continue going crazy, alerting everyone of her heightened state.

Just as the door to the room knocks open, she's screaming out again, "No. Please, God no. They can't be here. Take me to them. I'll be good. I'll do anything. Don't hurt them. Vince! Nick!!!"

Three nurses push us aside and begin to administer another round of what I assume are sedatives. Her face is bright red and etched in pain as she arches her back off the bed, fighting the restraints. It looks like she's in the middle of an exorcism with how her veins protrude from her neck and her body twists and lifts off the bed.

Then, like a switch is flipped, she whimpers and slowly slides back down on the bed before ultimately going completely lax. A nurse clears her throat, causing me to wipe away my tears and turn towards her. She has a big bruise on her face, which I assume is from Annie, but her gentle smile tells me that she holds nothing against her at all. "She'll be ok. I know this is hard, but we see it a lot in trauma victims," She soothes.

Turning towards Melissa, the nurse offers her a gentle smile. "She'll probably be out for an hour or so. The doctor wants to lessen the sedative so it gives her more time to make her way out of her nightmares."

Melissa nods and I find myself mimicking the movement. "Thank you," She whispers. The nurse nods once and moves out of the room. *Apparently, the others had already left and I didn't even realize it.*

"I need a minute." I whip my head towards the gut-wrenching sound Nick lets out as he spins from the room and out the door.

I don't think twice, I know he's going to need me so I follow right behind him.

He barely makes it three steps into the hallway before slamming his knees into the ground, curling over himself, and letting out a guttural sob from the depths of his heart. I move quickly to wrap my arms around him from the back and scoot us towards the wall. His body shivers violently under my arms but I don't move; knowing he'll need equal pressure against his back, chest, and stomach. Thankfully, no one casts judgment or pays us any mind as I hold Nick while he tears himself apart.

It takes a full five or six minutes for him to expel the torture from his heart. Pins and needles prick my legs and ass but it's nothing I haven't done before; I'll do it again a thousand more times to make sure he's safe and protected.

His sobs give way to silent tears and, eventually, turn into stuttered hiccups. Once he reaches up and squeezes my hand, I know I can start to loosen my grip. He turns, just a little, as my arms begin to fall away, and presses a chaste kiss to my lips. His lips tilt in a tight grin before he kisses me again. I breathe him in and kiss him back, trying to pour out every thought and feeling, hoping he understands that he's not alone in this particular brand of torture.

Knowing we're in a very public hallway, we keep it light and brief. When he pulls away, I see the faint glimmer of acceptance mingling with a calmness that was definitely not there before. With one more quick peck, we move to stand up, joining hands and walking back into the room.

Everyone's empathetic smiles greet us and it instantly reminds me that we are with family, we are safe, and we can do this; for her.

I squeeze Nick's hand once then turn to face the group. "I'm going to check on the other girls." My eyes widen at the realization that it may have sounded suspicious, so I quickly add, "Captain told me they brought in quite a few and, since I'd been working this case long before Annie was taken, I need to make sure the others are ok, too."

Melissa nods with a smile, a hand clutching her heart, and says, "Oh absolutely. Those poor women. Who knows what kind of hell they all went through. Or for how long. It's absolutely disgusting."

Satisfied that she's not questioning my motives, I place a quick peck on Nick's cheek, then turn to walk down the hallway. I find the nurses' station and am immediately glad that taking my police badge is so ingrained in my routine. I hadn't originally planned to do this, but I need to know.

I stand for about ten minutes, talking with the nurse about the most recent updates. Two women needed surgery but are both expected to make a full recovery. All of them needed stitches or sutures and a round or two of antibiotics.

Afterwards, I was pleasantly surprised to hear all of the women were on this floor and most had already had friends or family here or on their way. I needed more, though. That may be selfish and fucked up but, I need to know what the hell happened in there.

So, I took off down the hall to meet with each and every woman who was saved that day.

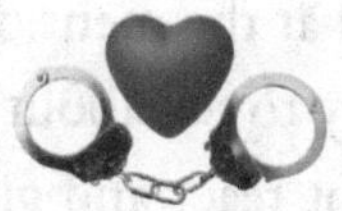

It's been almost two hours since I left Annie's room and I still had one more woman to meet with. I gently knock on her door and walk in to find a tiny little woman with big brown eyes. Fear runs through them but is quickly replaced with determination and strength. I grin to myself, hoping that means she won't let this shit destroy her life. It may be hard and miserable at times, but she's a fighter. Just like my Annie.

"Hello, Ms. Warton. My name is Officer Daniels. I just wanted to come check in with you. See how you're recovering." I flip my badge at her quickly and see the tension in her shoulders settle.

A small smile appears across her face before she waves a hand towards the couch that sits next to the bed. "Please, be my guest." I nod my acceptance, walk over to the couch, and then lower my large frame onto it. The fake leather squeaks as my body settles in and I try to get comfortable. Looking up at her, I find her head tilted as if she's assessing me.

Clearing my throat, I begin like I had with the others, "Ms. Warton, I *don't* know what you've been through. And, even if you tell me, I know I will *never* understand it. But, what I do know, is that we want to make sure you are all set up to heal, and to eventually live a full, happy, life."

Tears gather in her eyes as she nods her head. "Well, Officer Daniels, like I told the others, we were treated like dogs. Actually, worse than dogs. Barely food, occasional water..." She trails off, biting her lip as she looks down in her lap, picking at a loose thread in the blanket. "They wanted to prepare us. T-to be sex slaves. And if we didn't do as they asked, or comply correctly or fast enough, we were punished. Well, we were... or Annie was."

I try so hard to stay still at the mention of her name, again. Each woman had a different story to tell about Annie helping them and it was becoming harder to not react and give away what she is to me. But, I feel it so damn deeply. My hands tighten around each other and I squeeze until my knuckles are surely white.

Keeping my voice as steady as possible, I press on, "I've heard a lot about Annie from the others and what you have all been through, together. Or, at least, what was willing to be shared..." Then, I lost my words. *What the hell do I say? "I'm glad she was there to...help? To intervene? To be whipped or cut mercilessly so she could save them from one more bad thing?"*

Bile surges up like a volcano, ready to erupt, and I force myself to focus on swallowing it back down. I bite the inside of my cheek to keep my emotions at bay but, when I look back at Jodie, a soft smile plays on her face; her eyes distant.

"I had been taken only a couple of days before Annie had shown up. But, she was there the first time they, um…" Her voice wobbled and a breath got caught in her chest.

Clenching her jaw, she blinks away her tears and fixes me with a look that's filled with brimstone and fire. "I can't explain what she did the first time they took me. But she made it better. They had her strung up, whipping her, as that sick fuck took from me what wasn't his. And, though she couldn't physically help, it was in her eyes. She helped me almost push it away by just focusing on me and letting me get lost in the unwavering strength that flowed from her eyes. Like, I wasn't alone." Tears flow freely down her face as she re-lives whatever God-awful memory she has playing in her head. I sit in complete silence, knowing anything I say would be utterly pointless.

After another minute, she shakes her head and sighs heavily before returning her eyes to me. "Officer Daniels?" I tilt my head, giving her the go-ahead to ask me whatever she needs to. "An-Annie did some things. Some things that may get her in trouble." Her voice dropped low as her bottom lip trembled. Her glassy eyes search mine as worry etches across her features, "Will she get in trouble? For what she did? For us?"

Before she's even finished, I'm shaking my head. "Absolutely not. We're in Texas. Self-defense and defense of others are firmly grounded in our books. Even if it wasn't, we would never go after her. Ever." I say the last word just above a whisper and get lost in my head. We knew she killed a couple of men, but like hell would I hold that against her. I just hope she doesn't hold it against herself; once she wakes up.

"O-Officer Daniels?" I meet her eyes and see that whatever she wants to say, she's nervous about my reaction. "Yes, Ms. Warton? Whatever you're thinking, just say it." I give her a gentle smile and hope it's reassuring enough.

"C-Can I see Annie? I don't know where anyone else is but I keep thinking about them. I just want to see if they're ok. And I *need* to know Annie is ok. I heard one of the doctors say she was brought in from the house. And I think she's the one I hear screaming sometimes..." She trails off, looking longingly at the door to the room.

"I want to be there for her, like she was there for me. And, I think it would be a good idea to ask the others, too." She slowly turns her head back towards me, sits up a little straighter, and says, "I know it sounds stupid, but we were all each other had. And, as fucked as it was, I miss them." She huffs out a laugh but it holds no humor.

I start nodding in understanding. "I don't have a problem with it. Give me a few minutes and I'll see what the doctors say. I don't want to get into any trouble. I also want to ask Melissa, um, Annie's mom, if she's okay with it." The woman nods emphatically, looking a little excited about the prospect of seeing the others.

With one last smile, I rise up, give her my thanks, and tell her I'm going to start asking around since some of the women are set to be released soon. Heading out of her door, I feel a sudden pull of determination and satisfaction. Our woman is a fucking badass and maybe these girls can remind her of that.

14

Melissa

Vince left to speak with the other women a couple of hours ago. Checking my phone, I see that it's already 1:00. I need to leave by 2:00 to make it back across town in plenty of time to pick up the kids. I definitely don't want to cut it closer than that because one wreck could mean my grand-toodles will be forced to hang at the school.

Just under an hour ago, Jenson, I think, left in search of food. I finally talked the sweet boy, Cory, into lying down on the couch. He looked like he was in so much pain and I couldn't bear it. Before leaving, Jenson went and grabbed a pillow and blanket and I secretly watched as he got Cory all tucked in. The way he looked at the other one screamed a 'more than friends' vibe, but they never outwardly showed anything other than a close friendship; unlike Vince and Nick.

Nick has me sitting on the orange chair and he's on the floor, leaning up against the couch with his legs stretched out perpendicular to mine. We spent the first ten minutes in comfortable silence but curiosity got the best of me. I eventually had to ask Nick how he was really doing. He may have crazy blue hair and dresses like he's in a rock band but his soul is soft, sweet, fragile almost. I see the same in Annie. I didn't miss the way he briefly flinched when I hugged him but, once he relaxed into it, I knew he really needed it. However, nothing prepared me for the heartbreak I would feel over him falling apart at watching Annie freak out. His sobs carried from the hallway and it took all I had not to go bundle him up and squeeze him until the pieces of his heart were glued back together.

We've been quietly talking ever since. At first, he was a little wary of talking but, now, I can tell he's really relaxed. The way his eyes sparkle when he talks about their partnership with the Youth Center gives me a small glimpse of what Annie must have fallen for. His eyes lit up as he told me just how much helping those kids truly means to him.

A knock on the door interrupts my story about when I took the grand-toodles to the science center they partnered with and Josh exploded some concoction all over the table. He cackled, the girls squealed, and I was shocked in embarrassment. Thankfully, the girl working there laughed it off and exclaimed "Science rocks!" Then helped us clean it up.

The door opens and Vince walks in looking completely worn out. I can't imagine the stories he has heard over the last couple of hours. He quietly walks in and peers around the curtain towards Annie. His eyes find Nick's and the smile he gives him almost melts my own heart. These guys have the perfect type of love for my Annie.

Vince clears his throat and squats down next to the chair I'm sitting in. Not that it mattered much; he still towers over me. His eyes are filled with worry and exhaustion. I lay a hand on his arm, patting him lightly before I taunt, "You okay? Can I do anything to help with the giant boulder of other people's problems that you're carrying on your shoulders?" My smile tips up in a smirk and I hope he can see the semi-joke in my eyes.

He huffs out a laugh, shakes his head, then pats my hand on his arm. "I'm good. But, I wanted to ask you something. I don't have the right answer and, until Annie wakes, you get to make these decisions."

His eyes search mine and my body tenses in discomfort. "What is it? Just say it."

He nods his head, clears his throat then reveals, "The girls, women, the others that were saved, um, they want to see Annie. I can't share their stories, that would be up to them, but..." Tears fill his eyes and threaten to spill down his cheeks.

"But, what?" I inquire gently.

Indecision crosses his features as he works out his response. "Melissa, from what I gathered, Annie was made to be their trainer or something. The men told her she was basically their mama. She was in charge of cleaning them up, doing their laundry, tending to their wounds; stuff like that. If a girl didn't listen, *she* got punished, as well as the girl. If she didn't listen, or back-talked, she was pun-ished twice as hard. But, um, there were some other instances where Annie...intervened; knowing it would take the attention off the girls or, in some cases," he licks his lips and wipes away the tears running down his face. Breathing in deeply he finishes, "In some cases, if she saw the opportunity, she attacked them, getting the guys' attention off the girls entirely."

His body begins trembling as tears stream down his face. He is trying so hard to compartmentalize all the information and still stay strong for me, and the family he's made for himself. Watching him break, breaks me, and I join him in letting our emotions flow as we silently cry for the woman my daughter was forced to become. But, there is something he needs to know. I can't let him sit in sorrow for too long.

Tapping his chin to get his attention, I gently smile at him, "Vince, honey, I know it hurts. I can see the protector in you feeling like he failed but let me tell you something: No matter what the stories are, Annie is still a survivor *and* a victim. She's always been strong, always determined, and, even if she could never stand up for herself, she's always stood up for others. Whatever those women went through, they went through it together. So, yes, they can absolutely come see her. The type of terrifying bond they all must have is not something that should be messed with."

He smiles through his tears and squeezes my hand again. "Ok. Thank you, Melissa. I'll let them know." With one final smile, he stands, nudges Nick with his foot to wink at him, then walks back out the door.

Nick smiles up at me, takes my hand in his, and just holds it. He's so perceptive that he probably knows that even if I did say all of that, knowing Annie was hurt, for any reason, is ridiculously painful. And I don't know how to make it better.

* * *

Five minutes later, Jenson walks into the room with a huge brown bag from Panera and a drink tray filled with drinks. As he starts unpacking the bag, he looks over at me, red-tingeing his adorable cheeks. "I'm sorry, ma'am, but I didn't know what you liked so I got you four options. Green Goddess Salad, Fuji Apple Salad, Roasted Turkey and Avocado BLT, or Black Forest Ham and Gouda Baguette?" My stomach rumbles loudly at the options and the little shit chuckles.

Rolling my eyes, I say, "Green Goddess Salad, please. Also, a little hint: it's Annie's favorite, too. She never orders anything except that salad; unless it's breakfast of course." He smiles brightly and hands over the container overflowing with green goodness before rummaging through the bag and pulling out the piece of French bread that goes with it. My mouth salivates and I tear off a piece of bread, popping it in my mouth, and begin to soak up all of the carby goodness.

Before I even get the top off the salad container, Vince stands at the doorway, knocking to get my attention. His smile is wide and his eyes glimmer with hope and awe. "Melissa, there are some people here who would like to meet you."

I quickly push my food aside on the little table and stand as 11 young women quietly slip through the door. Their faces are gaunt, and the trauma that reflects in their eyes causes tears to flow down my cheeks without my permission.

The first girl, with big brown eyes, looks at me, approaching me slowly, "H-Hi. I'm Jodie." Her quiet words fill my heart and I have the overwhelming urge to hug them all. But, I don't. I keep myself rooted to my spot by the chair and smile while nodding at her. "Nice to meet you, Jodie."

Silence envelopes us as the others file in and stand around Annie's bed; all with varying expressions on their faces. The pain these women went through, bonded through, hangs heavy in the air. A few of the others eventually turn towards me and introduce themselves.

Cory's still passed out on the couch, facing toward the window. Jenson has backed himself into the corner between the chair and couch and looks to be actively avoiding the women. Not that I blame him; they're probably very wary about men right now. And sweet little Nick has his chin resting on his knees, head tilted to look up at Annie from his seated position on the floor.

Some of the women eye the guys warily so I quietly introduce them, "Cory's the one sleeping on the couch. He was recently in a bad car wreck so he's wiped out. Nick's the one here on the floor," I say waving my hand at him. He briefly looks up and smiles before gently lying his chin back down; focusing back on Annie. "And the goofball in the corner is Jense. I'm pretty sure he's trying to make himself invisible so you all won't feel uncomfortable. But, these men are important to me; important to Annie. Besides, I think Officer

Daniels over there could probably take them all down if they decide to be naughty."

Vince's eyes widen and I see Jense's chest bounce as he chuckles quietly. I beam a smile at all of them knowing they are good down to their marrow.

Some of the girls giggle and, most of them, relax a little. Jodie walks over to Annie's left side and I see a tear run down her cheek. She slips her hand into Annie's and speaks just loud enough that we can hear over the monitors. "Hey, Mama Annie. We made it. We're out."

She pauses looking at each of the girls with a small smile before looking back down at Annie. The other girls shift closer around Annie's bed, and one of them grasps her right hand. Tears and sniffles can be heard around the room as we all stand together in silence, hoping Annie will come back to us.

After a moment, one of the girls, closest to Annie's left foot, whispers out, "Do y'all remember when Annie took those big ass Channellock pliers to the bastard's skull who was... harassing Camila?" Her hesitation before choosing the word, paired with how wide her eyes got, hinted that *harassing* was not what was happening. But, I won't ask. It's not my place.

All the girls grin and nod, looking towards a blonde girl near Jodie. Her face splits into a huge grin, eyes sparkling with mischief, as her right brow raises, "Hell yeah she did. Those assholes were on one that day. I mean table pose for an hour then wailing on me when I went down? Stupid bastards." She shakes her head and appears to go somewhere deep in her memory before speaking again. This time, she's much quieter, her face distorted with a mixture of emotions. "I still have a bald spot in the back of my head where he yanked me by my hair." A tear falls from her eyes and one of the other girls wraps their arm around her.

Leaning her head on her friend's shoulder, she continues, "I felt so guilty for so long. When the first guy went down, I was in shock. But, by the time she was wailing on the brother, I just took it as my chance to run. I should have helped her. She helped me. Went up against them both, and then almost drowned for it." She hiccups on a sob as more girls gather around her.

Another woman brushes her hair off her shoulder and gently empathizes, "Girl, it's different when you're right in it. Besides, your arms were ready to give out long before they started beating you. You would have been hurt worse. Annie just wanted you as safe as you could be. She wanted that for all of us."

Silence blankets the room, minus the gentle beeping of the monitors. Then another girl tells her favorite story about Annie. Then another.

Over the last twenty minutes, the girls have rehashed terrifying stories, funny stories, and even conniving stories; all centering around Annie. She never gave up. She fought and lost, fought and won, fought and survived. *I just wished she'd fight and come back.*

Another minute ticks by before one of the girls, Clara, I think, furrows her brows in a deep scowl. "These need to come off." Everyone shoots their heads over to her as she starts unstrapping her right foot from the soft buckle.

I step forward, slightly panicked, "No, you can't. She gets stuck back there when she wakes up. She hit a nurse. She screams and she fights..." I look deep into her eyes, imploring her to understand. "It's as much for their protection as hers."

Jodie's brown hair swaying catches my eyes and I look over at her. "No. That's because they don't understand. Annie was cuffed more than we were. All the time; sometimes for hours. Even when she was being punished for something we did wrong, she fought back until she went to her safe place."

My brows furrow and I tilt my head. "Her safe place? What's that?"

She shakes her head, seeming to not know how to explain. Some girls nod, some chew their lips; all are struggling to find the right words.

Eventually, Jodie tries to explain, "Sometimes," she sighs heavily. Licking her lips, she nods once in finality, looks back at Vince for a moment, then to me again. "Sometimes Annie would, like, check out. It's hard to explain but, when the rest of us would scream or cry, she would just... stare into space. Almost like she could leave her body for long periods of time. Even when they gave her the paralytic that still forced us to feel everything without being able to move, her eyes would stay open and she would appear to just drift off somewhere. It usually took some coaxing to get her to come back; even after they threw her back in the cell."

She looks back down at Annie, head tilting as she assesses her. "Maybe that's why she's stuck. She feels the cuffs and leaves again." It almost sounds like she's talking to herself but I can tell by their expressions that the others feel the same.

With no further discussion, the women standing closest to each of the cuffs slowly, quietly, unbuckles them, then gently frees her limbs from the restraints. The others watch as Jodie moves the buckles out of the way and rests Annie's arm on the sheet; signaling with just a look for the others to do the same.

"Mama Annie: we're out and we're free. It's time for you to come back. You were the badass bitch fighting for us. Now it's time we fight for you."

Seconds tick by without so much as a twitch.

Jodie and another girl, Flora, grasp Annie's hands. And then, they do the strangest thing. They all start quietly humming a tune; almost as if they had done this before. Far be it for me to stop them because they literally went through hell but, it definitely took me a moment to adjust to the change.

Jodie abruptly switches from humming to singing, the others immediately joining in. I won't lie, when the word "bitch" came out of their sweet mouths in such confident, sassy tones, I jumped a little. It was so different from how they had been acting and talking. But soon, they were all quietly singing, smiles spreading across their beautiful faces as they sang the lyrics to whatever song they clearly all knew. It was a little risqué for my tastes but they deserved something to smile about.

The atmosphere became lighter, freer, and just a little more cheerful as the girls sang their power song, hand-in-hand.

15

Annie

The darkness swaddles me in peace and serenity. I love it here. No worries, no pain, no shame. Just me and the never-ending nothingness to float in. It's quite lovely.

I feel myself sway in its arms, as my feeling of euphoria slowly morphs into something else; something familiar. It gently tugs at my consciousness; like a thin strand of spider silk, glistening through the darkness. I want to ignore it. I want to stay here where it's comfortable; safe. But dammit if it doesn't continue to call out to me.

The more I follow it, the more my heart rips open, allowing

emotions to explode out of it. Hurt, pain, happiness, anger, fear, joy, pride. It all pours out of me, splitting right through me.

I think I hear a small whimper leave my lips before feeling the gentle squeezing of my hands. *Not my wrists.*

I twitch my foot and, though it doesn't feel like it moves far, I don't think it's restricted. That little piece of information has me crawling to the surface, pulling on the silky strand until it leads me to a blinding light. It sears through my eyelids but I don't care. The strange mixture of voices begins to filter through and around me. But, I don't feel fear. I felt content, silly, and maybe a little sassy.

I try moving my hand, just a little. It interrupts one of the voices near me but then she, *definitely a she,* keeps singing. "...she the devil, she a bad lil' bitch, she a rebel..."

A soft giggle falls from my lips as I recognize Doja Cat's Paint the Town Red as the song the girl is singing. *Wait, no... girls. Definitely more than one. We've sung this before. The girls!*

I need to see them. I need to see the girls and make sure they're ok. So I *try.* I start flicking my eyes, willing them to open, until light streams through the tiny slits. It shocks my system, forcing me to close them again.

Someone swipes a soft finger across my forehead and causes my hair to tickle me. It is so sweet and gentle and familiar that I think I feel myself grin. A gasp lifts over the singing and I distinctly hear shoes walking closer. But, the girls just keep singing. The singing becomes bolder, like a melody used to lift me right out of the pits of darkness and straight into the light.

Between wanting more of the gentleness and needing to see if the girls are ok, I go back to fighting against my closed eyes. I tighten my hands and find that they are both filled with small, feminine hands; which gives me the extra push I need. I'm supposed to be taking care of *them*; not the other way around.

Finally I crack my eyes open, pushing through the pain caused by the searing light. I slam my eyes back together, causing my face to squish with them. I groan in pain as my face comes back to life and I immediately consider going back to the darkness.

But, somewhere deep inside, I know it's time for me to leave it behind.

I try again; fluttering my eyes open and blinking through the harsh light. At first everything is blurry; just a bunch of strange figures standing around me. But, after blinking away the fog a few more times, the images sharpen and the figures come into view. Tears leak from my eyes as I scan their faces and I smile up at each of them.

Darting my eyes around, I take in their strange outfits. I hiss in pain when I furrow my brows in confusion, but I don't let that steal my attention. Gone are the skimpy chemises, dirty faces and arms, and matted hair. Instead, the girls all wear light blue and white hospital gowns. At least, I think the thin, stiff material that covers them from neck to past the plastic railing is a hospital gown. They each look like they've cleaned their bodies, and even their hair, recently

It takes me a moment to realize the singing has stopped and all the girls are crying; but also smiling so wide that it has to hurt. A squeeze on my right hand causes me to turn. As Jodie's face comes into view, I return her bright smile as much as I can, fighting the exhaustion and pain weighing heavily on my body.

"Hey, Mama Annie. Long time no see." I slightly tilt my head at her, assessing her closely. Her body isn't locked up in tension like usual. Her face and hair have been cleaned and the knots that I always had to work out of her long locks are gone.

"Wh-Wh..." My voice is a painful rasp. I try swallowing but there is nothing but a sandbox full of gravel in my mouth and throat.

A cup with a straw magically appears in Jodie's hand as she leans it towards me. I suck down two mouthfuls, grateful that it tastes clean and crisp and refreshing. She gently pulls it from my mouth telling me that I need to take it slow. I nod in acceptance before leaning forward for another sip.

Once I'm finished, she smiles wide and looks around the room. I lick my dry lips and try to talk again. "What happened? Where are we?"

Her smile grows, even as she cries. "We're in the hospital Annie. We're free. We're safe. We got out."

My brain was not ready to process, or accept, that information. Images bombard my mind of the last things I remember.

The boat.

The girls in black.

The gun.

Blood.

So. Much. Blood.

Can't move.

The big house.

Lukas.

Fucking Lukas

And Greaser.

My body shivers involuntarily as my mind replays the last few moments of my time with Greaser. I remember not being able to move, I remember him slapping my breasts. But, nothing else.

"How?" It's the only word I can get out. It's the only thing I can think of that may be able to help me wrap my head around it. *We're free. Really free?*

Cara speaks up first, "After the uh," she looks around between everyone for a moment before finding her words, "Well, after you sent that asshole on the boat straight to hell, they had to stop the transfer and turn around."

She looks at all the girls, smiling softly, before looking back to me. "We were all taken to the warehouse but they kept you there, at the house."

She swallows audibly, a slight tremor working its way up through her shoulders. A throat clears to my left and I see Flora, holding onto my other hand. "We had barely settled back into our cages when someone blasted through the door. A bunch of men in all black came running in, shooting the dickheads who had come back with us. Then they let us out of the cages, gave us food and water and blankets, and brought us here." She waves her hand around the room but I could feel the way my eyes widen at the sheer craziness of the story.

"Well, who was it? The police or FBI or something?" In my periphery I see Jodie shaking her head so I swing my head back to her, momentarily groaning as I give myself whiplash. I force myself to ignore the pain as I look at Jodie expectantly. "They weren't with any group like *that*. In fact, they specifically didn't tell us their names, even when we asked. They dropped us off then, poof, vanished."

She pauses for a moment, giving a pointed look to someone in the back of the room. *Not that I can see who it is past the wall of women surrounding me.* "Not that I'd give them up even if they had." With one last quirk of her brow, she turns back to me and says, "I told the officers as much. If they didn't know about them, they probably weren't doing it legally and I'll be damned if they prosecute people who saved our damn lives."

Her fire hadn't been snuffed out and I couldn't be more proud. I wanted to hug her but wasn't sure how to ask, or even move much at this point. So instead, I squeeze her hand and smile as wide as I can before she adds, "None of us were with you when they got you out so, unfortunately, we can't fill in those blanks. But, once we found out you were here," she pauses to look at all the girls standing guard around us before facing me once more, "Well, we all knew it really happened. *This* is our new beginning and, honestly, we owe so much of that to you."

Tears fill my eyes again as I let out a watery laugh. "I'm sorry I couldn't do more."

I look down at my lap; overwhelmed and completely exhausted. I take a deep steadying breath and look back over at the girls, trying to show my appreciation, admiration, and pride through my eyes.

Jodie clears her throat as she looks at the others. "Well, we know you need rest but we'll come visit later. Maybe we can convince them to let us have a movie night tomorrow." I laugh out at how sweet and innocent she still is; *thank God*.

Nodding my head, I return their smiles. Before they leave, Jodie whispers, "Besides there are some other people here who are anxiously waiting to set their eyes on you." I look at her in confusion but she just leans back with a wink.

Slowly the girls leave the room, taking part of my soul with them. My heart feels so full yet, so broken.

Before I can dive into those feelings, movement in the corner of the room catches my eye. A ghost, a mirage, a figment straight from my imagination. It has to be.

"M-Mom?"

Her face is drowning in tears, a wad of tissue is crumpled in her hand, and her whole body shakes. "An-nie!" She wails as she rushes over to my side. She abruptly stops the moment she gets to my side and fiddles with her fingers. I've never seen my mother look so unsure.

"What's the matter, Mom?" I asked, hoping everything else was ok.

She swallows hard before looking at me, tears blurring her hazel eyes and a small smile gracing her lips. "I, I just didn't know if I could hug you. I've heard a little about what happened while you were gone but, I just, I didn't..." she trails off, biting her lip with uncertainty. She is so dang cute.

I smile as wide as I can, wincing a little as the pain moves across my face, and slowly raise my arms. "I could really use a mommy hug."

That was all she needed. She leans in and bundles me up, wrapping both arms around my back and squeezing. We stayed like that for Lord knows how long, as we cried out our reunion.

Sniffling, she eventually returns to a stand, smiling widely at me. Then it hits me. My eyes widen and I gasp in fear, "Where are the kids? Are they okay? What have you told them? How long have I been, um, gone?"

Squeezing my hand, she gives me a gentle smile before relieving me of my anxiety. "They're in school. I, um, I told them you had to go out of town for work. They've been so upset you haven't FaceTimed them but, well, with your current state, I'm thinking we should try a different fib." Her lips purse to the side as she thinks up something to tell the kids.

While she does that, I tentatively look down at my arms and hands, twisting and turning them. The long, jagged cuts from my first day with Brute are almost healed but look disgusting. Based on how sore my face is, I'm assuming that doesn't look much better.

Suddenly, she claps her hand, her face lighting up with enthusiasm. "I've got it! You left for a work trip but got in a bad accident. It took them a while to find my number and you had to heal." She nods once, like it's been decided. I can't lie, it sounds as good as anything else. They are my babies and there's no way in hell I would tell them I was kidnapped out of our driveway and taken by a bunch of ruthless, spineless bastards.

I grin at her and nod my agreement. As I do, her phone starts chiming. "Oh crap. I have to go. Oh honey, I don't want to but we're near Clear Lake so I have to make it all the way back to the house to pick up the kids." Her eyes fill with tears at having to leave.

"It's ok Mom. Please go give my babies a hug. And maybe I'll get cleared soon. Besides, I'm exhausted and really do want to sleep." Her smile takes over her face before her eyes widen like she suddenly remembered something.

"Well, I hope you aren't too tired." She says with a sly smile. "You have one more set of visitors waiting for you. They scooted out when the girls came in so you all could have some privacy, but they've definitely been chompin' at the bit to see you."

I look at her like she's lost her mind because I have no damn clue who could be waiting on me. With one last, bone-crushing hug, and a kiss to my forehead, she walks back to her purse, picking up a container that looks like it has a salad in it, then says, "I'm just going to text them and let them know the room is theirs for a bit."

Looking back at me, she rushes over to my side, causing me to chuckle, and gives me one last squeeze. "I think your phone is still at the station but I'll call to try and get it back. Until then, I'm sure you can use the phone here."

I try to hold my tears back, but they come anyway. I know she has to leave to get my kids but, dammit, I want my mom. I hate that she's leaving but fully understand that we have no one else to get the kids.

With one final smile, she breezes out the door, leaving me in silence. *Well, except for the annoying monitors.*

Leaning back, I gingerly shift my body to try and get more comfortable. My muscles and joints protest the movement, as does my skin, rudely reminding me of the dozens of cuts and bruises that litter my body.

After I get comfortable, I take in a deep, cleansing breath before releasing it. Licking my dry lips, I realize that I'm still painfully thirsty. I take a quick glance around and am relieved to find that Jodie had placed my cup right on the tray next to the bed. Bringing the hard, plastic straw into my mouth, I suck the cool liquid greedily; each swallow feeling better than the last.

Setting it back on the table, I release another deep breath and start to close my eyes. A knock on the door startles me, causing my palms to break out in a sweat. "Co-come in." My voice is still raspy and there is absolutely a tremor in it but it was at least loud enough to alert whoever was on the other side.

The door handle clicks open, and I hear a set of footsteps walk into the room. *No, not a set, a few sets.*

Anxiety begins to claw at my chest, causing my breath to come out in weak pants. I quickly search for the brick-like device that has the nurse call button; just in case. Once I catch sight of it, just behind my bed on the left, I turn and reach for it. Groaning in pain, I twist my body and try extending my arm enough to reach it. Right as my fingers brush over the device, the sounds of footsteps stop.

"Do you need something, Sweetness?" My whole body freezes, arm suspended in mid-air, as my brain connects the voice, the nickname, the memories. *No. It can't be.*

My chin wobbles and more of those damn tears escape my eyes as I slowly turn around to face the men standing at the edge of my bed. All of them are wearing devastating grins that don't quite match the mixture of fear and relief in their eyes.

My eyes widen as I take them all in and I blink repeatedly in hopes that this isn't a dream or a dissociation. I try connecting the images in front of me with the ones that played out in my mind while I was *there*. But, fear tells me it isn't real. *They aren't real.*

Desperately needing them, all of this, to be real, I call out to them. In a barely there whisper, I look at the men in front of me and utter the only two words that I can, "G-Gospel Boys?"

16

Vince

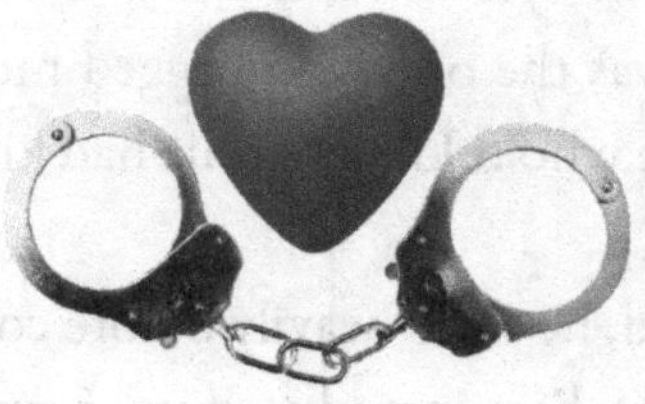

We all stood there watching as Annie slowly woke up; the girls surrounding her like angels in heaven. Cory had woken up while they sang, too, and I was impressed he didn't make a damn sound.

Once they started talking, the others slowly made their way towards the door, not wanting to overwhelm her. I stood by in the corner, not wanting to leave but also not wanting to make anyone uncomfortable. Once Jodie gave me 'the look' while telling Annie she wasn't telling anyone about who rescued them, I followed the others out. I think maybe I stuck around because I was worried someone would put pieces together.

The guys and I decided to head downstairs and eat our lunch while the girls and Melissa had some time with Annie. None of us said a word most of the time; each of us bouncing a knee, knotting up straw wrappers, tapping on the table. The urge to get back to Annie was strong but we collectively knew we needed to wait.

After Jense finishes his sandwich, he leans back and rubs a hand through his hair. "Dude, I thought for sure Jodie would recognize me. I was so glad Nick moved to head out because I had been itching to leave once I saw her face."

I look over at him, cocking my head to the side. "What do you mean? Is that why it looked like you were trying to blend into the corner like a chameleon?"

He bounces his head with a nod and rubs his fist roughly "Yeah, man. I talked with Jodie. Like, had a full conversation about Annie."

He finally raises his eyes towards me and I see them glisten with unshed tears. "She was the one who begged me to make sure Annie got out. And the one who told me Annie had killed people to protect them."

Lowering his head, he sighs heavily before continuing, "When she first walked in and Melissa introduced us, I swear it looked like she recognized me." He rubs at a spot on his chest. "I almost had a heart attack, man."

Nick chuckles as he leans over and thumps Jense in the shoulder. "Good thing we're in a hospital then, huh?"

For a moment, we're all stunned into silence. Then we burst out laughing.

I shake my head at them both before looking back at Jense, "Well, she's been more than adamant that she won't ever tell anyone about the people who got them out. So, I think our secret's safe." We all nod our heads absently and lapse back into a comfortable silence.

Our girl is awake, talking; just one floor above us. I've never been so terrified *and* relieved in my life.

I suddenly remember that I told Enzo that I would let him know when she finally woke up. Pulling out my phone, I send a quick message before clicking off the screen. I move to place it back in my pocket but it vibrates in my hand. Checking the screen, I see that I have a new message from Melissa.

Melissa: Girls went to rest and I need to get kids. She's all yours. Be good to my baby.

My heart thunders in my chest as I look between the guys. I try smiling but nerves flutter through my body. "We can go see her now," I say in a low, raspy voice. It takes the guys a second, just one, to process what I had said before we abruptly stand, clean up our mess, and make our way to the elevators.

The elevator ride is silent, tense. Relief, fear, and excitement swirl around the small space. I don't even need to look at the others to know they feel it, too.

Once the elevator whooshes open, we all step out and head for Annie's room. I'm sure we look like idiots trying to remain steady and walk casually. But, I'm pretty sure we look more like puppies scampering over each other to get to a treat.

Reaching the door, I steady my breathing and knock on the door. Her sweet voice, although hoarse from trauma, filters through the door. I look at the others, raise my lips in a tight grin, and open the door.

Walking towards the other side of the curtain feels like we're walking towards heaven's gates. Once we make it to the edge of her bed, we all freeze. Annie is twisting behind her towards her left side. She groans in pain as she struggles to reach something.

We take a moment to study her and the cuts that we can see on her body. A long, raised scar on her arm stands out more than anything. It's pink and puckered; like it wasn't stitched right. The blanket and hospital gown still cover most of her body but we can see her body tremble in pain, fear, or maybe exhaustion. She looks so damn vulnerable; smaller almost.

"Do you need something, Sweetness?" Jenson asks in a low voice. Her whole body freezes, arm suspended in mid-air, as she takes in his words.

She turns towards us and I can't help but smile at the sight of her; eyes open, body moving, *here*. Her eyes widen as she runs her gaze over each of us; blinking repeatedly like she can't quite believe that we're here. Her chin wobbles and her eyes fill with tears as she whispers out "G-Gospel Boys?"

My heart fucking shatters. I force myself to stay where I am even though every part of me wants to run to her. Instead, I give her my best smirk, shove my hands in my pockets, and try to make my voice as carefree as possible, "Hey, Angel. Long time no see." *Ok, that was just bad.*

Her eyes shimmer as tears fill them. "You-You're here?"

I release the breath I was holding and smile at her. "Of course, Angel. We were actually here when you woke up." I palm the back of my neck, unsure of how she would react. "But, we figured you may need some space and time to process, you know, with the others."

Her gaze freezes as she stares at the wall past my head, but she quickly blinks out of it. Clearing her throat, she moves her hands toward her hair, trying to flatten it out. Her hiss of pain has Nick moving. "Oh, Siren, hold on. We need to call the doc." He looks over his shoulder at me, "Did anyone tell them she's awake?"

Jenson immediately responds, "I'm on it" and strolls right out the door. Nick turns back to face Annie, smiles down at her, and gently moves his hands towards her face. Right before touching, though, he stops himself and drops his hand back down to his side. Her eyes follow his every movement then stares at his hand with a pinched expression.

Not wanting her to overthink anything, I clear my throat. Her head whips back to face me, eyes wide open as she assesses me. A tiny smile pulls at her busted lips and I feel my heart squeeze in my chest.

She then turns her gaze to Cory and gasps, "Oh my God! Cory! What happened?"

I look over at him and watch as his cheeks start turning pink. He lowers his head to the ground, a small grin tilting his lips. Scuffing his shoe on the floor like a nervous little kid he says, "It's nothing, Pretty Girl. Just got in a little car accident." The loud intake of her breath has us both shooting our heads toward her. Her hand covers her mouth and her eyes are wide with worry.

"Oh God. Come here. Let me look at you. Do you need to see someone? Did it happen recently?" Nick's chuckle brings her out of her anxiety-riddled questioning and she turns her head to glare at him. "What's so funny? He's hurt. Why is he here? He needs to be resting."

Cory chortles under his breath and steps up to Annie's bedside, "I'm fine, Pretty Girl. Just some bumps and bruises. Seeing you is way more important than resting."

Her eyes hold his for a moment before she tentatively reaches for his face, "M-May I?"

I can see his dimple pop out from over here as he leans in closer. "You can touch me anytime, baby. That will never change."

She initially flinches at his words but, like the strong, fierce, badass that she is, she recovers quickly and moves her hand again. His breath hitches as she ghosts her fingers over the bruises and near his stitches. Sniffling, she bats away a stray tear before smiling at him. "Is that all or is there more?"

Cory looks over at me, a silent question in his eyes, and I shrug. I mean, he might as well show her. Inhaling deeply and pushing it out, he slowly stands and lifts his shirt up to his neck. Her hand trembles and tears roll down her cheeks as she gently traces over the bruising left on his chest and ribs.

Her hands then follow the ridges of his abs, causing him to tense and flex. He sucks a breath between his teeth as she reaches the top of the V sitting just above his waistband. The sound startles her, making her quickly withdraw from him like she's been burned. The parts of her face that aren't bruised turn a gorgeous shade of crimson. She lowers her gaze to her lap as she clasps her hands together, squeezing them tight. "Sorry." Her voice comes out just above a whisper.

Cory rolls his shirt down and lightly places one finger under her chin, slowly guiding her to look at him. His full smile and dimples are on display and I watch as she melts into the hospital bed for him. "Never be sorry for touching me, Pretty Girl. It's all yours, anyways." He whispers with a wink, causing her to blush hard and suck her bottom lip into her mouth.

"Okay." She concedes.

Releasing a heavy breath she looks back at Nick and straightens her right arm out, palm up. "*You* don't have any bruises I need to worry about do you?"

Nick's smile widens at the sass in her tone that was obviously used to cover her worry. He looks from her to her hand, licking his lips, then glides his hand across her palm interlacing their fingers. "No, Siren. I've been a good boy."

I snort out a laugh that causes them both to look at me in question. Nick's look is more of a smug challenge to prove him wrong. Which, of course, means I level him with a raised brow and tilted grin. His smile widens, knowing exactly what's in store for him later. Glancing back to Annie, her questioning eyes flit between us, revealing that she is worried he's actually hurt.

I step up to the end of her bed, smiling wider as her eyes change from worry to surprise. "He's *fine*, Angel. But he's definitely *not* a good boy." Nick huffs a laugh and I grin, hoping that she'll understand that we're just playing around.

It takes a few seconds before she releases a breath, nods, then leans back into the bed. Her face shifts as she gets lost in her thoughts.

Whatever is bothering her, I want her to feel safe enough to tell us. "Hey, Angel, what's that look for?"

She chews on her lip for a moment before looking between the three of us. "Can I tell you something? It might be stupid but, I don't know…" All three of us are already nodding; willing to hear anything she wants to say.

I take a chance and briefly rub my palm up the inside of her leg, over her ankle. "Always. Tell us anything, everything, nothing. Whatever you want us to know, we'll be happy you shared."

Her eyes fill with tears again and she bats them away before releasing a water laugh. "It's so stupid." I start shaking my head to dispute it but Jenson strolls back in with a doctor and two nurses in tow, all wearing large smiles and looking genuinely excited to see her awake.

"Oh, sweet girl! I'm so glad you're awake." One of the nurses coos, flitting over to Annie's side and strapping the blood pressure cuff around her bicep. The other nurse brings over a little machine to check her temperature and oxygen levels.

The doctor flips through some paperwork before regarding us with a lifted brow. Turning back to Annie, his face softens, "It's good to see you. You gave everyone quite the scare." He walks over to her slowly and with measured movements. "I need to check your eyes and your wounds. The nurses will help and will stay with you the whole time. Is that ok?"

She gives a shaky nod and tilts her smile in a soft grin. "Yes, that's fine."

He nods and begins his assessment as the nurses slowly fold her blanket down to her ankles. The guys and I look at each other, then quickly turn away from Annie, giving her a little privacy.

Staring at the cream wall, I listen to every grunt, every groan, every hiss of pain. I have to flex my hands and inhale deeply to keep myself from knocking them out of the way so she stops hurting. The minutes tick by and I feel myself trembling as I fight against the visceral need to go to her, to hold her.

The doctor clears his throat and whispers something to Annie. Whatever she says, it's too low for me to hear. "Gentlemen, thank you for giving Annie some privacy. You may turn around now." We all turn back to her and I know we're all doing the same thing; checking over her entire body, face, everything; desperately wanting to catalog every mark on her beautiful skin.

Annie clears her throat and flicks her gaze between the four of us before landing back on the doctor. Nodding slightly, she gives a barely there grin. "It's ok. If they, um, if they want to stay, they can. It would be easier to hear it from you. And, I wouldn't have to try and explain it later."

Her smile wobbles as she peers at each of us through her lashes. "Um, only if y'all want to. You don't *have* to be here. I know we barely just... well, before, we had just started..." Her frustration is evident as she trails off, sliding the blanket under her nails like it's soothing her.

My heart breaks in understanding. We had just started a relationship when she was taken. Like, hours before. Now she's worried we don't want her anymore. Or, maybe she's worried that *she's* not ready anymore. We spent weeks showering her with love and attention and showing her every chance we had just how much we wanted her. And then, that asshole took her.

Before I can react, Nick is shushing her, gently twirling a lock of her hair. "Siren, sweet, sweet girl. We didn't "barely just" nothin'. We've been waiting, searching, spending every waking moment missing you. Whatever you want us to do, darlin', we will. We are still. All. In." He kisses the back of her hand to punctuate the last three words. The worry in her eyes melts away and a sweet, shy smile transforms her face.

Nodding gently she smiles at each of us, looking for confirmation.

And, of course, we give it to her. We each walk over, pick her hand up, and kiss it softly before repeating, "All in."

We stand around her bed, closer to her head and she gives Doc the go-ahead. He clears his throat and begins to go over her current assessments as well as the initial assessments they did when she first arrived.

For the next ten minutes, Annie's hand squeezes mine and Nick's as the doctor reviews some of the cuts that needed restitching, the results of her tox screen, and areas he's still concerned about.

At the end of it, he clears his throat for the final bit of news. Tense silence fills the air and some kind of unspoken conversation passes between them. Annie nods her head and straightens her shoulders like the little badass that she is. "When you first arrived, because of your condition, we conducted a rape test."

I suck in a breath as images of the room she was found in, with that fucker's limp cock still out, flash through my mind. I can feel my body vibrate with rage and anxiety. Annie's nails piercing my skin brings me out of my selfishness and back to her. I force myself to relax and kiss her hand once more. Doc takes that as a sign to continue. "The good news is there was no sign of penetration, bruising or tearing, and no bodily fluids."

Annie's loud exhale causes the rest of us to domino; releasing the breaths we were all holding. Her sweet little voice barely carries through the room, "Thank you. I know while I was *there*, they didn't, um, do that. But, that last night was really fuzzy and, well, let's just say I was told it was going to happen, so I thought it had."

The doctor nods his head and comments, "That makes sense. The amount of paralytic we found in your system, paired with the disassociation and shock from however you were rescued, probably sent your brain into overdrive trying to protect you."

Annie nods in understanding, chewing on her lip before looking back at him. "H-How did I get here? Do you know what happened?"

The doctor gives her a grim smile and shakes his head. "No, ma'am. The groups that saved you, and the others, dropped you off under the radar. Overrode the security cameras and everything. Witnesses said they were all in black, head to toe, and had their faces caked in black paint."

Annie quietly contemplates his response before quietly asking, "Is it wrong that I'm glad? I agree with Jodie, you know."

She looks up at me from the corner of her eye, unsure of how I will respond. "If I knew who they were... they obviously didn't operate on the legal side of the law but they *saved* us." Shaking her head, she tilts her lips into a small grin, then looks back up at me. "No offense, but, I wouldn't tell on them, either."

I nod and gently kiss the back of her hand, inhaling deeply. "I don't blame you. We're just glad you're back, Angel."

The smile she sends my way is all-consuming. The light in her eyes pierces my soul and I finally feel whole. Looking over at each of my brothers, then back at my girl, I feel like the last piece of the puzzle has finally slid into place.

17

Annie

It's been three very long days since I woke up in the hospital. The guys have spent almost every waking moment with me laughing, talking about the Youth Center, and watching random movies. I still get tongue-tied when they show up. Like, part of me is expecting them to decide it's too much; I'm too much.

But then, you get my mother in the mix and it feels so overwhelmingly perfect. Mom has been here every morning for a few hours. I guess we're near Clear Lake so she has to drive clear on the other side of town to get back in time to pick the kids up from the bus.

I won't lie, I was shocked that not only had my mother and Vince met, but that she already had an inkling about our *unconventional* relationship. Apparently, she called Vince out and he floundered trying to cover, but also didn't want to lie to her. She says she took mercy on him and laughed it off.

They did, however, assure me that the kids had not met the guys; yet. But, judging by how all of us have fallen right back into being safe, comfortable, cared for, I have a feeling that will be happening sooner than later. Well, after I'm healed, of course.

Over the last few days, she *and* all of my guys have spent hours in this sterile-ass room together. Joking, talking about their business, her work. The guys eat up every story she shares about my kids. Their eyes fill with light and genuine interest in the daily drama.

My body is littered with scars but, thankfully, a lot of the bruising has faded. I have a couple of fractured ribs but nothing else is broken, *thank God*. And, yesterday, I got to eat actual food! Well, hospital food, but still. No soup, tea, or Jell-O. *Gag. It's a texture thing.*

After my first real lunch, they let me take a shower and it was bomb-tastic! The feeling of actually being completely clean from head to toe, with hot water pelting my back, and the fragrance of eucalyptus filling my nose was almost orgasmic. But, I guess being gone for almost three weeks will do that.

Finding that piece of information made it more real somehow. It's not like we had windows or clocks so day and night meant nothing in there. But, three weeks: that was a lot of time lost with my kids. My anxiety always kicks up when I think about how they probably felt that I abandoned them.

Mom had brought my phone back yesterday morning so I was able to see their sweet little faces before bedtime last night. We all cried and, once they got over their initial feelings of seeing the markings on my face from the "car wreck", they talked my ear off about anything and everything.

After the thirtieth "I love you" and three rounds of "goodnight", we hung up. Then, I allowed myself to finally fall apart. With nothing more than the corner light on, and the beeping of the monitor, I allowed all the feelings to pour out of my eyeballs until I was a drenched, hiccuping mess. And, damn, it felt good.

As promised, the girls and I had a movie night, but we waited until the day after I woke up since I was so exhausted. The news came on, first, and we all stared in shock as the reporter gave an update on a warehouse and home bombing. Shock turned into relief, and, eventually, excitement. Those assholes were gone and we could truly move on with our lives. Starting with watching Pitch Perfect together.

Some of the women were discharged yesterday and some are being discharged today. We all swapped numbers and made our own group chat. We voted on "Warriors" as our group name; needing a little extra confidence to get through the next few days, weeks, months, whatever. It sounds strange to say, but I'm really going to miss them. They became my family in the most fucked up situation and I can only pray they all keep their fire and strength.

Glancing at my phone, I check the time and find myself excited for the guys to arrive. We usually get an hour or so to ourselves before Mom shows up. Not that I don't love her being here but, I'm still nervous they will back out. So, every time they're here, I'm filled with hope that maybe, just maybe, I can still live a full life with my mother, kids, and the guys by my side.

A knock on the door has me snapping my head up and grinning like a loon. "Come in," I call out, shaking with excitement. The door clicks open and one-by-one my guys appear.

Nick has another bouquet of Stargazer Lilies, making me chuckle. "Nick, seriously, are you trying to buy the whole floral shop?"

He grins wide and winks at me. "Nah, but I can if you want." I giggle, fucking giggle, and shake my head at him. Then he slowly leans in and brushes his lips across my forehead, causing me to blush immediately.

Jenson comes up to my other side and leans in, kissing my nose, and handing over a huge Cinnamon Crunch Bagel from Panera. My stomach growls in anticipation, causing them to laugh at me. *I don't even care; they're my favorite.* I bat my eyes at him and whisper out a "Thank you."

Nick busies himself with adding my newest bouquet to the line across the window sill. Cory takes his place, kisses my hand gently, then reveals a fresh, hot mocha with whipped cream. "What did I do to deserve all of this? You guys are spoiling me way too much."

"No such thing, Pretty Girl." He whispers before kissing my hand again.

Vince clears his throat, bringing my attention to him. I smile so wide that it pulls at my lip and lingering bruises, causing me to hiss. "I, uh, brought someone to meet you." He shifts from one foot to the other, fiddling with a button on his shirt. He's so damn adorable when he's nervous. Which shouldn't be possible with how damn hot the man is.

Knowing I trust these men, I nod once, giving my permission for him to let in my mystery guest.

A woman, about my age, steps around the corner with a dazzling smile. Vince smiles at me and introduces her as Gina. "She's a friend of ours. And, well," he clears his throat uncomfortably, looking even more unsure. "She's been through something similar."

He looks at her and she nods with a sweet smile. "We thought, maybe, it would help to talk with someone who understands. We will always be here to talk, cry, scream, or just listen to anything you want to share but, well, we just thought..." He trails off, palming the back of his neck, and looking like he's about to spin out. *I have to put this sweet man out of his misery.*

"Thank you, Vince. I really appreciate it." Turning towards Gina I smile at her and wave towards the couch. "Care to sit on a hard, shitty couch?" Her smile brightens and she practically skips over and flops onto the couch; the fake leather protesting loudly.

The guys all walk over and give me lingering kisses on my forehead. "Thank you, Vince, really," I assure him before he walks away. Nick tells me they'll be downstairs and to just text when I'm ready. Feelings, far too big, threaten to burst out of my chest but I suck them down. I settle on nodding my head with a smile before they file out of the room.

Turning towards Gina, I see her brow is raised conspiratorially. "What?" I say, instantly nervous. She giggles, covering her mouth with one hand, then flicking her long red hair behind her shoulder. "Damn, girl. I knew they had it bad but seeing you in the room with them all fawning over you; it's adorable."

Her voice comes out sweet and light-hearted but I still can't help the tinge of jealousy that lights in me. I take a moment to look her over, taking in her neon pink manicure, nude lipstick, and shining red hair. She's all perfect curves, definitely slimmer than me but not skinny. This woman is perfection.

She tilts her head at me, squints her eyes, and points one of her brightly painted nails at me. "Don't you go there, girlfriend. I met those four, recently, while they were looking for you. They reached out to my guys. Guys, as in three. I have more than enough D in my life and I'm not looking to add any more."

She blows out a raspberry, rolls her eyes and, I think, mumbles to herself. "I can barely handle the alphaholes I have."

Looking back at me, she smiles widely and says, "Besides, those boys are 1 million percent Team Annie." She sighs wistfully, leans back against the couch, and folds her hands together.

We spend a moment, quietly assessing each other. *Ok, I'm assessing her and she's just smiling sweetly.* Eventually, I decide I'm an idiot and give her a smile in return. "Sorry, low self-esteem and, well, yeah." I shrug my shoulder and she shakes her head as the smile stretches across her face. Her pale blue eyes sparkle as she leans forward, resting her hand on the guardrail of my bed. "Don't even sweat it. I get it. Heck, without my three, I wouldn't have made it out of that bunker alive. And I damn sure wouldn't be living my life free, and filled with love." She whispers the last part to herself.

Silence fills the space between us. I flit my gaze between her and my hands, squeezing together in my lap. Finally, I let out a deep sigh before turning to her. "How do you do it?"

She slowly raises her head towards me and the shadows that cross her gaze mirror my own. It's then that I know I can talk with her, share with her, fall apart with her. She understands wholly and appears to have moved on with a wonderful life.

A thin smile pulls her lips as her brows crease in concentration. Based on how she's looking at me, she knows exactly what I'm talking about. With a heavy sigh, she responds, "*I don't.* Some days, some moments, it's easy to forget. My partners and I have spent so much time *living* and just being in the moment with each other. But, sometimes the memories creep in, the smell of ham travels through the air, heck, the sound of a microwave has pushed me into a downward spiral."

She shakes her head, her eyes cast down as pain and sorrow take over her features. Sucking in a deep breath, she huffs a laugh and turns her sad smile back to me. "I can't tell you it gets easier but, what I can tell you is, your support system is where you draw your strength from. You have to be able to tell them triggers, even if you don't know them until after they happen. Talk with them about how to guide you out of panic attacks and flashbacks and come up with plans on how to handle them. It doesn't have to be with your guys, it could be with your mother." Her eyes sparkle mischievously as she cocks her brow at me, "But I can tell you, after seeing them interact with *my* partners, they'd do anything for you. And that includes helping you heal your mind and heart, as well as your body."

She reaches her hand past the guardrail, clasping my hand in hers. Something wet hits my chest and I realize I'm crying. But, so is she.

Squeezing my hand again, she lets out a water laugh and turns to grab some tissues, passing me one. We both giggle a little, sniffling and wiping away the waterworks. Once we're finished, she disposes of the tissues and comes back to stand next to me.

"So," she starts, sounding lighter than before, "If you're anything like me, you don't want to talk about what happened because we don't like to burden others, right?"

A smirk graces my face as I chuckle. Nodding my head, I sigh, already knowing where this is going. "Ok. What do you want to know?"

I look over at her and watch as she gets comfortable, bending her legs and tucking them under her as she rests her right arm and side against the side of the couch. "Dealer's choice. Beginning, most terrifying, wherever you want to start. It's all about getting it out."

Her gentle smile puts me at ease and I relax into the bed. Popping my knuckles, I draw in a shaky breath and search her eyes. "Do you, do you just want after I was taken? Cuz, um, Lukas was in my life far before that. Hell, him being a vile bastard is actually how I ended up pregnant; twice." Her brows hit her hairline, eyes widening in surprise.

After a moment, her face relaxes and she fixes me with a fierce flare. "Get it *all* out, girl. Right here, right now, with someone who not only understands almost any situation you've been through but knows the importance of talking to someone. I'm not going anywhere. My guys know where I am and the tracker Enzo put in my arm last year will show that I'm right here; where I should be." *Damn, I wish I was that brave and confident.*

"That, and they know better than to interrupt any semblance of girl time I may get. Lord knows I have enough peens surrounding me." Her eyes dance with humor as her smile stretches across her face. Laughter erupts out of me, shocking us both.

The surprise on her face must mirror my own because we stare at each other for a moment before falling into a fit of giggles. Happy tears flow down my face and my whole body aches from the movement, but it feels too good to stop.

Once the laughter subsides, we dry our faces, settle back down and let silence envelop us once more. I inhale for a count of four, hold for a count of four, then exhale for a count of four. Turning towards Gina, I take in her sweet, calm, aura. I've always had a hard time making friends, especially women, but I already feel so comfortable with her. I can trust her with my truth. I see it in her eyes, in the way that she holds herself. She's been through hell and is still standing to tell the tale. Not just standing, she's thriving, loving, living.

With a nod, I begin my twisted, fucked up tale; starting with dating Lukas O'Brian.

Gina and I spent over two hours sharing stories, crying, laughing until we cried, and just soaking up time with another person who understands our struggles. It physically pained me when she talked about being taken by men at 17 years old, then sold to multiple trafficking rings for over a decade. A decade! I barely survived three weeks.

But, she's here. She's living her best life with three adoring men by her side.

Her response about what she and her men do for work was strange, and she redirected the conversation quickly after that but, honestly, she seemed so pure and genuine that I chalked it up to not wanting to dominate the conversation.

By the time my mom walked in, Gina and I had already swapped numbers and loosely planned a meeting with each other once I was well. It felt so good to have another friend on my side; one that understood trauma and the fall-out from it. She gave me the best hug before skipping out of the door with a promise to send the guys up.

Mom and I have only been talking for about five minutes when someone knocks on the door. Mom calls out for them to come in, and quickly moves away from my bed as the nurse comes bustling in to take my vitals.

After the usual review questions, the doctor walks in and smiles wide. "Well, Ms. Annie, it appears that you've been recovering very well. Did you talk with your psychiatrist to make sure they can get you back on your meds, yet?" He asks me with a hopeful smile.

"Yes, sir. They're already waiting for me at the pharmacy. And, I believe, she sent the paperwork already."

The doctor nods his head in appreciation before smiling wide, "Good, good. I'll go check that once I'm finished here. If everything looks good for the rest of the day, I think it's time to get you relaxing in your own bed."

I stare at the man, dumbfounded for a moment. Then my brain comes back online, "So, I'm getting discharged? I get to leave?" Excitement courses through my body. Yes, I'm sore. Yes, I'm scared. But, dang it, I miss my kids, and my bed, and my dang bearded dragon.

The doctor chuckles and nods his head playfully, "Yes ma'am. Of course, should you need anything once you leave, you'll be able to call and ask, but it's time to go home."

I release a sound that is maybe one or two notches below a shriek. Tears decide to run down my face as the weight of my reality settles on me. The doctor sends me a sad smile, nods at my mother, then tells me he'll check on me after dinner.

Once he's gone, Mom stands up and rushes over to hug me. My body and skin protest but I don't forking care. And, judging by the bounce of her chest and sniffling of her nose, I'd say she needs it as much as I do.

We break apart when there's another knock on the door. Separating, we wipe our eyes before I tell the guys to come in. I figured it had to be them since Gina left a little while ago.

All four of my guys walk in with broad smiles across their faces. "Good news, Angel?" Vince asks with a knowing smile.

I can't help the blush that spreads across my face and chest. That low voice gets me every damn time. Tucking a strand of hair behind my ear, I look between them, smiling widely, and proclaim, "Looks like I'm bustin' out of here tomorrow!" The guys cheer and hugs are shared as we let the realization that I'm truly free settle.

Mom starts mumbling about making plans to get me home and rushes over to grab her journal and phone from her purse. Meanwhile, Vince walks over, takes my hand, and kisses my knuckles. In a tone just loud enough for me to hear, he asks, "I'm guessing you had a good visit with Gina?"

I look up into his gorgeous brown eyes, swirling with hope and adoration. "It was great, actually. Thank you." I whispered. Before I can second guess myself, I move into his space and fuse my lips to his. His hand tightens around mine for a brief moment and butterflies take off inside my chest. It wasn't a long kiss or a steamy kiss, but it was the first one we truly shared since *that* night. The night I was taken. So far, they've all been gentle with me, caring, and sweet. Never kissing more than my hand and the occasional forehead or nose kiss. I didn't know how much I needed that connection until this moment. Honestly, I wasn't sure how I would react with all of them around me since being taken but, these men had become a source of comfort and peace far before I ever admitted it to myself.

Breaking apart, I release a contented sigh. Vince's smile is so wide that it causes the corner of his lips and eyes to crease. Matching his smile, I bite my lip, knowing deep down that our story isn't finished. As far as I'm concerned, we're just getting started.

18

Cory

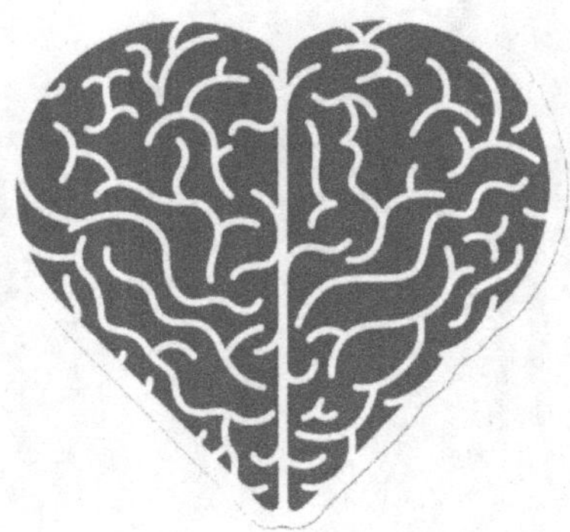

Making our way to the hotel room, an excited energy buzzes around us. Vince is in the parking lot talking to Enzo and Gina while the rest of us head to the room to pack.

We spent a couple of hours getting our butts handed to us playing Phase 10 with Melissa and Annie. I never would have thought our girl had a little competitive streak had I not witnessed it for myself. In fact, that naughty girl ripped some stitches on her belly when she loudly celebrated her sixth-round win. The howl of pain she let out, followed by the immediate reddening of her face, almost had me passing out. I have *absolutely* learned that I can't stand to see her in pain.

The only thing worse than that was her frantically waving us away when the nurse came in to restitch and rebandage her. She wasn't ready for us to see more than what was obvious on her arms. Yes, it was on her belly, but it didn't ease the ache in my chest when I saw the fear in her eyes when the nurse started lifting her gown. Of course, none of us argued. We never want Annie to feel uncomfortable but the look in her eyes was so...odd. It wasn't fear of seeing her body; like she had been nervous about before. This was something else. Something that made me want to cry, punch, or run. Or, maybe all of the above.

Once the nurse was finished, she jokingly told us to make her settle down so she could be discharged tomorrow. We agreed and the nurse hummed cheekily as she walked away. Walking back in, Annie made a pointed effort to not talk about it and decided to talk about favorite movies, instead.

When her mother left, Vince pulled the chair next to her bed, Nick sat in his lap, and Jense and I took the couch as we started a Back to the Future marathon. However, Annie barely lasted through the first one before passing out. Vince just shut the lights off in the room and turned down the TV.

Once she woke up, we all just hung out in comfortable silence. I sketched, Nick read on his tablet, Vince watched a movie on his tablet with his earbuds in, and Jenson and Annie worked together to color in an "adults only" coloring book filled with curse words and smutty jargon.

When it was time to leave for the night, Annie asked Vince for another "real kiss". He lifted his brow mockingly and said, "Oh, so you do know how to ask for what you want?"

When I say her cheeks went red, I don't mean a light blush. No, no. I mean God himself took the color straight from a red poppy flower and painted it on her skin. It was obvious by his tone, and his dominant smirk, that there was a story behind that. Thankfully, he remembered our girl needed some extra reassurance as he quickly winked and said, "Whatever you want, Angel."

The damn smile she had for him afterward almost sent me to my knees. But, the one she sent my way as I approached, all sweet and shy, just about killed me. I felt like I was ten feet tall when she held her hand out for me and asked if she could have a real kiss. I would have given her the entire universe if she asked me to. The moment her lips met mine, I had to physically fight myself to keep it sweet and chaste. I missed her taste, her smell, her little gasp of surprise; even if she was the one who asked for it.

Jenson got the same treatment, although he had to add his own flair; kneeling on the floor next to her bed before asking her, in the most ridiculous British accent, if she "could spare a kiss for an old, battered soul." We all rolled our eyes at his antics but he absolutely got what he was hoping for. Annie snorted out a giggle while she shook her head in exasperation. Her eyes were so wide, bright, and full of life and they matched perfectly with the smile she had stretched across her still-bruised face.

As always, Annie knew Nick needed to do things at his own pace. She slid her hand down the bed, palm up and open, and gave him the most innocent, loving smile. He interlaced their fingers before leaning in. She didn't move a muscle as he faltered an inch from her mouth. They stayed, suspended in that moment for what was probably seven or eight seconds, before he whispered something too low for us to hear. Annie nodded and leaned in, just a little, placing a light kiss on his cheek. When she leaned back, Nick's face looked like it had been painted with poppies and the look he gave her was comparable to a little boy who just got his first kiss from a crush.

"I'm going to wash the smell of hospital off of me," Nick calls out, walking into the bathroom and closing the door. I didn't even realize we had made it back to the room. But, now that I'm here, fatigue weighs heavy on my bones.

I cross the room and toe-off my Hey Dudes before mistakenly flopping onto the bed. Pain jolts through my chest and midsection, splintering out like a firework through my body. I groan through the pain and try to get my lungs to suck in breath as it all flew right out when I landed. I had been moving a lot better but, I guess I'm not as healed as I thought.

Jenson appears at my side and shifts me up the bed to my pillow. "You ding-dong head. Are you trying to take Annie's place in the hospital? She'd probably kill you. Especially since you severely downplayed your injuries." He had started walking off in the middle of his rant so I'm not sure if he is still talking to me, or himself. I don't even get a chance to find out as I hear the door open, then slam shut; cutting off Jenson's mumbled rant.

I continue breathing through the pain; closing my eyes, and gritting my teeth. Slowly, my body relaxes and, some of the pain eases. That jolt of pain caused me to expend the last of my energy reserves and I slowly feel myself leaning into sleep.

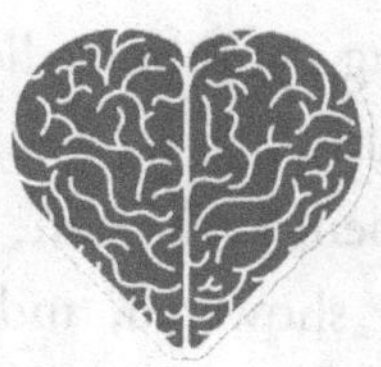

I jolt awake, heart hammering in my chest, as something ice-cold hits my battered body. "Ssshhh, easy Cor." Blinking past my initial shock, I turn and find Jenson lying on the bed next to me. It takes a moment for my mind to come back online. I groggily trace the path of his arm across my body and see his hand holding a towel, wrapped up like a giant dumpling, sitting on my chest.

I take in a shaky breath and lay my head back down, facing towards Jense. "Thanks. Sorry. I guess I was more tired than I thought."

His lips tip up in a barely there smile before he lightly shakes his head. "No worries. But, you haven't been icing it as much as you should since we've all been with Annie."

I barely nod my head as we both lapse into an awkward silence. Licking my lips, I take in Jenson's features. His brows are scrunched in a light scowl, his eyes look distant and haunted, even his hair looks like he's been running his hands through it a hundred times. "Th-thank you, Jense. I've been so worried about Annie and, you're right, I haven't been taking care of myself. So, thank you; for always knowing what I need, even when I don't."

The light of the room dulls the usual brilliance of his green eyes but they still pierce right through me as he flicks his gaze towards mine. Seconds pass as we stare at each other. I have no idea what he's thinking but, fucking hell, how I wish he would lean over and kiss me.

He doesn't, though. Instead, his smile widens, part genuine and part forced, as he says "Cor, I'd do anything for you. And, that's how this crazy little family works. We pick each other up when we're not at our best. Besides, Annie would kick my ass if I didn't help you. Then, she'd kick your ass for being a stubborn dickhead." We both chuckle, knowing just how true that is.

The bathroom door opens at the same time the front door beeps. Nick stands there, freshly showered, and waits for Vince to enter. They share a few quiet words before walking further into the room. Both of them scan my chest and abs and Vince raises his brow in question. Huffing out a forced laugh I grumble, "I'm fine. Just got a little too excited about lying down is all."

He and Nick both roll their eyes and walk towards us. "I called in for dinner a bit ago. It should be here soon. We all need to try and get some rest because I have a feeling tomorrow is going to be long in a different way." Vince says, sparking our curiosity.

Jense is the first to ask, "What do you mean? Did they find out we were involved? Are we going to jail? Fuck! My hair is too pretty to

go to jail." His whining coupled with his strangely hilarious theatrics cause us all to burst into laughter. His face contorts into mock outrage as he flings his luscious locks behind his shoulder. "Whatever, y'all are just jealous." His feigned haughtiness just causes us to laugh harder.

When he can't contain it anymore, he joins in. I wrap my arm around my abs to try and counter the pain from the laughter but it does very little to help. However, at this moment, with my best friends surrounding me, all laughing together for the first time in weeks, it feels good; perfect.

Once we all gather ourselves, only shaking in the occasional after-chuckle, we look back to Vince. Nick clears his throat, smiling wider than I've seen in a while, and taps Vince's shoulder with his. "Alright V, what's happening tomorrow?"

Vince's eyes turn from humorous to downright excited. He bites at his lip, second-guessing himself for a moment before shaking his head. "OK, I already talked with Gina and she's down to help. I've got a plan to make tomorrow extra special for Annie."

All chuckles have subsided and the air in the room shifts. We all subtly lean in and hang off every word as Vince shares his idea for tomorrow. Tears fill our eyes, smiles widen, and a new type of joy zaps through the air.

When we're all in agreement, Vince pulls out his phone, clicks on Melissa's name, and hits the speakerphone icon, "Hello? Vince? Is Annie ok?" Vince calms her quickly, getting right down to business. "It's ok Melissa. Annie is perfect."

She sighs in relief before Vince continues. "I've got the guys here with me. We have an idea to run past you but we need your help to pull it off."

19

∼

Annie

My room has been filled with anxiety, excitement, and hope for the last hour. My mother showed up with some fresh clothes for me and the guys showed up shortly after. We all waited until the doctor came in and finally cleared me to leave.

Knowing it was going to be another hour or so, I scurried into the bathroom to shower. I'm sure I'd want another once I got home but I wanted to feel fresh, clean, alive. I want to leave the hospital with my head held high knowing Lukas tried, and failed to destroy me. I mean, I'm not stupid. I know there's going to be a lot of healing, and I'm sure my nightmares will get worse for a while. But today, I get to see my babies. Today I get to start my life again. Today, I get to show the world, and myself, I fucking survived.

After washing up with my favorite shampoo and conditioner, I wrap a towel around my body and open the bag of clothes my mother brought for me to change into. I was a little nervous because when she handed me the bag, she looked like she was going to cry. She smiled, warming me from the inside out, and whispered, "I wanted you to be comfortable but I also wanted you to feel fierce. You, my baby girl, are amazing. You've been through so much in your life; so much in the last few weeks. But today is the first day of the rest of your life, and I want you to own it."

It was such an odd statement. Bold and inspiring but, odd. At first, it put me a little on edge but, the more I thought about it, the more I loved what she was trying to do. Lukas didn't break me. Not then, and not now.

Pulling out my panties and frilly black bra, I smile. I love this damn bra. It has always made me feel pretty, even if no one ever saw it.

Once those are on, I slowly pull out the black shirt. I have a lot of black in my closet but I instantly know what she had chosen. The feeling of empowerment flows through my veins as I unfold the shirt and take a moment to really appreciate the design.

A year or so ago, I stumbled across a FaceBook ad for a company called Beautiful Disaster; a company that caters to empowering women through clothing and other merchandise. I'm pretty sure it was love at first sight and I spent at least thirty minutes combing through every item they sold.

Many of their designs are switched out as new collections become available. And each collection, each design, and every post was made specifically to strengthen women emotionally and mentally. Their entire business is set on the principle that women should empower other women and, dang, I liked it.

I was immediately drawn in by a raven design that boldly

announced to not allow fear to determine fate. I remember holding my breath, praying that they had a size even sort of close to mine. What I found was a whole lot better. All of their- clothing, tanks, shirts, hoodies, leggings, all of it- came in sizes S to Curvy 3X! So, yeah, I added the Raven leggings to my cart. Then, I found a beautiful pair of sweatpants with a light blue outlined snake, also accompanied by a strong message. I love snakes and I loved the message so, those were added, too.

The last set I ordered that day is the one currently in my hand. Seeing the shirt in front of me, I guarantee Mom packed the leggings, too. At the time, I thought about my past and have made a home for the kids and myself. Now, the design brings a whole new meaning. One that brings tears to my eyes as my body begins to tremble.

I rub the soft material through my fingers as I take in the deep orange flames that swirl in the middle of the back. The fire disperses above and below the center in an ombre design from deep orange all the way to a pale yellow. Right in the middle of the flames, the words *From the Ashes I Rise* in bright yellow, jagged font pop against the black background.

I swallow the lump in my throat, praying to God that I can make that happen as I slide the shirt over my head. Releasing my wet hair from inside the shirt, I consider wiping the fog from the mirror. Other than to be careful while bathing, I haven't taken the time to look at myself. I'm not ready.

Anxiety swells when I remember that I'm leaving. Going back into the world. And, damn it's scary. I feel myself disconnecting so I force myself to breathe in deeply before releasing it, grounding myself in this moment. I whisper out words of encouragement in hopes that putting them into the universe will make them true. "Your past does not dictate your future. You are a Beautiful Disaster, and, from the ashes, you will rise. *I* will rise."

I stare down at the detailed image on the front of the shirt. The same yellow, jagged message is printed a few inches below the neckline. But, right in the middle, a gorgeous purple, orange, and yellow phoenix spreads its wings and appears to be lifting out of the flames surrounding it. The company's power term, Beautiful Disaster, sits at the bottom of the fire in a gothic-style font, lending me strength, confidence, and courage as I prepare for the next chapter of my life.

Mom knocks on the door quietly, letting me know the doctor is here to discharge me. I smile wide and slip into the softest damn yoga pants I've ever worn. *Not that I wore them for yoga.* The black pants are flared at the bottom, just enough to cover up half of my foot. Down the side of the right pant leg, an identical flame pattern from the back of my shirt is printed; spanning the length from the top of my thigh to just past my knee. The other pant leg has the phoenix image taking up most of the thigh section on the side, and a smaller flame rising at the bottom from ankle to mid-calf.

I quickly run a brush through my hair, brush my teeth, and step out to join the others. Yes, this is a very casual feeling outfit, but damn if it doesn't have me straightening my shoulders, ready to face the world.

Mom bats away a tear as I smile at her. She nods her approval and gives me a gentle squeeze. "Time to rise, baby," She whispers in my ear.

I watery chuckle escapes me as I walk back into the room and see my guys waiting for me. I'm not wearing anything hot or sexy, although the yoga pants do make my ass look amazing. But the smiles that stretch across their faces, mixed with their subtle nods and puffed-out chests, make me stand a little taller; smile a little wider.

The doctor makes quick work of going through my discharge paperwork. Vince is tapping away on his phone and Mom is scuttling around, making sure I don't leave anything behind.

Once finished, the doctor looks at me, almost like I imagine a father looking at his daughter, and says, "You've got a great support group behind you, Ms. Annie. What you did for those women, and for yourself, is nothing short of heroic. I can't imagine what you all went through, but it's patients like you, stories like yours, that make me proud to be a doctor." His smile is soft and caring as he takes in my outfit. Shaking his head a little, he smirks and bends down, just a little, and says, "Give 'em hell, Phoenix," Before walking out of the door.

His words further boost my confidence as I look around the room at my mom and my guys. "Ready, Pretty Girl?" Cory asks. I take in a deep breath, square my shoulders, and raise my chin, "Hell yeah, I am."

I look at Mom, huffing out a laugh as tears run down her eyes, and tell her, "Let's go home."

We make our way to the elevator and down the sterile hallway. The nurse's station is empty so I make a note to send them a "thank you" cookie platter of something later.

Cramming into the elevator, I quietly take note as Cory leans a little on Jense. But, I don't want to irritate him so when he catches me looking, I just smile shyly and face the doors again. My heart beats wildly in my chest as the realization that I'm finally going home sets in again.

The elevator bings, alerting us of our arrival, and the doors whoosh open. I swear I jump ten feet in the air as cheers and applause surround me. The entire lobby is lined with nurses, doctors, and the women I walked through hell with. Jenson puts his hand on my back and gently pushes me out of the elevator as tears stream down my face.

The nurses who cared for me wave, some give me gentle hugs, but they all smile and cheer as we walk by. The women I came here with all step up for tear-filled hugs as we lose ourselves in this moment. I was the last one released, but they're all still here; for me.

Eventually, we break apart, as the doctors and nurses say goodbye so they can go save lives and stuff, and Gina steps forward with three men I've never met. She hugs me fiercely and then pointedly tells me she needs to know where I got the "power suit" from. My laughter is watery and loud but wholly refreshing and I promise to send her the website.

She quickly introduces me to her men, Enzo, Rocco, and Mateo, who nod their heads at me before giving my guys their own version of bro hugs. Gina hugs me again, promising me she'll visit soon but needing to leave to make their flight home.

Just as they walk out of the sliding double doors, I hear, "Mommy!" My heart stops and I swirl around to see my three favorite littles, standing by the waiting room with big signs. Cheyenne's sign says "We missed you," Samantha's sign says "We love you, Mommy", and Josh's sign says "Welcome home".

I didn't even process that my feet had moved until I was on the floor in front of them, scooping them into my arms and sobbing loudly. Holding my kids is everything I needed and more. Pain stabs me at all angles but I will deal with it later. My babies are in my arms and I refuse to let them go.

Eventually, Josh says he's hungry, effectively pulling me out of my emotional state and causing us all to laugh. *Wait, is that?* I crane my neck to look into the waiting room to find Lana and Christina holding hands while smiling and crying.

"Oh my God!" I squeal. They both rush towards me and envelop me before I get to a full stand. "You're both here! How? When?" I'm not even sure who I'm asking but I'm also not sure I really care because they are, in fact, here.

Lana chuckles and explains that Mom called her to help Vince and the guys pull off this little departure parade. When she's finished, I turn towards Christina, confusion stretched tightly across my face. Her smile lights up the whole damn room and I realize just how much I've missed her. "Mama called me when you were first taken.

One day I called and Lana was with your mom making reward signs, which got us talking. Once we heard you were in the hospital, I made arrangements for Ryker to watch the kids when you were going to be discharged so I could be here and help out for a few days."

My eyes widened and my mouth dropped open. "You left Ryker, alone, with the kids, in another state? Are you nuts?" Silence settled around us before she snorted out a laugh; causing Lana and I to follow.

Once we get a hold of ourselves, I hug everyone, again, before turning to my guys. "Thank you. This," I wave my hand to encompass the whole lobby, "This was phenomenal."

They all wear matching smiles. Jenson steps forward, presents me with his elbow, and proclaims "Your chariot awaits m'lady." I giggle, like an idiot, and allow him to lead me through the lobby and out towards the lot.

Josh's hand slips into mine as he reaches his other hand out to Mom. Cheyenne and Samantha each hold onto Lana and Christina and excitedly gab about all the things they've been up to.

I take in a refreshing lungful of air, squinting as the sun that I've missed for weeks shines down on me. Looking around at the people I have surrounding me, I realize that I'm damn lucky to be alive; and I refuse to waste another minute of it.

20

Nick

Annie went home a week ago. I can't tell you how it felt to watch her leave that hospital. Her fire, her strength, her fucking courage was absolutely intoxicating. And since then, I've been consumed with thoughts of her.

Her best friend, Christina, had stayed with her the first few days. She insisted on staying to help her mom with the kids and making enough food to fill both of her freezers. According to Annie, she won't have to cook for weeks.

Christina went home two days ago and left Annie a blubbering mess. The good news is, she promised Annie she would fly back in after the holidays; and Annie is already planning a trip to see her.

I know her mom is officially returning to her own house this evening so, I'm sure she'll be needing some space as she heals and settles into a new routine. I just hope she lets us heal her, too. I don't know why I'm stressing about it. We've been talking every day, and she seems to be just as open and available as she was before. But the need to see her is growing stronger. After spending all that time with her in the hospital, going back to just messaging or talking on the phone is wearing on my nerves; and my heart.

Shaking the thoughts from my head, I focus back on my run. Needing something a little more to clear my head, I flip through my playlist. I land on Sickick's Official SickMix Part 3 and allow the oddly perfect mix of genres to flow through me. I don't know how he does it but the man is a musical genius. I give myself over to the music and push my body for the next twenty minutes.

By the time I'm ready to cool down, I feel lighter, less on edge, and ready for a damn shower. Guzzling some water, I wipe the sweat from my brow, then fling my towel over my shoulder. I make my way to the locker rooms, nodding at a few customers as I pass.

Once I'm in the shower, I quickly lather up and scrub my body clean. My phone rings from outside the curtain so I rush through the rest of my routine.

Shutting off the water, I wrap myself in a fluffy blue towel and walk over to the bench with my gear still on it. Clicking the button on the side, my heart does a backflip when I see that I missed a call from Annie. Fear tingles down my spine as images of her in the hospital bed flip through my mind. Swallowing hard, I quickly click on her contact and press the call button.

"Hey," her voice streams through the phone like a sweet, sweet tune. My shoulders instantly sag in relief and a smile works its way across my face.

"Hey yourself, Siren. To what do I owe the pleasure of your call." I'm secretly hoping my voice sounded strong and flirty because my nerves are still battling anxiety.

"Um, well..." she trails off. I hear some shuffling in the background and a loud exhale. "I know you're working but, is there any chance you're free for lunch today?"

I glance down at my phone and find that it's almost noon. I quickly run through the tasks I still have to complete today before ultimately deciding that I don't care. If she wants to see me, I'm going to be there. "For you? Absolutely. I know you aren't cleared to drive, yet, so do you want me to pick you up?"

She releases a heavy sigh before responding, "Um, if you want, sure, but, I'm not sure I'm ready to face the world. Do you-Would you like to come here?"

"There?" I question; sounding just slightly more man than mouse.

Her adorable giggle filters through the line, "Yes, here. You haven't been here before. It's just me. The kids are at school and I shooed Mom out so she could get her hair done before meeting up with her boyfriend? Manfriend? Ew, no." She huffs out a laugh before continuing. "Anyways, I could make us something if you want. But, it's whatever you want. I just miss you and want to see you."

And my heart explodes. Seriously, it's gone. Poof. Game Over. If I wasn't in a towel I would sprint there right now. Instead, I slow my roll, and offer to pick up lunch so she doesn't have to do dishes; which she enthusiastically agrees to.

As soon as we hang up, I'm throwing clothes on my body so fast that I'm surprised I don't trip over myself. Once I grab my lock and shove everything in my bag, I head out of the locker room. I don't even bother stopping in the office. I just send the guys a text and bolt right out the front door. *My girl wants to see me so that's exactly what she's going to get.*

* * *

Almost thirty minutes later, I'm pulling into the address that Annie sent me. Her Suburban sits in the driveway, the sight sending shivers down my spine. *I wonder how she feels about it? Maybe we should get her a new one?*

Pushing those thoughts away for now, I grab the food and make my way towards her door. A smile plays on my lips as an assortment of painted rocks fills the small garden in the front; clearly the kids' work. I also see pavers and mini-statues, also hand-painted by tiny humans. Most people always want the best and prettiest front gardens yet she allows her kids to fill theirs with art. *Damn, I love this woman.*

I skip the last couple of steps and knock on her door, butter-flies swooping through my chest. The door opens and her blue eyes smiling up at me almost knock me on my ass. Before I can react, her body collides with mine in a soul-altering hug. Dropping the bag of food, my arms wrap around her, trying desperately not to hurt her, but needing to feel her in my arms.

A broken sob erupts from her mouth. Even though the sound is muffled in my shirt, it penetrates my heart all the same. Instantly, I bend down, take a handful of her juicy thighs in my hands, and lift her. She releases a startled yelp but doesn't try to get down. If any-thing, she wraps around me even tighter.

I swipe my foot out, making sure the food is in the house and out of the way, then carry her over the threshold. Swinging my foot back, I search for the door until it catches on the toes of my Converse; allowing me to close it behind us. Moisture pools on my shoulder as she silently cries into my neck. Shushing her quietly, I scan the house to find the living room and beeline straight to the couch. Turning around, I move one hand from under her thigh to cradle her head while the other wraps around her back carefully; then I lower us to the couch.

My arms tremble with the war raging in my mind. I want to squeeze her, I know she needs it, but she's still cut up and bruised and healing. I don't know what else to do.

Her nose finds its way to my neck and her breath fans out, causing goosebumps to ripple down my arms. I gently shush her, softly rubbing down her back, and stroke my hand down her hair. "I'm here, Siren. I'm here. You're safe. I've got you," I whisper in her ear as I continue trying to calm her.

After a few minutes, her cries turn into cute little sniffles. She nuzzles deeper into my neck and inhales deeply, commanding my dick to attention. *Asshole. Not now.*

"Can I tell you something stupid?" Her voice is barely above a whisper. I dip my head in agreement, continuing to rub soothing circles across her back.

"I thought of y'all. A lot. When I was with Lukas, a long time ago, he, well, when things hurt I..." She trails off for a moment before sighing in resignation. "In full disclosure, I'm really good at disassociating. Like, *completely*; sometimes for hours." Her quiet words make me pause my movements as they settle into my brain. But she continues her revelation, "I typically dissociate to a memory; something fun or happy. Like my time with you guys." She leans her head back on my shoulder to peer up at me. Her ocean eyes shine with vulnerability and it takes everything I have not to tell her how much I love her right now. I opt for a gentle kiss on the nose to encourage her to keep going; sensing she's not finished. Her shy smile crawls across her face as her cheeks tint with blush. *Damn, she's gorgeous.*

"Anyways, I usually thought about my time with you all or about my kids; summer play days, art time, whatever. Except, that last night." She lowers her head back down to my chest, drops one arm from my neck, and begins running her fingers across my chest. I slide my hand up her back, gently stroking her hair, while idly rubbing circles on her back with my other hand.

"That last night, Greaser, th-the guy who, well, my kids, h-he..." I start shushing her again, pulling her deeper into my body. "It's ok, Siren. You don't have to tell me anything. You don't have to go through any of that again. I'm here and you're safe."

She freezes as she weighs the truth of my words. But, ultimately, she disagrees. "You need to know. That night, the last night, he was there. Lukas gave me the paralytic injection in my neck. I disassociated a few minutes later but, it was weird that time. Like, not how it normally is."

"What do you mean?"

Her fingers draw simple patterns across my chest in a soothing motion that both relaxes me and turns me on. I hear her swallow before she whimpers, "It wasn't a memory that time. You were all there, with my mom and my kids. It was almost like, well... Lukas told me that Greaser would have me for 24 hours, and then he was getting rid of me. So, I don't know. Maybe my mind just wanted to leave the world with a happy thought instead of a distant memory. But, then, the scene was distorted; vibrating with loud booms like fireworks and firecrackers. Even in my dissociation, I couldn't make sense of it. I still couldn't move. I was so scared and so fucking trapped, Nick. I actually wondered if maybe I was already dying." A shiver ran up her spine and I felt the evidence of her tears across my shirt. However, I stayed silent, allowing her to get it all out. Right here, with me.

Her words change from pained to borderline panicked. "I was so, so scared. The noises outside of my head didn't match what was inside but I couldn't physically open my eyes. I could feel my body being jostled around as the noises grew, then faded, and I literally felt like I was losing my grip on reality." She sniffles, then is quiet for a moment.

Slowly, she raises her red-rimmed, puffy eyes to meet mine. "The craziest part is, right before I lost consciousness, I *swore* I heard you. Your voice. It was *so real*. And, maybe it was my body wanting to help me to calm but, Nick, it worked. The words you've said to me before played on repeat and settled me until I passed out. Then I woke up in the hospital."

My hands were frozen mid-circle. She was looking up at me with so much hope and light and, *fuck! I can't believe she remembered. How could I have been so stupid?*

Before I could school my features, she furrows her brows and slowly picks her head and chest off of mine, raising up on her knees, thighs still spread across my body. Her brows turn from confusion to worry and she gently takes her finger and presses between my brows. "Don't do that. You're too cute to look so scared. I'm ok. I just wanted you to know."

The tension in her brows releases and she gives me a shy smile. But, I'm fucking stuck. I can't come up with a way to respond and the longer I stare at her, the more likely she'll know something's up.

"Nick?" *Dammit.*

She tilts her head and studies me. "Hmm?" I respond, raising my brows like I'm confused by her question.

Her face turns from nervous to a little suspicious. Suddenly, I blurt out, "Oh! The food! I left it at the door. Let me grab it really quick and we can finish this. I know it has to be hard to talk about and you need your energy."

Her arms band around my neck while her eyes narrow in suspicion. "Nuh-uh. What am I missing?"

Sweat drips down my neck as I dart my eyes between hers, trying to come up with something that sounds plausible but I can't. Her tits are pressed against my chest and I can feel her heat searing through her black leggings hovering just above my jeans. My fingers tingle and I dig my hands into her thighs, trying to keep the lust at bay but my damn brain keeps short-circuiting. So, I do the only thing my brain can process; I close my eyes and lean in to kiss her. She rears her head back, just out of reach, causing me to whimper out a groan.

Running her fingers through my hair, she pulls gently, sending another wave of lust straight to my aching cock. "Nick. What are you keeping from me?" Her voice is stern and commanding, reminding me a little of Vince.

"Nothing, Siren. I just need to kiss you." I still haven't opened my eyes and I try to lean forward again. This time, the grip on my hair stops me and my whole body trembles as I fight the *need* to keep our secret, and the need I physically have for her.

I can feel my brows bunch in agony, matching the internal war I'm having. I release a shuddering breath as I feel her lean closer to me. Her warm breath skates over my neck as she runs her nose all the way up to my ear before placing the sweetest fucking kiss behind it.

"Nick," she whispers into my ear, causing me to shiver. "Please don't push me out. You said you were all in. That means no secrets. I can't handle it."

Her breathy voice is mixed with want, pain, and deep vulnerability. I can't, I can't. I... "You heard *me*. It wasn't in your head. I really did hold you on the way to the hospital and it killed me to have to let you go but we could have gotten caught if I didn't. It was me, Annie. I'm so sorry. I'm so, so sorry!" I cry out.

By the time my word vomit came to an end, she had shifted away. Her legs are still straddling mine, but the slight tremor in her legs tells me she's having difficulty keeping the pose as she hovers above me.

"Wh-what? What do you mean?" Her sweet voice is shaking; whether from shock or fear or disgust, I don't know because I'm too big of a pussy to look at her.

I release a defeated breath, knowing that this is how we end. And I'll have to be the one to tell the guys I fucked it all up; for all of us. *Stupid asshole.* A single tear escapes from my eye as I drop my head down.

"Nick. I need you to tell me everything. Right now." The strength and conviction in her voice further remind me that I'm dealing with a badass. Equal parts vulnerable and brave. But, she deserves the truth; and we were stupid to think we could keep it from her.

She gingerly pulls her body away from mine, causing me to snap my head towards her retreating body. Thankfully, she doesn't go far, as she slowly lowers herself to the oversized ottoman a foot away from me.

I take a moment to truly take her in; assuming this will be the last time I see her. Her blue eyes still shine from the tears she cried and her beautiful cheeks and chest are kissed with pink splotches. Her black leggings have little lattice holes on the sides, while her heather peach shirt hangs off her left shoulder; showing her three black birds tattoo.

When I finish my perusal, I meet her eyes again. While there is definitely still pain behind them, I also see determination and grit. She's not going to let this go. Nor should she. Nodding my head solemnly, I prepare to tell her our only secret. The one that could land all of us in prison, or a shallow grave.

Nick looks absolutely wrecked. His fear is palpable which makes me incredibly uneasy. I just don't understand. *Why would he say he was there? And why didn't he stay? I'm so fucking confused and, maybe, a little hurt. Why wouldn't they tell me? We've had more than enough time alone together for them to say something. But they didn't. They kept it from me.*

Nick clears his throat, effectively ending my racing thoughts. He leans forward, resting his arms on his knees, and drops his head to the floor. "Ok, here it goes..."

* * *

We sit in silence. We don't look at each other. We don't move. We. Just. Sit.

I glance over at the clock on the wall and find that he's been here for an hour now. And the last forty minutes have been a mind fuck of *what-the-hell*ness.

Swallowing around the lump in my throat, tears fill my eyes. *Holy shit. They literally went to battle for me. For me.* All the pieces of information fly through my head and the more I process, the harder I fall.

As my tears begin to crash to the floor, I voice the one last question I have; for now. "Why?"

I see Nick's head snap towards mine, so I slowly raise mine to meet his gaze. Confusion stretches across his face before concern warps it into something so gentle and sweet.

"Because, Siren," his tongue peeks out as he licks his lips before he draws in the little loop on his bottom lip; tugging it between his teeth. He lets it go as his lips slightly turn into a sad smile before he continues. "We were lost without you. We needed, need, you. Police weren't able to get enough information on their own." He shrugged one shoulder quickly before, leaning back against the couch. "So, we used some of Vince's Dad's old connections. You didn't deserve to be there; none of you did." His voice slowly turns from broken and raw to strong and full of conviction. His eyes find mine again, piercing through my very existence. "And yes, it was hella scary. Yes, people got hurt; people fucking *died*. But you know what Siren, we can live with that because we got *you*. And those other women."

I go to speak when he sucks in a deep breath but he beats me to it; his voice turning much rougher and more demanding. "And you know what, I would do it all again. Could we go to jail forever because of what we did? Yup. Could someone from the Cosa Nostra or even Enzo's syndicate take us down if we were to give away any information about them? Also, yes. But you know what, Annie?"

His gaze burns into mine, hot and fiery, lighting an inferno deep within me. I can feel my eyes widen as he leans in closer to me. His chest rises and falls as he pants. His voice lowers into something similar to a growl, causing me to swallow hard and press my thighs together. "I would do it all again if it meant saving you. Even if you tell me to leave, right now, and never look back; I would still do it again because you are out; you are safe; you are free."

His eyes hold mine captive as I take in the last of his words. How this man went from nervous and shy to dominant is a mind fuck but I'm so here for it.

They did this for me. They risked their lives for me. And, even telling me puts them at risk. Holy Shit.

Without bothering to respond, think, or breathe, I stand and quickly climb into his lap. His eyes widen with surprise and he leans back against the couch; arms spreading out wide.

Hovering over his lap, I take his face in both of my hands, gently swiping my thumbs across the stubble. His brows pinch and raise in confusion as he tries to figure out what I'm doing. Leaning forward, I press my forehead to his, take a deep breath, then smash my lips to his.

He doesn't respond at first, but I'm not swayed. I put every ounce of emotion running through my body into the kiss. Then I slowly retreat, just enough that our lips are barely touching. Swiping out my tongue across his bottom lip, I take his ring between my lips and tug; forcing a moan from his mouth.

I let it slip free and go to kiss him again but his hands land on my hips, firmly pushing enough to signal for me to stop. I lean back, shaking as my weight bears down on my knees and I prepare for whatever he's about to say. He looks at me, eyes filled with questions and a few tears. His breath ghosts across my face, as he quietly asks, "What was that for? You're not mad?"

I huff out a humorless laugh and shake my head. "Of course I'm mad. I'm fucking furious! You all could have been in prison, or dead! I wouldn't be able to live with myself if something ever happened to you assholes!" I rant as my emotions ping between anger, sadness, relief, and love.

His frown deepens as his eyes close and he nods. "I know, Siren. I'm so sor..." I cut him off, pushing my lips against his again, and only release when we both start panting for air.

I press my forehead back to his as the tears we release slowly join together on his shirt. Shaking my head against his, I release a heavy sigh. "You guys came. You did all of that; risked it all, *for me.*"

Nick nods his forehead against mine and I sniffle, trying to stop any more tears from falling. Stroking my fingers across his cheeks, down his jaw, I watch as his Adam's apple bobs. Looking back at his eyes, I see my future; not my past. "Thank you," I whisper out. "Thank you for coming for me."

His fingers dig into my hips as he whispers, "Of course, Annie. We would do anything for you." Nodding my head, I brush my thumb across his lips before scowling. "Thank you for telling me. But, if you ever do something that stupid, that risks your fucking lives, I will cut off your balls. Got it."

Nick's eyes widen in surprise for a moment before settling; a mischievous glint adorns his eyes as he smirks. "I'll take that chance, Siren. Because we'd do it again for you. Always."

Before I have time to protest, he wraps his hand around my neck and crushes my chest to his as our mouths fuse together in a bruising kiss. The brutal force is not what I'm used to from him but I absolutely love it. His tongue snakes out to request entrance and I open my mouth on a gasp. His tongue chases mine back into my mouth, fighting for dominance. A fight I'm completely ok with losing.

Liquid heat pools between my thighs as his other hand leaves my hip and wraps around my back, effectively plastering our bodies to each other. My body begins to move on its own accord as my limbs tingle but I stop myself when the pain from holding my body over his, causes me to gasp.

Nick quickly pulls back and his eyes dart everywhere. I'm sure I'm a mess. My eyes are swollen from crying, my chest is rising and falling in quick bursts, and I can feel the heat from my body reddening my skin.

"You are stunning." He whispers just before his mouth crashes back to mine. His hands both lower down my body, dipping with every curve, all the way down my thighs. When he gets there, he squeezes them and groans into my mouth. But suddenly, he pulls back, scowling at me.

"Wha-what's wrong? Did I hurt you?" His head tilts as his scowl deepens. He takes a moment to lean me back, looking at the space between our bodies. I can feel my face burn with embarrassment and discomfort right before he growls, grabs my hips, lifts them up, then slams down right on his crotch.

I cry out as pleasure and pain collide and my vision swirls. I didn't realize I had closed my eyes until Nick's fingers grip my chin, quietly demanding that I look at him. When I flutter my eyes open, awareness of my body floods back in and I immediately try to shift myself back to hover over him.

His perfectly beautiful face should never look this angry. "I-I'm sorry. I didn't mean to hurt y-"

"No" he growls with a weak, yet eye-opening, smack to my ass. I release a yelp in surprise, a little pain, and fuck me, my panties are definitely wet, now. *It's weird that it excites me right? Why would I possibly like that when I have been beaten and broken?*

Seeming to read my thoughts, or some of them, Nick's hand gently rubs the sting on my ass away as his quiet voice takes on a husky tone. "Siren, you listen and you listen good: If you're in, you're all in. We would never hurt you. Ever. But this lap, *this* lap is yours." He pushes my hips back down and yanks them forward; forcing me to feel every ripple and bump of his jeans and the huge outline of his cock. A highly inappropriate moan filters from my mouth before I have the wherewithal to stop it. *I just had to wear fucking leggings.*

He leans in and flicks my earlobe with his tongue before

whispering, "We know *you* don't like your body, but we *fucking love* it; long for it; would gladly die for it and you. And you will not hold back with us. That includes sitting all the way in my lap like a good girl. Do you understand?"

His breath in my ear has my whole body on fire and goosebumps racing around my skin. My clit throbs like a greedy attention whore and my body shudders from his dirty, sinfully sexy words. *Holy fuck. When did he start talking like that? And why do I like it?*

Shutting my eyes tightly, I shake my head because it's too much. *I can't do this. I'm going to hur-*. His hand comes back down on my ass again, causing me to melt a yelp and a moan together as he quickly rubs it back out.

"I know it's hard, but let us take care of you. If something is too much, you tell us, ok? But you, sitting in my lap, is *never* too much. Got it?"

He leans back, and grasps my face with both of his hands before wiping away a few escaped tears. I reach up, and grab onto his forearms as I relent; letting him bear the brunt of my weight. The moment I'm settled, he surges forward and kisses me with such passion and need that I nearly self-combust.

He raises his hips, forcing his jean-covered cock to connect with my barely-there leggings, right into my clit. I tremble harder, moaning into his mouth, as he sucks my tongue. My fingers dig into the skin of his sexy-as-sin forearms as he continues his attack on my mouth. He briefly retreats, then sucks my bottom lip into his mouth, nipping at it, while slowly sliding his hands back over my curves. Once his hands find my ass, he squeezes and groans into my mouth. My hands find their way over the hard planes of his stomach, then greedily clutch the fabric of his shirt.

Much to my disappointment, he squeezes my ass once more before breaking our kiss. I release a pathetic whimper and slowly open my eyes. His lips are pink and puffy and so damn biteable. We pant for breath as we take the other in.

Then, like he can't stop himself, he grabs a firm hold on my ass, pressing me down and over his cock, and begins to pepper my jaw with kisses. He makes a pathway down my neck and my hips involuntarily buck. His lips leave my neck for a moment as he leans into my ear and says, "Wrap your arms around my neck, and don't let go."

I freeze, for literally two seconds, before this man squeezes my ass in warning. For some reason, I'm sure I'll dissect later, I wrap my arms around his neck, pressing my boobs further into his chest. "Good girl," he whispers in my ear. He follows up with nips, kisses, and sucks all along the side of my neck until he gets back to my ear. "Now, my sexy Siren, you're going to ride me until you cum." His teeth nip on the shell of my ear but I'm already shaking my head.

"I, I told you. I can't. I think I've had like four orgasms my entire life. Let's just get you to cum and that will make me feel better. I promise." I purr the last part into his neck and suck a smile area into my mouth before letting it go with a pop. The groan from the man underneath me damn near has me feral.

He does the same to my neck, in a similar spot, but bites down; earning him a squeak. "Nope." He pops his p confidently. "Even if we sit here for the next three hours, you're going to ride me. You're going to use my body. And I'm going to love every second of it."

Some kind of whine leaves my mouth as the thought of him clearly not understanding begins to mess with my head. "Ni-ick..." *Why the hell am I so whiny all of a sudden?*

"No." He punctuates with a smack on my other ass cheek. The shock of it has apparently worn off as I literally feel my pussy clench. *What the hell is wrong with me?* "*You* need to relax and let everything go; even if for a moment." He says as he rubs the sting out. I begin to squirm in his lap, looking for friction where I need it most.

He takes my face in his hands, again, and forces me to look up at him. His golden brown eyes seem unreal this close-up. Like looking into one of those pieces of amber that paleontologists dig up. After a brief moment, he nuzzles his nose against mine and takes a deep breath, before whispering, "Kiss me, Siren. Kiss me and let everything go. Let go with me."

His gentle words are filled with promise and restraint; longing and purpose. So, for just a moment, I let go. Crashing my lips back to his, I lock away every fear, every piece of pain, of the possibility of regret or rejection. For this moment, I let myself just feel.

One of his hands slides down to my ass, squeezing and pulling me over his erection. A wanton moan escapes me as he slides his fingers down my neck and collarbone, resting on my breast. He hesitates for a moment so I suck his lip into my mouth before toying with his piercing. A guttural groan vibrates his chest and he takes that as an opening to massage my breast with one hand as he continues guiding my movements with his other hand on my ass.

My leggings do nothing to prevent the bumps, ridges, and girth of his jean-covered cock. *And holy forkballs! There's no way that thing will fit inside of me.* I feel my pussy clamp down on nothing as my body flushes hotter.

Needing more of him, of this, of everything, I wrap one arm around his neck and bring the other to rest along the stubble on his cheek. My heart beats out its own tune as my body takes over completely, brazenly chasing the more. Our breaths mingle and our kisses turn sloppy as our needs release a symphony of moans, groans, grunts, and whimpers.

What I can only describe as molten heat pools in my panties, probably soaking through my leggings. My body feels like a live wire and there is absolutely nothing I can do to stop it as I ride him mercilessly. I'm too lost in sensation; buzzing, lighting, zinging through my body.

Nick releases my boob to grab my head, forming a fist at the roots.

He forces my head to rest on his and pants out, "Eyes on me, Annie. Eyes on me when you cum for me."

My eyes snap open and an orgasm barrels right through me. Like a tsunami, it felt like every sensation, every feeling, every part of my body went almost numb; as I floated backward into oblivion. Then it raced through with a force that had me screaming out his name while tears filled my eyes. Never in my life had I felt something so strong, so intense, so surreal.

Second by second, my body relaxes as the tension drains away the last of my reserves. I sleepily close my eyes and feel a smile grow across my lips. Nick sighs, taking the hand on my ass and rubbing soothing strokes down my back while gently massaging my scalp. He removes his forehead from mine, giving me a tender kiss, and bringing my head to lie on his chest.

I hum out a contented sigh and am just about to doze when his phone chimes. I tense, suddenly realizing what the hell just happened. My eyes pop open and I go to move off of his lap. Nick, tightens his hold on my back, continues stroking my back and hair, then rasps, "I can hear the wheels turning in your head, Siren. If it's not one of our voices, it's wrong. That was hot as fuck. If I didn't have to head back to work, I would absolutely do it again."

He turns and presses a kiss to my forehead before snuggling me deeper. I chuckle quietly and shake my head. How this man knows me so well astounds me. But, if he's currently ok with what just happened, then so am I. *At least, that's what I'm going to tell myself until my inevitable freakout happens later.* Right now, though, I'm content to just sit here in post-orgasmic bliss with him. This crazy, sweet, beautiful man who not only chose me but went to war for me. *How the hell did I get so damn lucky?*

21

∽

Jenson

The last few days have been a whirlwind of catching up with work issues, a few members causing issues and making sure all of our programs are running smoothly. The youth classes started this week and, I can't lie, watching these kids look at our various instructors with curiosity and an eagerness to learn has been the sunshine I so desperately needed in my life.

Yes, Annie is home and away from that vile bastard, but, other than messages and a few phone calls, we haven't seen her. Not like the hours we spent in the hospital before. It may or may not be getting to me. I swear I'm trying to give her space and I know she needs to rest and heal but, damn, I'm dyin' here.

Three days ago, Nick came back to work looking cheeky as hell.

Whatever happened on his lunch break, he wasn't willing to share with the class. But I have a sneaking suspicion that he got to see Annie. I should feel upset, I think, but out of the four of us, he's probably better suited for her needs right now.

Sliding out of my sandals, I toss my towel onto a chair nearby. Stretching the cap between my hands, I lean down, pressing the inside seam to the middle of my forehead, and pull it over my bun and ears, before allowing it to snap at the base of my skull. I take a couple of seconds to make sure my ears aren't bent and my hair is all in the cap before moving to the edge of the pool. I remove my goggles from my wrist, snap them into place, and shake out my arms. I need this swim. I need to quiet the noise and the anxiety that threatens to bury me with each passing day that I don't see Annie in person; in all of her sexy glory. Between her and Cory, my heart feels like it's constantly on the verge of exploding.

I walk to the edge of the pool, bend over, and move my body into track start position. Taking in a deep breath, I count down from three before diving into the cold water, allowing it to wash away my thoughts, feelings, nightmares; everything.

* * *

My body is completely spent so I'm slow to make it back to the locker room. I definitely over-extended my abilities, by at least four laps. But, as soon as I thought I needed to finish up, my heart squeezed painfully and my thoughts would start to muddle again. So, instead of slowing, I would complete a flip-turn at the wall and start another lap.

By the time I'm staring at my locker, and unlocking my lock, I'm pretty sure my body is too tired for my brain to care about thinking. *My stomach swirls, or my head, or is that the room? Fuck. I know I overdid it but, I shouldn't be this dizzy. This, weak. Maybe, I just need to sit for a minute. Yeah. That's good.*

I lean against the lockers and slide down to the floor a little quicker than I mean to. My head feels dizzy, fuzzy even. I lean over resting my head in my hands and groan. I try breathing through the world whirling around me but I can't concentrate or focus.

"Jense! Jense man, you ok?" My head feels too heavy to lift so I try to reassure whoever it is, but a weird whimper rings out, instead.

"Dammit, man. Hold on." I faintly hear the scuffle of shoes across the locker room floor. My body feels completely depleted. *Maybe I just need some sleep.*

"Alright, Jense, let's go." Two arms lift my legs as two more curve under my arms before I'm lifted and placed on the long, hard bench. A warm body slides underneath my head, propping me up and patting my cheek. "Hey buddy, I need you to open your mouth. We need to get this in your system. Come on bud."

I fight through the fog weighing me down and finally open my mouth enough for them to squeeze something sweet into my mouth. It takes me a moment but I finally swallow it down before they ask me to take in more.

After a few swallows, a straw is pressed to my lips with one command, "Drink." The apple juice feels good as it coats my tongue. After the first sip, I can't seem to stop. I end up guzzling until obnoxious sounds from the straw trying to grasp the last bits of liquid fill the room.

Leaning my head back down, I'm comforted by the warmth radiating from the person below me. I lull my head into his lap and feel my breathing start to even out as I try to drift to sleep.

"Nu-uh, Jense. Gotta finish this. You can sleep at home." I groan out my displeasure but open my mouth when the plastic tube of, whatever, is pressed to my lips. When the smooth, sweetness hits my tongue this time, I realize it must be a Go-Gurt; something berry flavored.

Once I'm finished with the contents of the tube, a warm hand runs across the top of my hair. "When was the last time he ate?" The voice comes from the other guy. It's deep but filled with a southern twang. *Vince. Hey, at least my brain is noticing shit now.*

The voice belonging to the person stroking my head replies, "I don't know. We've all been so busy catching up with stuff, we haven't even been eating together." *Cory.*

My cheeks flush hot as I think about him taking care of me and part of me despises it. I shake my head with a groan and try to sit up; feeling at least a little less fuzzy than a few minutes ago. But a hand on my forehead stops me, pinning me to Cory's leg. "Nope. You lie right there for 5 more minutes until the yogurt and juice hit your system. Then, I'm driving you home and making sure your dumbass eats."

I mumble my response, still too tired to argue. Vince takes it upon himself to *Big Daddy* me as I'm clearly not able to get away at the moment. "Jenson, I know things are busy but you know for damn sure you pushed yourself too hard. You're obviously not eating enough and, yet, you still push. You can't force your body to use from an energy source you aren't filling. You know better."

"S-sorry. Acs-dent." My tongue feels so damn heavy but at least I'm a little more aware of what's around me.

Vince exhales heavily before patting my arm. "I know. But," he sighs loudly as he moves to stand. "If you do this shit again, I'm going to tell Annie."

My eyes snap open in shock that he would stoop so low. Seeing my panic, he and Cory start chuckling at me. "All right All Star, let's get you home. Can you stand for me?" Cory asks as he lifts my head off of his leg.

"Ye-yeah," I grunt out. "Thanks guys." Vince nods and Cory stands. They both reach their hands out for me to take and they slowly lift me to stand.

"We need a family meeting. We're all falling apart at the seams. We have to talk, together, and it can't wait."

Cory and I guiltily nod our heads in agreement as they help me into my sweats, not caring about the still-damp suit underneath. I grab my phone and slide it into my pocket.

Vince slings my bag over his back as Cory maneuvers to my side and we slowly make our way out of the locker room. Vince swipes open his phone and sends off a message. Mine pings and I take it out just in time for it to ping again.

Vince: Got Jen-Jen and he's fine. Thanks for the heads up. Emergency family dinner. Tonight @6.
Nick: And what if I'm late?

I can hear Vince chuckle as a grin slides on my face. "Ooo, he's in trouble." Cory glances my way so I show him my phone. After he reads it, his smile widens and he shakes his head.

Vince: Don't push me, Pretty Boy. It's been a long time since I reddened that ass.
Nick: I'll get the playroom ready big boy.

Vince shakes his head and shoves his phone into his pocket while Cory and I laugh. Nick just loves to push his buttons. Not that Vince truly minds; he loves Nick's brat side.

We wave goodbye to Cathy as we pass the front desk and head out to the parking lot. The sounds of the nearby traffic make my skin buzz in annoyance but I do my best to shake it off as I clumsily climb into Cory's SUV. Once he pushes the ignition button, his Bluetooth automatically syncs and begins to play In This Shirt by The Irrepressibles. The haunting melody glides through the vehicle and swirls through the air as the memory of a night we once shared filters through.

"Fancy another?" Cory asks, walking back with the bottle of Crown Royal Black before plopping himself on the couch next to me. It's the

middle of winter and it's one of very few days during the year that temps have dropped below freezing. I came up here a couple hours ago needing to get lost in a book and warm up near my fantastic-ass fireplace. It's one of my favorite things in this whole house. Sometimes, when no one is home, I'll crank the AC down just so I can use the fireplace. It reminds me I'm safe, cared for; home.

"Suuurree" I drawl, holding out my glass. As he pours another couple of fingers worth into my glass, I can't help but admire how the fire's shadows dance across his face. I didn't bother with lights when I came in because I really just wanted to read by firelight tonight. It felt so, right. But, as I feel my erection grow in my sweats, I realize that may have been a bad idea.

I haven't always been attracted to Cory. It's only been about a year since my, er, feelings, started to change. It wasn't even immediate. More of a gradual change in how I felt when I was with him. In fact, I wasn't entirely sure how it was changing until I saw him running on a treadmill one day and my body, well, reacted. It wasn't anything I hadn't seen before but it sure the hell made me slow my reps on the rowing machine. The overly analytical, hyper-focused, extra-organized boy I grew up with had definitely turned into a man. One that bends over backward for those he cares about. One that takes everyone's burdens and selflessly makes them his own.

As I watched the sweat pour down his back, muscles bunching and flexing from his precise movements, I realized that my heart had already been trying to tell me who this man truly was to me. His mom left; my dad died. His dad preferred booze and women; my mom preferred men and didn't care how bad they were. We were two children, forced to grow up far too soon. Two souls lost but still trying to make our own way. His heart, his soul, his very being calls to mine.

Cory clears his throat, bringing me out of my thoughts. "So, what's your dream within a dream, Jense?" He pushes up his black-rimmed glasses, framing his oddly beautiful hazel eyes. The flicker of light from the flames makes the green in his eyes pop a little more as his pupils drown out the brown. He lazily smiles, propping his hand behind my head on the couch as he takes a sip from his drink. I watch intently as his Adam's apple bobs, swallowing down the deep amber liquid.

Taking another swig of my drink, I clear my throat before considering my answer. "I don't think I have one." I huff out a humorless laugh. "If anything I have nightmares within nightmares. And sometimes," I shake my head, staring down at the floor. "Sometimes when I wake up, it takes a while to remember that I'm safe. I'm not there anymore. I'm not that scared, broken boy." I angrily bat away a stray tear as I toss back the rest of my drink.

Leaning my head back against the couch, I take a deep breath. We sit in silence for a minute before I roll my head to face him and ask, "What about you? What's your dream within a dream?" He quickly diverts his eyes and stares down at his glass. His hand absently begins stroking my hair; having left it down after my shower.

My eyes close as his hand soothingly makes its way through my hair over and over again. A quiet moan escapes my lips as the whiskey heightens the sensation. Cory's movements stop for a second. My eyes open as I look at him; confused by his reaction. I'm just about to ask him what's wrong when he slowly lifts his head and turns his eyes, to meet mine. The intensity in his gaze makes my breath catch. I blink a few times, trying to push through the alcohol-haze then sit up, turning my body towards his. Emotions flit through his eyes, too fast for me to identify. His face transforms into a cross between a frown and a scowl. Licking his perfect lips, he inhales deeply before pushing it out. His voice is raspy and filled with emotion as he says, "You."

Before I can ask what he's talking about, he surges forward, crashing his lips to mine. Surprise only lasts for a moment; then he tangles his fingers into mine, and I lose it.

Groaning into the kiss, I nip his lip to request access. He eagerly opens for me and our tongues clash in a rough and bruising kiss. Without thinking, I pull him onto me, situating him on my lap and we both groan as our cocks line up through the barrier of our sweats.

I'm so hard and I can already feel pre-cum leaking from my tip. I surge up to thrust into him and he molds his body to mine, sliding the hand not in my hair up my chest, landing over my heart. Cory abruptly breaks the kiss and we both suck in greedy gasps of air, chest to chest; our skin layered with a light sheen of sweat.

Cory's eyes bounce between mine for a moment. Fear, excitement, worry, and lust all fight for dominance. He shifts in my lap, causing me to curse under my breath, and I yank his head back to mine in another bruising kiss.

"I need you, Jense. God, I need you." His voice is huskier than I've ever heard it as it drips with lust.

"Take me, Cor. Use me. I'm yours."

With that, his hand slides down my body, slowly dipping over every ripple of muscle until he reaches the point where we are connected. Our kiss slows into a more languid pace as our bodies tremble with the urge to rip each other apart.

Just when I'm about to take over, Cory slips his hand in my sweats, pushing them down a bit, and relieves my aching cock. He breaks the kiss to look down, his eyes widening in surprise. "When did you get those?"

I chuckle quietly and nibble on his ear before whispering, "A few years ago. You like 'em?" I nip his ear, enticing a grunt from his mouth as he circles my tip, spreading my pre-cum around.

"Yes," He hisses. "I know that one is a Prince Albert but, wh-what's the other?" He says on a moan as I suck a patch of skin on his neck.

Licking over the reddened area, I whisper, "It's called a pubic cross." I can feel his body shiver underneath me as he begins pumping me. After a few hard tugs, I have to suck in a breath to prevent me from completely messing myself.

"Cor," I grit out. "I want to taste you." His hand freezes and eyes widen as they search mine. Leaning up, I grab him by his neck, squeezing gently, and rest of my forehead on his. "Please Cor. Let me make you feel good." I give him a gentle peck and wait, frozen in time, as he makes his decision.

Eventually, he nods his head and hoarsely agrees, "Okay," before clearing his throat. That's all the confirmation I need. Grabbing him by his lean hips, I lift him off of me and turn him so he's lying on the couch next to me. Scooting back, I bite my lip as I slowly reveal his hard length; long, veiny, fucking beautiful.

I've messed around with guys a few times. Nothing crazy, just some fun but, this is Cory. My best friend. My ride or die. And the one person I shouldn't be falling for; yet, here I am.

I kneel down between his legs and look up at him. His hands are gripping the couch, his chest heaves with each breath, and he's never looked sexier. Fuck this is going to blow up in my face.

Batting away the errant thoughts, I wrap my hand around the base of his dick and give it one good tug, twisting slightly as go. He hisses out a breath and bucks into my hand. Smirking, I lean down and swirl my tongue around his tip, before licking through his slit; gathering his sweet drop of pre-cum on my tongue. I'm rewarded with a porn-worthy moan as his head falls back and his eyes close.

I slowly take his length into my mouth, to meet my hand, then hollow out my cheeks and suck back to the top. Cory's hands fly to my hair, pushing some of it out of the way, and begins to slowly thrust into my mouth. I work his dick in time with my thrusts, making sure to suck on every pull and lick on every drop.

Not even two minutes later he's grabbing my hair, panting, groaning, and grunting. I feel his body tighten under me so I move my hand away from the base and take him all the way into my mouth; then I hollow out my cheeks. "F-u-u-uck!" He yells to the ceiling. As soon as the first splash of his cum hits my throat, I start swallowing him down.

When he's completely spent, I leisurely lick every last bit from his now softening cock; earning me another groan and a twitch of his hips.

Pushing myself up, he meets my gaze, eyes hooded in exhaustion and his orgasm hangover. A small smile plays at his lips, enticing me to kiss up his body until I am hovering directly over him. "That, was, amazing." He pants out.

A smile stretches so wide across my face that it actually hurts but, seeing him blissed out, dimples and all, is so worth it. I lean in and kiss his neck, then jaw, and finally place a chaste kiss on his lips.

I move to lean back, he wraps his hand around my neck and pulls me back in, kissing me with vigor. Licking the seam of my lips in a silent plea to open them, I let him in. As our tongues stroke and dance together, I feel him smiling into the kiss. Breaking apart, he brings my forehead to his before whispering, "We taste good together." I chuckle at his corniness but, yeah, I agree.

With one last peck, I climb off of him, dragging up my sweats over my hard-as-steel cock, and walk out to the bathroom. Grabbing a washcloth, I turn the water to warm and soak it so I can go back and clean him up. However, when I turn to leave, he's in the doorway with a smirk and a cocked brow. "What?" I ask him, not sure what to do with the now wet cloth in my hand.

"How 'bout you come to my room and find out?" Without another word, or even a backward glance, he vanishes from the doorway. It only takes me five seconds to get my ass in gear as I sprint towards his room.

We spent the rest of that night entangled in each other. Kissing, licking, sucking. It was absolute heaven. Since it was our first time together, we didn't go for penetration. We just explored every exposed inch of each other until we fell asleep, cuddled into each other.

The next morning, Cory laughed it off and said we could pretend it never happened. My heart was completely destroyed but there was nothing I could do. I didn't fight or argue because if it isn't something he wants, then that's fine. And I wasn't losing my best friend just because I felt more; deeper.

It took about a week before we got back to normal. Thankfully,

Vince and Nick hadn't noticed anything amiss so we went back to our regularly scheduled lives. While I don't regret it, I sometimes wish that I could forget. Because the memories bring the same pain; every time.

We take a turn and I realize we've already arrived home. Anxious to shower and eat something, and probably do something about my now raging boner, I pick my bag up off the floor and set it in my lap. Cory barely parks before I hop out and run inside, desperately needing to get away from everything and, unfortunately, him.

22

~

Annie

Another week has passed by. Other than that day Nick came over, I haven't seen any of the guys. Between nightmares, trying to soak up every moment with my kids, and conversations with my psychiatrist, I just haven't made the time. Don't get me wrong. I absolutely *could* have. I've just been, scared...maybe?

I don't even know what it is. Emotionally, I'm all over the place. Then, the incident with Nick happened and that was just one more thing to over-analyze and stress out about. I can count on one hand how many times in my life I have orgasmed. But, dry humping that man like a horny teenager?! I mean, how do I come back from that?

I can't even tell you what came over me. *No pun intended.* Once he told me about all of them risking their jobs, their lives, I had a deep urge to show my appreciation; to show my love. We're not ready for that word but I was dangerously close before Lukas had even taken me. Then hearing about them saving me, saving those women; yeah, I was done for. *Here's my heart; signed, sealed, delivered.*

Stepping out of the shower, I wrap my oversized trowel around my body, then bend over and wrap another one around my hair. Lifting my head back up, I'm forced to make a decision. One that my psychiatrist has urged me to make for over a week. It's been my only "homework" every day and, every day, I fail. *Big, fat failure.*

I exhale raggedly as I stare at the mirror on the opposite wall. It would only take two steps to get to the counter, 4 swipes of a cloth to clear the condensation, and 60 seconds to look over my body. It's supposed to be a 90-second exercise. One that, theoretically, should lead to me healing internally as most of my wounds have healed externally. I mean, of course, I have seen the marks and watched as the bruises faded, and I definitely had a few that I needed to take care of each day but, I've never allowed myself to look in a mirror. To put all of the "little" things together and see the full picture.

I hated seeing my reflection before all of this. I hated the rolls, the dips, and the curves and how everything felt so disproportionate. How could taking inventory of my new scars, new reminders, on top of my same body possibly be a good idea? I asked my psych as much but she just lifted a brow in challenge. I both love and hate her.

My heart rate increases and I feel my lips begin to tremble as I consider my decision. Maybe this is why I haven't tried seeing the guys. Maybe I subconsciously know that I can't possibly give anything more to the guys without knowing what to prepare them for; or at least knowing what's there for them to be disgusted by.

Shaking my head, I repeat the mantra that we've been working on; partially thanks to Nick's words that night. "I'm safe. I'm free. I'm ok.

I'm safe. I'm free. I'm ok." I suck in a deep breath and take two timid steps towards the counter. I see my foggy reflection; just enough to see the white towels and paleness of my skin. But nothing else.

"I'm safe. I'm free. I'm ok." Another deep inhale, and careful exhale. *Step 2, Annie. You can do this.*

Slowly, I reach up and unwrap the towel sitting on my head. I spend a second shaking out my hair and letting it fall to my shoulders before lowering my hand to my side. A shiver runs down my body, causing an outbreak of goosebumps across every inch of my skin.

"I'm safe. I'm free. I'm ok." I begin to lift my hand, still holding the towel, and lean over the counter towards the mirror. Suddenly, I'm holding the towel to the mirror! *I have never made it this far. This is it. I can do this. Just a few swipes and that's it.*

My phone pings in my bedroom with a message, causing me to jump. The action causes me to wipe away a small clearing against the mirror where I can see the now-healed scar near my hairline. It's just far enough down my forehead that the thin pink line is sort of notice-able against my pale skin. My eyes dart towards my mouth where a tiny scar sits on the bottom but you can't really see it unless you're looking really closely.

I slam my eyes closed as images flash through my mind of my time with the various assholes I was forced to deal with. Something wet splashes on my cheeks, causing me to look back into the mirror. Tears are now flowing down my face. I look weak, hideous, pathetic. I notice my cheeks are still chubby, catching every tear falling down my face. Although I did lose some weight. *I guess one good thing came from all that.* I scoff at how awful I am to myself.

Shaking my head, thoroughly done with this whole exercise and more disgusted with myself than I was before, I quickly cover the little two-inch long thorn brand with a little burn ointment and fresh dressing. It's almost healed, thank God, but I can't wait to get a tattoo to transform it. Once I'm finished dressing it, I turn to make my way out of my bathroom.

Entering my bedroom, I drop my towel and put on my undies. As I put on my skull and snake sports bra, I realize I never pulled the clothes from my closet. Which, of course, means I have to pass by the counter-length mirror again. Sighing in aggravation, I turn back towards the bathroom and hastily make my way to the closet. I find some soft, black workout leggings and begin to search for a suitable top. I refuse to wear a short-sleeved shirt, acutely aware of my hideous scars.

After a moment, I settle on one of my Beautiful Disaster zip hoodies. We live in Texas and I have never had an issue with my lower arms so I prefer to live in regular tees, saving the sweatshirts for winter. But, desperate times and all that.

Unzipping the heather gray hoodie, I grin at the smiley face on the left side. The design is a simple smiley face made of bones and out-lined in purple. The back has a peace sign, also in bones and outlined in purple, a skull outlined in purple, and the same smiley face as the front; running vertically down the center. Peace, Love, Happiness, is written along the bottom. I smile as I think of my little family and the guys. *Maybe I can have all three one day.*

Sliding each arm through the sleeves and zipping it up, I take a moment to appreciate how damn soft this thing is. The insides of their hoodies always make me think of a soft blanket; now I want to go cuddle up in bed. *Nope. You are getting out of the house. You are going to the gym. You are going to live; not just survive. Pull up your big bitch panties and fake it til you make it.*

Damn, Christina must be rubbing off on me because that was totally her voice in my head. A giggle escapes me, causing me to smile wide.

Throwing on my Asics, brushing my still-wet hair into a messy bun, and grabbing my bag, I head towards the garage.

Once in the Suburban, I quickly lock the doors and pull out. I don't even turn the music on until I get to the stop sign because I refuse to be blindsided again in my own driveway. Yes, I'm aware that's silly since all of those douchebags are dead but, then again, so is taking a shower before going to the gym. However, they are both part of the new "routine" my psych and I worked on to help me get back to normal.

Needing to choose something quickly, when I see I'm only third in line behind the stop sign, I click on Alone by Kim Petras and Nicki Minaj. It ends up being perfect with just enough beat to get my head ready for being out in the world. It's also just mellow enough to not overwhelm me.

Another message pings on my phone but I don't look at it, yet. I just focus on my primary task for the day. Getting to the gym, and maybe working out some of this damn trauma.

Pulling into the gym, I find that there are a few more cars here than normal this time. Not that it's bad because that's good for the guys. It's just... more people.

After parking, I inhale for four, hold for four, and exhale for four, then nod my head and throw my phone in my bag. Take my keys, I climb out, fling my bag on my shoulder, and shut the door, glancing around quickly before walking up to the door.

Entering the gym is both comforting and terrifying. Cathy is standing behind the rounded front desk, scrolling on her phone. Her perfect blonde hair is up in a perfectly straight high ponytail. She's wearing a neon pink sports bra that is barely covered by her super-cropped black hoodie. Her toned stomach is on full display along with her perfect tan.

Shaking out the jealous thoughts, I approach the desk to scan my card. When the scanner beeps, she jumps and snaps her head towards me. "Annie!" She squeals loudly, causing me to flinch. Embarrassment floods my face and neck as I see the few people in the cardio space nearby look towards us.

She begins to walk around the counter so I try to give her my best smile. "Hey, Cathy. How're y-" She abruptly cuts off my words, and my air, as she slams into me, hugging the life out of me.

At first, I jolt in shock; partly from lingering pain but mostly from physical touch being a little weird still. Then I remember that Cathy is safe, *I am safe*, and I return her hug. After all the tension leaves my body, she steps back, looks around, and lowers her voice. "I don't know what happened, but, between the news reports and how the guys had been acting last month, I just-" She chews on her lip; her eyes fill with so much sympathy and sincerity that I have to look away before I cry. "I just want you to know that I'm here for you. And, I'm glad you're back." Her smile turns up slightly in understanding before the door behind us opens. She squeezes my shoulder once, nodding her head, and wishes me a good workout just in time for a couple of women to walk up to the counter.

I stand there, like an idiot, and feel a real smile form on my face. Suddenly remembering where I am, I clear my throat and make my way towards the back. "Thanks, Cathy. I'll see you later."

I make my way to the back studio but stop short when I see the long hallway that leads to the back offices. For all of 5 seconds, I consider going down there to say "hi". I miss them terribly but, I didn't exactly tell them I was coming. I mean, before my shower I wasn't even sure I would finally make it here.

Shrugging it off, I decided to just slip into the boxing studio and figure I'd text them on my way out. I really could use one of their hugs. And maybe a reminder that they're real and not just figments of my texting imagination.

Turning into the closet on the right, I drop my bag and take out my water, gloves, and phone. I scroll through my workout playlist to decide what I should start with. I know I need a release but, I also need to be super careful. I was just released to drive and start slowly working out again. It's not even my arms, the doc is worried about. It's my ribs. That and, you know, *trauma*.

Tag You're It by Melanie Martinez catches my eye. I actually love this song while cleaning or just flitting around the house. But, the lyrics. *Do I dare?* I look around the studio, the place I can be utterly and completely myself. Cutting myself open and laying myself bare as I take my aggressions out on a heavy bag has always been so cathartic. Maybe, just maybe, these dangerously familiar lyrics can help me in this new chapter I've found myself in.

Not bothering to spend any more time thinking about it, I press play and put my phone down. The first notes fill the vast studio space and I close my eyes, breathing it in, as I pull on my gloves.

Shaking out my arms, I begin walking around the room a couple of times to get warmed up. The lyrics cause images of the dungeons to flip through my mind like a fucked up slideshow. A tear slips down my cheek as anger and humiliation run rampant through my veins. Knowing I need to keep going, I pick up my pace from a simple stroll to a brisk walk. My muscles protest the movements, even as they begin to warm up, but I push through. A few more laps around the studio and I finally feel my muscles give in, flexing with the movements instead of resisting them.

The song ends and I make my way to the bag. After rolling my shoulders a few times, I drop my right foot back, squat slightly, and put my fists up. P.I.M.P by 50 Cent starts up and I immediately burst out laughing. It's so freeing, so overwhelming, and so damn amazing, that I have to bend over to try and catch my breath. I haven't heard this song in forever and the fact that it's playing, today of all days, during my first workout after what that asshole put me through; yeah, I think it's funny. I used to sing this song loud and proud and loved every minute of it. The instruments, the beat, and of course the lyrics brought me so much joy.

After a moment, I finally catch my breath; feeling lighter than I have in weeks. With a smile on my face, I move back into my stance and begin making purposefully, careful jabs to the bag. I have to re-adjust my stance a few times, and I'm definitely not able to put my all into it, but it still feels wonderful.

I only had about ten minutes in me today. Exhaustion still comes pretty quickly but I did it. I fucking did it. A prideful grin shines on my face as I drop my stance and start my cool-down walk. Dropping my head to roll out my neck, I turn around, with my hands knuckles against my hips. My hoodie sticks to me uncomfortably but, it is what it is.

A throat clearing startles me and, like a damn cat, I yell out and jump. Cory, Nick, and Jense are all standing against the wall, right inside the door, wearing matching grins. Cory's in a pair of khakis and a light blue long-sleeve shirt; his sandy-blonde hair is perfectly styled. He's leaning against the door jam, arms crossed over his chest, and legs crossed at the ankles, showing off his perfectly white shoes. He has the whole sexy professor thing going on. And those damn dimples. *Focus, Annie!*

Jense is leaning his back against the wall, shirtless, with a light sheen of sweat making him look ethereal in the lights of the studio. The tattoos along his arms and chest pop against his skin. Finally, a pair of gray sweats desperately hangs onto the V of his lower abdomen. *Dear Lord, give me strength.*

Next to Jense is Nick, looking every bit of a Rock God/computer genius. Black and white checkered Vans adorn his feet; one planted on the ground and the other casually placed on the wall behind him.

Dark gray distressed skinny jeans leave nothing to the imagination as the bulge in his pants shifts lightly. I flush fast and hard remembering what I did to him just over a week ago. A worn Pearl Jam shirt stretches across his lean muscles, stretching just right to accentuate his biceps. His hands are shoved into his pockets and he's playing with the damn lip ring. *Oh fork nuggets. I'm going to need to change my panties.*

Jenson's chuckle brings me out of my blatant perusal and I snap my eyes towards his. His eyes sparkle with amusement, matching the look on his hot-as-hell face. "See something you like, Sweetness?"

"Huh? No. I mean, not no, but no I wasn't. Um..."

Cory shoves Jenson, causing him to drop his sexy-ass stance. "Don't listen to Jen-Jen. He held his breath in the pool too long and it killed some of his brain cells."

Nick chuckles quietly but he never takes his gaze off of mine. "So, how was your session today?" He asks, tilting his head towards the bag behind me.

Chewing on my lip, I consider my answer. "Um, good. I think." I sigh heavily, pursing my lips in a small pout. Lowering my voice, I explain. "I couldn't work as long as I used to. And, I'm definitely sore."

Cory leaves the doorway and slowly walks over to me. "That's understandable. Is it just sore muscles or," he clears his throat, "or is something *else* hurting?" He continues walking until he's maybe a foot away. His eucalyptus and bookstore scent envelopes me and I find myself closing my eyes, inhaling him in.

Warmth on my face causes me to flinch, flinging my eyes open. Cory had apparently stepped closer after I closed my eyes. He releases my face as if I burned him; pain and regret are written all over his face. "No, no." I quickly say, reaching for his hand, and pulling it back to my cheek. I immediately snuggle into it, soaking up the connection. "You just startled me is all. Don't retreat from me. I've," I swallow thickly, staring deeply into his eyes. "I've really missed you. Don't be afraid to touch me, Cory. I won't be able to handle that." My voice sounds hoarse as I whisper my truth.

Cory smiles down at me, both dimples on full display. "I've missed you, too, Pretty Girl." I swallow hard, looking into his consuming gaze. The green in his hazel eyes almost overtakes the brown as he sucks in a deep breath. His other hand comes up to my other cheek and he rubs both thumbs downward, gently caressing my lips. Leaning in closer, I can feel his warm breath skate over me. "Annie, can I kiss you?"

A smile breaks free and I chuckle lightly. "Please."

I barely finish the word and his lips find mine. It's not hard or punishing. It's sweet, exploratory. Almost too gentle. I pull back a little and notice his whole body is slightly trembling. A small frown takes over my face. "What's wrong? Do you not want to?"

Cory's eyes widen in surprise and he starts shaking his head. "No, baby. No. I absolutely want to. I just don't want to hurt you."

I don't know why, but something inside me snaps. I quirk my brow, grinning up at him. Before he can react, I grab him by the collar and yank him towards me; stopping just shy of our lips touching. "Cory. I am not glass. I am almost healed and, dammit, you said you were all in. So if you still want me, show me, and don't hold back."

His lips crash into mine before I can even take a breath. His hands leave my cheeks and he wraps one hand behind my neck, positioning me just where he wants me. His other hand lands on my lower back and slowly travels down to grab my ass. Our tongues dance together and a moan escapes me as he presses me into his body. I can feel his hardening cock through his pants, sitting at the base of my stomach.

A throat clears behind us and I realize we are right in the middle of a very open studio, and I'm basically dry-humping Cory for anyone to see. My cheeks flush with heat as we break apart. Cory's smile is so wide that his glasses move up and his dimples are prominently displayed.

Jenson speaks from behind me, "I may not mind sharing you with these assholes, but no one else gets to hear those pretty moans. Let's get outta here, yeah?" I look behind me to see that Nick is holding up my bag and phone, a knowing grin pulling up his face.

Jenson walks right up to me, helps me out of my gloves, then swings an arm around my shoulder. My entire body zaps with electricity. He kisses my cheek as we walk through the studio door. This fine-as-sin man is half-naked, walking through the gym, claiming me as his.

We reach the front desk and I wave goodbye to Cathy. She smiles brightly at us and waves goodbye.

Once we walk outside, Jense walks over to the blacked-out, gorgeous, Suburban. Opening the back hatch, he unzips an Army green duffle, pulls out a navy tank top, and slides it on. My throat goes totally dry as I watch the flexing and bunching of every lean muscle; all the way down to...*holy banana hammock!*

Jenson chuckles, slamming the hatch down, causing my face to burn brighter than any sunburn I've endured. "All in, Sweetness; and all yours." He whispers in my ear before kissing my cheek. Leaning back, he winks at me and I have to slap his arm as I laugh at his antics.

Nick walks over, toying with that damn lip ring, and nods to Jense. His smile widens and he claps excitedly, "Yay! Field trip?"

I tilt my head at him and shake my head as I laugh. "OK, I know you guys are busy. But, I'm glad I got to see you. M-Maybe I can come back on Monday? I'll definitely need a couple of days to recover. I may or may not have overdone it just a bit." I mumble the last part more to myself.

Cory moves in behind me, and carefully wraps his arms around my shoulders. "Or you could come with us? Lunch and maybe shopping down Main?"

I start shaking my head, "No, um, I don't have a change of clothes and I'm already a little overheated. And, then I have to get the kids from the b..." Jenson moves in closer to me, effectively cutting me off.

"You hear that, Nick. Our girl is too busy for us." His tone is light and playful but oh so confusing. He leans in just a little more, my body trapped between his and Cory. A shiver works its way down my body and my pussy clenches thinking about being between them but, with fewer clothes on. *Stupid hussy.*

"You haven't checked your phone in a while, have ya?" My brows furrow even further. "What?" Suddenly, Nick is presenting my phone to me. It takes a moment to realize that I'm surrounded on three sides by my men and the other side is hidden by the Suburban next to us.

Clearing my throat, I desperately try to get a handle on my thoughts, and hormones. I look down at my phone screen, clicking it on. I see I have two messages from my mother and a missed call. *Shit. I forgot to check my phone when I got here.*

Clicking on her contact picture, I press the phone to my ear as it rings; my anxiety slowly builds due to missing her so many times.

"Hey. Did you get my message?" My mother sounds cheery which immediately puts me at ease.

"Oh, um, no. Sorry. I went to the gym." I rush to add, "Is everything ok?"

My mother hums happily as the sound of her car door closing travels towards me. "Yes, yes. I just, well, don't be mad at me."

My hackles rise. She's never done anything particularly bad but I can't help my fight, flight, or freeze responses recently. Hell, I screamed bloody murder when my oven timer went off while I was making dinner one night. "Okay..."

"Annie, I love you. But, I'm worried about you."

"I-"

"No, please, let me finish." My mouth snaps shut and my jaw clenches. I hate when she worries.

"I am so proud of you and how far you've come since returning to us. I am freaking overjoyed that you even got out and went to the gym. You could tell me you walked to the locker room and right back out and I would still want to celebrate. But, since Christina left, and I left, you...haven't. Except for right now. You've always done this alone. I've tried to help when you let me but, baby, it's not just me anymore. You have your guys. The ones who spent more time at the hospital with you than even I did. I saw how they care for you, how much you mean to them. You deserve to be cared for, loved, even. So..." She inhales heavily, blowing it out quickly, then states, "So, I called Vince yesterday. I'm picking the kids up from school early today and taking them to Main Event. Tomorrow we are going to have a whole zoo day and then you can have them after church Sunday."

I look up for the first time since starting the call. All three guys are standing in my line of sight with various looks of smugness. I narrow my eyes at each of them before responding. "Okay, so what does Vince have to do with this?" I'm so damn confused and it's giving me a slight headache. Not to mention my sweat has long since dried and the sun has definitely heated the air enough that my hoodie feels like it's suffocating me.

"Vince is going to make sure you leave the house. Even if it's just for dinner or a walk in the park. I knew if I just got the kids, you would probably curl up under your weighted blanket with a book for the weekend and not emerge until Sunday."

I pinch the bridge of my nose, squeezing my eyes to the point they hurt a little. Sighing heavily, I look at the guys and watch as their smirks slowly dim into slight frowns. Gritting my teeth, I will myself not to cry, then I suck in both cheeks, biting down to help ground myself as anxiety tries to choke me. It's not that I don't want to spend time with them, it's just that I don't want it to be forced. I don't want *them* to feel forced.

"Thanks, Mama. I'll, uh, I'll be home in a bit to pack their bags and stuff."

When she responds, she takes on a gentler tone; like she's soothing me. "No need. I've got it taken care of. Just, please, take some time to get out, remember to live your life. You deserve it all and more."

I nod my head before I realize she can't see me. "Ok, Mama. I love you." I say almost too quietly.

"I love you, too, Annie. We'll text later. Don't worry about the kids. Just, do something for yourself. Bye, baby."

"Bye," I murmur before I take a deep breath. Staring down at my phone screen, I take a moment to gather my thoughts and feelings before looking back at the guys. They're silently watching me, trying to read my every thought and emotion. It's heady and overwhelming, yet, powerful.

Licking my lips, I look at each of them in turn. "So, Vince called you?" I ask with my brow raised.

Nick nods silently as he assesses my reaction. I swear the man can see into my damn skull and it's still a little intimidating. I break eye contact, shuffling from one foot to another, shaking my head slightly. "Look,"

Nick steps closer, wrapping one hand around my neck and bringing the other to caress my cheek as our foreheads connect. His bright, amber eyes shine in the sunlight as his gaze locks on mine. "No, Siren. Whatever it is you're thinking, the answer is 'no'. We weren't conned into this, or trapped. We aren't doing this against our will. We were ecstatic about the opportunity. Although, we did assume you knew already." He huffs out a laugh, shakes his head, then presses the lightest, most tender kiss on my lips. It's over before it really begins and he looks down at me again. "Please, Siren. At least let us have lunch with you. You can shower, get changed, and we can even order pizza. Then, if you want to go home and be by yourself or go home, change, and go out, we can do that, too. Whatever you want."

His eyes bounce between mine before that little shit pouts. Like, full bottom lip out, batting his lashes; pouts. It shouldn't work with the damn lip ring but, fuck, it does. I giggle at his ridiculous behavior and nod my head. "Ok, but, you don't fight fair." I playfully narrow my gaze at him, poking him in the stomach.

He chuckles, quickly kisses me again, and whispers, "All's fair in love and war, Siren." Then he winks and stalks off; leaving me with my mouth open in shock. *Did he just...? No. Definitely didn't mean that.*

Shaking my head, I look at the other two goobers, grinnin' like kids that were just told they're going to Disney World. Chuckling, I ask, "Okay. Now what?"

23

Vince

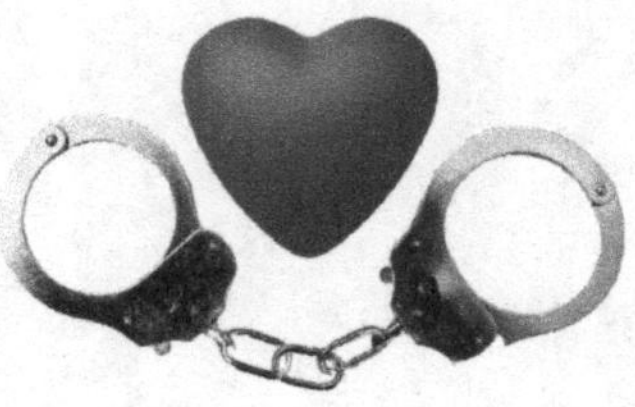

I'm just packing up my bag to head out for the evening when my phone dings. Fishing it out of my pocket, it dings two more times. I quickly see that our group chat is slowly blowing up.

Cory- Annie just talked with her mom. It took her a minute, but she's in.

Nick- She was here today! Kicked her a little ass but she may have overdone it so we all need to watch.

Cory- Have an emergency with the gym. She's going to head to her house and grab some things. Are you going to be home soon?

Jenson- Dude, chill. She'll come back out.

Cory- Are you sure? You saw how she looked when her mom was on the phone.

Nick- It's not her. It's us. She thinks we feel obligated now that she's out of the hospital. She needs this weekend as much as we do.

Me- OK, ok. You guys take care of the stuff at work and I'll call her. I'm about to head out.

Pocketing my phone, I toss my duffle over my shoulder and head out. Once I get to my truck, I open the door, throw the bag in the passenger seat, and step in.

Turning on the truck, I take my phone from my pocket, making sure it's synced to the truck, and dial Annie. After three rings, her sweet voice flies through the speakers. "Really?! They couldn't just trust me. I said I'd be there." She was so sassy and maybe a little irritated. I couldn't help but chuckle because, even irritated, she was cute.

"Well hello to you, too, Angel. It's good to hear your voice; even if it is being mean to me." I made sure my tone sounded playful and sarcastic since my girl loved to overthink things.

She blew out a breath, causing a little raspberry sound, before saying, "I'm sorry. Just. I'm sorry." Clearing her throat she started again, "Hello, Vince. What are you up to this fine Friday afternoon?" While she still had the bratty edge, she did genuinely seem to be trying to get out of her own head.

"I'm just leaving work. Was thinking about you and thought maybe you'd like me to pick you up. Since, as you know, you're all ours this weekend." Oops. My Dom side slipped a little, but I chose to let the promise stand; just in case.

Her giggled tinkles through the cab. "Yeah, I heard. So glad my mommy is setting up playdates for me now." Images of her in Nick's playroom flashed through my mind. Tied up, taking both of our cocks, completely at our mercy. *Fuck! Not the time.*

"But, anyways," her voice brought me back to our conversation, "I'm ok. You don't have to pick me up."

"Well, here's the thing. You may want a glass of wine, or three, you may get tired, hell, you may just really enjoy our company and stay out past your bedtime. Either way, I'd rather have one of us drive you home than you drive back by yourself."

A long, tense pause fills the cab. I know we're both thinking about it. About the last time she had left our house late at night. That was the night we lost her. I hadn't even meant to bring that memory up, but, now that it was out there, I was no longer asking. I would be picking her up, and one or more of us would drop her off.

A sound like a choked sob broke off my thoughts. "Annie..."

"No, it's ok. I know. Um. You're right, though. So, yeah. If you don't mind, I'd like it if you picked me up, please." I could hear the slight tremble in her voice but, over that, I could hear her resolve tighten. She was still going to hang out with us. She wasn't going to hole herself up in the house. She was going to live.

* * *

Fifteen minutes later, I pull up into her driveway. The last time I was here, I was talking with her mama about her disappearance. And now...

Shaking my head, I clear the images of the past. I need to be strong for her. If she has to move past it, I will, too.

I glance at my phone and read the digits to her garage code. She didn't want me to wait outside but needed a shower. I let myself into her house, closing the garage as I step in. The garage door is on the opposite side of the kitchen from where I usually enter so it's easy enough to find my way to the living room. She told me to make myself comfortable so I plop on the couch and stretch my feet onto the ottoman.

I pull out my phone, letting her know I'm here so I won't startle her. Then I text the guys. Apparently, a child had been running around the pool, slipped, and cracked his head. So, Cory and Jense had to give statements about the incident, which also meant Nick had to have security footage available. Then, there was clearing the pool area, cleaning; all the things. Jense was following the ambulance because he wanted to make sure he was going to be ok. His heart is just that big.

A door in the hallway behind me opens, then squeals closed. Annie walks out in a pink and black tie-dyed hoodie, black-ripped skinny jeans, and black slip-on Converse. She is so damn beautiful and so damn cute. I notice that her hair is still wet from her shower and she's blushing slightly.

I rise from the couch with a smile. "Hello, Angel." I beam, holding my arms out towards her.

"Hi," she shyly whispers as her blush moves down her neck. She slowly shuffles in between my arms, resting her head against my chest, and wrapping her arms around my waist. I inhale her unique scent; something like eucalyptus, lavender, and citrus.

"Thanks for picking me up."

Shaking my head, I let her pull back to meet my eyes. The smile she gives me almost brings me to my knees. I very slowly lean down, watching as she tenses slightly, just before relaxing. Kissing her soft lips is everything right now. But, I don't want to push, so I break the kiss. "Any time, Angel."

Smiling wide, she moves out of my arms and begins packing a bag for her kids' weekend away. After that, she writes them each a note, stuffs them in their bags, then turns and makes her way to the kitchen.

She grabs out two water bottles, clicks off the lights, then dang near skips back to me. "Ready?" She asks happily, reaching her hand out for mine. Loving this playful side of her, I grab her hand, kiss her knuckles, then lead her to the garage before muttering, "More than you know."

Annie and I are snuggled up on the couch watching John Wick. I think I almost had a coronary when she said she had never seen it. I knew the guys would be a while so we picked up a few half sandwiches at a local deli, figuring we could at least have enough to last us until dinner.

For the eighth time in less than 20 minutes, I feel her shift against me. After a minute, she sits up and my arm drops down to my side. I look over and her whole face is unusually flushed and it looks like she's sweating. "Are you ok? Running a fever?"

I reach out and press the back of my hand to her forehead. She quickly swats me away, rolling her eyes. "No. I'm just hot. And you're," she flings her arm up and down above my body.

"Hot?" I say with a wry grin.

She giggles and nods her head. "Yes, *that*." She pulls at her hoodie a few times, trying to cool herself off. Tilting my head, I look her over. I mean, it's a little chilly-ish for "Texas Fall", but not cold in the house.

"Take off your hoodie, Angel. We'll be here a while waiting on the others. And, you should always feel comfortable here." She quickly shakes her head, taking the ends of each of the sleeves in her hands and holding them for dear life.

"I'm good." She brings both of her legs under her, criss-crossing them. Then, she leans her elbows on her knees, resting her chin on her knuckles. She stares at the TV, actively avoiding me, like she's trying to convince me that she's fine. *I don't buy it.*

Picking up the remote, I pause the movie. Her jaw clenches but she doesn't move or utter a sound.

Leaning slightly towards her, I whisper, "Annie, baby, talk to me." Assessing her profile, I see the tremble in her chin, the tears sitting on her lower eyelids, the knuckles of her hands turning white as her breathing slowly picks up.

"Annie, I'm going to wrap my arms around you. I'm going to bring you to my lap, and snuggle you." She blinks once, causing a few tears to spill.

When she doesn't object, I lean over, moving one arm around her back and the other under her crossed legs. Then I lift her up and over to my lap, placing her sideways so her legs drape over my left leg. I adjust my arms so that my hands clasp across her right arm; her left arm and body pressed against my chest. She curls her body into me and begins to softly cry.

Knowing she isn't ready to talk, I run one hand through her hair and whisper in her ear. "Let it out, baby. I'm right here. Whatever you need; we've got you. You're safe. I'm not going anywhere."

Thankfully, it only takes her a couple of minutes before she calms down, but I don't stop running my fingers through her hair.

She shifts her head, looking up at me through her now wet lashes. Her voice comes out so small and scared when she whispers, "I-I don't usually wear long-sleeve shirts. Even in winter. But, ever since," She pauses, licking her lips. "Brute. The one who I, um, taught me most of my *lessons...*" she spits out the last word with so much vitriol that I tighten my arms around her. She sucks in a deep breath then lets it out. "The first night or day, whatever. The first time I met him, he had cut the clothes off of my body. One long slash on each arm and leg. Those were, are, the deepest cuts; the ugliest scars. But there's another set of scars. I was punished for hurting one of the guys..."

She trails off with a heavy sigh as I hold her; trying to tamp down my anger over what she went through.

Her voice is even lower as she continues, "I just don't want you guys to see them, any of them, and be reminded of where I was; who I had to become. I don't want any of you to be disgusted with me." Big, wet sobs wrack her body as she falls apart in my arms. I know she isn't ready to hear my truth, our truths, yet, so I just hold her to me for a few minutes.

Once her crying turns into adorable fucking hiccups, I push my chest out, encouraging her to lean back. When she does, she looks deep into my eyes. The crystal blue quality of her eyes nearly takes my breath away. Even sad and crying, she is the most beautiful woman I have ever seen.

Taking my hands, I gently hold her cheeks, imploring her to hear, and feel, everything I am about to say. "Annie, *you* are more than your scars. But, most importantly, we *want* you. All of you. Past, present, and future. You are ours."

She shakes her head trying to look anywhere but at me. "You don't understand. They're bad. And they aren't the only ones. I just…You guys deserve better."

"Annie, look at me." I wait for her eyes to slowly drift back to mine. "You, Annie, are *everything*. When we said, "all in", we damn well meant it."

When it's clear she doesn't believe me, I slowly lift her to stand. Her eyes widen in fear but I grip her chin, just hard enough to halt her brain from spinning out. "I want to show you something but I need you to trust me. Do you trust me, Annie?"

Her face transforms into shock but she quickly nods. "Yes." She whispers. I smile wide at her then stand from the couch. Grasping her hand in mine, I gently tug her to my room. She quietly follows but I can hear her breathing pick up as anxiety takes hold.

Opening my room, I hold my arm out, gesturing for her to go

first. She does, smiling shyly up at me. When I step in, I see that she's taking it all in. "Annie," I say softly. She turns to face me, a question in her eyes. "Door open or close?" Her brows furrow in confusion and she glances between the door and me a few times. Suddenly, her eyes widen as the realization hits; then she smiles. *Fuck me. She is an angel.*

"Open. Thank you for asking." She grins and a little shiver runs down her body.

I tilt my head, narrow my eyes, and grin. "Oh, we *will* be talking about whatever thought you just had, naughty girl. But first, come here."

I walk over to the far side of the room where a floor-length mirror is positioned. Holding out my hand, I silently ask her to join me.

She considers me for a moment before making her decision. Stepping over to me, she places her hand in mine and allows me to maneuver her to stand in front of me. She gulps audibly as she looks at the mirror. My hands lightly rest on her perfect hips as I lean down and whisper in her ear, "Good girl." Her body shivers against mine and my cock throbs in my jeans.

"Now, look in the mirror." She chews on her bottom lip as she contemplates. "Obey or I'll spank your sexy ass."

She gasps in surprise, her eyes meeting mine in the mirror. At first, I was afraid I triggered her. But the heat and desire I see there sends white-hot need flashing through my body. "Not now, Angel," I growl, nibbling her ear. "Right now, you need to see what we see. Eyes on my hands, and if it truly becomes too much, your safeword is *red*."

Her eyes widen comically but she nods quickly. I kiss her neck, sucking slightly on her pulse point. "Good girl. Now, lift your arms up." I let the command hang in there and watch as her lip trembles and her body shivers. Anxiety flushes out the lust in her eyes. After another second, I reach back my right hand and pop her ass. Not too hard; just enough to startle her. She yelps and her cheeks flush as desire blows her pupils wide.

I chuckle against her back. "Oh no! My good little Angel likes that, don't you?" She doesn't respond but, I know. "It's ok. We'll work on your responses later. Right now, we have something far more important."

I reach back, gripping her hips firmly, and slip back into my dominant voice. "Now, arms up." She oh so slowly raises her arms above her head. I dance my fingers from her hips, up to the hem of her hoodie. "I'm going to take this off now, and your shirt is going to go with it."

She starts to lower her arms, shaking her head adamantly, "No, no, no, no. No one's, well, I've never..."

I pause, tilting my head, and narrowing my eyes. "You've kept this sexy body hidden from everyone?" I say, hoping my playfulness comes through even though I'm honestly shocked.

She slowly nods her head and shrugs one shoulder. "I've either kept a shirt on or turned the lights off." Her whispered confession makes my head swim and my fingers tingle.

I slowly nod my head and smile. "Well, today that changes. It's just me and you, Annie. Let me show you what we see. What *I* see. Please."

She gulps, indecision warring across her face before raising her arms again. Nodding once, she inhales deeply and I can see her suck in her stomach. I don't like that. *One thing at a time Vince. That's not the goal today.*

I raise the hoodie, with her shirt, up over her head before she can second guess herself. Flinging them behind me, I face the mirror in complete awe. I see the various scars but they don't deter me; until I land on one. Squinting my eyes and leaning in, I grit out, "He branded you?"

Deflating, she nods her head as her shoulders drop, and I immediately want to kick my own ass. "Hey, Angel. It doesn't make me feel any different about you. It just makes me want to do the same to him.

Three hundred times. A day. For all eternity." She releases a wet giggle and rolls her eyes.

Tension begins to leak out of her again and I see a little bit of a smile curving her lips. *Good save, dumbass.*

I run my gaze over her bare upper body and hot damn. Even her scars turn me on, showing that she fought like hell and is *still* standing. Her boobs are perfect handfuls; maybe a little more. Her curves are soft and inviting, and her collarbone is prominent, begging to be kissed. And, is that... "You have a belly button ring?"

Quietly, as if she thinks I'm judging her, "Y-Yes. Why?"

The fear in her tone causes me to look at her face in the mirror. She's flushed from her cheeks, down her neck. But, just as I suspected, her damn eyes are closed. I notice her arms wrapping around her front, trying to block my view. Tsking low in her ear I say, "No, Angel. Don't hide from me. Open your eyes and *see*, baby."

I lightly trail my hands down her shoulders, her arms, and over her hands before interlacing my fingers with hers. With my hands on top of the backs of hers, I slowly control her movements. Stretching her fingers out a little, I move her to rub against the pink and butter-fly ring she has hanging in her navel. "This is so damn sexy, Angel." My voice comes out husky and sexual desire drips off of every word. Then, I take control of both hands; running them down the curves of her sides, "You're so soft. It's addicting. *You're* addicting. I want to spend my days touching your skin."

Her eyes start to flutter but she keeps them open, staring straight at me in the mirror. I grin mischievously as the red trail of flush begins to bleed across her chest.

Curling her hands inward towards her belly, we slowly make our way up to her chest. I gently flex my fingers open, silently command-ing her to open her hands for me. When she does, I move them up to her breasts and cup them.

Her breaths are coming in short pants and her legs are trembling, ever so slightly. I can only feel her smooth skin against my fingertips but I see how her hands fit over them; or should I say, *almost* fit over them. A low groan works its way up and out of my chest as I lean in and kiss her pulse point. "Perfect. Absolutely perfect. Do you see, Annie? I want all you bared before me. I want to touch, lick, kiss, every goddamn inch of you. Can I touch you while you watch baby?"

Her gulp is heavy and fills the otherwise silent room. Her eyes are wide but are a much deeper blue as lust takes over. She whimpers and bites her lip. I can feel her squeeze her own tits under my palms and I grunt in satisfaction.

"Okay." Her whisper might as well have been a shout and my dick did its very own happy dance.

"Good girl." Her body shivers, and I see her thighs clenching with need. I can't help it, I grind into her from behind, providing just enough stimulation over my jean-covered cock to groan.

The sexiest fucking moan leaves her mouth and I almost lose it completely. "I've got you, Angel. Remember the rules: eyes open, and keep your hands right there where I can see my girl."

The air is charged and I would love nothing more than to bend her over the bed and sink into her. Knowing it's not the time, I force myself to slow down.

Unlocking our fingers, I trail my own hands down her ribcage, over her stomach, and to her pants. I flick the button on her jeans, my eyes glued to hers in the mirror. Dragging down her zipper, I tell her, "I'm going to take your pants off now." Giving her a light kiss on her shoulder, I drag her jeans down her body, then help her step out of them.

I catalog every scar, making a note to paint a path of love over them later. Tears are brimming in her eyes as she shakes from a mixture of anticipation and worry. "Annie, you know the rules. Why are you covering up *my* stomach?"

She shakes her head, chewing both lips together. A tear falls down her face and I wrap my arms around her. "Ok, Angel," I kiss her cheek. "Ok, tell me "red," Annie. Tell me "red"."

She shakes her head again. On a choked sob she wails, "It's not that. But, the scars. You were making me feel so good and then, they were there, and I didn't... I don't..." The dam breaks and tears flood her eyes. I scoop her up in my arms and carry her over to my bed. With the hand under her knees, I rip the comforter open before gently placing her on the bed. She's still holding her arms around the bottom part of her stomach where her jeans had rested. Not wanting to make things worse, I cover her with the comforter, lie on top, and move her closer to me. She immediately snuggles in deeper as her tears soak my shirt. But, I don't care. I pushed her too fucking far. I *am* the asshole.

"I'm so sorry, Angel. I pushed way too hard, too fast. I'm so sorry." I could feel my own eyes filling with tears the longer I held her to me; rubbing the back of her head with one hand, and her back with the other.

Taking deep, steadying breaths, I hold her against me until her muffled sobs turn into quiet whimpers. I don't say a word. I can't because there is nothing I can say to fix the pain I caused. I just hope I didn't ruin this whole relationship. I would never forgive myself.

24

Annie

Sighing into Vince's chest, I sink deeper into his embrace. He smelled so, *Vince*. Like, Sandalwood mixed with Lavender and maybe a hint of clove. It is intoxicating. I feel like a complete moron for breaking down on him. I didn't want to say "red". I wanted to give my whole self to him; to all of them. And I fucking ruined it.

Goosebumps break out over my body as I remember his hands on my body. Not even that, but *my* hands on *my* body. Feeling what he felt, seeing myself through his eyes was... there isn't a word for it. But, now that I had that little taste of freedom, of power, I crave it.

Shifting my head to rest on his shoulder, I slowly uncurl my body from the fetal position. Vince doesn't say anything. He doesn't rush, or try to help. *Damn, he's wonderful. And so fucking hot. And good gracious, that mouth should be illegal.*

Suddenly very aware that I'm still stark naked under his comforter, I press my thighs together. Remembering the way his large hands felt sliding down my body, the way he whispered his desires in my ear. *Fuck... Ok, I can do this. I need to do this. For me. For us.*

"Vince," my voice is scratchy from crying but I can tell he hears me by the flinch of his body.

"Yes, Angel?" He hums, almost sounding like he was drifting off to sleep.

Biting my lip I raise my right arm out of the blanket and lay my hand on his chest, feeling his heart beat out a steady rhythm. Shifting my head back a little, I look at him. His beard has been trimmed since I got back from the hospital. His hair is getting a little long on the sides but it doesn't look bad on him.

Reaching up, I slowly take his cheek in my hand, gently turning his head down to meet my gaze. He takes a moment to search my eyes. I'm not sure what he sees, or what he's looking for, but he eventually leans down and meets my lips. His soft, plump lips meet mine, just briefly, before he leans back. His smile almost blinds me and the golden flecks in his eyes shine with...something I'm not sure I can name.

Before I can chicken out, I blurt, "I want you to see. *Please.* I just... the cuts' *there* are not like the others. One of the guys was mad at what I did to his friends; the guys I hit with a tool because they were hurting Camila; then found out, the brother died. Anyway, he cut the bottom of my stomach. Left a nice little note behind. And that's going to be there forever. Do you understand? *Forever,* forever. And, if you can't handle that, if the others, then.....I just... I need to know now. Because I think I'm falling in love with you and I need to know if it's too much for you before I fall deeper." I suck in a lung full of air, having barely stopped as the word vomit poured from my mouth. My heart feels like it's in my throat and I angrily swipe away a runaway tear.

Vince tucks his pointer under my chin, and his thumb just above it, squeezing lightly. "Look at me, Angel." The deep timbre of his voice is like a sensual caress, causing jolts of electricity to shoot from my stomach straight to my core.

Raising my eyes to meet his, I trip over a breath as his eyes bore straight into my very soul. "I will do whatever makes you comfortable. Nothing would make any one of us see you as anything other than sexy," *kiss*, "Beautiful," *kiss*, "Amazing," *kiss*, "Breathtaking." When he finally leans back, I can't contain the smile that spreads across my face; nor do I try to.

I take a deep breath, bite my lip, then nod my response to the question in his eyes. Sitting up slowly, he gives me the most hopeful grin I have ever seen. He moves cautiously off the bed, maintaining eye contact as he stands. "Standing or kneeling, Angel?" I consider his question. If he's standing, he can see, well, everything. But, if he's kneeling above me, he sees it up close. If he's standing and he gets grossed out or something, then he can leave quickly and that will be that. No awkward maneuvering, or feeling the deep loss of his body warmth. *Shit. Why is this so hard to answer? Just make a decision.*

"Standing. Please." His smile is sweet; and understanding. As he moves around to the end of the bed, I roll onto my back so I can track his movements. He moves slowly, purposefully, making sure to not startle the scared, defenseless animal. A little shiver of lust zips through me and flutters through my pussy. *Not now hussy.*

Vince stands to his full height at the end of the bed, looking at me with a fantastical mix of lust, desire, and...that thing I still can't name. "Annie, when I remove this blanket, I won't be able to stop myself from kissing every inch of you. Tell me now if you don't want that."

My pussy clenches with need as I begin to pant. *This damn man...*

With a slight nod of my head and a painful swallow, I force myself to relax.

The soft pull of the blanket down my chest and over my breasts causes my nipples to peak. A shiver passes through my body as the cold air whispers across my skin. Lower still, the blanket slides down my stomach, right past my navel. Sucking in a breath, I slam my eyes shut, drop my head to the pillow, and clench my hands; letting the bite in my skin from my nails ground me.

The blanket drops past the bottom of my stomach. I feel myself tense, expecting him to drop the blanket, maybe throw out a random apology, and then run out of here. Instead, I'm shocked to feel the blanket continue its slow descent.

Hissing in a breath, I can feel the air move as Vince rips the rest of the blanket off with a flourish. My muscles are taut, shaking with fear, as my heart pounds a chaotic rhythm in my chest.

"Fucking stunning," Vince whispers in a groan. My eyes fly open and I watch as his gaze slides over every inch of my body, leaving a path of fire in its wake. His chest inhales and exhales in rapid succession and he's vibrating with restraint.

Suddenly, he's climbing onto the end of his king-sized bed, causing my eyes to widen. Smoothing his hands down the curve of my foot and up my shins he grins in pure delight. "Fuck, Annie." He kisses the inside of my left ankle, then repeats the movement on the right. The moan that leaves his mouth as it skates up my shin is downright sinful; causing liquid heat to pool between my legs and my clit to throb.

Each kiss that lands, lights up every nerve. His coarse beard against my leg causes lust to climb higher. I moan and tip my head back as he gradually makes his way up my legs; overwhelming every nerve-ending. His hands skate up my outer legs, then land on my love handles. Groaning, he continues his path up both legs, straddling mine and hovering over them instead of forcing me to widen my legs.

"So soft," *kiss,* "so smooth," *kiss,* "so fucking irresistible." He kisses the top of my mound, right in the center, and I shudder out a gasp.

He chuckles before moving his body further, kissing a path from my right hip until he reaches the scars on my lower belly. "You know what I see when I see this filthy word on your perfect skin?"

Lust and anxiety rip my insides apart as they fight for dominance. "N-no. What?" A single tear drips down my face.

"Annie, eyes on me." Breathing heavily, I look down my body and see his face hovering, just above the jagged word 'cunt' etched into my skin. It's the first time I've looked at it since, before. I've purposefully not looked at it. I barely even wash over it in the shower. But, now, I see it. And him. A tear breaks free again as I take in this beautiful man hovering over such an ugly scar.

His head lowers, and I watch with curiosity as he stops just above the word. My breath catches in my throat as his tongue peeks out and begins to trace each jagged letter. A whole damn butterfly garden riots in my chest as he says, "I see a woman who fought for her life." *C* "I see a woman who always protects others." *U* "I see a beautiful, sexy angel that never gives up." *N* "I see a Goddamn warrior." *T.*

He straightens his arms, pushing himself up as he levels me with his piercing gaze. As his eyes burn into mine, I finally see the truth, the sincerity, the absolute, unwavering conviction of this man. He crawls over me until we're face-to-face, nose-to-nose, breathing the same air. His voice is a raspy whisper, thick with emotion, "I see a fucking survivor and I'm damn lucky you chose me, chose us, to stand by your side; to stand in your light."

Surging up, I wrap my arms around his neck and slam my mouth against his. Fire and ice war through my body as our tongues tangle. The kiss is not sweet and slow. Nope. It's passion, it's need, it's all-consuming. Air is no longer important but this man *absolutely* is.

He tangles his hand in my hair, positioning me just as he wants.

Nibbling my nip, a groan rips out from somewhere deep inside. "Vince, please." *Was I begging? Seriously? What am I even begging for?*

Vince's hand slides down to my jaw, before resting on my throat. He doesn't squeeze, just lays it there as he continues his assault on my mouth. A groan rips free and my eyes roll back as I feel myself getting impossibly wet. He applies just a little pressure and nips my bottom lip one more time.

Releasing our kiss, he hovers over me and locks his eyes with mine. My breath startles in my lungs as he slowly removes his hand from my throat, barely brushes my collarbone, and trails down my chest, over the swell of my breast. His hand engulfs my breast as he begins squeezing and massaging. It feels good that he's touching me but my boobs aren't sensitive to me. I don't know if they ever were, to be honest. But, I don't have the heart to tell him that. *What is it with men and boobs?*

I glance down and see he is rolling my nipples in sweet circles between his thumb and pointer but it honestly doesn't register. *Why am I so damn broken? Why can't I be normal?*

Pushing that thought away, I bite my lip, I do what I do best; I fake it. "Oh, Vince, yes." I pant out. He pinches my nipple, hard, and I yelp out as a spark of electricity shoots straight to my clit. "Don't lie to me, Angel."

Flinching, I flash my eyes open to meet his as I shake my head back and forth. "I didn.." He cuts me off with a brutal kiss, sucking my lip into his mouth and biting down gently. He abruptly pulls away and I whine at the loss. "Pretending to like something you don't like, is still lying, baby. I only want to know what you like. Don't hide from me." His voice turns from stern to sweet, "Now, let's try this again." His breath ghosts over my lips and a shiver runs down my spine.

Leaning back, he reaches his arm behind him and whips his shirt over his head and holy forks and spoons. I must be dead. This man's upper body looks like the NFL is missing a player. And the tattoos...

fuck me. *No really; please fuck me.* My mouth goes dry as my eyes bug out of my head. I imagine I look like Bugsy from Bedtime Stories.

His chuckle brings me out of my obvious ogling and I lift my gaze back to his eyes. Fire burns in their depths and my skin flashes with fever. Leaning back down, he presses his tantalizing lips to mine, way too fast for my liking. A low whine pushes from my mouth and he chuckles, pressing another brief kiss to my lips. "I know what you need, Angel. Now lie back, and let me worship this body like I promised." My breaths are coming in shallow pants and I barely manage to nod. What the hell else was I supposed to do? I don't think I've ever been so turned on in my life.

Vince is clearly enjoying how desperate I am because he *slowly* makes his way down my body, kissing every damn inch; just as promised. Pleasure sparks with each kiss, each swipe of his tongue, and with each gentle scratch of his beard. I try to squeeze my thighs together to get some much-needed friction but I realize that he's already made himself comfortable between my legs. *When did I spread them?*

He licks a trail across my mound, kissing each of my inner thighs. "You know," he says casually, "The guys call these fantastic bits 'hot pockets.'" He sucks a hickey into the middle of one of the embarrassingly jiggly sections on my inner thighs. "I never understood it," He groans and sucks the same spot on the opposite thigh. "But, now I do. So warm, so biteable. Mmmm."

I moan out, trembling with need, no longer caring that he is touching something I hate so damn much. His voice is like a drug and makes me ache in all the best ways.

Looking up through his lashes, he locks his gaze on mine and lowers his head, right above my slit. "NO!" He startles and immediately sits up. Confusion distorts his beautiful face as he tilts his head. Shame and embarrassment burn across my face. Closing my eyes, I release a breath before blurting, "I've never, well, I mean..."

Vince reaches down and holds my hand, squeezing it firmly in his grip. "Words, Annie. It's ok. I will never judge you. Just tell me."

Blowing out a raspberry through my lips, I say, "So, you know I haven't, um, had sex in..."

"Almost ten years." He nods and gently smiles.

Nodding my head I continue, "Well, even, um, *before*, no one has ever, um, done *that*."

His delicious chuckle sends goosebumps across my arms and my heartbeats in my clit. He slowly leans back over me, bringing his face down to mine. Our lips just barely touch as his eyes dance with mischief. Smirking, he leans further to the side, nuzzling his face into my neck. I can feel his lips move against my ear as he says, "*That* as in, no one has ever tongued your delicious pussy? No one has ever had the joy of feasting on you until your cum drips down their face?" He accentuates his fantastically vulgar questions with a lick up my ear from lobe to helix.

A moan rips free and I grab onto his waist, digging my nails into his jeans. "Oh, God." I half pant, half scream as I thrust my hips upward wantonly. "No, no one." That's all I could puff out before he nips at my ear lobe.

"Good," Is all I get before he disappears.

Flashing my eyes open to meet his, I watch as he carefully rolls himself back down my body. Kneeling between my legs, he bends over, never breaking eye contact. He settles on his stomach and gives me a panty-melting grin. *Well, if I still had panties on to melt.*

He wraps an arm under and around each thigh before bracing both hands just below my pelvis, pressing down. Leaning forward he inhales deeply. *Oh. My. God!* Flashing me a knowing smirk, he sticks out his tongue and swipes from the bottom of my slit, right to my clit. I yelp and jump, startled by the sensations, but his large hands keep me firmly in place. Groaning low, he mumbles, "Fucking delicious," before leaning back in and tonguing me thoroughly.

"Oh, shit!" I moan out as my body lights up like a Christmas boat parade. Fisting the sheets, I drop my head back as he begins to lavish every inch of my intimate area. I feel my pussy clench with need as I try to breathe through the trembling. *He's barely touched me and I'm falling apart.*

Vince shifts, bringing one hand from around my thigh. Then, suddenly, his finger is at my entrance. He doesn't enter, instead remaining just outside of my opening while applying pressure in slow, measured circles. His tongue licks my clit, which surprises me because I actually feel it. The more he circles or zigzags or whatever he's doing down there, the further my body tenses.

My feet begin to cramp, only adding to the sensations zipping through my body. Then, when I feel like I'm about to die, his long, thick finger enters me. At that exact moment, a whole damn atom bomb explodes; surging from the middle of my being and lashing out through every limb. I'm vaguely aware that I can no longer breathe but, I can't seem to care.

In some distant dimension, I feel him increase his tempo and press on...something; something deep inside, and just as I feel like I may recover from the energy striking out in every direction, it turns inward and compresses. I suck in a gasp, my whole body locks up, my back arches off the bed and a scream tears out straight from the pits of my very soul. Blackness spots my vision before taking over completely.

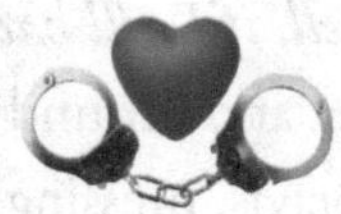

Watching Annie give herself to me was more than I could have ever hoped for. But to find out my Angel is also a damn unicorn. *Fuck me. She's perfect.*

I remember her telling us about her medical conditions. Cory, being Cory, looked them up and gave us all the deets. Apparently, it's difficult for people with these conditions to orgasm, but not impossible. The good news is, she has four men who are more than willing to try anything and everything; including toy play.

Licking my lips, I relish the taste of her and can't wait to do it again. The first taste almost had me cumming in my pants. But, sliding my finger into her sweet pussy. *Lord Jesus help me.* She was so fucking hot, so fucking wet, and so fucking tight. I had to be gentle out of fear of hurting her, but the moment I entered her, her pussy clamped down on me and squeezed the shit out of my one finger. *One finger! Good God.* We have to take things slow with her. No matter how painful our dicks get.

Her face was absolutely gorgeous as she gave herself over to her orgasm. I wanted to keep her high going so I doubled my efforts. Then, she surprised the hell out of me. As her back bowed off the bed, her pussy contracted in ripples like it was trying to push my finger out. Afraid I was hurting her, I removed my finger from her G-spot and slid out. But then, the gates of heaven rained all over me as she shouted up to the ceiling.

Our girl is apparently a squirter. And it was the hottest thing I've ever seen!

Her body relaxed into the bed shortly after she came. I take a moment to appreciate the dark, wet patch that is all over my bed. *Mine.*

Panting heavily, I crawl my way back up her body. Brushing my hand across her cheek, I watch as her eyes flutter and her nose wrinkles adorably. Leaning down I whisper, "I'll be right back, Angel," then place a kiss on her nose.

I can't tell if she's just exhausted or passed out but I know she'll need some time to recover. Sliding off the bed, I quickly make my way to my bathroom, wash my hands then run a clean washcloth under the warm water. Right before I leave the bathroom, I snag a large towel, too.

Returning to the bed, I gently wipe her face, then clean her up. Folding the oversized towel in half, I shimmy it under her hips until it completely covers the wet spot and I can't help the satisfied smirk that crosses my face.

Annie lets out a small sigh and I realize she is completely passed out. Chuckling, I maneuver her completely off the towel, and further up the bed so she can rest on my pillow. Grabbing the blanket off the floor, I cover her beautifully naked body. She curls to her side and inhales deeply before snuggling further into my pillow. A small smile forms on her face and I feel my heart expand.

Before leaving to let her rest, I step back and look her over. I had moved her hair off of her face and neck but it's still a sexy mess. Her face is still blushed out but her usually worried or anxious expression is gone. She looks *peaceful*.

Not wanting to spend any more time creeping on her, I grab my shirt, tug it on, and look at her one more time before slipping out of the room. As I walk down the hallway, I think about the words she'd said to me. She's falling in love with me; with us. Thankfully, I'm already there. I want her. I want to love her, to care for her, to spend every day finding new ways to make her smile. I want it all.

Hitting the bottom of the stairs, I make my way through the kitchen to grab a note card and a pen along with a couple of bottles of water. Scribbling out a quick note for Annie, I head back to my room, place the note on the pillow next to her, and set the water on the nightstand. With a final, soft kiss to her temple, I walk out of the room, closing it quietly behind me.

The alarm beeps downstairs, alerting me that at least one of the guys has returned. I hurriedly make my way downstairs in hopes they won't yell out and wake her. All three come into view and their eyes meet mine in question. Subtly shaking my head first, I nod towards the kitchen.

Once we enter, I crack the lid on my water and guzzle down half. I grab out the sandwiches and snacks we bought earlier and place them on the raised section of the island. "She's sleeping," I say quietly, allowing a bit of a warning to show through my eyes.

Looks varying from confusion to worry cross each of their faces. I can't help it; I smirk. Jenson is the first to put it together and he chuckles, shaking his head while Cory grunts right before taking a bite of his sandwich.

Nick slides up next to me, squeezing my ass before bringing me down for a kiss. "Oh, shit!" He breathes in heavily before licking my lips again. "You two taste perfect together."

I chuckle as he captures my mouth in his. Opening up, I allow him this rare moment to control the kiss. A groan slips out of his mouth, suddenly bringing me out of our little bubble. Pulling back, I nip at his lips once more before facing the others.

"So, we need to talk." I nod my way to the table, quietly asking them to sit before trying to figure out how to tell them what happened, and what to expect, without invading Annie's privacy. *Lord help me.*

25

Cory

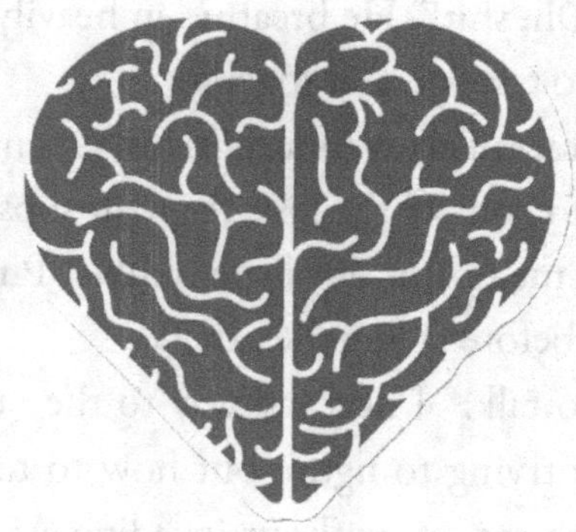

Vince decided to give us a heads-up about a few marks on Annie that she's the most concerned with. Hearing what those bastards did to her makes me want to puke. We'd all seen a few scars in the hospital but never imagined anything like that. It also explains why she was working out in a damn sweatshirt.

Sighing heavily, I lean back in my chair and take in the somber faces surrounding me. "I'm glad you told us." Jenson's head snaps toward me. "I, I don't know how I would have handled seeing the word on her beautiful body, making her feel less than perfect. And branding her. I mean shit."

Shaking my head, I work through the rest of my thoughts before choosing one to share. "I was going to say I can't believe she had never been, bare, in front of anyone but, knowing what we do about her past, it makes sense."

We all sit in silence as we work out the new information we have learned. After a few minutes, Jenson leans forward in his chair, the wood creaking slightly, and questions, "OK. So, what do we do tonight? We originally wanted to walk Main, but since Vince orgasmed her into a coma…"

We all chuckle and Vince grins cockily, shrugging one shoulder. "Hey, Cory was the one that said it wasn't impossible. Honestly, she just needs to get out of her head."

We all nod in agreement because it absolutely lines up with what we know about Annie. "What about we give her a few options? Movies, in or out, walking Main Street, maybe Putt-Putt?"

We all nod in agreement and make our way out of the kitchen. I call out that I'm going to shower while the others plant themselves on the couch.

My excitement grows as I make my way to my room. Tossing my clothes off, I throw them all in the hamper before walking into my ensuite. It's not as big as Vince's but I have the better bathtub.

Turning the faucet to reach my preferred temperature, I brush my teeth really quickly and then climb under the spray. Relief floods my body as the water sluices down my body. The water is just a couple of notches above boiling and is perfect for massaging my aching muscles.

Thoughts of Annie naked and waiting just down the hall makes all of the blood rush to my dick. I can't believe she's here and she still wants us.

I ignore my dick and force myself to think about the weekend. I'm looking forward to the time with Annie, and with the guys. Going from spending every day with her at the hospital to barely seeing her has worn me down.

Shaking my head to scatter the solemn thoughts, I reach for the shampoo and massage it through my hair. The smell of Eucalyptus and Peppermint lift through the shower as the steam wafts through the air. Quickly rinsing the suds from my hair, I reach for my body wash and lather it across my body. Ever since Vince found the Viking Revolution products for men, we've all been obsessed. It smells great but I swear my skin and face have never felt better.

Not wanting to miss her if she wakes up, I hurry through the rest of my shower before shutting off the water, then step out. I rush through toweling off my body before securing it around my waist.

Walking out of the bathroom, the cool air causes goosebumps to scatter down my arms. The ache in my balls reminds me that I'm still painfully hard but I do my best to will it away. Crossing the room, I pull open my drawer and pull out a pair of black boxer briefs. Dropping the towel to the floor, I hear a sharp intake of breath and immediately turn around. My eyes widen and I freeze as I see Annie standing just outside of my very open door. Her eyes are comically wide and her face has the most beautiful flush to it. Her pink sweatshirt seems to swallow her but her black skinny jeans caress every curve that I can see.

I watch as her eyes rake over my body. I subconsciously puff my chest out like a peacock. Why? Who the hell knows. Men aren't notorious for being smart around beautiful women.

A squeak from her mouth has me looking back at her face in time to see her slap her hand over her eyes. "Oh holy shit, I'm so sorry. I- I didn't mean to. I was just, just um, walking..."

At first, I was confused by her embarrassment. Then, the startling realization that I'm stark-ass naked in front of her hits me. My hard cock strains toward her like a sunflower searching for the sun. "Oh, fuck," I rush out, fumbling to get my briefs on.

Of course, the universe couldn't be nice to me. My uncoordinated ass gets my foot tangled in my briefs, my pinky toe snagging on the opening in the middle, and I fall to the floor; hard. With a loud *oomph*, I collapse. I barely have time to catch myself, but I still bang the shit out of my knee.

Groaning out, I take a moment to collect my breath. The shock from my unmanly fall and the pain radiating through my knee takes all of my attention. A warm hand on my back causes me to flinch. Immediately, I miss the warmth as it retreats. "I'm so sorry. Are you ok?" Annie's voice is soft and comforting, like a warm blanket on a cold night.

Even then, I kind of wished the ground would swallow me whole, because I literally just stumbled and fell, with my actual dick hanging out, in front of her. My cheeks burn with embarrassment as I shake my head. "I'm good. Just, you know, needed to clean this spot on the floor before it stains." Yes, I heard it. *Now would be a great time to die.*

I hear a soft snort behind me, quickly followed by what sounds like a muffled giggle. Still in prone position, I turn my head to look behind me and see that she has both hands covering her mouth. Her shoulders shake with barely contained laughter and her eyes are wide and sparkling with amusement. For the briefest moment, I get lost in how breathtaking she looks. Her eyes look happy and bright, not even remotely clouded with the demons of her past.

She gradually brings her hands down and rests them on her lap. Her eyes smile as wide as her mouth does and damn it does something funny to my heart. Suddenly remembering I'm still very much naked, I snatch the towel that, thankfully, is right in front of me. Standing quickly, I wrap and secure my towel, tucking my leaking dick behind a barely-there wall of cloth.

Leaning my hand down to her, she looks at me with those sparkling eyes as she chews on her lip. An image of her on her knees with her mouth wrapped around my dick has my cock jumping for attention. Coyly, she slides her hand into mine and lets me pull her up.

"Hi," I stupidly say. Because, I'm the 'smart one' when it comes to our business, but I'm a total dumbass when it comes to this girl. Shit, I had more conversational skills the night I met her. But, that's normal when I'm there.

Her smile widens like she can hear my inner thoughts and she peers up at me from under her lashes. "Hi. Um, sorry again. I'll, uh..." She points to the hallway and makes her escape, pulling the door behind her and leaving me staring at the closed door like a goob.

Exhaling a raged, "Fuckin' idiot," I rub my hands through my hair, then get my clothes on. This time, though, I don't fall.

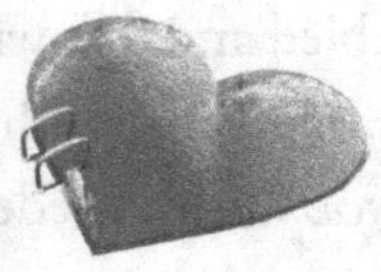

I'm half-dozing in the recliner while Nick and Vince are curled up on the far side of the sectional. Deadpool plays on the TV but I'm too wiped from all the police crap we had to deal with today.

A familiar giggle tinkles at the end of the stairs, causing us to glance over. Annie makes her way to the living room; a bright smile playing on her face.

"Hey, Angel. Did you sleep ok?" Her face immediately turns the shade of a tomato and she ducks her head as she whispers, "Yes, thanks," then begins to nervously play with her fingers.

Standing up, I stride over to her and gently tug her bottom lip from between her teeth. "Good," I say in a hushed voice. Dipping my head, I place a kiss on her lips and hold it until I finally feel her relax.

Stepping back I wink at her, grab her hand, then drag her over to "her chair." Plopping myself down, I fold her into my lap and she immediately snuggles into my chest, releasing a sound akin to a purr.

Raising her head, she looks over at Vince, "Thank you for the water, and the note. I'm sorry I fell asleep but the note at least helped me get my bearings."

Vince smiles at her and nods his head, "No problem, Angel. Besides, I figured you really need the rest." Ending with a wink. I feel the shiver roll down her body and, of course, the nosey bastard in my pants decides to wake up. I knew the moment she felt it under her ass because she tensed up and side-eyed me warily.

Leaning forward, I wrap my arms around her and kiss her neck. "Ignore him. He doesn't make the rules around here."

Giggling, she looks over at me with a quirk of her brow, "Are we talking about Vince or your dick?"

Throwing my head back, I laugh hard, then respond, "Both," with a shrug of my shoulder. She breaks out into a fit of giggles and I take a deep, contented breath. Leaning back, I bring her with me until she's lying on her side, still snug in my lap.

"That checks out since I accidentally caught Cory with his pants down." Without my damn permission, my stupid cock jumps at the thought. The other two goons are cracking up but I don't miss the question in Annie's eyes. I give her a passive smile and hug her back to my chest, so she doesn't try to see behind my mask.

At Vince's playful adamance, Annie tells us about Cory literally fumbling over himself and we all lose it. Poor bastard. He is so confident, smart, and organized when it comes to almost everything in his life. But, unless we're at Sky's the Limit, he's a total goober when it comes to women. Sometimes, he can override it but, when something doesn't happen that he anticipates, he can totally lose it.

Just as our laughter dies down, Cory walks into the living room. His face looks a little pinker than normal and I give him a knowing grin. Rolling his eyes in exasperation, he makes his way towards Annie. Leaning down, he moves a lock of hair behind her ear and says, "Sorry, I didn't get to say hi properly," before kissing her breathlessly.

Watching the two of them almost has me groaning in a mix of

pain and pleasure. I can feel the jolts of electricity shooting through my balls and my dick. When they finally come up for air, I can see that Cory has well and truly recovered from his earlier embarrassment.

Stepping back, he walks to the other side of the couch before plopping down. He spreads his legs wide and his deep blue shirt pulls across his arms and torso perfectly.

Clearing my throat, I look towards Nick and Vince. "So, what're we doing?"

After discussing the options, Annie decided we could go out tomorrow but would prefer to stay in tonight. Which is totally fine by me. Melissa already let her know that she had fed the dragon and picked up the kids an hour ago.

For dinner, Annie requests Chinese food. Then, we decided to have a Pirates of the Caribbean marathon. Splitting up, we each head to our rooms to dress in comfier clothes since we plan to do nothing but relax tonight. As I pull on my gray sweats, I remember that Annie is still in jeans and a hoodie. Swiping another pair of sweats, I grab one of my old goofy tees and pad back downstairs to the living room.

Strutting over to Annie curled up on the couch, I grin like a smug bastard as I catch her eyes lingering below my waistline. *Girls and sweatpants.* Shaking my head I put a little extra swagger in my steps. "See something you like, Sweetness?"

Her eyes snap up to mine and her face blushes in the adorable way it does. "And if I said, yes?" Her coy smile and light-hearted tone causes me to chuckle. I love sassy Annie.

Groaning dramatically, I rub my chest. "Don't tease me, Sweetness. I can't take it."

Her laughter fills the room, simultaneously filling my heart. Handing her the clothes, she looks up at me in confusion. Shrugging a shoulder, I try to sound nonchalant when I say, "Just figured you may want to get comfy."

With a dazzling smile, she takes the clothes from me then stands.

"Thank you, Jense," is all she whispers before giving me the briefest of kisses. Before my body can catch up to my brain, she's pulling away and shuffling towards the downstairs bathroom.

"You ok, there, Jen-Jen?" Nick mocks.

That pulls me out of my stupor and I flip him off. "Fuck off, dick."

Laughter filters around me and I realize that everyone else has made their way back into the living room just in time to see my brain glitch. Groaning, I rub a hand over my face and mutter, "Fuckers," as I stroll into the kitchen. Grabbing a few waters and beers, I bring them back to the living room and set them on the coffee table. Before anyone has time to comment, I head back to the kitchen and grab plates and forks since I know the food will be here soon.

Just as I walk out of the kitchen, the doorbell rings. Passing Vince and Nick on their way to the door, we all share a genuine smile. Things are already much better than we could've hoped considering....*everything.*

Just as I set the plates down, Annie walks over to me and wraps her arms around me from the side. Maneuvering a little, I wrap my arm around her shoulders and she snuggles straight into my side. "Thank you. These are super comfy. But, I left your shirt on the sink."

"Ok. No worries. Glad the sweats worked." I feel her nod against me and give a slight squeeze before letting go.

Nick and Vince come back with a ridiculous amount of food and start taking all of the boxes and tiny bags out of the large brown paper bags. "Good gracious," Annie exclaims. "You'll have food for days." She says it playfully and even bumps her hip into my thigh.

"We're growin' boys, Annie." Vince chuckles, patting his belly. *Yeah like there's anything but muscle there.*

She chuckles, shaking her head, and swats him in the arm. "Ok, *that's* the story we'll stick to, big man." Her eyes roll and her smile deepens as we all laugh with her.

We return our attention to the table and make our plates before settling around the living room. Annie decides to sit next to me on the couch and Cory snags her other side.

Tucking into our food, we begin to watch the first movie in the Pirates series. A sense of calm, rightness, blankets the room. For the first time in over a month, it feels like home.

26

Annie

I startle awake and immediately panic as something tightens around my feet. Adrenaline and fear kick in and I begin kicking out, flailing my body wildly until I land on the floor with a heavy *thump*. Groaning out, I flutter my eyes open. Finding beautiful hardwood floors I frown. *What the hell?*

As my breathing slowly returns to normal and the haze from the space between asleep and awake begins to fade, I realize that my hands aren't secured. Testing the weight around my legs, I feel my frown deepen. Rolling over with a groan, I look down at my legs to find... a fucking blanket.

Flattening out on my back, I drop my head to the floor with a dull thud. "Fighting with blankets, Annie? Really?" Shaking my head and rolling my eyes, I catch sight of the ceiling and realize: it's not mine. But, neither are the floors.

Leaning up to rest on my forearms I look around. There's a light on in the bathroom down the hall and another light coming from behind the couch. But, everything else has been turned off. *The guys' house.* The visual affirmation helps to calm me and I start to filter through the memories of last night.

Damn, I guess I fell asleep. I really need to go home, though. Shit. What time is it?

I slowly make my way up off the floor, stretching each muscle as I go, then pad into the kitchen. I remember I put my purse in there earlier. Thankfully, one of the guys must have put my phone next to it when I passed out.

Pressing the screen on, I see that it's 5:30 am. *Holy cracker balls. I must have been tired.*

No messages or texts from Mom, so that's good. I did talk with her and the kids between the first and second movies.

Clicking the phone off, I grab water from the fridge and immediately drain half the bottle. I don't remember the nightmare exactly but, it was enough to ensure I will most definitely *not* be going back to sleep any time soon.

I walk down to the bathroom and empty my bladder. Then, after washing my hands, I splash some of the cold water on my face and neck. This hoodie is suffocating me but I'm not willing to take it off, yet. I was braver with Vince than I thought I would be. So, there's that. I'm just not ready for the others to see. Especially Cory and Nick. Nothing against either of them but, like calls to like, and those two would probably not handle the macabre artwork slashed across my body.

Once I've cooled down a little, I make my way back to the living room and yelp as a dark figure steps out from the long hallway at the back of the living room. Nick's vibrant blue hair comes into view; hands up as if he's scared I may shoot. "Sorry, Siren. Was just coming to grab some water. I didn't know you were awake yet." His voice is just above a whisper but carries perfectly in the otherwise silent area.

Exhaling deeply, I smile at him. "Sorry. And, um, I'm sorry I fell asleep. I really was going to go home." Chewing on my bottom lip, I look over at him. The harsh shadows of the dim living room make him look like an edgy rock god. His lip piercing glints in the light and his lean upper body is on full display.

Where Vince is broad and muscular, *everywhere*, Jense has a sculpted upper body that tapers down to a trim waistline and powerful legs. Cory, on the other hand, is all lean, long muscles. Not super defined, but fit nonetheless. Similarly, Nick is all lean muscle but has a more definitive six-pack. His upper arms aren't as defined, but his forearms, *fuck me.* I can practically trace their protruding veins from all the way over here. Overall, he is beautiful. If that wasn't enough, tattoos are scattered across his chest and arms bringing that rock god image back to mind.

Clearing his throat, I realize that I am absolutely staring and it probably makes him uncomfortable. Squeezing my thighs together, I feel the wetness that has pooled there. I'm immediately thankful it's dark in here because I legitimately feel my face catch on fire.

Stepping towards me, his face forms a worried frown. His voice is low and soothing as he says, "It's ok, Siren. We don't mind that you fell asleep. Hell, it makes us feel good that you felt safe enough to do that."

Huh, I hadn't even thought about it like that.

I offer a shy smile, not knowing what else to say, then look around the room. I quickly realize that I'm trying not to make eye contact as I shift from foot to foot.

Tilting his head, he quietly assesses me. I can hear the questions running through his mind but, most of them I'm not ready to answer, yet.

"Can I show you something?" His voice startles me out of my meaningless perusal of the room. His eyes hold so much hope but, a flash of nervousness is what makes me realize this is something for him. This is him wanting to share with me. My heart flips knowing that Nick is generally a private person, minus the guys in this house, and he's offering to really, truly let me in.

My smile grows and I walk towards him. He holds his hand out to me, a silent question in his eyes; one that I immediately answer by sliding mine into his.

The smile he returns makes mine widen, almost to the point of pain. He gently squeezes my hand and turns to walk down the hall he had come from. I hadn't seen this side of the house but I do notice a home gym through one of the open doors.

At the end of the hall, is a door on the right. It looks like every other door in the house but he squeezes my hand and waits for me to meet his gaze. His brows are drawn down as he pulls on his lip ring. Reaching up, I gently tug it out, rubbing my finger on his lips. "Is this important to you?" He nods once. "Are you scared I'll run away?" Another single nod.

I smile gently and reach up on my toes to plant a firm kiss on his mouth. Leaning away, I assure him, "You stayed with me after finding out about my past. Then, you helped find me. You helped *save* me. And you've been here ever since. I'm not going anywhere, Nick. I want to know all of you." He looks a little concerned, like whatever is behind this door may really freak me out and it's scaring him.

Squeezing his hand once, I grin and try my best to bring out my playful side. "I'll show you mine if you show me yours."

He pauses for a second, his eyes widen, then he laughs out loud. "You did *not* just say that." Hearing his laugh is so pure, so joyful, so overwhelming, that I instantly vow that I will do anything to make this man laugh like that every day.

After a moment, his laugh simmers to a chuckle and I respond, "I did. And, I mean it. I have something you should see, too. So, now's as good a time as any, right?"

The adoration and understanding beam from his eyes and it feels like standing in sunshine. Breathing deeply he smiles, nods his head, then turns the knob.

My hands are sweating but I don't let that deter me. She's been through so much already and the last thing I want to do is make her uncomfortable. I also don't want to continue this relationship and then have her find out about my, *preferences,* and feel like she's trapped. I just want it all out there. For all of us.

And, I need to share my story. If she can be vulnerable, so can I.

Flicking the lights on, I take three steps into the room then stop. Head down, I wave her into the room, as nerves riot through my body. The red lights scattered through the room give it a dim, sexy vibe. There are no other lights but it's bright enough to see everything.

My heart rate has climbed to an uncomfortable level but I remind myself to take calming breaths as I see her step up beside me, then slowly move in front of me. Eventually, her hand slips out of mine as she walks further into the room.

I force myself to raise my head and watch as she takes in the room. The closest item to her is the bondage bench. She gently walks past it, running her fingers across the smooth leather. I see her snap her hand back so as not to touch the eyelets for the restraints.

Swallowing heavily, I begin to second guess whether or not this is a good idea. Before I have a chance to make a decision, I freeze as she wanders over to the St. Andrews cross. As she stands in front of it, her head just barely clears the horizontal beam that runs between the middle of the top of the cross' arms. Like most of the room, the X-shaped cross is made up of natural wood but covered with oil and wax; painted black, and polished smooth.

We ordered *this* cross because it included 6 softer pads on top of the hardwood of the X frame. The upholstery is made of high-quality, artificial leather with four-inch foam inserts. The middle of the X has a pad that stretches almost the length of a torso. Each arm, and leg, of the cross contains six-inch pads to rest against semi-comfortably. There's also a board that runs a few inches above the top v of the X. It connects to both arms and provides a four-inch wide cushion to rest your head. Additionally, the arms and legs all have soft, leather cuffs chained to them for easy access.

Her breath hitches when she sees the cuffs secured to the back. Unease ripples through me but I stay rooted to my spot by the door; waiting for her to run.

Backing away slowly, she turns and makes her way toward the California King, four-poster bed in the middle of the far wall. A black wooden headboard with red leather upholstery, in an intricately curved shape, spans the wall. Black wooden beams rise up on each corner, touching all the way to the wall. The beams are also connected by thick, black beams on each side; acting as a trim for the ridiculously large mirror looking down at the bed. Each of the four side beams has four eyelets, evenly spaced, running down them. Soft black bamboo sheets cover the bed along with a couple of king-sized pillows.

Annie's eyes haven't stopped their perusal as she takes in every tiny detail. Her face is completely impassive. I have no idea what on earth she's thinking. But, she hasn't run, or cried, so that's good I suppose.

I shift from one foot to the other, then slide my hands into the pockets of my basketball shorts. I pinch some of the polyester between my fingers, rubbing them together to try and keep myself from fidgeting outwardly. I don't want to startle her or rush her.

I track her movements as she makes her way to the wall on the left. Over half the wall is filled with black upper and lower cabinets. The lower cabinets are covered in stainless stop counters. Each end has an eyelet screwed into the counter for rope work. Thankfully, I religiously clean this place. Other than my computers, it's the only space where I'm as particular as Cory is.

I hear her fingers skim the surface before stopping in the middle. Pausing, she turns to me and quirks her brow, nodding towards the cabinet.

"We have nothing to hide. Please," I tip my chin to the cabinets, giving her the permission she was seeking. Chewing on her lip she regards me, silently seeking answers that I'm more than willing to share. With a small grin, I silently assure her that it's her decision, and hold my breath as she turns back around.

Opening the cabinets directly at her eye level, I hear her sharp inhale. Clenching my hands into fists, I dig my blunt nails into my skin, forcing myself to stay right where I am.

Slowly, Annie reaches her hand up and delicately runs her hands down the various paddles and floggers in that particular cabinet. *Fuck, there's no way she's going to accept me and Vince. Not after what she's been through.*

After a moment, she quietly closes the doors. Taking a few steps past a couple of sets of cabinets, she randomly opens another. Her brows pinch in confusion as she rises on her toes, reaches her arm in, and pulls out a purple silicone butt plug. My eyes bug right out of my head. I'm not sure why, this is who I am; unapologetically so. But seeing her soft hands roll it around, looking at it from every angle like she might be... interested, *maybe*, is a *totally* different feeling.

My cock hardens in my pants which is really the last thing she needs. I was doing so well as she perused my space, my solace. But one damn buttplug...

She turns to me and it's my turn to suck in a breath. In the glow of the red light, her eyes sparkle in the most bewitching manner. Her grin is playful as she tilts her head, shakes the plug around a little, and says, "You or Vince?" Her voice lights me up inside and the bluntness of her question collides with the actual point of this little trip.

A self-deprecating chuckle tumbles from my mouth and I rub the back of my neck, briefly avoiding her gaze. I can feel my face heat with embarrassment but, not shame. Never shame. This is who we are; she needs to know that.

"Usually me but, every now and then, Vince," I answer. She hums in response and gently places the plug back on the shelf, then closes the cabinets.

Walking closer to me, she comes to a stop at the small black table that holds the Bluetooth speaker on it.

"Do you want to dance?" My eyes widen as I realize, *I* fucking said that. Her head snaps towards me, likely shocked by the random question. *Jesus, Nick. Get it together.*

Before I can even try to backtrack or play it off as a joke, her face transforms as she smiles wide. Nibbling on her lip, she considers me, dips her head, then shyly asks, "Music or no music?"

"I have music." To my horror, I realize that my voice has rudely decided to play the puberty card. Brushing off the embarrassment, I quickly pull out my phone and randomly click on one of the Playroom playlists. Turning on the speaker, I push play on the first song, slide the phone into my pocket, and hold my hand out to her.

The first notes fill the room as Can I Be Him by James Arthur begins. It's loud enough that we can move to the middle of the room and still hear, but not so loud that it should wake the others. It's not even remotely a dancing song but, I don't care. With her eyes consuming mine as I rest my hands on her hips, I refuse to take even a second away to change the song. Besides, it kind of feels like it's saying all the things I'm currently feeling.

Her arms slide around my neck and I move close enough that our chests brush. We don't grind, we don't two-step; we sway. Like junior high dance, sway. And it's fucking perfect.

Her eyes never leave mine and I swear I could dive right in and swim the depths of them. Up close she looks every bit the angel that Vince calls her. I tentatively slide my left arm from her hip to her lower back. She doesn't even react other than to swallow. Her eyes continue to bore into mine; searching, flying, falling. And dammit do I want to fall with her. *I think I already have.*

By the third chorus, we're completely entranced by each other, reveling in this little bubble we've created. I bring my right hand up, caressing her cheek softly. She closes her eyes, leans into my hand, and sighs. A lone tear rolls down her cheek and I wipe it away with my thumb.

"What's wrong, Siren?" I whisper, just loud enough to be heard over the song.

Inhaling deeply, she opens her eyes; shining with a buildup of tears she's trying to fight off. "What if I'm not enough?"

I barely hear her but it still hits me like a punch to the gut. "Why would you say that? You. Are. Everything." My brows furrow as I try my damndest to see what's going on in that head of hers.

Taking out my phone, I turn off the music, immediately thrusting us back into silence. "Talk to me, Annie. Whatever it is. Just, don't hold it in."

Chewing on her lip, she darts her gaze around the room. "I don't think I can like all the same things y'all do." A few more tears escape as she shakes her head lightly.

Bringing both hands to her face I smile and wipe her tears away. "Oh, baby. You don't have to. Vince likes some things, I like others.

I'm sure Jense and Cory have their own kinks. I'm not asking you to like everything we do. It's not why I wanted to show you this room."

Her brows raise and her eyes widen. "It isn't?"

Chuckling at how fucking adorable she is a shake my head slowly. "No, Siren. I didn't want any surprises for you later. I wanted you to know me, us, and not be scared or worried. We would never, ever, ask you to do anything you don't want to." Her brows lower a fracture but pinch slightly like she's not totally sure she believes that.

"Ok, for instance, I like a little pain, *sometimes*. Paddle, flogger; *not* canes. And Vince knows just the right amount of pressure to have me straddling the line of pain and pleasure. However, Vince isn't a masochist. He's a sadist, for *me*, but that's because it pleases me."

Nodding her head she worries her lip as she works through the information.

"So, he's a top and you're a bottom." Rolling my head back and forth I don't really commit. "I'm a switch. I like to be a top with women, but I'm a bottom for Vince. 99% of the time, that is."

"Okay."

... that's it. She adds nothing, barely even blinks.

"Okay, what?" I ask, trying to figure out if *now's* the time she's going to bolt.

"Okay... so, like at the club, there are hard and soft limits. I've, um, looked into BDSM quite a bit but, you know, never..."

She trails off and shrugs like a little kid. Smiling wide, I put my pointer under her chin and lift until she meets my eyes. "Yes and no. Yes, these are conversations that will be had if you ever want to explore this. No, we don't have to. Ever. I just wanted you to know that sometimes, we like to take things out of the bedroom and explore other things. Not always, really not even weekly, but it does happen. And if the time comes and you want to watch, experiment, whatever, it's here. If not, you never have to walk into this room again."

Time seems to stand still as she considers my words, chewing them over, and processing them individually. Leaning up on her toes, she brushes a kiss to my mouth and whispers, "Thank you for showing me and for trusting me with this."

Taking a step back I blink back my shock as she smiles up at me. She holds her hand out for me and I take it, locking our fingers together. "Okay," I say.

"Okay." She repeats with a giggle.

Then we walk back out of the room; flicking off the light, before shutting the door.

27

Annie

Nick and I left the playroom and snuggled back onto the couch. He had spread his legs along the chaise part of the sectional and pulled me to snuggle right up against him. It took me a couple of minutes to fully relax after he pulled my head to lie on his chest, as he wrapped his arm around me and ran his fingers through my hair. Eventually, my muscles loosened and I cuddled further into his side, laying my arm across his stomach and resting a leg over his.

I'm not sure how long we've been here because my mind has been looping the images of the playroom the whole time. And, if I was honest with myself, I was kind of intrigued. I definitely don't want to be hit, or handcuffed, but I did like it when Vince swatted my ass. And, the thought of watching the two of them together had my panties dampening.

Shifting subtly, I realize just how naughty my thoughts turned. My panties are not damp; they are straight-soaked.

A throat clearing behind me has me almost falling off the couch. "I got you, Siren," Nick assures me as he pulls me closer.

"Sorry, Annie." Cory's sleepy voice comes up just behind me so I carefully extract myself from Nick's body and turn around to face him.

"Go away. *My* snuggles." Nick complains petulantly as he maneuvers his own body to stretch out behind mine and pulls my back into his front. One arm is behind my head while the other rests on my hip.

I smile and my chest bounces with a barely suppressed giggle. Cory smiles wide, even though his eyes are still weighed down by sleep. He looks so different in the morning. He's relaxed, comfortable, like he hasn't placed all of the burdens of the world on his shoulders, yet. His navy blue shirt hugs his torso and shows off the lean muscles in his upper and lower arms. He's also in a pair of red sweatpants that hug his package.

His semi-hard package.

His semi-hard package that is slowly growing harder.

I squeeze my eyes shut as he walks towards me. I feel his presence in front of me and my face lights on fire. At least that's what it feels like.

"Good Morning, Pretty Girl." His warm breath holds a hint of mintiness as it passes over my face.

"Morning," I squeak out. His chuckle scatters butterflies through my chest and I feel myself getting impossibly redder.

His smooth lips kiss my temple before his warmth vanishes. Opening my eyes, I see that he has taken a few steps back and is assessing me quietly with a smug-as-hell grin.

"Coffee?" He asks. "Yes," Nick and I pipe up simultaneously.

With a final wink, Cory strides towards the kitchen.

Nick's contented sigh and little nuzzle into the back of my shoulder reminds me of something. Quietly I rasp out, "I know I still owe you the "show you mine" portion but, if you don't mind, I really need to wait for everyone. It's..." I trail off and sigh heavily. Barely above a whisper, I admit, "It's something you should all know and I don't know if I have it in me to do it more than once if it ends up as bad as I-"

I'm silenced by Nick's finger held to my lips. "OK, Annie. Whatever you need." His satisfied sigh as he moves his hand away and settles it back on my hip cuts off any additional argument I may have had.

I force myself to settle into his embrace and I take this time to savor the connection; just in case it's the last one I get after my reveal. The scent of fresh coffee fills the air and I hum out a little moan and wiggle happily. Nick's hand immediately squeezes my hip, halting my movements. "Sorry," I whisper.

"Don't be." He grunts near my ear. "But if you keep doing that, I'm going to have to leave this snuggle party to go take a shower." My body goes still as confusion flusters me.

A few seconds later, I begin to sit up; relieving him of snuggle duty since I have apparently made him uncomfortable. However, his arms tug me back to him before I can make it far. "Whatever you're thinking, it's wrong. I want you *right* here. But, every time you move, well, let's just say that having you in my arms, pressed up against my body is doing things I really can't control."

Again, confusion. *What the hell is he...Oh. OH!*

Rolling in his arms, I come face-to-face with Nick. I need to see if he's full of shit or just wants to make me feel better. His lips curl into a grin and he licks his bottom lip, pulling his ring into his mouth. Letting it go, his brows pinch in the middle as he leans his head back a little to study me. "Please don't tell me you really believe that having your soft, warm body snuggled anywhere near me doesn't get me hard."

Rolling my eyes, I lightly shake my head. "You don't have to pretend but you're sweet for wanting to make me feel good."

Something erupts from his chest; a half growl, half groan. Removing his arm draped across my back, he takes my hand in his, locks our gazes, and quirks his brow. Before I can decipher the look in his eyes, he's pulling my hand down between our bodies and turning my hand to palm his *very* hard erection. A hiss leaves his gritted teeth as I gasp leaves mine.

Pulling his hand away from mine, he brings it up to move some of my stray hair behind my ear. "Never underestimate the power you hold over us, Siren. I am *always* aching for you." He leans forward and gives me the sweetest fucking kiss. My whole body erupts in goosebumps.

But, all too soon, he breaks the kiss and smiles sweetly. "Coffee's ready," he whispers. I'm absolutely frozen in a plane of disbelief and undeniable longing.

He takes an exaggerated glance down between our bodies and I'm instantly flooded with embarrassment as I realize that my hand is still cupping his cock. *Oh, please kill me now.* I release his hard bulge so fast that I hit myself in the stomach.

He chuckles good-heartedly before kissing my nose. "Coffee?"

Imitating a bobblehead, I quickly begin to extract myself from his warm body and hurriedly shuffle to the kitchen where Cory is pouring coffee into 5 mugs. "Are the others awake, too?"

Cory turns around and I have to force myself to look at his eyes. Just his eyes. Only his eyes. Because if I let my gaze travel... *no, bad Annie.*

Cory's returning smile reveals his damn dimples and his eyes shine with a sense of understanding. *Too much understanding if you ask me.* Thankfully, he doesn't comment on my current inner turmoil.

"Vince's alarm should be going off soon. He and Jense usually grab coffee and head out for runs when they're both home in the morning."

Nodding, I take the mug he offers me and inhale the decadent life-saving beverage. Nick rounds the island, opens the fridge, and takes out three different creamers.

"If you need a different one, just let us know and we can make sure it's here." He says casually. Like, me being here in the morning is as normal as the sun rising.

"No, they're fine. I'm not picky." He smiles and nods as he accepts the coffee from Cory.

I stir in a couple of spoonfuls of sugar-free Vanilla and call it good. The first taste hits my mouth and I moan out. The warmth of the coffee mixed with the subtle sweetness of the vanilla is like a balm to my exhausted soul.

Cory groans, causing me to lift my head towards him as he grips his mug like he might break it. Meanwhile, Nick drops his head to the cabinet in front of him with a dull thud. "What?" I ask.

Nick straightens and turns to face me. "Remember the talk we just had on the couch?" My ears and face heat and I swallow another gulp of coffee.

"Well, hearing you make those sweet little sounds has the same effect. On each and every one of us. Always has."

It takes a minute for my brain to follow the proverbial cookie crumbs but, once I find the candy house, I get it. My mouth drops into an 'o' shape and my brows climb to my hair. But, for some reason, I get stuck on one word. "*Always*?" I know the meaning, but I don't think I moan that much.

"Always, what?" Jenson's voice comes from behind me. I jump out of my skin, causing the coffee to slosh over my arm. Hissing through the burn, I start apologizing as I run to the counter and grab the roll of paper towels. My eyes burn with tears. Shame, embarrassment, and a little bit of fear, all fight for dominance as I mop up the caramel-colored liquid.

"Annie. Annie, stop!" I don't know who's saying it but my fight, flight, or freeze kicks in as flashbacks of Lukas handing me my ass whenever I made a mess filter through my mind.

I fight against the person's hold, barely feeling the tears now streaming down my face. "I'm sorry. I'm so, so sorry. I'll clean it. I promise."

Something warm and solid covers me from the front and the back, as something else very cold and very wet jolts me out of my swirling panic; but I'm still flirting with the line of past and present.

"...keep pressure on her front and back but don't prevent her head from being able to move." I hear a voice, calming, reassuring, sweet. "Ask her to do the count."

Count? What count?

Big warm hands run down my sides, arms, and thighs. A smooth and smokey voice filters through the haze from behind me. Calm, anchoring, kind of sexy. "Annie, tell me five things you see." Shaking my head I fight to claw my way back to the voices. I like them.

With a squeeze of my arms, a little more of the fog clears and he says again, "Five things you can see."

I dart my eyes around as my vision starts to clear. "Raven tattoo, skin, nipple ring..." swallowing around a lump in my throat, my gaze travels up. I slowly study the man in front of me before whispering, "You have a nice smile."

My voice has taken on a soft, wondrous quality but, can he blame me? He's stunning to look at. I tentatively reach up and rub the spot between his brows. "Don't scowl. You're too sexy to be all scowly." His rich chuckle vibrates through my body and I realize the person behind me is chuckling, as well.

Blinking a few more times, I come out of my panic-induced haze and take in the rest of my surroundings. Jenson's very naked, very sexy chest is pressed up against mine; his hands running a path up and down my hips and thighs. Turning my head behind me a little, I see Cory; worry reflecting behind his glasses. A stinging sensation pulls my head to look on the other side and Nick is rubbing some kind of ointment on my inflamed skin. His face is twisted in concentration and he's so focused on taking care of me. *Woah.*

Clearing my throat, I rasp out, "Sorry," feeling sheepish and a little overwhelmed.

Jenson takes his hands from my hips and places them on my cheeks. In a low tone, a smile tips his lip as he says, "Don't be. Accidents happen. We were more worried about your burn than a little coffee. Coffee's replaceable, you're not."

I feel as much as I can see the tears fill my eyes. His expression is so open and sincere that it causes me to feel first, think later. Reaching on my toes, I close the distance between us and seal his mouth in a kiss. I'm vaguely aware that Nick is still holding my hand, although he's not rubbing anything on my arm anymore, and Cory is still pressed up against me; hands now roaming my sides and hips.

Jenson pushes the kiss further by sliding his tongue against my lips, silently requesting access. Once I open for him, there is no more request, just pure heat and need and control. Letting go of my face, he runs one hand through my hair, fisting it into a loose ponytail while wrapping the other gently across the front of my neck. My entire body floods with desire as we straddle the lines between rough and gentle, demanding and requesting, dominance and submission.

With another stroke of his tongue and a kiss on my nose, Jense releases me and steps back. The visceral shock of his retreating warmth, and the knowledge that he isn't going further, causes me to actually whimper out. All three stupidly attractive, panty-ruining men chuckle around me.

I open my eyes and pout like a brat. "That's so not nice," I whine playfully.

Jense leans in, barely brushes a kiss to my lips then whispers, "Soon, Sweetness." Once he steps back, Nick brings my attention to him as he steps up next to me. "We have all the time in the world. No rush, Siren. And we still have some things to discuss." He gives me a pointed look, forcing me to nod my agreement, then kisses my hand like he's some British gent. I can't help it, I giggle. And the grin I'm rewarded tells me that's exactly what he was hoping for.

Once he retreats, Cory uses my hips to turn me to face him. His damn dimples are out; not played up in a huge smile, but subtle with a careful grin. Squeezing my hips, he dips his mouth towards my ear and says, "Don't worry, Pretty Girl. We will give you whatever you want. But, we know some things need to be discussed first. But don't think for one second we aren't all aching desperately to strip you down and have our wicked way with you." His tone is sweet and teasing, as is the glint in his eyes before he kisses my cheek. But my body freezes at the thought of them stripping me down and seeing, well, anything and everything. *Fuck. They're right. I need to just get it over with so I can go home and take care of this little horny problem myself. If I even can.* Nodding my head at all of them, I plaster on the best fake smile I can muster.

Then, I fucking chicken out. "You're right. Sorry, I didn't sleep great. Oh, and sorry for falling asleep. Let me just go grab my phone and I can call a rideshare. I'll be out of your hair. I really, really don't make a habit of imposing. And, thanks for the coffee." I snatch the wad of paper towels off the counter, making sure the mess has been soaked up. Keeping the momentum, I launch it into the trash as I head away from the guys to the far right counter near the dining room. Swiping my purse and my phone, I hurriedly blow them all a kiss, thank them for a fun night, and walk out of the kitchen furthest away from them. Darting through the living room, I open my phone and swipe through the apps. I don't do rideshare. EVER. I'm way too rigid and cautious but, I don't have a choice right now.

Finding one that seems popular, I click on it so it can download. I'm almost through the foyer when I crash into a fucking wall. No, not a wall. A Vince. *Fuck. He must have just come down the stairs.*

With both hands on my shoulders, he steadies me as he chuckles. "Woah, there Angel. You okay?" His southern drawl is particularly tasty this morning and... *holy gumballs!* He's shirtless and wearing a pair of blue basketball shorts. *Why are they all half-naked? Are they trying to kill me?*

Tamping down the whore that now lives in my vagina, I plaster a smile on. "Morning. Yeah. I'm fine. Just didn't mean to fall asleep 'cause, you know, but anyway, I'll let you guys get on with your day. Bye!" I make a move to pass him for the door but his hands don't retreat from their spot on my shoulders. Chancing a look up at him through my lashes, I see that his beautiful whiskey-colored eyes look stormy and irritated. I immediately feel myself recoil from the intensity and suck in a sharp gasp.

Blinking a few times, his body relaxes, and the storm in his eyes fades into more of an overcast, but his brows pinch in worry. "What happened? And how are you getting home?"

Pulling on my carefully curated mask of acceptance and sweetness, and throwing in a spark of sass to throw off his scent, I reply, "Nothing happened." I scoff at him like he's being silly. "I just didn't mean to fall asleep and you all have lives to get to. Besides, I need to feed Reginald. So, have a good day, and text me later." I sweeten the deal by rising on my toes like a sweet little girlfriend and pecking his lips before moving around him. This time, he lets me go. Opening the door, I quickly slip out, looking into the house once more to find the other three are standing behind Vince looking as dumbstruck as he does.

"Bye, guys." And with that, I close the door and fly down the driveway.

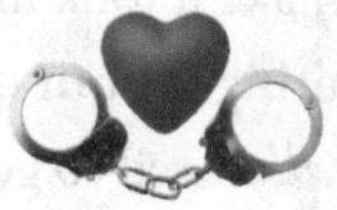

The whirlwind that is Annie flew in and out of the foyer like a dust devil. I stand there, completely perplexed, and stare at the front door. The closed front door.

"We should…" Jenson doesn't even finish the rest of his sentence before Cory blows past me; flinging the door open, and jumping off the porch. "Annie!" His voice travels through the almost closed door, effectively bringing the rest of us out of our own stupor.

Rushing the door, we file outside and catch a glimpse of Cory turning right at the end of the drive. Rushing after him, we hit the end of the driveway and stumble into each other as we see Cory two houses down, wrapping his arms around Annie. Looking at the other two, we all shrug like we're not sure whether we should stay put or follow after them. When he leans down to say something to her, she shakes her head, then nods it, and then laughs. The breeze carries her laughter towards us and forces some of the tension to drain.

I can't see her face clearly but her body language suggests she's embarrassed or nervous about something. Especially since she can't seem to stop shifting from foot to foot.

Eventually, her shoulders droop and she nods at whatever Cory says. I look at the others and nod my head back to the house in a silent order for them to follow; which they do.

Once inside, I turn to them and say, "What the hell did I miss?" Nick and Jense look at each other and subtly request we head to the kitchen.

In the time it takes them to explain the good, and bad, parts of the morning, Cory and Annie walk back through the door. "I don't mind getting a rideshare." Her voice drifts down the foyer to us and we abruptly break apart to make it look like we aren't standing around like "good boys" waiting for our owner to return.

"Don't be silly. If you *really* need to go home, one of us will take you. You don't need to get into some stranger's car at 6:30 in the morning." As she steps into the kitchen, she rolls her eyes as if she's exasperated by his concern.

I turn my body towards her, resting my back on the edge of the island, and smile. "I can take you, Angel. But, you don't have to go if you don't want to. We really were hoping you'd spend the day with us."

Gnawing at her lip, she considers each of us before sighing out an irritated huff. I just can't tell if she's irritated with us or herself.

"I do need a change of clothes. And I need to feed Reginald. But, if you want to hang out, I can do that. As long as I'm not imposing." She threw the last part out with her eyes narrowed in warning.

"You could never impose, Angel," I say as I step closer to her with a wink. She rolls her eyes but I catch the grin on her face.

"And..." Cory pauses as he walks around to the other side of the island. "We promised a talk." He cocks his head at her and I can see his planning brain working in overdrive. It causes me to look back at her and I see the subtle changes in her body. Her face reddens, her shoulders hitch up, and her face drops into a mask. One I've seen her wear way too often.

"How about we order some bagels and we can talk? Then, we can plan what we want to do today?" I say as I bounce my eyes to the others. With nods, I turn back to look at her, hoping that my excitement is noticeable.

"Okay." She slightly nods her head and looks at each of us before stepping back. "Living room?"

Once we're all situated around the living room in our normal seats, Annie begins to fidget. I can see how hot she's getting under her hoodie but I don't want to call it out. Not yet anyway.

With a deep inhale, and a rough exhale, she curls her legs up under her, grabs the hems of her sweatshirt with her hands, and pulls the frilly pillow she likes to mess with into her lap.

"So..." she begins slowly. I can see her working out her words and fighting off her demons as she pulls on the edges of the pillow. "I saw the playroom."

I don't know what I was expecting but *that* wasn't it. Swallowing around a giant ass boulder that has now formed in my throat, I lean forward and brace my elbows on my knees. "And you know that you never have to go in there. But, if you do, you never have to participate in anything," I hedge cautiously.

Nodding her head, she absently picks at the pillow. "Nick mentioned that." She sighs again and brings her gaze directly to mine. A whole conversation passes through us and I finally understand what set her off. What this whole thing is about.

I feel my face soften as I tilt my head just a little and give her, what I hope, is an encouraging smile. She studies my face, and my unspoken words, for a moment before a tiny grin pulls at her lips.

"I'll show you mine if you'll show me yours." Nick's voice brings us out of our conversation and I can't help the scowl that rearranges my face; or the growl that rises up. Before I can ask him what the hell he's doing, Annie bursts into a fit of giggles.

Nick sends me a smug grin and a wink. I'm glad that was her reaction because I for damn sure have never heard Nick talk like that. But, I guess it means something to her as she nods while trying to contain her laughter.

I look over to see Jense and Cory equally perplexed so it's clearly a her and Nick thing.

Suddenly, Cory leans forward and shocks the hell out of us when he says, "How about we talk about how our last relationship ended? It may help with anything you want to share. Or it won't. But, at least you'll have all the information."

We all freeze. Cory NEVER talks about Amber. Her arraignment, her trial, her sentencing; not one time did he want to talk except to relay the exact facts when asked by police or lawyers.

Cory's gaze moves over to Nick and I follow. He's frozen in fear and awfully pale. While Amber was truly a psycho bitch, Cory and Nick got the worst of it. So, this is their story to tell.

I hesitantly slide my hand onto his thigh and wait for him to meet my eye. His eyes are already glazed with memories, and not just the ones from that night. He gives me a barely perceptible nod before closing his eyes and inhaling deeply.

"Coffee?" I ask quietly. His answer is a squeeze of my hand.

As I stand up, Jense follows hot on my heels to help. I kind of wish we were heavier drinkers because this conversation absolutely calls for something stronger. But, maybe this needs to happen right now. Maybe this will be the thing that pushes all three of them to heal and form something breathtakingly beautiful out of the shattered glass. At least, that's what I hope.

28

Annie

The atmosphere is thick with tension and so many feelings that it's almost suffocating. I've been so blinded, so fucking selfish by my own past that I never once bothered asking about theirs. I mean, we've talked a *lot,* but it's been about present-day things. I always assumed they didn't want to bring up the past because, well, who does?

After Jense and Vince came back with coffees, I pointedly ignored mine and sat it on the floor because no way was I embarrassing myself again.

Nick started our group's walk down the trail of horrors by telling me about his mother. *Pfft. Fucking* mother. *Egg Donor and Piece of Shit is more like it.*

Angry tears rolled down my face as he gave me a condensed, but no less disturbing, overview of what he went through for the first 14 years of his life. I was so disgusted but I also wanted to make sure he was aware the disgust wasn't aimed at him. Who the hell drugs and sells their kids to pervs? They all laughed about my quiet comment hoping that karma had kicked her ass. I never admitted aloud that I wasn't kidding.

When we lapsed into silence, I made my way over and waited to see if I could touch him, hold his hand, anything. He ended up pulling me down and curling me into his side. With his arm firmly around me, my head resting on his chest, he shared his recollection of their time with Amber; glossing over the two years they spent together and focusing on the pieces he remembers of the last night.

My stomach had revolted in the middle of his story, causing me to take an emergency bathroom break. Much to my embarrassment, Vince doted on me even though I tried pushing him off, insisting that Nick and Cory were the ones who needed attention. Not that it did me any good.

A cold cloth, a couple of swigs of Pepto, and half a bottle of water later, we're making our way back to the couch. But, when I moved to sit next to Nick, he shook his head softly, grinned solemnly, then kissed my knuckles. Pulling me forward, he whispered, "Cory's going to need you for this next part."

I felt the blood drain from my face and tears already formed in my eyes. I took my spot next to Cory, resting my head on his shoulder as he told me his part in the story. Since Amber had drugged, and raped, Nick, he didn't have the actual memory of how she was caught. Nope, that fell on Cory. Catching his girl raping one of his best friends had to have been truly terrifying. But, to have her stab him, twice?! Yeah, I now had two people I wanted to pummel into the ground.

The only good news was that Amber was a complete idiot and had used her credit card to check in to a hotel near Dallas. Once they caught up to her, the police had uncovered that she had been wanted in connection with a dozen other cases, under multiple identities. All the charges stacked up and they threw the book at her.

Cory chuckled as I checked over his scars as if they had just happened but I needed to see. I was fuming but relieved they were all still living. Still, I wanted to find her and punch her. *Hopefully, someone had made her their bitch.*

It's well past 9:00 and I've single-handedly gone through half a box of tissues. Apparently the guys think I'm cute or something because they all keep grinning at me and chuckling.

Cory chortles as I run my fingers over one of his scars. It's only a few inches but the raised skin puts me in a trance as I think of what mine feel like. "Really, Pretty Girl, I'm fine." He says in a low voice, rubbing his hand down my arm. Unfortunately, it doesn't pull me out of my mind. He looks so good and his scars are a little, dare I say, sexy. But the story still pisses me off. It fills me with a rage that I'm not sure I have ever felt; except during the time I was captive.

I feel tears begin to fill my eyes, again, but this time, it's not about the awful things they went through. Nope, my mind goes the selfish route and I start pondering how they will feel about my body. Not just the fact that I'm big, or extra curvy, but I have huge, hideous, uneven scars. Thick pink, puckered scars. Scars made by hot steel pressed into my skin. Scars that spell out a disgusting word; making me feel even less desirable than I had before.

A warm hand gripping my knee jolts me out of my self-pity. Vince's soulful eyes are searching mine, shining with understanding. I smile at him, hoping to hide my current thoughts. But, I should have known better. His hand reaches up to wipe away a stream of tears, momentarily causing a gap in the waterfall. "You don't have to if you're not ready." His voice is soft but deep, causing my body to warm.

Cory's arm is still draped over my shoulders, his hand rubbing soothing circles on my arm as I lean into him. "He's right. Just because we were ready, doesn't mean you have to be. I'm just glad you're here." He says, leaning his head down and placing his lips on my head for a kiss.

I cast a glance over to Jenson, leaning back in *my* chair, arms casually folded across his chest and legs spread like he doesn't have a care in the world. But, even across the room, I can see the worry in his eyes. But, not just for me. Every now and then his gaze dips to Cory's stomach and I see his jaw clench ever so minutely.

Looking over to Nick, he's resting his head on the far arm of the couch where Vince had previously sat. After I moved to sit with Cory, Vince maneuvered Nick to lie down in his lap. While I curled up with Cory, Vince ran his hand lovingly through Nick's hair but, I'm pretty sure it was equally a comfort for Nick as it was for him.

Feeling all of their gazes on me begins to suffocate me and I slowly start to overheat. Clearing my throat, I go to sit up. Cory's hand squeezes my shoulder once before allowing me to slip out from underneath him completely.

I unfold my legs and go to stand up. Vince makes a move to stand, as well, but I catch his face first, feeling the gentle scratch of his beard under my palm. Leaning in, I kiss him briefly. He moves to hold on to me but I retreat before he can. "I *have* to do this," I whisper and stand before he has the chance to offer a rebuttal. He stands from his squatting position, towering over me in a way that is both comforting and a little overwhelming. He grins down on me, presses a kiss to my cheek, and slowly backs up to claim his spot back on the couch.

My heart plays a pretty mean drum solo in my chest as I slowly make my way to the center of the living room. Fire and ice burn through my body as I tremble. Chewing on my lip, I look at each of my guys in turn. Silence stretches out between us as I take in every detail from the color and shape of their eyes, their lean, trimmed, beautiful bodies, even the twitch of each of their fingers or jaw; desperately needing to soak up this exact moment.

The moment before they decide to just be friends.

The moment before they see my imperfections.

The moment before they realize that they deserve so much better than me.

I stare at the wall behind the couch, unable to meet anyone's gaze, as I prepare to put myself on display; inside and outside. I can feel the tears begin to fall but don't acknowledge them. My whole body trembles with fear, and extreme sadness, as all the worst scenarios play out in my head. Sucking in my cheeks, I bite down, hard, and move my hands down to the hem of my hoodie.

Slamming my eyes shut, I grasp the hem of my hoodie and dig my nails into the fabric. Thankfully, other than the water I drank, my stomach is already empty. The way it cramped and curled told me that lightning bugs were participating in a full-ass mosh pit in there. Swallowing a lump of air, I shift from one foot to another.

"Do you want help, Angel?" Vince's raspy whisper comes up from behind me, causing me to yelp in surprise. His big, warm hands provide gentle pressure on top of my shoulders as he patiently waits for me to control my breathing.

After a couple of deep breaths, some of the trembling has subsided, but not all. "I can help, Angel. Remember, we've already done this. I already know, and I told you, you're perfect. So, if you want my help, I can help. Whatever you need, Annie."

I don't open my eyes to see if the others are looking because I just can't bear to see their reactions, yet. With a less-than-obvious nod, I acquiesce to his request for help.

"Words, Angel. Be a good girl and use your words." His use of "good girl" causes something in my psyche to break; in the best way. The demanding tone he uses sends electric shocks through my body as images of him between my legs flash through my mind. His warm breath skates over my ear, just before he nips at my lobe. Warm hands slowly move from my shoulders, down my arms, then grasp the bottom of my hoodie.

"Please." It's not much, but it's all I can get out.

With a single kiss to the side of my neck, Vince whispers, "You got it, Angel. Remember your safeword?"

I nod then quickly remember, "Yes. Red." I whisper out.

"Good girl." He responds huskily, causing a wave of lust to ram into the fear.

Screwing my eyes tighter, I fist my hands, digging the nails into the fleshy part of my palms, and try to stand completely still. A stuttered breath is sucked through my nose as I prepare for him to move.

Finally, he begins to lift my hoodie, taking my shirt with it like he did yesterday. Once he moves halfway up my ribcage, I suck in a breath, feeling the cool air hitting my lower belly. "Lift, baby."

I don't know why, but I immediately lift my arms above my head. It's like my body subconsciously yearns to obey this man at all costs.

I hear a gasp, somewhere, and maybe a hiss, as Vince pulls the hoodie and shirt up and off over my head. My hair swishes down, brushing against the top of my back, and causes goosebumps to erupt everywhere.

The telltale thunk of clothing hitting the ground somewhere behind me startles me back to the very real situation I have found myself in. Anxiety rushes through my body and I begin to shiver with an overwhelming need to cover back up. Just as I have that thought, my arms begin to rise so I can cover myself.

"Ah, ah, ah, Angel." Vince tsks playfully. His hands find their way down my arms again, clasping my hands in his as he slowly pulls them behind my back. I flinch in fear of being restrained before he pauses, "Just hold onto my belt, baby. Don't move."

With shaky hands, I open my fingers and close them around his belt, very aware of how this position pushes my breasts forward. "Good girl." He whispers, causing another whimper. *This man is turning my brain to mush.*

I feel his beard on my neck just before he kisses down the column of my throat. I move my neck to the side, giving him more access. One of his strong hands wraps gently across my throat while the other gingerly runs a finger down my collarbone, dipping to trace the curve of my breast, before traveling down and flicking the butterfly of my belly ring.

His hand travels a little lower, landing on top of the button on my black jeans, and flicks it open without preamble. Before I have a moment to breathe again, the zipper is pulled down swiftly; the sound loudly filling the still silence.

My whole body tenses and my hands tighten on his belt. This time, when I whimper, I hang my head down in defeat and resignation. "Breathe, Angel. It's just us. And my God you're beautiful, baby. Let them see how beautiful you are." He presses gentle kisses on my neck, sucking a patch of skin, before licking away the sting. It's just enough to distract me as he releases the hand from my neck and moves it to the top of my jeans. "Hands up baby, just for a second."

Obeying immediately, I raise my hands. I immediately miss the warmth at my back as he uses both hands to roll my jeans down my legs, pressing gentle kisses to the side of my thigh, and down my calf. Tapping my ankle twice, I raise my foot up, allowing him to remove the jeans before raising my other foot.

The A/C cools my overheated body and causes me to shiver. His big, warm hands grasp the outsides of my ankles and leisurely make their way up; ensuring a gentle caress of both ass cheeks, before resting on my hips. "Belt, Angel." He orders. And I obey without complaint.

For a moment not a damn sound is made. Even with Vince's warmth behind me and on my hips, I can't help but feel way too fucking exposed. Way too raw. Way too vulnerable.

My head dips, again, as a few tears escape my closed eyes. "Angel. Open your eyes." I'm shaking my head before he even finishes his command. His right hand leaves my hip and swiftly *waps* my ass cheek; then rubs over the sting causing me to flush with heat.

"Angel, open your eyes and see what I see." He says with a little nip to my neck.

"I can't," I whisper through tears.

"Do you remember what I said, Angel? What I *did*?" I squeeze my thighs together thinking about him tracing the scars with his tongue before using that same tongue in my most intimate parts.

"Yes," I rasp.

"Good. Now open your eyes, baby. See how they're looking at you. How bad they want you." Confusion wars with uncertainty as I process his words. Until curiosity wins out.

Peeking through my lashes, my eyes land on Cory first. His fists are clenched on top of his spread knees, he's leaning back like he's holding himself back from doing or saying something. His eyes though, his eyes are burning with fire. The intensity behind his glasses threatens to burn me alive. Quickly, I divert my gaze for fear that I will do something stupid. Then, I make the mistake of landing on the tent in his pants. *Oh, holy crackers.* My mouth opens in surprise and I suck in a gasp.

"He can barely contain himself, Angel. Cory is always prepared, organized, and controlled. But one look at you and he's completely unraveling." As Vince speaks into my neck, he tenderly traces a path up each side of my body, eliciting more shivers to erupt.

"Look over here at Jenson. He's two seconds from falling to his knees in front of you. *You* do that, Angel. Only you." Turning my head to my left, I see Jenson, still sprawled out in the oversized chair, rubbing his thumb across his lip as his gaze sears across every available inch of my body. His long brown hair is free, hanging in waves and resting just over his shoulders. His Adam's apple bobbing brings my attention back to his eyes and the emerald quality has turned darker, hungrier. He squirms in his seat, causing me to glance at his sweatpants and the very hard bulge straining to be set free.

I feel liquid heat pool between my legs and I whimper as Vince takes my breasts in his hands, slowly massaging them. "Vince" I plead as my head drops back, resting on his chest.

"Yes, Angel. What do you want? Do you want to see how Nick sees you? Do you want to see what watching me run my hands over your naked body is doing to him?"

Squirming again, I lift my head, dazed and feeling like I'm floating. My eyes meet Nick's scorching gaze, and I officially turn into a puddle on the floor. His blue hair is a hot mess, likely from Vince running his hands through it. He's sucking on his lip ring, biting on it, then flipping it around. His breathing is coming in shallow pants and his palm is squeezing... *Oh. My. God!*

I moan out, rolling my eyes into the back of my head, as I thump back into Vince's chest. His chuckle vibrates through my back, causing another overwhelming wave of lust to burst through my body. "You okay, Annie? Too much?" He teases.

"Nooo," I don't know if it was a whimper, a whine, or something in between but it causes all of them to chuckle out.

Vince's warm breath continues to annihilate my senses as he asks, "Do you need me to touch you, here?" Wrapping one hand around my throat loosely and another through my hair. "Nmph..." I don't know the sound I made but it was all my brain could supply.

"Hmmm," He considers, sliding his hand out of my hair, and tracing his fingers down my side, over my hip, and across my mound. My hips buck without my permission but he doesn't slow down as he draws his finger back over the path he just came.

"P-Pl-Please." I stutter out.

"Please what, Angel?" He nips my ear lobe, then sucks it into his mouth. *Damn asshole. I don't do dirty talk. Or asking for anything. He's trying to kill me. I just know it.*

"I don't know," I yell out as frustration and desire blow through my body.

"Oh, Vince," Jenson's playful, yet raspy voice causes me to flinch. When I look over at him, I realize he's now standing almost directly next to me. His smile is disarming, and playful, and I'm sure could charm a nun out of her panties. "Don't be so mean." He chastises. He comes to a stand right to the left of me, leaning down just enough to bring himself eye level with me. "She's been such a good girl. Letting herself be vulnerable with us, open; so God damn sexy." His tone turned from playful to downright sinful. I squirm again, feeling all kinds of things in my panties.

Hell, I've been turned on before, but nothing like I have been with these men since I met them. I've also had more orgasms in a few weeks than I did in my entire relationship with Lukas. *Ew, no. He's gone. You're here. Even if I don't have another orgasm, they're worth every moment of my time.*

"Need some help, Sweetness?" Jenson asks with a smug as fuck grin. If I wasn't about to combust, I would call him an asshat. He leans in closer, nose touching mine, and briefly kisses my lips.

He's gone before I can blink and I go to chase him. Unfortunately, Vince's hand around my throat stops my movement but heightens every nerve-ending sending lava erupting through my veins. *I'm going to die. I'm going to burn up from the inside out and melt in a puddle of indecipherable goo.*

Jenson's pupils dilate impossibly further as if reading my thoughts. Releasing a single groan he slams his lips back to mine, coaxing my mouth to open for him. At the same time, Vince's hand travels back to my breasts, pinching just enough that I can feel it, before running back down to my hip.

I move to release my hold on Vince's belt so I can wrap around Jenson's neck but Vince lands a steady *thwap* against my ass cheek again. Then rubs out the sting, causing me to moan out. Jense laughs into the kiss, leaning back slightly. "Oh, hell, our Good Girl is also a little naughty, huh?"

Another *thwap* to my ass has me rocking back into Vince. "Hands on my belt, Angel. Remember?" I whimper out, grasping hold of his belt behind my back like it's a lifeline. My entire body trembles with need; overwhelming, blinding need.

"Good girl," Jense murmurs, causing my knees to buckle from under me. Strong hands catch me before I fall and heat rolls over me.

Nick hums in my ear, causing me to whip my head away from Jense; startled by finding him standing there. His eyes are wide, the amber color almost completely dissolves as his pupils continue to dilate. His smile is gentle, not smug or overly charming, but sweet, and tender. I melt into the warmth around me as Nick whispers, "You, are absolutely, stunning," breaking up the soft words with three kisses. The last kiss turns from sweet to passionate. It's like he's trying to force me to truly believe his words through each swipe of his tongue; each groan of satisfaction.

Warm, patient hands run from the outside of my thighs and travel up to my hips. Nick's tongue plunges into my mouth as he demands acceptance. Soft fingers trace over the scars on my lower belly, causing me to suck in a breath and try to move my head to watch. "Ah, ah, Siren. Get out of your head." Pulling back enough to lock gazes, he asks, "How did you feel seeing Cory's scars?" The low huskiness of his voice threatens to undo me but the seriousness of his tone allows my lust-addled brain to clear; just a little.

"Mad. Pissed. Sad..." Nick nods once, a tiny tilt of his lips graces his beautiful face. After a brief second, he tilts his head towards Cory, who's now standing directly in front of me. I move my head to face Cory, Vince's hand squeezing lightly in reassurance as Jense begins kissing down my shoulder to my collarbone. He then trails his lips back up to the dip in my neck before whispering in my ear. "Do his scars bother you? Do they disgust you, Sweetness?"

Shocked and maybe a little outraged, I squeal, "Not at all! Why would you say that?"

Jenson's deep, green eyes snap up to find mine. "Tell him." He rasps, maneuvering my head to give him access to my neck, again. "Look in his eyes, and tell him."

A full-body tremble makes its way through me as I meet Cory's eyes. The hazel has been washed out by his pupils but a tiny sea of brown and green provide the perfect outline. "Cory," I whisper. "I would never, your scars are part of your past; not your future. And, to be honest, they're kinda hot. But, if I had the chance, I'd still knock her out for what she did."

I feel more than hear Jenson chuckle against me, as Cory steps even closer. I feel his hand wander over my scars, bypassing them and continuing their path up my ribcage. His voice is low and simmery like a hot toddy; seemingly innocent with a bold kick. "Then why would we feel different about yours? This body..." He says as I feel 7 hands sliding all over my body. "This body is sexy and gorgeous and perfect. These scars make me crazy because they show off your fierceness, your strength, your ability to constantly overcome all the shit life has thrown at you."

Sliding his hands onto my cheeks he leans in, my whole being narrows in on the pure, unfiltered sincerity shining in his eyes. Just as I suck in my next breath, he slams his lips down on mine, swallowing the moan that vibrates through my chest. His kiss is the opposite of how he usually holds himself. It feels like he's fraying at the seams and silently begging me to unravel with him.

Cory abruptly breaks the kiss, leaning his forehead against mine.

Our breaths are harsh pants and the shirt he's wearing brushes against my breast with each labored breath.

Jenson's voice bursts the bubble around Cory and me as he pleads, "We can't make you believe us, Sweetness, but we can spend every day convincing you; if you'll let us." Labored breathing surrounds me and I realize I'm not the only one that is wound up tight.

"P-please," Is all I can whisper before strong arms wrap around me. The world spins as Vince swirls me around to face him. "Words, Annie," is his only demand.

I step out of his embrace, feeling Cory move to stand next to Jense. Backing up a few more feet, I take them all in. All four are sporting some impressive tension in their pants, but the tension in their bodies calls to me. Their eyes are wild with need and bodies are primed to strike. It's heady to think these amazing, gorgeous, sweet, caring, strong men want *me*.

Lifting my head, a smile curves across my mouth. "I want you. All of you. Whenever, however; I want to be yours."

Jenson runs a thumb over his lip as he chortles. "Oh, Sweetness, you already are." And with a smirk, he stalks towards me.

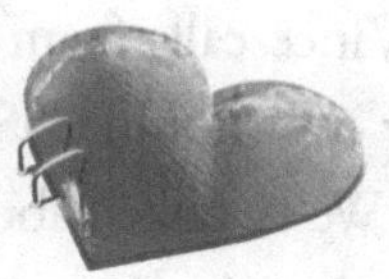

I'm so damn hard I'm pretty sure I could use my dick as a steam roller. I can't even tell you what I love most about today. Watching her open up to us, for us, seeing her eyes glaze over as she submitted so beautifully to Vince, or her standing, on her own, giving herself to us completely.

Stalking over to her, I slam my lips down on hers in a bruising kiss.

I want her, all of her, forever. That thought has me snapping my head back in shock. *Holy shit. I've never thought that about anyone before.*

Her lips are puffy and glistening from all of the kisses she's received. Her chest is panting out a tune that matches mine. Her eyes, *my God*, her eyes are shining brighter than I've ever seen as she waits for one of us to move.

I smirk at her and whisper, "Where to?"

Her brows pinch in confusion, causing her to look absolutely fucking adorable. Then, her eyes widen a little when it clicks.

"I don't care." Nodding once, I turn my head towards the other, tilting my chin towards the hallway.

After their silent agreement, I search her gaze again. "Trust us?"

Her sharp inhale causes me to pause but is quickly covered by a wondrous, "Yes." Her sweet smile makes my heart flip.

Shaking the thoughts from my head, I scoop her up in my arms, resulting in a startled shriek from her. I laugh her off as she protests loudly. Nick barrels ahead of us and opens the playroom door, flicking the light on as he goes. It's the room with the biggest bed and, honestly, upstairs is too damn far.

"You're going to hurt yourself!" She squawks.

"That's one, Angel," Vince calls from behind me. I see her lean her head back to see over my shoulder. Stealing a glance, I see her eyes narrow in irritation. "We've talked about this." His Dom voice is low and gravelly and I watch as her eyes grow round and her cheeks pinken.

Once my knees hit the bed, I carefully lay her on top of it and she scurries back to the headboard, tucking her knees up and trying to lift the black comforter.

"No, Siren. No hiding." Nick's voice is strained and there's a vein in his neck that looks like it may burst with the effort it's taking him to restrain himself. *Same, man; same.*

Vince leans over, pressing a soft kiss to her lips. When she sighs into him, I see her body slowly relax as Nick kisses up her arm, to her shoulder.

"We know it's been a while, but we will take care of you. I promise." She nods gently before steeling herself.

Looking at each of us, she bites her lip, as she pierces each of us with those alluring blue eyes. Swallowing hard, she looks down, fiddling with her fingers. "How, um. I don't..." She trails off and it looks like she may cry. "I don't want anyone to think I like someone more than another and I'm not sure how to even do this and..."

Cory cuts her off, "Stop, Annie. Would you..." he pauses and looks around. "Would it help if you were blindfolded?" Her eyes turn into small saucers. Fear and desire clash in their depths.

"Nothing else, and you have a safeword." Nick gently reminds her, tucking a strand of hair behind her ear.

Vince chimes in, "It may help to keep you in the moment, too. And if you don't want a total stop, you just need something adjusted, you can say "yellow". But, regardless, not a damn thing will happen that you don't want."

His demanding and assured tone helps her to relax. Nodding with a smile, Nick moves across the room to grab a silk blindfold from the cabinets. Not able to wait any longer, I prowl onto the bed, hoping to take her mind off of the other things. Smiling down on her, I kiss her nose, hovering just over her body. "Hi, Sweetness," I say with a grin.

"Hi," she answers with a giggle. Then, I lean in and kiss her. I put everything I have, everything I feel, everything I want into the kiss. Her arms find their way around my neck, fingers tangling in my long hair. With a gentle pull, she rips a groan out of me. My hips thrust forward as I try to fight off my need to bury myself deep into her right this second.

All of a sudden, Nick is standing there, eye quirked playfully as he nudges me over. "Ok Casanova, ease up a second. Crawling backward off of her, I slip off the bed and stand next to Nick as he smiles down at her like she's the most precious thing in the world.

Vince and Cory are standing on the other side of the bed, looking equally enamored. *Damn, she really is perfect for us.*

29

Annie

With a quick look towards all of the guys, I check again to make sure there are no looks of regret, disgust, discomfort. All I find is adoration, lust, desire, lo... *Nope, not now.*

Smiling shyly, I nod once to Nick, silently giving my permission to proceed.

Then I'm cloaked in darkness.

My body automatically tense but Vince's soothing hush helps a little. I hear the rustling of clothing and pull my knees into my chest.

"Now, now, Pretty Girl. Please don't hide this beautiful body." Cory's whisper washes over my neck as warm, smooth hands rub my ankles. I flinch momentarily, "Sorry, Sweetness. Just me," Jenson says as he moves his hands further up my legs.

"Lie back." Vince's calming shush has been replaced by his rougher, commanding voice. Goosebumps coat my body as hands with long fingers, *Nick*, grabs my hips and lifts me towards the middle of the bed. I feel the four of them climb onto the bed, surrounding me.

My head is turned and my gasp is swallowed by a strong mouth, thick lips, and perfect beard. I moan into his mouth as someone's hands travel up my body, gently nudging my thighs apart. Reflexively, I move them together, but strong hands keep me from succeeding. "Fuck me," Jenson's voice is laced with desire and my breath stutters in my chest.

Nick's voice is in my ear as he strokes my right breast. "Is that all for us, Siren?"

They must see my forehead move in confusion because he quickly follows with, "You're soaked right through your panties."

Embarrassment floods my system. Maybe it's my new meds but I've almost always needed lube; whether it was used or not is a separate question but, I've never...

My thoughts are cut off by Vince nipping my lip. "Get out of your head, baby. Seeing your arousal through your panties is fucking addictive." The coursing lust in his voice lights my whole body ablaze and I nod lightly. "Ok," I whisper with a tremble.

Vince's lips are a breath away as he calls out, "Just how wet is she, Jense?" The answering groan sends a spark straight to my clit as my pussy clenches down on nothing.

Someone's mouth closes over my left nipple at the same time a hand comes to lie on top of my neck. I jolt and cry out just as Vince claims my mouth again and something snaps around my waist. Before I can ask what happened, two long fingers swipe from my opening straight to my clit. The moan that leaves me is indecent at best. Jenson groans long and deep before teasing my entrance, barely pressing the tips into me. "She's fucking soaked." He grunts out.

His warmth leaves me, and I whimper at the loss. I can hear Cory and Vince chuckle before Vince's low voice commands, "Taste her, Cor."

I brace myself as I prepare for Cory and Jense to switch places. But a garbled moan gives me pause. "Holy shit," Jense whispers.

Vince chuckles and Nick's hand flexes over mine. A sucking sound followed by a loud pop can be heard just before Cor says, "Fucking delicious."

No one moves. No one speaks. My mind is racing a million miles an hour as uncomfortable silence wraps around me. My breaths start coming in short pants as I think about them maybe deciding to leave but Nick's delicious voice stops me from spinning out. "You're ok, Siren. We just watched Cory suck your juices off of Jenson's fingers. He's never done that and, it was fucking hot." He rasps just before taking my lobe into his mouth.

The mental imagery he supplied, paired with the magic he's doing on my ear, causes me to moan desperately, bucking my hips and meeting nothing. Vince chuckles, "You like that, Angel? Thinking of watching Cory and Jense together?" The teasing in his voice makes it obvious that he's baiting them. Which kind of falls in line with a few things I had noticed during our time together.

"Mm-hmm." I moan as he applies a little pressure on my throat. "What about Nick and I? Do you want to watch us, too?"

"Yes," I gasp as fingers swipe through my wetness. This time, I get more than the tip. One thick finger enters me at the same time that two long fingers pull my labia wider, opening me up to them completely. A warm mouth closes over my barely there clit and my hips buck at the sensation.

Hands, so many hands, tracing, pinching, squeezing. Warm licks, nibbles, sucks, and kisses. My whole body is compressed tightly like a spring coil squeezed under intense pressure. My back arches up as Jense, or Cory, I'm not quite sure, adds another finger. He begins twisting the hits- "Fuuucckkkk!" I scream to the ceiling as the spring releases, flooding my body with a blinding wave that causes my toes to curl.

Through the haze, I hear Vince command, "Pull out," just as two calloused fingers land on my exposed clit, sliding over the wet bundle furiously.

The blinding wave turns into an explosion of colors as my entire body locks up. Deep, guttural groans leave my body; as does all sense of time and space.

Something cold and wet touches my forehead, rousing me from a dream-like haze. The blindfold is still in place but I can smell them. My guys. A small smile curves upwards as Vince asks, "You back with us, Angel?"

Tilting my head I frown in confusion. Jense's deep chuckle vibrates my stomach as he plants sweet, open-mouthed kisses up my body. "That was so hot." He groans before sealing his lips over mine. Tasting myself on him should probably turn me off but, honestly, it turns me on.

Bucking into him, my body ramps up for more. I *need* more.

Jense pulls back and I pout before someone turns my head and kisses me deeply. It's sweet but has an edge of possession that makes me clench my fists.

I smile, "Cory," I whisper as I grab his face with my hands. He stills, panting heavily. "How did y…" I snort a laugh at his bewildered tone. "I can tell." Groaning in satisfaction, he dives back in with another claiming kiss.

Mouths begin to roam all over my body, gently nipping and sucking, and my core starts to tighten once again.

"Who do you want first, baby?" He rasps against my mouth.

Shaking my head, I blink back the feelings that threaten to consume me. "I don't...I can't..."

With a quiet shush, someone swipes my sweaty hair off my forehead. "It's ok. You don't have to decide."

Nodding in appreciation, I smile under my blindfold and chew on my lip. A low growl comes from my right, turning my chin towards the source. A thin finger presses on my lip, forcing me to set it free. "Mine," Nick growls before slamming his mouth to mine. Fever racks my body and my pussy clenches with need.

Suddenly, I feel bodies shifting around the bed once more.

"Gotta open you up a little more, Angel. We don't want to hurt you." Nodding my head without breaking Nick's kiss, I lash out with my left arm, connecting with a strong, very naked hip. A soft hand wraps around the back of mine, urging it forward until velvety smoothness connects with my palm. Groaning out, I wrap my hand around the hard shaft, tugging a couple of times as I get used to the weight in my palm. A hiss is released and I grin knowing it's Jenson.

Nick breaks our kiss, breathing heavily, and asks, "Remember your words, right?"

I nod ridiculously fast as I say, "Yellow, need to change. Red, please stop."

"Good girl," Vince says from between my legs as he gathers up some of the wetness and pushes his thick ginger into me. I buck at the intrusion, trying to get closer *and* further away.

Vince slowly works his finger back and forth, allowing my body to adjust, again. Jenson's hand begins to guide mine up and down his shaft as Nick shifts away. After a few pulls, I feel something bump my pinky when it hits his body. Freezing, he chuckles, "Pubic cross." Then he drops his voice lower. "Good for clitoral stimulation."

What. The. Fuck.

I buck into Vince's hand as he grunts out, "So, damn, tight."

Bringing my hand back to the tip of his dick, Jense says, "That's not the only one I have." It takes me a minute to realize there's a Prince Albert looped through the tip. Smearing the wetness leaking, I toy with the piercing and get a feel for it, then drop my hand back to the base in a slow, squeezing motion.

He hisses out a few curses and I smile with pride. Just then, Vince adds another finger, stretching me impossibly wide. Not a second later, he begins twirling his tongue over and around my clit. "Oh shit, Vince. Please," I pant out. I try my best to time my strokes with Vince's building thrusts.

After another minute of riding Vince's fingers while jerking off Jenson, I huff out in frustration and lower my hips back to the bed. "Vince, you can stop now. I know what you're trying to do but, I told y'all, orgasming is super difficult. It doesn't mean it's not enjoyable. But, you really don't have to waste all that time on me."

A firm slap comes down on my pussy and I gasp in shock. The little sting of pain did absolutely nothing to curb my desire. "Don't tell me what I can and can't do with our pussy, Angel." His command leaves no room for argument and, if I'm honest, it was hot as fuck.

Not knowing how else to respond, I groan, "Yes, Sir," setting off a chorus of lust-filled groans.

Vince begins to build me back up again, one lick, one flick, one thrust at a time. Then, Nick reaches down and guides my hand to his cock. It's warm and thick under my palm but I shriek when my fingers hit metal. *A lot* of fucking metal.

"Jacob's ladder," he whispers, then plunges his tongue into my mouth when I gasp.

The sounds that fill the room are like a soundtrack to a porn video. However, they're raw and filthy, and utterly delicious.

As my hands become acquainted with Jense's and Nick's cocks, their hips begin to piston faster. As if in sync, Vince thrusts his fingers in time with Nick and Jenson's movements.

Suddenly, they all pull away.

"Nooooo!" I scream, or shriek, or, really, it's a loud whine.

Before I can comment about their absence further, a lean, warm body slides between my legs, opening me up even more to him.

From the general direction, Vince says, "Condom?" And it takes me a moment to realize he's asking me. "Um, I'm clean. And, I can't have kids anymore so…" I let it hang out there and hear a mixture of quiet curses and low groans ping around the room.

"Us, too. We've never done anything without one but we're clean, too." I nod my head in understanding and suck in my breath as anticipation threatens to drown me.

Everything goes completely silent and it feels like the universe has zoomed in and slowed down this particular moment. Two hands slide up the inside of my thighs, grasping the jiggly section with a tight squeeze. "Hands on the bed, Angel. No touching. Let us make you feel good."

My nod is barely finished when I feel a blunt tip slide through my folds. Groaning out, I thrust up, desperately chasing the sensation. Two fingers find my clit again as he gently pushes in. Someone sucks my neck, another attacks my breast. The warring sensations threaten to overwhelm me in the best way possible.

I feel myself stretch as, whoever pushes in another inch or so. My moan never leaves my mouth as it bounces through my chest. I haven't had so much as a finger inside of me since these men and I feel like I did when I originally lost my virginity. Only, way more turned on.

His cock retreats and I feel my pussy clench down, desperately trying to keep in place. The fingers on my clit continue a steady pattern of hitting the nerves and missing them. If I didn't know how difficult my body was, I would assume the person knew exactly what he was doing.

Two hands grip my hips hard, bringing me back to the moment, and, with a final thrust, a very large, very hard dick is completely buried in my pussy. Our groans swirl together like a couple dancing as my body adjusts to the sensations. *Or tries to.*

My hands have officially wrapped parts of the sheets wrapped around them as I try to breathe through the pain and the immense pleasure that accompanies it. With a heavy exhale, the pain resides and I buck up. "Please," I beg.

That was all he needed; all *they* needed. Fingers swirl, tongues lick, and someone drowns out my moans with their mouth as the person between my thighs begins to piston his hips. Tears leak from my eyes as a kaleidoscope of sensations bursts from my core, lashing out through my limbs as I cry out with another intense orgasm.

Over my cries, I faintly hear muffled curses and words of praise. I come back to reality just in time to feel his cock swell inside before he spills into me.

A shiver travels down my body as his body comes down to lean over mine, pressing gentle kisses along my belly, up my ribs, and landing on my lips.

Wrapping my arms around his neck, and my legs around his waist, I sink into the kiss. It's lazy, languid, and so damn sweet. Running my fingers through his hair, I let him deepen the kiss as my body slowly comes back down from the high.

When he breaks away, he's still panting for breath but it's much calmer than before. Smiling softly I whisper, "Thanks, Cory," before dragging him back down for another kiss.

A spank echoes around the room, causing us to break the kiss. Jenson cackles as Cory mutters, "Fuck off," before pecking my lips once more. I can't help it, I giggle along. I don't know why but the image my mind makes does seem comical.

With a final breath, Cory slips from inside of me which causes us both to groan at the loss. Before I can protest, two strong arms lift me and I'm spinning around. Settling my knees on each side of his thick thighs, I can't help but rub my hands up and down his chest; tracing every contoured line.

Ducking my head, my smile grows. "Hi, Vince," I say shyly. "Hi, Angel." He responds huskily before sliding his hands from my hips, up to my arms, and placing my hands on his shoulders. "Keep your hands right there, Angel." Before he's even finished, I'm nodding my head like an eager puppy.

"Good girl." He whispers as his teeth graze my jaw. "Now you're going to ride my cock while the others watch you get yourself off." My body locks up. A rebuttal is on the tip of my tongue but before I can even get it out, his hand lands on my ass cheek with a smart *whack*. It's a little harder than he did yesterday but, like yesterday, he immediately massages the pain away. "Whatever bullshit you had in your head just now has no place here. Unless you need to safeword, you're riding this cock, baby." *Holy dirty words, Deadpool.* His dominant side is so damn hot.

A shudder ripples through me as I say, "Yes, sir. But, if I hurt you, or it's not comfortable will you..." I don't even get to finish before another *whack* stings across my other cheek. As he massages that one out, grunts and groans fill the room; every one of them dripping with desire.

"What did I tell you before, Angel? We can all handle you. We all want you. You are ours and we are yours." He dives in with a breath-snatching kiss, his tongue easily dominating mine with every swipe before he abruptly pulls back.

Like a wanton little hussy, I begin squirming in his lap, trying and failing to connect with his rock-hard cock longer than half a second. "Say it. Say it and I'll give you what we both want." He whispers between kisses along my jaw.

My mind has melted and apparently, all that's left is a little subby who needs to be praised, owned, and desired. "Yes, Sir. I'm yours and you're mine. Please. Please touch me."

With a chuckle, he wraps one hand around the nape of my neck and slams my mouth into his. As soon as his tongue swipes for entrance, his hand reaches between our bodies and his glorious dick finally connects with my willing cunt. The moment the tip breaches, I can feel my resolve shatter as I drop my weight into his lap. He breaks the kiss with a deep, guttural moan that feels even better than he sounds. I can feel the blindfold soaking up my tears as it feels like I may have very well ripped myself in half. *But, it is glorious.*

Apparently, I recover faster as I steady myself on his shoulders, lean up, and drop back down. His answering hiss was all I needed to hear before I rode the high. *Or should I say, before I rode him?*

After a few more bounces on his cock, my knees began to ache but I try to ignore it; especially when his hot mouth connects with my nipple, biting hard enough to feel it. His beard brushing across my chest adds to the overwhelming sensations coursing through every cell of my body.

But the pain in my knees becomes unbearable. So, I ask for help. "Can you please lie down? Um, my knees..." Vince's answer came so fast that I didn't even have to finish. Within three seconds I'm leaning over him, breast to chest, dick still firmly in place, and he gave me no reason to feel bad; he just went back to attacking my breast and even added a hip thrust for good measure.

Leaning further, I plant my hands on either side of his head, move my knees for a better angle and lift my ass. Then, using my thighs for leverage, I start to bounce my ass up and down repeatedly. The new angle means that his entire dick isn't jammed up inside me. However, the tip keeps flicking a spot inside of me that makes my toes start throwing gang signs. His hands grip my hips tight and he begins to pant out, "Oh fuck. Angel. Oh shit. I can't. I'm gunna..." His roar shakes the entire bed as he slams me down on top of him, bottoming out completely, and cums; and cums; and cums. Each jet is like a shock to his system as he twitches underneath me.

After a moment, he slams his mouth to mine and fucking devours me. It is not sweet and lazy. Oh no. This is hard, fierce, and powerful. Perfect.

With a ragged exhale, his head drops down, and mine falls to his chest. My whole body is slick with sweat but I don't have it in me to be self-conscious about it.

"Fucking hell, Angel. Where did that come from?" He asks between pants, sounding like he's confused and maybe a little in awe. I huff out a laugh, not able to provide anything additional as I relax my body. His arms come up to band around me, squeezing me to him before kissing my head.

"Don't freak out. Just relax." He whispers in my hair. I have no clue what the hell he's talking about. But then, I feel a tongue come up from the underside of Vince's cock, slowly softening inside of me, and running straight up to my... I jump with the contact as Vince chortles in my ear.

Behind me, I faintly hear Nick mumble, "Best flavor ever. That is so Goddamn sexy," Followed by a humming sound. Right as Vince tightens me against him, Nick's tongue comes back, flicking its way over, around, and even a little... *in*. My eyes widen in surprise but I don't move because, dammit, it felt so fucking good. And naughty.

The taboo nature of it all had my sex-crazed hormones kicking into gear again. As he slurps and sucks, I start squirming and rocking, Vince groans, lifts me a little so his cock can slip out, then places me back on his chest; snuggling into me. "Stay right there." He whispers in command.

My mind tries to understand the reason for the quiet command but then, hands are grasping my hips, and the tip of a hard cock nudges my entrance. My body is already shaking in anticipation as he circles my entrance with his tip. The additional lubrication, mixed with the knowledge of what the lubrication *is*, has me mewling for more.

Vince lifts my head as I rock my ass back into Nick's groin. He places one hand on my throat, still just pressing it there, and wraps the other in my hair. "What's wrong, Angel? Do you need more?" Nodding is hard but I do my best. "Does Nick need to slide his hard cock into your tight, wet pussy while my cum drips out of you?" A truly indecent groan falls from my mouth as I thrust my ass back, briefly feeling the tip of Nick's cock enter. "Are you ready, Angel? Ready to feel how amazing each and every one of those barbells will feel in your pussy as you milk his cock?"

I'm about to cum; or die. But, hopefully, cum, then die. "P-please," I beg.

Nick raises my hips and I immediately feel the stretch of his cock pressing in. I can feel his hands tremble with effort and his fingers dig into my hips in a biting, yet blissful pain. "So. Damn. Tight. Fuck!" Nick grits out, as I feel the first barbell settle inside me. His hands squeeze my hips again and his breathing comes out in loud pants. "Fuck, Siren. You're so wet and so goddamn hot. Shit. I don't want to hurt you." His voice comes out pained and I want to make it better. I need to make it better. So...

Grabbing onto the front of Vince's shoulders, I dig my nails in and slam my body back. Nick's cock pushes allllll the way into me. I'm pretty sure his dick is currently talking with my stomach. His yell is a mix of horror and immense pleasure and it causes me to explode.

My body ceases to exist in this realm. It's all fragments of sounds, lights, and sensations, swirling around me and through me. My orgasm splinters the very fabric of time. *Ok, that sounded a little too Dr. Strange but, nothing else can describe it.*

Groans travel around me and the exquisite push and pull, slide and glide of Nick's Jacobs Ladder has my orgasm dragging on spectacularly.

With what I think is a grunt, his head comes down between my shoulders. I'm flattened on top of Vince, poor dude, as he whispers sweet words into my hair. Hands are running all over my body and gentle words of praise surround me as I begin my descent down from the clouds. With a final kiss between my shoulders, Nick carefully slides out, causing a sound that is more whimper than whine to spill out, as the barbells rub my overestimated insides.

I can feel Vince's chest vibrate with a chuckle as Nick lies on Vince's side and brushes a hand down my hair. "You are perfect," Nick whispers in awe and I can't help but preen at the compliment.

My body is sated, my heart is full, and I'm so deliriously happy that I can't help but smile.

Exhaustion slowly takes over my body. I've never had so many orgasms in one day. *And* this was the first time I've had sex in years. Honestly, it was perfect. The best balance of sweet and spicy. Want and need. But, there's still one more man I need to connect with.

"Jense. I need…" A soft hush comes from behind me as fingers trail up and down my spine. "We have all the time in the world, Sweetness. Just relax."

And then, sleep drags me under.

30

Jenson

I'm stirring a pot of chili that's simmering on the stove. It still has a couple more hours until it's perfect. Speaking of perfect... Images of Annie flip through my mind like a live porno. At no point have I seen something so erotic yet so emotional. Watching Annie go through all the stages of vulnerability then ending the night sexy, sated, and sleepy. I only got to taste her, touch her, but that was more than enough for me. Of course, seeing her turn Nick into a blubbering three-pump chump was pretty great, too.

The only thing sexier than Annie giving herself to us was Cory sucking my goddamn fingers into his mouth. *What in the actual hell was that?* She may not have seen it but I swear to God my dick almost exploded. The look in his eyes had my brain short-circuiting. It was like he was asking for permission, but also initiating a challenge. One that I definitely wanted to agree to.

Hissing in pain, I flinch my hand back. I had completely blanked while stirring the big steel pot, successfully burning my hand on the inside. Cursing under my breath, I turn to the sink behind me and flip the cold water on.

"What happened?" Cory inquires as he walks in with wine and one of those cheesecakes with different types in the same box. He pushes them onto the counter and rushes over to me. Pulling my hand closer, he studies the burn from all angles, brows furrowed in concentration.

"Come on," He orders and pulls me out of the kitchen and to the bathroom down the hall. Grabbing the first aid kit under the cabinet, he cracks it open and lays out the things he needs, lining them all up just so, and in order of when he will use them.

A smile tugs at my lips as I look over his face. His thin brows are pulled down in concentration; the black rims of his glasses have slid down his nose so that I can see the tops of his lashes. His hair is perfectly styled and pushed out of his face. Very different from the disheveled look it had yesterday.

As he rubs ointment into my burn, I notice he's wearing his forest green polo with a pair of khaki pants. *So Cory.* It took us years to convince him to try ball shorts or sweats when hanging out at home.

This close I can smell the Eucalyptus and Peppermint Viking shampoo and conditioner. That, paired with the undercurrent of something that's simply Cory, infiltrates my nose and floods my system.

With a final nod, he steps away and begins cleaning up the trash, packing the materials just right, then washing his hands. I haven't moved. I can't. With all the stuff that's happened with Annie, I've realized just how much I need this man. We almost lost her and I refuse to let her go a day without telling her how amazing she is. So, why wouldn't I do the same with Cory? My best friend. The man that I've been in love with for the last four years.

Swallowing heavily, I stop the swirling thoughts, "Cor." My voice is just a hoarse rasp but he whips his head to look at me. Sensing something's wrong, his eyes flit over every part of my body assessing anything that he may have missed. When he finds nothing, he meets my gaze and freezes.

I'm silently pleading, begging for him to see me; all of me. "Jense, wha..." I don't let him finish. Words won't help. Not right now. I wrap one hand around the back of his neck and slam my mouth to his. For just a moment, neither of us moves. We're both frozen in time as our lips melt together.

Then, the dam breaks. We're all teeth and tongues, grunts and groans. His fingers tangle in the back of my hair, still left down from my shower earlier. We spend what feels like forever devouring each other, flirting the line of fighting for dominance and completely submitting to the other.

When the need for oxygen becomes too much we break apart, panting for breath as our lips brush with each inhale and exhale. My hand tightens on the back of his neck and my voice cracks as I whisper, "Tell me now, Cory. Tell me right fucking now if I'm wrong. I've loved you for years and I tried, damn have I tried, to give you space after that night. But I want, no need, you to know: I want you. All of you. Every day." My breathing has sped up as I divulge my longest-kept secret. The only one I had left.

The silence draws out until a high-pitched ringing in my ears threatens to drive me mad. The longer we stand there, the worse it gets.

"Yes," his voice whips out through the ringing leaving me momentarily stunned as my brain tries to process. "Always, yes. I've loved you since high school. Since you first saved me from losing my shit when those bastards filled the balloons with penis confetti, I knew I wanted to be close to you. You help me relax, help me be me, but, more than anything, you are unapologetically you and I love you for it."

His confession brings tears to my eyes. This brilliant, sweet, sexy man. "Fuck," I rasp out before slamming my mouth against his once again.

****

Cory and I spent quite a bit of time making out like horny teenagers in the bathroom. We heard Nick and Vince talking in the kitchen and decided we should probably go out there. And we did, hand in hand, with stupid ass smirks on our faces. They both paused their conversation when we entered, the look of surprise on their faces was almost comical. Then, they started hollering and clapping leaving both of us more than a little confused.

"It's about time!" Nick cheered before slapping me on the back. He walked over to Vince, dramatically laid his head on his chest, and fluttered his eyelashes as he wiped away a pretend tear. "Look, baby, they're all grown up."

With that, we all burst into laughter, shooing them away and getting back to our tasks.

We still had a little over an hour before the chili was ready. And the cornbread wouldn't take long so I told the guys I was going to wake Annie and try to convince her to get cleaned up before dinner. I did my best to clean her last night but, doing it while she was passed out on top of Vince felt wrong, so I stuck to the insides of her thighs and didn't go elsewhere.

Now I'm sitting in the bathroom connected to the playroom, watching the tub fill with hot water. The jacuzzi tub is technically large enough to fit 4 or 5 people, not that we ever have. I pour in a generous amount of lavender Epsom salts and flick on the jets.

Once it's filled, I turn the faucet off and head back into the room. Annie's hair is a hot mess. Her face is rumpled with sleep but, damn if she isn't the most beautiful woman I've ever laid eyes on. Nick had found her a blanket once they all extracted themselves from under and next to her. Granted, they didn't move for the first 30 minutes she was sleeping. Not that I minded, or would have done differently. I took a quick shower, relieving the tension in my balls before skipping down into the kitchen to figure out a dinner plan. I highly doubted she wanted to go out after all of that. And it was *a lot*. Tantalizingly so.

Crawling onto the bed next to her, I move some of the hair off of her face and smile as her nose twitches adorably. Unable to resist, I move in to kiss her forehead, then her nose, then her lips. "Annie," I whisper. "Come on, Sweetness. We gotta get you cleaned up."

She mewls like a little sex kitten as she stretches out. "No. Need sleep. Come snuggle." She murmurs through a yawn.

I can't help but laugh lightly as she nuzzles further into me. "Nope. Come on beautiful, move that sexy ass and I'll snuggle you in the warm tub."

Her eyes pop open in surprise. "You ran me a bath?" She asks in surprise. My smile widens as I see her blue eyes dance with excitement. "Yes, Sweetness. We, uh, didn't get to clean you after. You fell asleep. I at least wiped down the insides of your thighs but wasn't comfortable with anything closer while you were sleeping."

Her answering smile causes my heart to stall in my chest. "No one's ever run me a bath before." She says in a giddy little voice.

"Good, then you'll only ever have the best." Leaning up, I lightly pop her on the ass, enough for her to feel but it was definitely muffled by the blanket. Then I rip the blanket off of her. "Let's go sleepyhead. I have 30 minutes with just you and me before I have to finish dinner."

"You're making dinner?!" I can't help but laugh at her incredulous tone.

"Yes, but I'll ruin it if you don't get a move on. Now, up." I grab her hand while she weakly protests, even though she's sliding off the bed towards me.

On wobbly legs, she follows me into the bathroom and inhales heavily.

"Wow," she breathes out.

Stepping towards her, I lean down and kiss the side of her mouth. Backing towards the tub, I whip my shirt over my head; her eyes widen with intrigue and delight. Then, with a saucy grin, I hook my thumbs into my sweats and drag them down my legs. Stepping out of them, I make a show of turning my back on her and stepping into the tub; letting out an exaggerated sigh as I lean my back against one of the jets.

"Your turn," I say with a cheeky grin.

Her face blushes and I watch her tense when she looks down to realize that she is still stark naked. "Don't even think about it." My voice startles her just as she begins to cover herself. She drops her hands back to her sides and I grin at her before murmuring, "Good girl. Now, get that sexy ass in this tub so I don't burn dinner."

The smile she sends me is enough to last me a lifetime, but I'm a greedy bastard and want to see it every day.

She shuffles forward, lifts her leg, and dips her toe in, hissing quietly. Then she plunges her leg in, swinging her other over the lip of the tub. My hands move to her hips and I help her slide down to sit between my legs. Sighing in contentment, she leans her head back on my shoulder and I feel every ounce of tension drain from her. Wrapping my arms around her, I hug her tight to my chest and breathe her in.

We sit for a few minutes in comfortable silence with nothing but the sounds of the jets filling the room. "Um, Jense," the hesitation in her tone makes me chuckle. "Yes, Sweetness?"

"We didn't, well, I fell asleep. I'm so sorry. It was..."

"A lot," I finish for her. She nods against my chest. "No need to be sorry. It was perfect in every way. We have the rest of our lives to make you feel good." She hums as if she doesn't fully agree.

Wanting to bring her out of her head, I lean her forward, moving my hand to her forehead and gently pushing it back towards me so I can begin washing her hair. When I massage the shampoo into her hair, she moans out. My stupid dick pokes her in the back as it hardens. I had hidden it well but when she lifted back and I sat up, it found her like a beacon of light. *Needy asshole.*

Once I rinse out the shampoo, followed shortly by the conditioner, I lather up some kind of lavender body wash into a new loofa and begin washing her arms. Her body melts back into mine and she rolls her head to the side. Her neck becomes too tempting to resist so I lean down and press a gentle kiss to the base. Her body shuddering against me encourages me to kiss another part of her neck. Then another. Then another.

My hand glides the loofa across her chest, dipping up and around each breast before traveling down her stomach. I gently run down the area she hates the most and add in a lingering kiss just behind her ear. "Thank you for being ours, Annie," I whisper and watch in fascination as goosebumps flutter over her skin.

When she doesn't recoil, I smile against her neck and slide my hand between her thighs. I make small circular motions with the loofa and am rewarded with a sweet groan. Her hips buck up to meet my hand. "Jense," she rasps out with a shaky exhale.

I don't have time to form a reply before she lifts herself and turns. I can feel the confusion cross my face and I fear that I've pushed too hard. But my fears vanish as she settles in my lap, straddling me, and wraps her arms around my neck. "Kiss me." She mutters. Even though she tried to sound commanding, her anxiety caused her to waver a little.

With a playful grin, I murmur, "Yes, ma'am," before slanting my mouth over hers and sucking her lip directly into my mouth. The groan that leaves her has me primed and ready to explode. I sink my tongue into her mouth, wanting to memorize every moan, every shift, every whimper.

She chuckles as I try to follow her mouth as she leans away. With a raised brow, and the sassy little smirk that I first fell for at the club, she lifts up, wraps her hand around my shaft, and twists as she tugs once, twice... then encases my entire fucking dick in the warm heat of her pussy. We both release a deep groan as we breathe through our teeth. She is so deliciously tight and her pussy is choking the life out of my dick. "Oh fuck, your piercing. Oh..." She trails off on a moan as she swivels her hips in slow, methodical circles, getting used to the stretch. My hands clamp down on her hips and my fingers dig into the perfect handles there.

"I'm not going to last long," I grit between my teeth. "Oh, Annie, you're perfect. Fuck. Perfect." My mind ceases to work correctly as she rocks forward. The pubic cross is clearly doing something because she just continues rocking, upping her tempo, and splashing water up the sides of the bath. Her moans become louder, more sensual, as she takes what she needs, grinding down into me, and rippling around my aching cock.

It's only another minute before I'm groaning out her name, holding her down on my lap as my cum paints the insides of her cunt. "Jenson!" She screams. Her pussy convulses repeatedly around me, pulling even more cum from my balls.

Once her orgasm recedes, she rests her forehead against mine as we both fight to catch our breath. "Shit. Now I can't make fun of Nick for being a three-pump chump. Your pussy is heaven." I mumble, causing her to chuckle and shake her head.

We moan simultaneously as she moves to let my softening dick leave the warm embrace it so badly wants to live in.

Unplugging the drain, she helps me wash and rinse my hair and we make sure to rinse off any remnants of our not-so-clean bath time.

With a final kiss, I leave her to change into the sweats and tee I left for her on the bed.

Walking out of the playroom, I can't help but relish in the smile that's pulled across my face. Cory wants me, Annie's ours, and life is feeling pretty fuckin' great right about now.

31

Annie- Two Weeks Later

Smiling at myself, I replay the events of my last weekend with the guys. Life-altering sex, stolen kisses, movie marathons, and the immense satisfaction of knowing that I found love. Real love. Consuming love.

After the most drool-worthy chili and cornbread for dinner, Jense and Cory sat me down to talk about them wanting to pursue something together and I laughed out loud. They were both dumbfounded when I told them I had wondered if something more was going on. But, the tension in their shoulders bled out when I whole-heartedly told them that they better make each other happy or I'd kick their ass. Of course, they had also laughed; but I was serious.

Later, Vince drove me home. After feeding Reginald and letting him run around for a bit, I packed a small overnight bag, unable to say no to their puppy dog pouts when they all begged me to spend another night.

I had been deliciously sore, only bleeding a little. But tingles still race down my body whenever I think about them. I finally have people who see me. The real me. And they aren't embarrassed, ashamed, there's no pity. Just pure acceptance and a desire to want to be with me as much as possible.

I've only had time to meet with them for a few lunches or breakfasts, stealing hot kisses and playful touches. Being with them is so much easier now. It's like breathing. It's like home. And a huge part of me is really excited to see what happens next.

My phone rings with an incoming call just as I'm packing up the last of the food to transport to Mom's. My kids are playing with Legos in Josh's room and actually getting along. It won't last through the day but, I'll take what I can get for now.

Swiping my phone off the counter, I see Jodie's name and smile as I connect the call. "Hey! Happy Thanksgiving!" She guffaws down the line and says, "More than you know."

The cryptic nature of her response had me pausing. "Everything ok?" I ask hesitantly.

"Yes! Sorry, got distracted. Have you seen the news?" I hum out noncommittally and go back to packing the rest of the food I'm taking to Mom's. "No, trying to get the last of this food packed up before going to my mom's. Why?"

My phone pings with a message that contains a link. "Open the link. I'll wait." My face twists into a scowl. Putting her on speakerphone, I open the link and watch as the red banner scrolls across the screen boasting 'Breaking News'. Coroners, detectives, agents, and a whole group of other people wade across some beach near New Jersey.

Lukas' mugshot flashes across the screen and my whole body freezes. Bile splashes the back of my throat and my vision begins to tunnel. Turning the volume up, I hear the report say, "...body was found with clear signs of torture. Sources say that a vile word had been carved across his body and he's missing many pieces of..."

I closed out of the link. Ice made its way down my spine as I worked on controlling my breathing. "He's been alive this whole time?" I mumble out.

A heavy sigh coming from the phone startles me and I remember Jodie is still on the line. "Yeah, but it seems like he's spent the last few weeks of his life being tortured. So, that's good. Right?"

Nodding my head a few times, I think about the fact that he's been alive this whole time. But, supposedly spent that time being tortured. *How do I feel about that?*

Jodie breaks the silence, "It really is over." I can't tell if she's talking more to herself than to me but I feel a smile grow on my face. "Happy Thanksgiving indeed."

After we wrapped our heads around the breaking news story, we spent a few minutes catching up. Therapy is going well for her and she opted to not go back to her apartment; instead, she's staying with her family for a while. I was overcome with joy when she said she even had a talk with an advisor at a college close to her and was considering taking 1 or 2 classes next semester. *I'm so damn proud of her.*

A tear-filled goodbye and promises to catch up later felt almost like a new beginning. Having a positive confirmation that he was dead filled me with a peace I didn't know I was missing.

* * *

Once we arrived at Mom's the kids took off to watch the parade as we heated the last of the food. Mom's boyfriend, Nate, is so damn sweet and I love how he treats her; even if it is a little sickening.

Dinner, well lunch, was filled with giggles, laughter, and overall amazingness.

We're all gathered in the living room, eating dessert and watching A Charlie Brown Thanksgiving. Things are good, great even, and I feel truly, undeniably happy. But, I feel like something is missing and I'm having a hard time keeping the tears out of my eyes.

My guys.

The realization hits me like a ton of bricks. *Is it too soon to love them? Each of them? Is it too soon to want them part of my kids' lives?*

I guess my face reveals my thoughts because Mom nudges me with her foot. Her face is gentle, all-seeing, and filled with certainty.

"It hasn't technically been a long time..." My mother starts. Her grin tips up as she considers her next words. "But you've been through hell and back since then. And they never stopped searching or caring. They're *still* here. Do you *really* think they're going anywhere?"

She raises her brow, daring me to challenge her. I smile, huff a laugh, and bat away a runaway tear. "No. But, what if it's too fast? I could never forgive myself if the kids get attached and they leave."

"Annie, do you really think they're going to leave you? For *anything*? Those men sat by your bed day in and day out waiting for a sign of you to wake up. I also have a sneaking suspicion they may have been involved in your rescue, too. But I understand our legal system enough to know they would probably be in trouble for it; so I never asked."

I try, and fail, to suppress a grin. The Sunday of our weekend together, I let the bomb drop that I may or may not have forced Nick into divulging their secrets. Their shocked faces were absolutely hilarious. But, I made sure they understood my full appreciation with my mouth on their cocks, and thanked them probably a hundred times.

There were some tears in there somewhere but, it was mostly a relief to have it all out there.

Then, Vince told me who Gina really is and I'm pretty sure I successfully nailed the 'deer in headlights' look. Not that it made me think any less of her or Enzo. If anything, I wanted to thank them even more. It's still crazy for me to think that Gina and I message or talk almost every day and she has not once alluded to who her husbands are. *Crazy.*

Shaking my head from my thoughts, I look back at Mom and smile. "You're right. I don't think they're going anywhere."

"Good. Now, call your men. I'll keep the kids tonight, and probably tomorrow." With an excited pat on my hand, she nods then takes our plates to the kitchen before I can even argue. Or, try to.

32

Vince

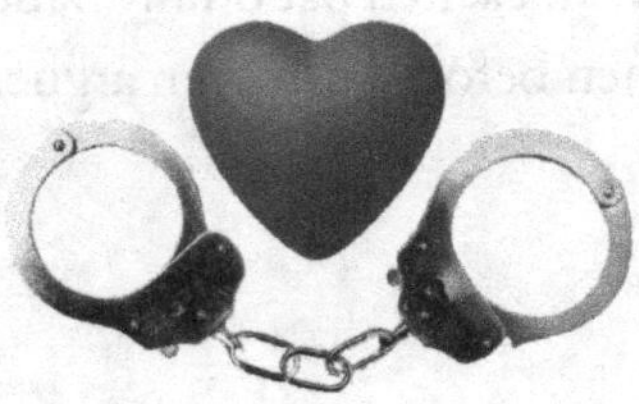

The guys and I are busy cleaning up the leftovers from our little meal together. Dad left thirty minutes ago, claiming that his chair was calling out to him. I huffed out a laugh because he's such a dork.

Our phones ping simultaneously. I dry my hands on the towel next to the sink where I've been elbow-deep in dishwater.

Sliding my phone from my pocket, I see the group chat has a new message. Excitement thrums through my body and the smile on my face almost hurts my cheeks.

My Angel: Happy Thanksgiving

I turn the sound down as pings begin echoing through the house.

However, they eventually taper out, signaling that the others did the same.

> **Cor:** Happy Thanksgiving. How's Mama?
> **Jense:** Happy Turkey Day! Although, we had ham.
> **My Love:** Happy Thanksgiving, love. Are the kids happy with a food hangover?
> **Me:** Happy Thanksgiving to you, too. Miss you.
> **Cor:** Miss you more!
> **Jense:** Miss you most!
> **My Love:** <eye roll emoji>
> **My Angel:** <laughing emoji> I miss you all. Mama is good. Nate is good, too. He seems good for her. And, no, the kids don't get food hangovers. They are bottomless pits.
> **Jense:** We have so much in common!
> **Cor:** Like Jense!
> **My Love:** He better be good to her. No one messes with Mama.
> **My Angel:** Agreed! Good thing I have a few badasses at my beck and call.

Damn, this girl. Her sassy side has come back in full force over the last two weeks. Occasionally she still tries to hide but, since that first night with all of us together, she's opened up spectacularly.

> **Me:** Damn straight.
> **Jense:** Yeah, especially Cor. <eye waggle emoji>
> **My Angel:** So, what are your plans for the rest of the day? I've suddenly found myself sans kids for the evening. Reginald has eaten and we have so much dessert left over. I actually think Mom secretly baked more hoping she would see you. <eye roll emoji>

I look up to see the guys strolling into the kitchen with various dopey grins on their faces. We all look up at each other before smiling and I send off another text.

Me: You're always welcome here.

I've barely set the phone back on the counter when the doorbell rings. My head jerks up to see Nick's confused face. Cory looks just as mystified, but Jense rushes out of the kitchen, cackling like a hyena. *What the hell?*

A loud "whoop" and a squeal of laughter echoes through the house. That sets the rest of us in motion; running through the foyer to see Annie's hair flying around as Jense spins her in a circle.

He sets her back on her feet and kisses her deeply before she even has a chance to recover from the spinning. A little moan slips out of her and my cock stirs in my pants.

When he finally breaks the kiss, they're both panting heavily. She turns to face us, a shy smile on her face. "I, um, I was already in the driveway." I guess my face was still turned in confusion. I feel it stretch and form into a wide smile as I step up to her. "I'm *so* glad," Is all I mutter before slamming my mouth down on hers.

After a couple of minutes, and Nick and Cory have had their turns kissing her luscious lips, we make our way back into the living room. Right before I sit down, her hand on my arm stops me. Looking down at her, I see her eyes shining with so much affection and vulnerability that it takes my breath away. "Can I talk to you? Alone?" She whispers.

With a wide smile and subtle nod, I grab her by the hand and lead her upstairs. "We'll be back," I shout over my shoulder and a round of lame protests fill the space. Her joyous laughter makes me huff a laugh as I pull her down the hallway and into my room.

Closing the door behind us, she takes me by the shirt and pushes me into the door. Startled doesn't even match how I feel, but all thoughts flee my head as she leans up and kisses me.

Sighing into the kiss, I release all the tension that had been building in my muscles and wrap my arms around her hips. Her tongue swipes out, asking for entrance, and I happily oblige. Her tongue is soft and warm in my mouth as she chases mine. All too soon, she pulls back and pecks my lips one more time before her eyes lock on mine. "Thank you for seeing me. Thank you for saving me. Thank you for freeing me so that I can just be me. Unapologetically, unabashedly, me. I love you, Vince." The last four words were just above a whisper but the aftermath leaves me decimated in the best damn way.

Smiling widely, I bring my forehead down to hers, gazing into her gorgeous eyes. "I love you too, Annie. Always. You have given me light, hope, and more love than I knew was possible."

With another bruising kiss, I fill her with every ounce of love that I can, before hugging her to my chest.

After a few more minutes of just holding on to each other, she pulls back and tells me she wants to talk with the others. Hand in hand, we head back to the living room. My heart is so full that it feels like it may explode out of my chest and I'm sure I look like a lunatic.

All eyes are on us when we enter. Nick quirks his brow in question and I just shake my head, lean down, and capture his mouth with mine.

Over the next twenty minutes, she disappears with each of them; and they each come back with a similar look of dazed blissfulness that almost makes me wish I had taken pictures. We are all so wrapped in this woman. I know for a fact we've been in love with her since before she was ready to even date us. Now, though, everything feels right; perfect.

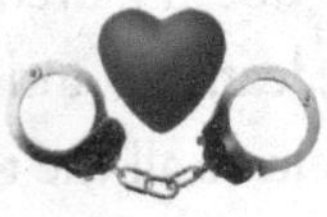

We spent the rest of the afternoon watching various shows and polishing off the desserts that Annie's mother may or may not have made us. I even made a point to send her a thank you text. All she responded with was a winking heart emoji. It made me smile.

Annie told us about her conversation with Jodie this morning. Not wanting to lie, we revealed that we knew he had been captured with the shipment in Jersey. We also explained that we didn't tell her because we knew he would never escape, and we found out before she had woken up.

We all waited patiently while she processed the information. We all wore similar looks of guilt at having kept it from her. Thankfully, she ultimately agreed that it was better she didn't know. But, she did make us promise no more secrets; to which we adamantly agreed.

Afterward, Cory and Jense showed off their library where she spent at least an hour gawking at it and squealing about how amazing it was. Cory then let her snag one of the books off the shelf to borrow. All she said was it was the first in a series and she had read it a couple of years ago. Her little happy dance made us laugh and I know that Cory and Jense are happy she loved the library. I barely caught a glimpse of the cover, showcasing a woman twirling upside down, as she skipped across the living room.

The sun has set, and, while none of us are particularly hungry, we decide to make popcorn before turning on The Fall of the House of Usher. It's some show Jense had been interested in because of the ties it had to Edgar Allen Poe's works. When Annie beamed in delight and started dramatically quoting "Annabell Lee", it was basically a done deal. She said she watched The Haunting of Hill House and The

Haunting of Bly Manor and gushed about how great the storylines were. Combining that with her apparent love of Edgar Allen Poe, we all agreed to watch. Horror-type shows aren't typically my jam, or Cory's, but neither of us wanted to wipe the looks off Jense and Annie's faces. Although I did catch the heated look Cory sent Jenson when they talked about Poe.

We've all changed into much comfier clothes and were equally dumbfounded to see Annie walking out of the bathroom with a black, comfy, t-shirt dress that falls off her left shoulder, and drapes down to her knees. There's a giant skull with flowers surrounding it. It almost looked too big but she appeared perfectly happy as she walked out, head held high, the scattered scars on her legs and arms on display. She was a vision.

Nick and I snagged Annie, plopping her between us. Jense is sitting in the recliner to our left and Cor is sitting on the other end of the sectional to our right. We grabbed a huge blanket we bought for the Playroom bed and threw it over our legs. I propped mine up on the table, crossed at the ankles and Nick did the same on Annie's other side. Annie had pulled her nightdress down over her knees, stretching the fabric out, as she crossed her legs underneath her.

I can't lie, I've watched her more than the show. She is absolutely enthralled, occasionally dropping the popcorn in her lap as whatever was happening on the screen shocked her.

The screen casts a light glow across her face, allowing me to see as her emotions change from one scene to the next. She truly is perfect for me; for us.

A sudden gasp leaves her mouth, causing her mouth to drop open. My cock stirs in my sweatpants as I think about those sweet, soft lips wrapped around it. Her gag response is very sensitive but we do our best to make sure she isn't uncomfortable. We know full well that not everyone can control it, and there's no way any of us want her to push herself to the point of getting sick. *Yeah, that's not on any of our kink lists.*

Cory did a lot of digging about her conditions. Sometimes we can get her to orgasm quickly, sometimes it takes longer, and, occasionally, she doesn't cum at all. We have learned that the same ministrations don't always work but enjoy watching the pleasure etch across her face as she lets go. Her clit and surrounding area may retreat or be less sensitive at times, but that just means we move to find another erogenous zone. Hell, she's the first woman I've been with that isn't phased when we suck and lick on her nipples. She says she barely feels anything at all except when we bite or pinch hard. Not that we ignore them, but we don't spend hours on them, either. Her body has too many other sweet spots that we all enjoy exploring.

An idea forms in my head and I lift the blanket over my shoulders, pretending to settle further into the couch. Instead, I slowly slide my hand down, placing it on her covered thigh, and make slow circles with my thumb. She's too engrossed in the show to react but I'm not stopping there.

After a moment, I begin rubbing my hand back and forth, careful to not hit the blanket and give away what I'm doing. I see her eye me from the corner of her eyes, a small smile teasing her mouth. She goes back to watching the show and I reach down, over her knee, and slowly peel back the taut material covering her knee. Moving it up her creamy thigh, I let it rest around her waist, then go back to slowly running my hand over her thigh. Goosebumps scatter across her flesh and I have to fight off a smirk.

From my position, I can see her eyes widen but a quick glance at the screen tells me it's not about what's happening in the show. Moving my hand closer to the inside of her thigh, I grip her little hot pocket and squeeze, digging my blunt nails in, and grunt as desire fills my veins. Thankfully, something loud happens on the screen and it covers up the sound.

My hand travels just a little higher, barely grazing the panties that are covering her mound. A slight hitch in her breath is the only thing she gives before biting down on her lip.

I'm about to move again, but then another finger grazes mine; both freezing at the contact. I see Nick slowly peer over Annie's head. I can tell by his eyes that he's trying not to smile and I have to force myself not to chuckle. *Game on, Pretty Boy.*

Leaning into Annie, I whisper, "Trust us?" She turns her head, nose grazing mine with wide eyes. I hold my breath as I wait for a response.

With a single nod, the smile on my face widens. I peck her lips then whisper, "Keep watching the TV. Be a good girl and don't make a sound." With the light of the screen, I see her blush, teeth pulling her lip in. She smiles and turns her face back to the show.

My cock threatens to burst through the seams of my sweats but I tell him he can wait a damn minute. Rubbing my hand over her thigh and down to her knee, I curve around and pull her knee towards me, silently commanding her to unfold her legs. She slightly turns, raising her brow in question, but obeys as soon as I narrow my eyes in challenge.

Once her legs are uncrossed, I drag her left leg over my right one. I can tell that Nick does the same with her other leg as her body shifts with the movement. The blanket gets pulled a little higher and her breathing begins to come out in slow, steady pants.

I take a few leisurely passes of my hand over her creamy thighs, dipping occasionally towards her middle before moving back. On the last venture, her hips raise and the tiniest of whimpers escapes her mouth as I retreat. I squeeze her little hot pocket, wanting to edge her as long as possible. Then, I go back in, over her mound, and travel closer to the area covering her clit. As if we share the same thought, Nick's fingers brush mine, and we slide down together, finding the wet patch on her panties. I bite my cheek at the feeling of her so wet and ready for us, almost losing the war with myself to go slow. Nick continues to rub over the wet patch and I glide my fingers back to where her clit is buried.

Her breath hitches as I rub her panties over her clit. Once she starts bucking into us repeatedly, I stop. I don't want to give her fabric burn. (Yeah, that happens.) Instead, I lean in, and murmur, "Move your panties aside. Let us feel how wet you are."

Her cheeks blaze and I hear her swallow audibly. After a deep breath, her hand finds mine under the blanket and she hooks her fingers in one side, lifts her hips, and pulls them open across her mound.

"Good. Now hold them there." I murmur against her neck before nipping at her shoulder. Taking one finger, I slide through her wetness until I reach Nick's hand. Without any warning or conversation, our fingers work together to slide her wetness around, up, and over her clit, circling it twice, then back down. Once we reach her entrance, I dip two fingers just inside and come back out. I feel Nick do the same before we start to rub teasing paths around her clit, her entrance, even stretching her lips out for the other to play.

One hand latches onto my thigh, her nails digging into me. Chuckling softly, I lean closer, licking the shell of her ear before teasing, "What's wrong baby? You want us to stop?" My tone isn't lost on her as she jerks her head to meet my gaze. "You know I don't. But, I need more. You're so close yet," she trails off with another huff as I circle around her clit again.

"You'll have to ask Nick. I like keeping you on edge. But, remember, stay quiet or the other two will know what we're up to." Her eyes darken and I see a shiver run through her. "Oh, you naughty little minx." I lean forward and suck her lip into my mouth before letting it go with a pop.

Then, I turn back to the show as if nothing is happening. My fingers dip down, gathering up more of her arousal, and languidly move through her most intimate area. I see her glare at me out of the corner of her eye so I press down on her clit, one time, before retreating.

With a huff, she turns her head towards Nick. I feel the moment he must enter her because her stomach clenches, her body jolts upward, and then she bucks her hips.

A turn to watch her as she throws her head back in bliss and begins to ride Nick's finger. Then, I decide to head back down. Feeling that he has two fingers deep inside her pussy, I swipe some of her juices off his fingers before circling her clit with more pressure. Once, twice, then I pinch it between two fingers and her whole body locks up. Her head is thrown back, her eyes are closed, and back is arched. It's the most beautiful thing I have ever seen.

Her body slowly relaxes, twitching with aftershocks, as Nick helps to bring her back down. Nick whispers something in her ear and she stifles a giggle; her chest vibrating with quiet laughter.

Jense's face appears between Annie's and I, his voice is husky as it rumbles in our space. "That was so hot." Annie startles, screaming and slapping the back of her hand against his face. Once she turns to see him, her eyes turn from surprised to concerned. "Oh my God! Jense, I'm so sorry!"

Nick and I almost fall off the couch laughing hysterically. Jense is rubbing a spot on his jaw, his expression is stunned but impressed. "Damn, Sweetness, that was kinda hot, too." Another round of laughter bursts out from all of us, including Annie.

"Well, it serves you right for sneaking up on me when we're watching..." her hand flails out to the TV, encompassing the show.

He quirks his brow, tilts his head, and remarks, "Watching TV... right. And do any other shows cause you to make your O face?"

Shock and a little outrage cross her features as she blabbers, "O face? Really? You knew?" Her pitch gets higher as her face blushes.

He dips his head closer to hers and groans "Oh, baby, I could practically feel your arousal across the room."

Her mouth drops open in surprise before she narrows her eyes. She swings her head to the other side to look at Cory and his face is so red he looks like a tomato. She groans as she slides her body down and pulls the blanket over her head.

"Aw, Sweetness, don't be like that. Want me to kiss it and make you feel better?" She chokes on a laugh, popping her head back out of the covers.

"God, y'all's mouths should come with a warning." Her face is all blushed and I can see the desire in her eyes.

Jenson chuckles, leaning forward where his mouth is right at her ear. I watch as goosebumps trail over her skin. Then he whispers, "That wasn't a no," before taking her lobe into his mouth and sucking hard. The moan she releases is absolutely sinful and my cock jumps in my pants.

Her back bows and I lean forward to see Nick's hand has disappeared under her shirt. "Do you wanna stay here or go somewhere more comfortable?" I ask as I make circles along her thighs, smirking as I feel her muscles bunch under my touch.

She turns her head and looks at Nick, tilting her head. "Um, it's the biggest bed but if you don't want us in your..." Nick cuts her off with a devouring kiss. It's messy and passionate and so damn hot.

Jenson appears in front of us, hair flowing down his back and looking like he's two seconds from losing all control. Not able to wait, he tosses the blanket behind him, causing her to gasp in surprise. The break in her kiss with Nick is all he needs. Without giving her a moment to protest, he scoops her up, flips her over his shoulder, and half runs down the hallway; laughing like a maniac. I vaguely hear her say something, her tone sassy yet outraged. Then a slap echoes down the hall. I hear her gasp in shock and then moan out.

And *that* was all I needed to get me up and moving toward the playroom, Cory and Nick hot on my heels.

33

Epilogue

The last 6 months have been a whirlwind of activity. The guys and I spend a ridiculous amount of time together; individually, as threesomes, in a group. We try to have breakfast or lunch at least three times a week and we almost always find a way to see each other on the weekends.

Over Thanksgiving weekend, the guys showered me with love, joy, and hope; and so much sex. I had never felt so cherished or loved in my entire life. But, I had kids to think about.

When Christmas break started, I officially asked the guys to meet the kids. I won't lie, I was shocked that they were so excited about it. Vince thought it would be best to meet outside of the house. Jenson, the overgrown child that he is, suggested meeting us at Santa's Wonderland. It's a huge production each year and is only about an hour away. So, we did. And the kids LOVED it. At first, they were super shy around the huge, towering men, but after the hilarity of the guys' reactions and narrations on the hayride tour, they warmed up to them.

I won't lie, it was one of the best nights of my life. Samantha, who usually is very shy in front of new people, eventually, and quietly, took Nick by the hand and never let go. In fact, I had to convince her to let go long enough to take her to the bathroom. It was so damn cute. And Nick, if I hadn't already been hopelessly in love, that night would have sealed the deal. His face was surprised when she first took his hand, almost a little panicked, but once she leaned her head on his arm, he was a goner.

Josh immediately bonded with Vince and Cory. He's always been pretty particular about things; including needing to have his jacket sleeves perfectly placed around his wrists; he hates when it's too long, or too short. But, he's also my most energetic child. If Roger Rabbit had been a kid, he would be Josh. He dragged the two of them everywhere; sledding, snow fights, the bull ride. We had to remind him to wait for the girls more than once but Jenson and Vince were more than happy to let him lead them around. At one point, we were watching the live music at the center of the food area and Vince lifted him onto his shoulders. The sheer joy radiated off Josh and I think I turned into goo.

Cheyenne didn't pick favorites. She bounced around between all four guys, talking their ears off about anything and everything. And, of course, decided to wow them with all of her knowledge of everything winter, all the animals in the petting zoo, and anything else that her little mind had soaked up. Where Samantha is my reader, and Josh is my active kid, Cheyenne is my science lover. I swear she knows more about animals, weather patterns, and other random science topics than most grown-ups. It wasn't lost on me how she and Cory got into a little scholarly discussion while riding the train. They talked so matter-of-factly about how many lights they assumed were used throughout the park and which lights would be best to use for brightness vs. energy saving. It was absolutely ridiculous but completely unsurprising.

The kids immediately woke up the next day asking when they would see the guys again. It was so sweet and was the perfect opportunity to talk about how they may be in our lives more. Needless to say, they were completely on board.

We try, at least, every other weekend to do something together with them. And I've never regretted it. In fact, I think it cemented their place in my life.

Gina and her guys came in a couple of weeks ago as summer heat began to fill the air. We had an absolute freaking blast as we tore through the Kemah Boardwalk like teenagers. All the guys competed to see who could win the best prizes for Gina and me. We even rode all of the rides; laughing and soaking up the sun. The next day, we boarded Enzo's big ass yacht and were treated like royalty. My bathing suit was a tankini that covered up my belly but showed off the brand I turned into an ice cream cone. The artist was very careful to not touch the now-healed burn marks, and the three scoops of ice cream dripping off the top are beautiful. Each one is a different color representing the kids' favorite flavors.

As for the other scars, if people don't like them, they can look away. It's their problem, not mine, and I fucking earned the right to love myself.

The tankini also covered my latest surprise but it wasn't ready to be revealed, yet. Tonight, though, it is. Smiling at the memories we've made, I brush a hand over the corset I'm wearing. A ping on my phone snaps me out of my memories, reminding me that I have to finish getting ready.

Mom: Taking kids to the drive-in. Call me tomorrow. <kissing emoji> Have a great night!
Me: Have so much fun! I will. <heart>

I head back to the bed and pull on my off-shoulder, black butterfly top. The black butterfly is a little shiny, bouncing off the lights just enough to catch your eye. I'm already wearing my black distressed jeans that hug my ass perfectly, and hide the secrets I have underneath. I quickly pair them with some glittery black flats and I'm good to go.

Lana did my makeup in an understated manner; small cat eye, mascara, and a hint of blush. I ended up pairing it with a lip stain that was a little more red than I usually go for but it makes the rest of the black outfit pop.

Lana also curled my hair in gentle waves and finished it with one single clip, pulling it up on the right side. Then, she left me with an air kiss and a wave goodbye. She had plans tonight so she couldn't go to the club with us but, that's ok. I have plans for the guys and I don't want to feel bad for blowing Lana off later.

I drive myself down to Sky's the Limit and park in the lot in front. Looking at the clock, I see that it's just after 9, but the lot is dang near empty. There are a couple of trucks, two small cars, and Cory's black Suburban.

Swallowing heavily, I will the butterflies that are stirring up chaos in my stomach to settle down. Sliding my mask on, I make my way to the front door. It opens wide before I reach it, causing me to jerk back a step. Charlie opens the door, gesturing me inside. His smile is wide and friendly but something about it makes me search his face for a hint of whatever secret he's clearly hiding. He doesn't even speak but his eyes sparkle with mischief. His grin tips up on one side before he slides a key into my hand. Confusion twists across my face but he only smiles wider, says, "Have a good night," and walks out the front door.

I stand there frozen; completely dumbfounded and gaping like a dying fish. The clicking of the locks from the outside has my eyes widening and I'm feeling a little more on edge.

Music starts up in the main room. Curiosity forces me to walk through the thick curtain that leads to the main club. Once I pass through the other side, the music hits me and I immediately start smiling so wide that my lips and cheeks already sting with the strain. The slowed remix of Dandelions by Muppet DJ & SECCA Records plays through the club and excitement races through me.

Stepping through the curtain, I see that the club is almost empty. The black curtains still adorn the windows but rows of string lights cover each of them, giving it a more magical look; especially since there are no other lights on.

Hesitantly, I step further into the vast space. Something is in the middle of the dancefloor but it's so far from the walls with the twinkling lights that I can't make it out. Suddenly, four tea lights, clearly battery-operated, are turned on, casting beautiful shadows across the faces of my four stunning men.

My breath catches in my throat as I step closer and see that they're all down on one knee looking at me like I'm the whole damn world. Their eyes sparkle with a mixture of love and adoration and their grins and smiles cause my heart to race for a totally new reason.

I take a few more steps, confused as to what the hell is going on. "What are y..." My question dies on my lips as a low light is turned on. It's just enough to shine down on them, but not so much that it ruins the atmosphere.

My heart pounds against my ribcage as I greedily run my eyes over each of my men. Vince is wearing what looks like a classic black suit with a matching vest, a white shirt, and a red tie. It fits him and his broad shoulders perfectly and does amazing things to my lady bits.

Jenson looks like he belongs on the cover of a magazine. His long hair is pulled up in a perfect man bun and his suit and vest are a gorgeous charcoal color. Like Vince, they're paired with a white shirt and red tie. I have to squeeze my thighs together as I see the heat in his eyes.

My eyes travel over to Nick and I have to suppress a giggle. Nick's suit is *so* him. Navy with black lapels, a navy vest, a white shirt, and a red tie. I've never even seen him in slacks and, *crackerjacks, he looks yummy.*

Finally, I roam my eyes over Cory. Cory basically lives in slacks but holy hot damn. His suit and vest are silver but he's also wearing the same shirt and tie as the others.

"Wow," I barely puff out. They are a vision and, thank you, God, they are *mine.*

I step closer, my cheeks hurting from smiling so hard, and a shiver runs through me. The song is lowered a little bit, as I come to a stand about a foot away from them.

Vince's voice is low, calm, and sure as he begins, "Angel, you've had me wrapped around your finger from the first time I was called to your house. You're the light when there's so much darkness. You are an angel amongst demons and we will spend every day making you feel every bit as special as you are." Tears begin blurring my vision as I gulp around a lump in my throat.

Before I can respond, Jenson says, "Sweetness, my heart was yours when I heard your sweet giggle followed by the sass you gave me for ordering kamikazes. Since then, your quick wit and sassiness have filled my days with more sunshine than thunderstorms. If you'll let me, I want to spend the rest of our lives as your partner in crime when you're feeling mischievous, and your shoulder you cry on when things get rough." I release a watery chuckle as I swipe away the tears that are now cascading down my face.

Nick clears his throat, swipes his tongue over his bottom lips, and says, "Siren, I was drawn to you before Cory had even invited you to the table. I know you've told me before that "like calls to like" and I think I knew, even back then, that you were our missing piece; *my* missing piece. You've seen each of us at our worst, at our best, at our most questionable..." he trails off and everyone chuckles. "But I truly hope you'll let us stay by your side to love you, comfort you, spoil you, because you're the best thing that has ever happened to us, and we promise to never take you for granted." His voice breaks off at the end as a few tears slip free. Of course, seeing a man cry sets me off more, and now I feel like my makeup is a nasty blob of goop by now.

I move my eyes to Cory who seems like he's reciting his speech in his head. The thought makes me smile and I have to hold in a chuckle. Swallowing audibly, he fixes his eyes on mine and recites, "You are everything I ever wanted and so much more. Your purity, your resilience, and your inherent need to protect others make you a rare diamond amongst a sea of pebbles. I want to spend every second showering you with all the love and happiness you deserve in hopes that you will never know sadness or despair another day of your life."

They all look at each other and Vince pulls out a little box, flipping it open to reveal a beautiful ring that shines brighter than anything I've seen in person. I don't get a chance to inspect it, through blurred eyes, before they say, "Will you marry us?"

I'm nodding my head so fast that I make myself dizzy. "Yes! Yes!" A watery laugh escapes me as they all stand and rush towards me.

Jenson beats everyone, picking me up and twirling me around as I laugh and hang on to his neck. Dizzy, he sets me back on my feet and doesn't give me a second to recover before he smashes his lips on mine. It's bruising and consuming and over far too quickly. As if sensing my disappointment he leans in, his breath tickling my neck, and says, "Can't hog the whole celebration, Sweetness."

With a final peck on the lips, he steps back and Nick immediately wraps around me. The hug he gives me feels transcendent. Like, this moment truly is as important to him as it is to me. He pulls back just enough to smile at me before slanting his mouth over mine. It's slow, sweet, and causes me to cry, again. My heart feels like it's bursting with too many emotions in the very best way.

When he breaks our kiss, the look in his eyes has me reaching out to slide my hand over his freshly shaven face. He leans into my touch, turns his head slightly to kiss the tip of my thumb, then smiles. "I love you, Annie. Yesterday, today, and always."

"I love you, too, Nick. Forever and for always."

With a wink, he slowly backs away from me and Cory fills my vision. Cory stands tall and proper, shoulders back, and chest out. I bite my lip as he appraises me. "Pretty Girl," he purrs. "I can't wait to spend forever with you." His smile turns into a smirk as he wraps his hand around the nape of my neck, pulling me to him, and kisses me deeply. His body presses against mine and I can feel his hard cock against my lower belly. He's so damn particular but, when he lets go, it's intoxicating. I feel the moment his carefully constructed persona falls away. His body relaxes as his tongue tangles with mine in a fiery dance.

All too soon, it's over. We're both panting for breath, pupils blown wide, and hearts racing wildly. With a kiss on my forehead, he quickly moves to the side and allows Vince to step in. I can feel the other three crowding in behind me. When Vince smiles down at me, he also presents the ring. I look at it for all of two seconds before launching myself into his arms. I can tell he's shocked, at first, but he quickly recovers. His arms wrap around me, lifting me up under my ass, and nudging me to wrap my legs around his waist.

His kiss is intense, charged, and dominant. There is no dueling for dominance. Not with Vince. He dominates and I am all too happy to submit. My panties are officially drenched and my heart is so full that it may explode.

Abruptly he breaks the kiss and slowly slides me down his body. A dirty moan rips from my throat as I slide down his pant-covered cock.

Once my feet hit the floor he chuckles out a deep laugh that sends shocks through my system. "Would you like your ring, Angel?" His tone is husky and playful and makes me giggle as butterflies crash my system.

"Yes. Please." He takes the ring out and slides it on my finger. It's perfect, unique, and utterly gorgeous. My breath catches in my throat as I get my first real look at it. It's a black gold ring, which I freaking love. The back of the band is solid but breaks into four thin bands going up on each side. The ones on the outside are stretched a little wider and dip up to touch the rim of the main stone setting. The middle two bands are crossed in the middle, on both sides, and the tops meet just to the side of the outer bands. All four bands on each side are dotted with beautiful diamonds. The setting on the top is circular and boasts a half-carat, round blue diamond. It sits atop a circular black setting and is surrounded by 17 little diamonds. According to Jense, the ring has a total of 102 round SI diamonds. It's jaw-droppingly stunning and I have to keep wiping away the flood of tears from my eyes so I can look at it.

Cory's voice is a low rasp when he wraps his arms around me, snuggling his chin on my shoulder. "Judging by your silence you either really like it, or you're trying to find a way to tell us you hate it without hurting our feelings."

Laughter bubbles out of me at how casually he said it. It's a little watery but it echoes around us. "It's absolutely...it's just...what's a word better than phenomenal? Or perfect? Or extraordinary?" I choke on a sob as the reality of the situation really hits.

Jense steps up to my left side, tucking his finger under my chin to lift my eyes to meet his. "You," he whispers before leaning in and kissing my lips tenderly. I giggle through the kiss but don't retreat until Vince coughs out to get our attention.

With a final quick peck, we all turn towards Vince who's smirking with his eyebrow raised all sexy like. *Damn, he looks fine.* "Care to toast?" His voice slides down my spine like honey and I nod my head enthusiastically.

We step up to the table and I release a shocked laugh. "Really?" I ask playfully.

Jenson steps up next to me and says, of course. "It's a reminder of the night that changed our lives forever."

With wide, cheesy smiles, we each take a glass and down the kamikaze shot. I giggle at how silly it is but, also, how perfect.

Looking at all of my guys I raise an eyebrow and grin, "So what now?" I ask, making sure I put in a little extra sass in my voice.

Jense chuckles then spreads his arms wide. "Whatever you want, Sweetness."

A sly smile forms on my lips as I take a few steps back. "In that case, room 6; five minutes." Without another word, I turn on my heel and head to the other side of the club. The key is burning a hole in my pocket and I'm so damn excited to show the guys the little secret I had prepared for tonight. Well, secrets.

* * *

The lights are dim around the room. A large four-poster bed sits right in the center next to a cabinet filled with all kinds of toys. The bed is made with the most luxurious red sheets with black damask swirls covering it. It's soft and silky and I can't wait to feel it under my skin.

I lie out a few tubes of lube on the dresser and check my reflection in the mirror. My cheeks are already pink and flushed. My lip stain stayed perfectly in place, even after the guys kissed the life out of me. *Thank you, Maybelline.* The vibrant red stands out against my almost porcelain skin and is the perfect match for what's underneath.

Realizing I'm wasting time, I slip off my shoes, push them into the corner next to the dresser, and then whip my shirt and jeans off.

Carefully sitting on the edge of the bed, I squirm a little as my surprises rub in all the right ways. Digging into the sides of the corset, I slide the ropes I had hidden over my arms and rest them on my shoulders. Standing again, I hurry into the ensuite bathroom, one of the reasons I chose this room, and freshen up.

The three-minute timer on my phone goes off and I take a quick look in the mirror to take myself in. The guys and I, Nick especially, have been playing a lot with bondage. I still can't stand my hands or ankles tied, but I do let them secure me in all kinds of positions using rope or satin. Although, Jenson's favorite bondage tool is definitely my panties. Not that I'm complaining because the primal look he gets is otherworldly.

Today, I spent an hour working on tying myself up for the first time. Using a long black rope and a long red rope, I fashioned my own corset and "fishnet" stockings. The loop of red rope rests on my left shoulder while the loop of black rope rests on my right. Then, they crisscross and twist starting beneath my breasts and continuing down my torso. Each line of the corset consists of the red rope, looped with the black rope, and knotting in the middle for symmetry. It's nowhere near as complicated as Nick can do but it's my first time doing it to myself.

The bottom of the corset ends just above my lower belly where the souvenir that jackass gave me sits. However, I've been hiding something from the guys for the last four weeks. It has been so hard but, thankfully, the kids had end-of-year celebrations and they've all been busy with the youth center program and launching their summer programs. It was a little harder to make sure it was covered and secured when we were on Enzo's boat but we were always with them so there was no chance for any private time.

I fondly trace a finger over my now-healed tattoo. A few weeks ago, I got together with an artist who is known for his coverups and bright colors. He worked his magic and it's miraculous. 'Warrior' is inked in thick Benjamin Franklin Font. The 'i' is replaced by a semi-colon, reminding me that I never gave up; even when I really wanted to. Hanging off the 'W' is a pair of handcuffs, the 'o' is filled with a brain in the shape of a heart, a pool shaped like a heart is just a little above the last r, to the right, and underneath is a rope wrapped in an intricate heart knot. The entire background is set in flames, yellow at the bottom with a subtle ombre from orange to red. It perfectly covers the disgusting word so, to anyone looking, you wouldn't know it's even there. I think only I can pick out where the scars are but, thanks to the guys, *my fiancées*, I no longer care. I was *that* girl, so I could be *this* woman. And I wouldn't have done a single thing differently.

Looking past the tattoo, I trace the red and black ropes attached to the middle of the bottom of the corset, running straight down, grazing over my naughty bits, then running back up and attaching to the middle of the corset in the back. Every time I walk, one of the ropes rubs against me and causes a shiver to travel through my body.

The final part of my little outfit consists of a black rope on my left side, and a red rope on the right side. Each strand is attached to the corset and runs down the middle of my thigh until it reaches mid-thigh. Then, it's wrapped in a loose fishnet pattern, creating large Xs down the front, and back, of my legs and tied on the sides to form little rhombuses. It's tied off at the bottom in a little bow because, honestly, I was tired by then.

With a deep breath, I grab my phone, connect it to the Bluetooth in the room, and wait for them to show. I barely get situated on the bed, leaning up against the headboard with one knee bent and the other outstretched, when they finally knock.

Pressing play, I fluff my hair quickly and raise my shoulders, summoning my inner sex goddess. *I've been hanging out with Jense too much.*

Milk of the Siren by Melanie Martinez fills the room as I call out, "Come in!" I hold my breath and watch as my four devastatingly handsome men walk into the room. Even though this corset pissed me off a hundred times, their looks are totally worth it. Various expressions of awe, lust, amazement, and desire cross their faces.

Nick steps forward, "Siren," his voice almost sounds like a warning as he stalks closer to the bed. His hand makes contact with my outstretched leg and runs over the entire length of the rope, causing heat to pool between my thighs. He ends his perusal by sliding a finger in the loop acting as a spaghetti strap on my shoulder. "Who did this, Siren?" His voice is husky and I can already see the hard imprint of his cock punching through his slacks. My mouth goes dry and I stick my tongue out to lick my lips as visions of him shoving it in my mouth assault me.

Vince steps to the other side of the bed, running his finger over the ropes that run over my mound and through my slit. "Angel, Nick asked you a question. Who did this?" His finger barely pushes on the rope, ripping a moan out of my mouth before he takes away the pressure.

With a gasp, I whimper out, "Me. I did it." Vince's hand pauses above my mound and I start trying to rub my thighs together.

"Good God almighty. Marry me?" Nick groans out, squeezing his dick through his pants. With a chuckle, I reply, "I already said "yes" to that." He bites his lip, shaking his head, then leans forward and slams his mouth on mine.

I immediately groan into the kiss as his tongue devours my mouth. He moves my head to get better access and it causes the corset to pull the rope running down my slit. I whimper at the feeling of basically edging myself for the last three hours, but I also know it will be worth it.

He breaks the kiss and leans his hand out for mine. Sliding my hand into his, he tugs me gently, silently pulling me from the bed. Once my feet hit the floor, he moves me to the middle of the large space and they all circle me like vultures ready to consume anything they can. Fingers roam over the ropes, eliciting small sparks of electricity to run through my veins.

"Absolutely perfect," Nick whispers from behind me.

Jenson's eyes catch on my belly. "Annie?" His voice is choked and I know he finally saw the tattoo. They were all too focused on the ropes to notice anything else. "Is that, is that real?" He asks incredulously.

With a shy smile, I nod my head, not sure how they will feel about reminders of each of them being permanently inked on my skin. "I've been hiding it for a few weeks so it could heal."

At some point, he'd taken off his jacket and rolled the sleeves on his shirt up, showing off those stupidly sexy forearms. *Yes, it's a thing, don't fight me.*

He spends so much time looking at it that I begin to worry he doesn't like it. Then, he falls to his knees, kisses each side of the tattoo, just outside the lines of the color, and looks up at me. My breath stutters in my lungs as I see his eyes have filled with tears.

Cory, Vince, and Nick join him on their knees and I take a little step back so they can all see. Eventually, Cor jumps up and smashes his mouth to mine. "That is so hot, so perfect, and so you. I love you, Annie." I don't even get a chance to respond before he's slanting his mouth over mine again. All of his emotions pour from his mouth straight into my soul and I wrap my arms around his neck, desperately needing to be closer.

Without further preamble, he grips my ass cheeks, massaging them for a minute, before picking me up so I have to wrap my legs around his waist. He chuckles into my mouth when I release a gasp, quickly followed by a moan. *Oh, yeah, that...*

My entire body is filled with fire and I start to tremble as my desire ramps up. "Cor..." We just started and I'm already begging.

The guys all chuckle, almost making me scowl but Cor begins to walk my back to the bed, moving *all* the things, and I groan out.

"What do you need, fiancée?" Vince asks. My heart almost stops and I have to look at him to ground myself. "I need you. All of you. I want...I want us all to be connected."

We've done a lot of things together, individually, and even broken off into threesomes but there's one thing I haven't had anyone do yet. Today...today I put all the fear behind me and embrace this next chapter of my life with my sweet kids and these amazing men.

Jense steps up, assessing my face as he narrows his eyes. "Connected?"

Biting my lip for half a second, I decide it's time. I can do this. I can ask for what I want with no judgment and, if someone doesn't want to, that's fine. I also know that if it becomes too much, I can safeword and they will stop. Thankfully, that's only happened twice; both times *I* tried to have my wrists or ankles bound, and I only lasted for all of two minutes before beginning to disassociate. The nightmares after were absolutely terrible but, just as promised, I used my safeword, the scene stopped, they took care of me, and not once did they make me feel bad about it.

Straightening my shoulders and jutting my chin up, I share my vision for tonight. "I want Nick in my pussy, while Vince fucks him into me." A chorus of groans and choked coughs echo through the room. I very rarely offer more than a couple of words and I *never* talk so, dirty. "I also want Jense in my ass, while Cor fucks him."

At that, the room falls in complete silence. Looking at Jense and

Cor I remind them, "It's not all about me. If you aren't comfortable that's fine. I'm absolutely game for other variations but, I've never seen Cory…" I flail my hand out between them like an idiot then move on. "But, it's whatever you want. I just want us all to be together."

Jense looks at Cor and smiles with so much lust that I almost feel like I'm intruding. With a single nod, he looks back at me and furrows his brow again. "I'm not so sure about placement, to be honest. We've played a little with your ass but, only a finger or two. I don't want to hurt you." The sincerity in his tone threatens to unravel me in the sweetest way, but then I remember my last secret.

Grinning at them, I roll to my stomach, slowly transferring my weight to my upper body. Then, I bring my knees closer to my chest and stick my ass high in the air. Turning my head so I can breathe better, I slide my hands slowly down the sides of my body, gripping my ass cheeks and spreading them wide.

"Fuck, shit, *oomph*, oh hell." I don't know who says what over my heart beating away in my ears but their comments do make me feel a little of the nervousness fade.

With a little teasing ass shake, the tension warps in the room. A hand comes down on my ass and is immediately followed by a long, cool lick of someone's tongue. "Not only did you walk around with this sexy outfit hidden under your clothes, but you've been wearing a butt plug with a blood-red gem, too?"

"Y-yes," I stutter out. "I put it in at home, so it maybe would be easier."

Someone releases a low throaty groan and I swear the ropes are soaked through. Feeling the heat of their gazes on my ass causes my body to erupt in goosebumps and I clench down, feeling the plug rub over my inner walls.

A voice clears and Vince drops into his Dom roll. "Dirty girl." He runs the tips of his fingers from my pussy all the way to the plug;

gently pushing on it. I gasp at the sensation before pressing my ass back to him.

"Roll over, Angel. Legs spread as wide as you can." He helps me get situated. My feet are sitting right on the edge of the bed, legs spread wide and bent at the knees so they can see *everything*.

"You are so perfect, so wonderful, and so *ours*." He accentuates the final word with a low growl before nodding his chin towards me while looking at Nick. Nick smiles mischievously, stalks over to me, then slices through the ropes over my mound with a knife that I hadn't even noticed.

"Holy shit," I whisper out; turned on way more than I anticipated.

Jense and Cor move towards my head on both sides. Jense presses his lips to mine slowly, sweetly. His tongue languidly reaches out and swipes my lip, asking for me to open; which I do. At the same time, Cor leans down and takes my nipple in his mouth; biting just enough that I can feel it. I moan into Jenson's mouth and he pushes his tongue in further.

My body is overheating already and they've barely touched me.

A long, wet tongue hits the spot right next to the plug eliciting a yelp and buck of my hips. Two strong hands hold my hips down as the tongue comes back and makes one long, firm line from the plug to my clit. My eyes roll to the back of my head as a finger slides through my wetness. Fingers prod the plug while another slips into my pussy. Tears leak from my eyes as the sensations overwhelm me.

Cory reaches over and pinches my other nipple at the same time he bites down on the other. Lightning shoots to my clit at the same time someone sucks it into their hot mouth and I rocket off the bed. My orgasm is so intense that I lose almost all feeling for a moment. Darkness takes over my vision as I feel the loss of Vince's finger and can faintly hear the wet sounds of someone rubbing my clit rapidly, as my body turns into waves of euphoria.

Once my soul becomes one with my body again, and the last

quivers of my orgasm ripple through my body, I blink my eyes open and take in my surroundings. Vince takes Jenson's place and kisses me hard; our tastes combining in my mouth. When I groan into his mouth, he swipes his tongue through my mouth once more before pulling back and staring down at me. "Good girl. I love it when you squirt for us." I can feel myself preen at the praise; even if it is still weird to me that they love making me squirt.

Movement between my legs catches my eye, and they immediately widen at the sight of Cory and Jenson making out. It's not the first time I've ever seen it, but it turns me on every damn time.

"Go get them ready for you, Angel," he commands, sending a little happy shiver through my stomach. "Yes, Sir," I respond and watch in delight as his eyes turn impossibly darker.

"Brat," he grits out, swatting my ass when I slide from the bed. Nick tosses me a pillow, always focused on caring for me. I rest my knees on it for support as I look up at the two delicious men in front of me.

Cory and Jense are both lost in each other so I sit on the back of my legs and take a moment to enjoy the show. Both of them have lost their shirts, socks, and shoes. They have their pants unbuckled, hard cocks free, and Jense is jerking their cocks together in his large hand. After a few strokes, he pauses, just briefly, to rub their pre-cum back over both of them.

I moan out at seeing it up close and feel the wetness dripping from me. Jense and Cor break apart, both peering down to take me in. "Sorry," I whisper with a little chuckle. Jenson raises his brow in challenge and Cory looks down at me like I'm everything. "It's still fucking hot but, I didn't mean to ruin the moment." I toss in a flutter of my eyelashes knowing Jense can't resist my "innocent act"; his words.

"You didn't ruin it, Pretty Girl." Cory coos sweetly. Then he looks at Jenson, deferring to him. "But, you can make it even better." Jense is technically a switch for Cor but he's always dominant with me. Not as stern and commanding as Vince, but just as effective.

As one, they both turn to me, their lips are red and swollen and their cocks are straining to reach out for me. With the sweetest look I can muster, I rise up on my knees. Both of my hands wrap around their velvety smooth shafts and I give each one a gentle pump from base to tip. Leaning in, I lick Cory's saltiness from his tip and swirl my tongue around it while pumping Jenson. I don't give him time to finish his groan before I pop back off and do the same to Jenson.

For a couple of minutes, I tease the shit out of them by switching between sucking and pumping. Just as soon as they release a sound of pleasure or jerk their hips, I switch to the other. My mouth aches in the best way as I go deeper and deeper each time.

Jense eventually snaps, pulling me off his cock with a loud pop, with his finger under my chin and his thumb squeezing just enough for me to know that I succeeded in driving him mad.

With a smug grin, I raise my eyes to meet his gaze and my pussy clenches as I see the fire burning in his eyes. "Bed, Brat." *Oh, yeah. When he uses fewer words, I've taken him to the edge. Score 1 for me.*

Fluttering my lashes I slowly stand and move to crawl on the bed. I may or may not sway my hips a little more, stretch my legs a little wider, and move achingly slow across the bed. A resounding pop lands on my ass causing me to squeal, and plop down on my stomach.

Almost instantly, Nick is whispering in my ear. "You ready, Siren?" His voice glides over me and is both soothing and heady.

"Y-Yes." At once, four mouths are on my backside. Two gently kiss my ass cheeks, causing my cheeks to flame brighter. The other two kiss my shoulders and I squeeze my thighs in anticipation.

"Roll on your back and help us get them prepped." I'm confused for a moment until I roll to my back. Nick crawls onto the bed to my left while Jense crawls on the bed to my right. Jense steals the air from my lungs with a kiss that makes my toes curl. Then, he breaks the kiss and nudges me to Nick. Nick's kiss causes me to tremble as he gently explores my mouth.

Both of them are gloriously naked and I wish I could see them better at the same time. Pulling away from them, I lean against the headboard and take both of their metal-filled cocks in each hand.

I hear the sounds of lubricant being opened come from both sides as I focus on slowly pumping, tugging, and twisting. "Ready, Pretty Boy?" Vince asks sweetly, leaning Nick further over me. "Yes, Sir," he rasps and I continue working his cock as Vince slowly eases into him. Watching the tinge of pain morph into pure pleasure gets to me every time and my pussy clenches at the sight. Not able to resist, I lean over and take Nick's mouth, continuing to pump him and Jense.

As Vince moves, Nick breaks the kiss to breathe and I turn to watch Jense. "You ready, Baby?" Cor grits out. "Yes. P-please," he chokes out. His arms are trembling as the anticipation overtakes him. In the background, the slapping sounds of Vince moving in and out of Nick are fucking filthy, and turn mean even more. I see that Jense is starting to lock up and I move in to kiss him. Slowly encouraging him to play tag with my tongue, I continue to slowly pump and twist his and Nick's hard cocks.

Cory releases a string of curses as he seats himself deep inside Jenson. Jense looks like his arms are about to give out and he's clenching his teeth. With a final kiss, I move back so he can see my eyes. "That is so damn hot."

I look at Nick and Vince, then back to Cory and Jenson. Leaning back, I trail my hand down my body and tentatively circle my clit. A moan rips from my mouth as the guys give a tantalizing show filled with grunts and groans.

Suddenly, Vince grits "Move in." Seemingly as one, Cory and Vince both move Jense and Nick closer to me. Excitement course through me as I realize what they're doing. I scoot down, just a little, so both of their dicks are hanging right at my mouth. Without further instruction, I take Nick all the way to the back of my throat, gagging for a second, then I suck in hard and move my mouth back up to release him. Nick's guttural groan and pinch of my nipple encourages me to move over to Jenson and do the same thing.

"Fuuuucccckk," Jense draws the word out like it's a full sentence and it sends my arousal through the damn roof. His thick cock in my mouth muffles the moan I release as someone, presumably Nick, dips his fingers through my wetness then swirls it carefully around my clit; not quite giving me enough pressure but still causing my core to tighten.

I move to roll Jense's balls when I hear Cory groan, "I-I can't. Damn, baby. Your ass is perfect." My eyes nearly roll straight to the back of my head at the dirty words. Cory is rarely vocal in bed but when he is, *cross my clit and hope to cry*, it sets my whole body on fire.

Vince must be feeling the same as he rasps, "Nick, Jense, take care of our girl."

My heart is beating against my chest as the anticipation rises. My body is trembling with need but, I also wouldn't mind just watching my men pleasure each other. The sight is absolutely intoxicating.

Hisses and groans release around the room and Nick and Jense quickly lie down next to me. Hands roam my body as their tongues flick and suck and nip every inch of my neck, jaw, chest and shoulders.

When I thrust my hips in the air, and whimper like a wanton little hussy, Nick kisses a path up my neck as Jense's mouth and fingers trail down my body. The moment he spreads me wide and barely grazes my entrance, Nick swallows my moan, sucking my tongue into his mouth.

Nick moves my head, adjusting our position so he can take our kiss deeper as I wrap my free hand around his head, pulling him impossibly closer. When Jenson thrusts two thick fingers into me, I rake my hand through Nick's hair and groan at the intrusion.

My breaths start to come out as harsh pants and I feel my pussy clench down on Jenson's fingers. With a suck of my clit, I bow away from Nick and dig my nails into his shoulders as the sensations ripple through my body. Just before I think I may go over the cliff, Jenson's fingers and mouth disappear completely.

A tear leaks out of my eye as my body plummets away from the edge. Nick chuckles low in his throat, nipping at the edge of my jaw.

"Did Jenson leave you needy, Siren?" I whine out, nodding my head like a drunk bobble head and they all join in mocking my pain with various chortles.

"Want me to make you feel better?" He whispers.

"Please!" I've been on the edge since I left the house and I'm beginning to wonder about my sanity.

Nick smiles wide, kisses me softly, then gently lays us both on our sides. Running his finger through my hair with one hand, he uses his other hand to lift my left knee up and over his hip. The barbells of his Jacob's ladder rub through my slit as he kisses me with more adoration than I can put into words. He breaks the kiss, leans down between us, and notches his cock at my entrance. Once he's lined up, his eyes bore into mine. A whole universe of emotions passes through our gaze. With a gentle nod, he thrusts forward, plunging into me completely.

My back arches, eyes slam shut, and my breath is forced from my lungs. He gives me a second to adjust to his size, and the feeling of his piercings rubbing perfectly inside of me. I feel so damn full. Between his cock and the plug still buried in my ass, it's taking me a little longer than usual to relax.

But once I do, *holy forks and spoons*, it is life-altering. I start rotating my hips, slowly getting used to the feeling, and a deep groan is pulled from the very essence of my damn soul. When I finally meet Nick's eyes, I smile and peck his lips. That's all he needed to start thrusting into me with slow, measured movements. My toes begin to tingle and sparks dance across my vision.

Just when I begin to lose myself in him, a kiss on my shoulder and a hand on my leg reminds me that we are definitely not alone. Suddenly, pressure is put on the plug, causing me to mewl at the sensation. I turn my head to look at Jense and he gives me his signature panty-melting smile. Cory's rubbing my leg and Vince is rubbing the thigh that's lying across Nick's body.

I focus on the feeling of him moving the plug in slow circles before he starts sliding it in and out. Cory leans over and squirts some lube on Jenson's fingers as he slides the plug out.

A finger under my chin turns my focus away from Jense and Cory. Vince's handsome face comes into view and he leans over Nick, capturing my lips with his. When he releases me, he whispers, "Breathe, Angel. Just breathe."

I nod my head in understanding as Jenson's fingers probe my back hole. I have to actively fight the knee-jerk reaction to disassociate as he moves from two fingers to three. It's not that it's painful, like, well like before, but the pressure is just weird.

Vince reaches an arm over Nick, expertly finding my clit between our bodies. Nick slowly rocks his hips and he works in tandem with Vince setting a slow, torturous pace.

Cory rubs a hand from my leg, up to my ass. His hand grips my cheek and pulls me open even more as Jenson continues pumping, twisting, and scissoring his fingers into me. Fire burns through my face at being so damn vulnerable but I don't have time to dwell on it as I feel his slick tip line up.

A smack on my ass causes me to gasp, forcing me to flood my lungs with oxygen that I had apparently stopped providing. "Breathe, Annie." Vince's tone is commanding but laced with concern. Honestly, it helps more than I can say.

I suck in another breath as Jenson slowly pushes in. "Push back a little; let him in." I don't know whose voice that is but I exhale heavily and begin pushing back.

Vince rubs my clit faster as Nick rotates his hips and I get swept up in the sensations and begin matching their movements. Each time I move away from Nick, I press myself further onto Jenson's cock. After a few more thrusts, I finally push back enough that he's fully seated, deep in my ass. He and I both relax into each other, savoring the connection, as I get used to the feeling of being so damn full.

Neither of them says anything as I slowly move my body, testing the sensations until pleasure consumes me. Then, I let go as my body takes over and I start fucking myself on their cocks. It's overwhelming and glorious and I'm cursing myself for never doing this before.

I feel the bed shift and lose my rhythm, popping my eyes open to look around. A smile stretches so wide across my face that my cheeks ache as I watch Vince settle in behind Nick, then turn to see Cory settling in behind Jense.

Lust and desire flood my system as Nick and Jenson prepare to be entered. Wanting to distract them, I begin rocking between them again. Reaching behind me, I put my hand on top of Cory's, gripping Jenson's hip, as he sheathes himself deep inside. Then I turn back to Vince. He must read my expression as he reaches across Nick and holds on to my hip, resting on Nick's leg.

And then, *oh and fucking then*, we move. Words can't describe the feelings, the sounds, the sensations of having all five of us connected. Rocking and grinding, mewls, groans, grunts, and moans echo around the room as we lose ourselves in each other.

After a couple of minutes in sweet, slow ecstasy, the guys up their pace. Jense and Nick work together to fuck me in tandem; then take turns sawing in and out of me. I'm full, so fantastically full. I swear all I can feel every inch of their cocks, and their piercings, rubbing into me deliciously. I'm lost to the sensations and open my eyes in time to see Vince drop his and find my clit. With a perfect pinch, and then twist, he sends me skyrocketing off the cliff I've been suspended on.

My ears ring, tears stream down my face, and blackness completely covers my vision.

Shortly after, each of the guys falls over the edge with me. We relax into the bed and spend time coming down from our highs in a sticky, sweaty mess of limbs; and love.

Thankfully, the club has multiple rooms with various-sized tubs. Vince makes sure Nick and I get the aftercare we need, while Cory and Jense take care of each other. Thankfully, Cory pulled some sheets from the office and put them on the bed; which is awesome since these little shits made me squirt, again. Vince makes sure we all drink plenty of water, including some Liquid IV, and munch on little sandwich boxes he had the staff drop off before they left.

My guys thought of everything. And, as I lie, fabulously naked in the middle of a huge bed, surrounded by these marvelous men, I realize just how different my life is; how different I am.

My life has had so much darkness, but these men helped me conquer it, overcome it, and continue living after it. My kids are happy and healthy, and my men are comforting and caring. If anyone ever asks if I'd do things differently, I can honestly say no. I wouldn't change a damn thing.

Note from the Author

Oh, gracious! I am equal parts sad and happy that Annie and her men found their happy ending. But, who knows...maybe we'll hear from them again someday.

Thank you so much for supporting me as a new author and I truly hope you enjoyed the journey.

A huge thank you to my editor, beta readers, and ARC group! I would not have made it this far with you.

Also, shout out to Kayla for always talking me off the ledge and assuring me the book was just fine after the eleventh edit.

Follow me on Facebook and TikTok for information about upcoming books and overall ridiculousness.
Facebook: https://www.facebook.com/groups/1422660571980693/
TikTok: https://www.tiktok.com/@triswynterswrites

9 798989 804573